About the Author

Andrew McDonald is from Coventry and is a dedicated husband, father and grandfather. He has successfully released three books to date, with *The Calling* being his fourth. He juggles his time between work, family and writing, and hopes to bring the same level of entertainment to people through his books that he has got from others. He believes everybody should have a dream and you are never too old to chase one.

The Calling

Andrew McDonald

The Calling

Olympia Publishers
London

www.olympiapublishers.com
OLYMPIA PAPERBACK EDITION

A CIP catalogue record for this title is
available from the British Library.

ISBN: 978-1-80074-816-3

First Published in 2023

Olympia Publishers
Tallis House
2 Tallis Street
London
EC4Y 0AB

Printed in Great Britain

Dedication

For Mary: my world and my inspiration

Acknowledgements

An author's work isn't always just his own thoughts and ideas; sometimes it's aided by the people around him. I would like to thank my enduring wife, Mary, who has by the very definition stood by many hours of plot ideas, discarded devices and endless talking about the myths and legends of Britain. I would also like to pay special tribute to my children, Laura, Peri, Kiara and Tegan without whom my dream of writing would still be a dream. My grandchildren, Ivy, River, Castiel and (at the time of writing) an unborn fourth who I hope will be proud of my legacy. My aunts and uncles have provided me with support over the years. I would also like to thank friends who have encouraged me during this project: Mark, Robert, Dawn, Laz, Scott, Colin. My colleagues who have had to listen to me during our shifts: Steve, Graham, Julie, Tracey, Chris, Robert, Dawn, Debbie, Norman – I promise no more talk about Camelot. I'd like to give a special thank you to Nikki who has given a lot of her time and most of her Easter holiday to proof read this book. And finally, I want to thank King Arthur without whom this story would not be possible. Thank you, my Liege!

1.

The King Is Dead

"The king is dead, long live the king!" The old man stood in the centre of the small congregation of knights with his arms flung high above his head reaching for the ceiling as he stood close to a flat stone altar.

The walls of the cavern were moist and dripped with tiny droplets of condensation which chased each other as they traced the contours of the rock. The sound of silence within the cavern was broken by the relentless pressure of water falling from the damp ceiling onto the floor below and mixing with the small puddles which lay scattered over the rough terrain of the cavern surface. He slowly approached the altar and adjusted his stained robes over his body. The lines on his face etched in with sorrow and were masked by a dirty greying beard which fell over the ragged clothing which hid his wiry body.

The light from a flaming torch cast shadows up the walls of the cavern and thrust the varying aspects of the twisted figures across the walls. He placed his hands on the edge of the stone altar and buried his head deep into his chest and breathed heavily. "My Liege," he whispered as he sank to his knees.

"Merlin," whispered one of the figures circling the altar. He pulled himself from the shadows and placed a hand gently on the shoulders of the old man. The light from the torch played across his battered body armour as he knelt quietly by his side and looked at the unmoving carcass on the stone.

"Galahad," said the old man softly. "Please... I am fine." Galahad nodded his understanding but remained in his own kneeling position beside the old man. He looked at the knight and stared into his eyes, his own filling with salty water. "Why?" he asked desperate for an answer.

The question fell upon deaf ears as Galahad sadly shook his head in response. "I am sorry, I truly am but I cannot answer."

"He was like a son to me," bemoaned Merlin. He knelt in the moisture by the altar, tears trickling freely from his eyes and mixing with the grime on his face and disappearing into the strands of his facial hair. He searched Galahad's face and peered deep into the knight's eyes as though searching his very soul, before tracing a line towards the remaining five figures still hidden by the darkness.

Slowly he pulled himself to his feet, using the rock to aid him and summoning the last vestiges of energy, he forced himself to turn his attention to the six men in his company. He sighed heavily and rested his hands on the altar and stared down at the sombre scene before him.

Galahad pulled himself away from Merlin and joined his fellow knights scattered around the edge of the cavern. His vision was drawn to the figure lying on the altar before him as tears blurred his eyesight. He could feel the energy draining from his body as he watched Merlin mourn over the body.

The body before him on the altar was bequeathed in the finery expected of a figure of his position. The fine embroidery which threaded through his armour sparkled and shone in the dim light of the cavern. The armour he wore was laced with golden trim across the breastplate, gauntlets and helmet, and a simple golden crown rested around the crest of the silver helmet. The figure held a large sword between his gauntleted hands, which lay impressively almost the entire length of the figure's body. The knights around the altar all held their heads and bowed with respect as Merlin circled the altar and the prone figure resting upon the stone.

"Galahad." He looked towards the knight as he spoke. "Gawain, Kay, Tristan, Bedivere, Percival." His eyes flicked and played upon each figure as he spoke. "We few come here to respect the final resting place of our King Arthur Pendragon." His voice quivered and tremored with emotion as he spoke. "Here deep within Avalon we pay tribute to the gracious king of the Britons, cruelly taken from us in battle."

He placed a hand on the forehead of the figure on the altar and breathed in the dank atmosphere of the surroundings, studying the faces of the knights surrounding their king. "We few, and we few alone, know of the king's death… We are the final survivors of the battle of Camlann and to this end it is with the power bestowed to me that I declare that none may know of this dreadful day." He stared at each knight in defiance to the decree, meeting each of their gaze one by one.

"Merlin," started Gawain quietly as the light bounced off his prominent green armour, "surely the people have the right to know?"

"No, Gawain," reaffirmed Merlin, "for the safety of Briton and the sanctity of its people, no-one but us must know of the king's demise."

"Surely, Merlin," said a new voice, "Gawain is right; the peoples of this nation should have the right to mourn the death of our Liege."

Merlin walked around the altar and looked into the eyes of the young knight who had raised his concerns. "My Lord Tristan," he said gently, "as we have seen, there are forces abroad and across the country that are waiting for the opportunity to seize the throne for their own ends." He turned and raised his arms high above his head and moved before the altar and his king, turning his back on the waiting knights. "Morgan Le Fay, Lancelot, Balin… all wait for the opportunity to lay siege to the kingdom. If any of these have any idea that the king is dead, then chaos will straddle the land." He paused allowing his words to sink in before continuing. "We must, for the safety of Briton, lead the people to believe that the king is alive and well."

"My father would not lay claim to the throne! He was a loyal servant!" protested Galahad angrily, stepping forward through the darkness as his hand drifted to his sword.

"I am sorry, Lord Galahad, but your father is not what you think he was. He was a gallant knight and an incredible fighter, but he was a hostage to his own sexuality. It was the actions of Lancelot with Queen Guinevere that led to Mordred uprising." He looked kindly at the knight and continued, "Your bravery and your dedication to the king is noble, my Lord, but your father is a danger to the kingdom. You must not contact him – for the sake of the people you must choose. Do you understand?"

Galahad nodded his understanding. "Today I have lost a king and a father," he commented sadly.

"I do not wish to cause you any increased heartache, but what I say is for the greater good."

"Will the people not question the king's absence?" asked Gawain.

Merlin considered the question; the thought had not struck him until now… But yes, people would. He would be conspicuous in his absence, both at court and throughout the country.

"It is well known, widespread across the land, that the king and Mordred were to battle at Camlann," began Merlin cautiously. "Both armies are now laid to waste with only we seven as survivors." He circled the cavern as he spoke with his arms folded behind his back as he considered his words carefully.

He stopped at the entrance to the cavern and gazed down the winding passage which stretched to the thin opening in the distance, at the far end of the tunnel and spoke into the open space. "The king has been injured during battle and has withdrawn his person here to Avalon to recover." He turned back to the waiting throng of knights who all stood close to the walls of the cavern. The knights stood in silent respect around the body of the king lying on the altar.

Merlin approached Arthur and reached forward towards the body and pulled the sword from the figure's grasp. "My Lord Bedivere," he spoke softly. A tall figure moved from the edge of the waiting group and knelt before the figure of Merlin. "Take Excalibur," he said and held the sword out in his hands towards Bedivere.

The knight looked up from his position on the floor and stared at the mighty blade resting in the palms of Merlin. "Return it to the Lady." Bedivere stood and took the sword from Merlin and pulled the object close to his body and nodded. "She will be waiting."

"And the scabbard?" Bedivere queried.

"That will be cared for…" He trailed off and peered down the tunnel. Through the shadows Merlin watched as a shape detached itself from the tunnel wall and pulled itself along the uneven floor. It walked slowly and dragged a leg behind its body, scraping the dead limb behind its large bulky frame.

"The Fisher King," whispered Kay.

"Yes," confirmed Merlin. "The Fisher King."

"Is this wise?" demanded Kay watching the figure as it dragged itself down the corridor. "The creature is an abhorrence to man!"

"That abhorrence was once one of the bravest knights in this kingdom!" snapped Merlin. He turned to the corridor and nodded, glancing between the oncoming figure and Sir Kay. "He is the keeper of the Holy Grail, and for that reason I see no-one better than to care for the scabbard than he."

The figure entered the cavern and stretched itself to its full height in the confined space. He stood at eight feet and stretched as water dripped from his body. He stood and examined the knights as they in turn examined him, staring at the hulking frame swathed in old rags and an elongated robe flowing from his body. He hung desperately to a crooked staff which held him upright and from around his waist a small plain chalice hung from a

14

belt. "My Lord Merlin," he stated simply in a muted tone. His voice was low and cracked as the age of time had ravaged his body and spirit.

Merlin walked to the figure and held his hands out in his direction. "My old friend," he gushed as he gripped the free hand of the Fisher King. "The years have not been kind to you," he offered as he considered the figure before him.

The Fisher King glanced down at his scarred body. "My wounds have not yet healed… but one day, God willing."

"I am sorry, but you are cursed to protect the Holy Grail," apologised Merlin. "For that thoust must bear your wounds as a symbol of honour."

The Fisher King nodded sadly. "I wait for the day of my release…"

"How can this… this… cripple protect the scabbard!" demanded Kay clenching his fist in frustration. "Please, Merlin, reconsider. Allow me to protect its honour."

"No… It has to be the Fisher King," said Merlin softly. "He bears the weight of responsibility to protect the Grail – who better to protect the scabbard as well?"

"I dismiss your logic, Merlin!" shouted Kay and stared defiantly at the old man who stood by the looming shadow of the Fisher King. He glared at them for a moment before turning his gaze away reluctantly and conceded. "But I do accept your wisdom and yield to your decision."

He watched as Merlin presented the Fisher King with the scabbard. "The scabbard is worth ten of the sword," he breathed quietly as he handed over the leather-bound object into the deformed hands of the Fisher King who bowed his head in silent acknowledgement. "One day," he whispered quietly towards the giant before him, "you will be called on again… Until then you must sleep and guard this item with your life."

"I understand," replied the Fisher King and slowly he turned and dragged his form down the passage leaning heavily on the stick and disappeared down the tunnel.

Merlin turned back to the attending knights. "Be about your business," he said, "and guard this country. Your king needs you now more than ever." He glanced towards the body on the altar and lowered his head in respect. "One day, my friends… one day the king will resurrect, and we must be ready." He trailed off and walked slowly towards the back of the cavern and lowered himself onto a large damp stone. The moisture stained his clothing as he closed his eyes, guarding them against the darkness.

One by one, the knights quietly bowed and left the figure of Merlin in quiet contemplation with his king.

"One day," mused Merlin, "one day."

2.

Come To Me…

The women stood waist deep in water as she beckoned towards the shoreline. Francis Pendragon stood on the beach gazing out at her form as she stood waving in his direction. He glanced at the floor and watched as the water lapped up against his trainers, the tide washing over the edge of the white trim of the predominantly black footwear.

"Come to me," she whispered seductively from her position within the water and teased a hand through her golden hair. Francis watched as her golden locks fell over her shoulder and draped its way over her naked breasts. Water teased his senses as it slowly ran over her flat stomach from her hair as it worked back into the lake.

"Francis," she called and pointed towards the young man on the shore. Her fingers beckoned to him as her other hand fell absently into the lake, stirring up the water and causing ripples to circulate and play around her naked waist. Her smile was illuminating, and her eyes flashed with a seductive stare, and she tilted her head slightly to the side. She smiled and spoke with the voice of an angel. "You know you want to," she called as the water circled her body.

Francis pulled his eyes away from the woman and back to his fully clothed body before he once again raised his gaze to meet the eyes of the woman. The big blue eyes burnt into his soul. Slowly he edged one foot into the lake and allowed the water to cascade over his trainers. His eyes remained focused on the woman in front of him as she toyed playfully with the water around her, letting the liquid slip and run through her fingers. Francis could hear singing drift across the still water towards him, pulling him further into the water, urging him more and more, closer and closer to this naked woman. He strained his ears at the sound and realised the tune was hypnotic in nature and together with her voice and demeanour it pulled him further into the water.

He could feel the cold of the lake bite as it surrounded his ankles, and he forged his way through the water. Each step felt like treacle as he pushed one foot before the other. He waded out further into the lake. The thought of the cold biting at his senses through his clothes flirted with his mind as he watched the woman circling her hands through the water, a smile constant on her face and she continued her insistence towards his advances.

"Francis, come to me," she begged softly over the sound of the singing. "It's warm in the water," she teased, a hand snaking towards the hair draped over her right breast. Francis watched her stroke the hair and as her hand followed the lines of her body, he could feel a stirring in his loins, but still he followed the sound of her voice. "You want to come," she cooed. "Closer… closer…" Francis was aware of the water chasing over his trousers as each step took him closer to the woman. "Nobody is forcing you," she purred. "But you want to… you want to come into the water. You want to come to me. You need to come to me. Your destiny awaits."

He was close to her; he could see his reflection in her eyes. He could feel the warmth of her body, even though the cold biting water as his jeans were now completely encapsulated by lake as the liquid encased his waist. She laughed as he reached out towards her and spun in the water causing the water to shimmer and ripple around her body, sending a thousand tiny sparkles across the calm sheen. She backed away from his reach slightly and smiled back to him over her shoulder. Francis could see the water lap around her waistline and pushed himself further into the water as she smiled at him. One more step, that is all it would be.

"Come to me," she urged again. Francis continued forward, closer… closer… Water traced its way around his own waistline. He reached out his hand towards her again, she was just within reach, just a little closer… a little nearer. The cold bit at his waist as he stretched his arm forward. She was within touching distance. Her smile was intoxicating. Her eyes made him drunk with sexual excitement… closer… closer.

Water swamped him. Francis could feel the sudden rush of water surge over his head – engulfing him completely. Panic rose in his mind; the sudden trauma of the inrush of cold swept him off his feet. Through the sudden coldness of the lake, Francis could see no sign of the woman as he struggled against the sudden tide. He thrashed against the current of the water as it threatened to drag him further into the mire. His legs kicked and his arms swung as the sensation of the water subdued him and threatened to dull his senses and overwhelm him.

Francis struggled against the water, casting his head upward and forcing his eyes open. Francis tried to pull himself above the water and see the surface of the lake, attempting to see the light from above, but nothing. His vision was blocked by darkness as the water engulfed him completely and weighed him down. The water pressed heavy against his body as he struggled for air. He could feel it solidifying around him as he fell deeper and deeper, darker and darker. The sensation was deafening.

The sudden pain in his shoulder forced Francis to wake, wrapped in the confines of his quilt. He sat on the floor of his bedroom and took several breathes, gratefully accepting air into his screaming lungs. A dream... just a dream, he told himself. His eyes cast their way around the darkness of his room, and he sighed as the light from his small alarm clock blinked out towards him. Almost four thirty, he thought as he picked himself up off the floor and sat on the edge of his bed and breathed heavily.

"Francis... Francis... Is that you?" the sound of a woman's voice echoed from the hall outside his door.

"Yes, Mum," he called back. "Sorry, bad dream." Francis listened to the mumbling from his mother but could not make out the answer to his admission.

Another nightmare, he thought to himself as his eyes played over the mess of clothing piled across his bedroom floor. Third night in a row, but this one... this one seemed so real... it seemed so different. The others had involved fighting... knights... and worlds of chivalry, but this was different. He scratched his head as he remembered the visions broadcast through his dream.

The woman, the lake – it had seemed so vivid, so real. But here he was sitting in his bedroom reflecting over dreams lost and pondering his future. Twenty-three years old, single and still living with his mother in a two-bedroom flat in the heart of Charlton. All his hopes, all his dreams – where had they gone? He held down a kind of good job in a local garage, but it was unfulfilling, and he had a niggling feeling that he had just settled for this life. He could do so much, he knew it... but how? He sighed and forced himself up from the bed and shuffled through the piles of clothing, coke cans and assorted wrappers swimming on his bedroom floor and reached for the handle of the door.

The coldness from the hallway bit at his naked torso as he pulled open the door and stared down the corridor. He glanced towards his mother's room before moving out into the hall. He placed his hand on the flowered wallpaper and traced its pattern as he walked carefully and quietly down the corridor towards a small door near the end of the passage.

Placing his hand flat against the door, Francis pushed at the barrier to the bathroom and slowly opened the door and taking one more glance towards his mother's room, stepped over the threshold into the small space beyond. His hand hovered for a moment over the light switch as he pulled the door behind him and stood for a moment as the darkness of the bathroom enveloped him. A quick flick of his finger illuminated the room, and he stood by the door surveying the shower cubicle and porcelain basin; he needed a wash, he realised, as the sweat from his body invaded his nose. Once again, he sighed and shuffled forward towards the toilet, taking a seat on the porcelain throne after pushing his pyjama bottoms to the floor.

Francis sat on the cold plastic of the seat, slowly lowered his head into his hands and cast his mind back to his dream. He had never bought into those people who analysed dreams and visions, but the woman… he could not shake the feeling that this had been different. What the hell was he doing? he asked himself and raised his head towards the shower. He needed a wash, that much was evident; he could feel the pearls of sweat cling to his body.

"Come to me." Francis frowned and glanced around the bathroom as a female voice whispered through the pipework which ran along the edge of the ceiling. It sounded like the voice from his dream and the words were the same as she had spoken.

He shook his head and ran a hand through his dishevelled hair. Now his mind was playing tricks on him, he thought. He briefly glanced down between his legs as his yellow urine mixed with the clear water of the toilet bowl. After a brief respite, he stood, discarded the remnants of his clothing and stepped before the shower cubicle completely naked. He reached into the confined unit, twisted the knob of the shower and watched as cold water forced its way out of the shower head.

He closed the door and returned to the toilet and sitting down on his bathroom throne, surveyed his kingdom as he waited for the water to heat up. He watched as the steam from the shower rose through the cubicle as the water turned from cold to hot and cascaded down the walls of the clear glass. Small droplets of water raced each other down the side and teased their way down the glass as they made their way back to the confines of the pipework and into the drain.

He stood and paused to listen at the door, mindful that his mother slept only a few doors away. Happy that there was no sound or movement from her room, Francis pulled open the cubicle door and stepped tentatively into the shower, allowing the water the play over his skin. He moved slowly under the flow of the water as his body temperature rose in tune with the heat in the shower, until finally he thrust his head under the waterfall from above. He closed his eyes and allowed himself to become immersed by the water. That felt better, he thought as the water washed away his grime and the dreams which had haunted his night.

He lowered his head under the flow and opened his eyes, staring at the water swirling around his feet for a moment, before reaching out to the small shelf at shoulder height which housed several small bottles of fragranced liquids. Grabbing a small black bottle, he forced the contents of liquid into his hand and rubbed it over his body, allowing the soapy substance the lather over his skin. Bubbles mingled and swirled around the plughole and chased each other as they tripped around his feet, the water washing over his body.

Francis raised his head and closing his eyes, allowed the water to wash over his face and down his neck. As he swayed his head from side to side, he allowed himself a wry smile as the sensation of water splashing against his body felt good. He rubbed his eyes and turned, letting the water strike his back and once again he closed his eyes in anticipation of the sensation of the ensuing waterfall. He lent forward and placed his palms against the cold glass of the cubicle and let the water flow over his back and haunches, and smiled as the sensation of flowing water warmed his buttocks. He closed his eyes as his hands strayed to his groin and using the moisture of the soap, slowly rubbed his growing genitals as he remembered the naked woman in his dream. Her body had seemed so perfect, so pure. His hand moved faster as his breaths increased as he rubbed quicker and quicker… faster and faster… until…

"Come to me." That voice again.

Francis snapped his eyes open at the sound of the female voice. His excitement turned to panic as a figure stood before him – no with him under the flow from the shower. She looked down at his naked body, then straight into his eyes as she moved nearer. His mind raced with a panic; standing in the shower before him, between his arms was a woman… a naked woman…

no… *the* woman… The woman from his dream.

She stood in the shower with him and smiled. Water struck her body and shimmered as steam rose from her body heat. "Come to me," she whispered again as the water flowed freely over her naked torso and down her waist and legs. Her long blonde hair once again covered her breasts as it had in his dream, but from his position he could see the mould of her breasts contour against the strands of her hair. "Come to me," she whispered again.

Shock overcame Francis and he fell backwards hard against the back of the shower cubicle and as darkness swam into his head, the vision of the smiling woman stood over his prone body.

3.

Arthur

"What?" roared the king. He stood from the throne and towered above the knight kneeling at the foot of his throne. The knight gazed up at his king, winced at ferocity in his eyes and quickly lowered his gaze away.

"Yes, my Liege," he stammered. "I saw it for myself."

The king stepped from the throne and placed a gauntleted hand on the shoulder of the knight. "Rise, Lord Kay, and tell me what you saw."

Kay rose and stood before his king looking up from the floor and taking in the regal figure before him. The king stood before the throne in full ceremonial dress, bequeathed in lavish robes and jewellery. The light from the torches scattered around the hall bounced and reflected off the small jewels set deep into the golden crest perched around the flowing dark locks of hair on the king's head.

"My Liege, forgive me," begged Kay staring into the king's brown eyes.

"No... forgive me, Lord Kay. The information that you partake is not your fault, but please thoust must tell me what you have seen."

"It was Lancelot, my Liege, of that I am certain," he glanced around the room as he spoke as though guilty of the admission to the king. "I saw him entering the bedding chambers of the Queen."

"You are certain?"

Lord Kay nodded and winced as King Arthur roared towards the ceiling before collapsing back into the throne. "My Guinevere," he whispered almost inaudibly. "Guinevere." He shook his head sadly and placed his hands on the arms of the throne, a look clouding over his features. "Give me your sword," he commanded Lord Kay.

"My Liege?" Kay queried.

"Your sword, Lord Kay. Give me your sword, that I may run it through that dog!" Kay frowned and placed his hand on the hilt of his sword locked deep within the scabbard hanging around his waist. "Give me it too me, man, or does thoust wish to feel my rage!" he demanded. "I shall not use

Excalibur on a slur like Lancelot!"

He thrust his hand out towards Lord Kay who knelt at his feet once again and withdrew his own sword from its scabbard and held it aloft towards the king. Anger flashed over his face as he held the sword in his hands for a moment and considered the knight before him. "Begone, Lord Kay, you can retrieve your sword another day," he said through gritted teeth before storming through the hall and squatting at a heavy curtain hiding the corridor beyond. His head bowed, and his eyes clamped tightly shut as he whispered a silent prayer before pulling at the curtain and plunging into the cold corridor beyond.

"Lancelot!" he roared down the corridor as he gripped the handle of the sword in a vice like grip. The sound echoed down the corridor as his voice bounced off the walls, disturbing the resting vermin hidden in crevices in the castle.

Francis stirred from his position on the floor of the shower cubicle, water pounding on his body. A sudden pain gripped his back, and he tentatively reached a hand around his body and gingerly touched the sore area. He could not feel anything and shook his head to clear the confusion in his mind. The water from the showerhead splashed over his face and Francis rubbed his eyes and cast his gaze around the room. There was no sign of the woman, but he knew she had been there in the room with him. Not just the room, but in the shower!

He remembered the mixture of shock and excitement before he had passed out. A tinge of embarrassment flushed over him as he suddenly recalled collapsing backwards during the exchange before several questions flooded his mind. Who was she? How did she get in? Where was she now? And was he going mad? In his heart of hearts, Francis knew there would be no way that a naked woman could have got into the shower let alone the flat, but still the sound of her voice echoed in his head and the smell of her invaded his nose. He rubbed the end of his nose and took a strong sniff and could smell the faint odour of… apples? He shook his head and forced himself to his feet and stabbed a finger at the shower controls turning off the flow of water through the nozzle.

"Francis! Francis!" came a woman's voice from outside the door. "Are you still in there? What are you doing, boy?" demanded the voice. "You better not be doing what I think you're doing… Not in my house!"

"Mother!" snapped Francis. "I'm not… I'm fine, just washing."

"Still!" she snapped back.

"Go back to bed, Mother. I'm all right!" he called through the door, covering his body with the large red towel which hung over the radiator by the door.

"Go back to bed!" she howled. "Go back to bed! It is almost nine o'clock!" she called as she banged on the bathroom door. "You're going to be late for work. If your father were still here…"

Nine o'clock? How could it be so late. Francis looked around the room in confusion. He had been in here for nearly four hours. He did not understand what was happening to him – the woman? He frowned and ran his hands through his hair. He could hear the strained voice of his mother filtering through the door, but there was something else… another voice, not the woman but another… a man's. He was shouting.

"*Lancelot!*" It stormed faintly then drifted off through the ether of the steam in the room.

"Yeah! Well, he ain't, is he!" he snapped back through the door unaware of the rest of his mother's sentence. "He walked out years ago, didn't he!" Francis immediately regretted his words even before he had finished speaking to them and the guilt weighed heavily on him as he heard a gush of emotion from the other side of the door followed by footsteps rushing down the hall. He cursed inwardly and opened the door and peered through the darkened hallway. "Mother?" He paused to listen. "Mum," he attempted again. "I'm sorry," he whispered into the air and closed the door and moved back into the bathroom.

He leant on the sink and gazed at the clean white porcelain basin and cursed loudly at his stupidity. He cast his gaze at the mirror above the sink and frowned as the glass was covered by a condensation sheen over the surface of the mirror. He raised a hand and swiped at the glass, wiping away great portions of moisture and peered at the face gazing back at him from the shined surface.

Francis recoiled in horror as the face which gazed back at him from the reflective surface was not his own.

He did not recognise the face and he could feel a sensation of panic rise through his body as the face of an elderly man gazed back through the glass and cast a shadow on the wall behind him. He stepped away from the sink and thrust his body towards the door, desperate to escape the nightmare which his life was becoming. He pulled at the handle and pulled the door open, casting a quick glance back into the room and into the heart of the mirror and into the eyes of... the eyes of... the eyes of himself.

He stopped himself from moving out of the door frame and peered at the mirror and at his own face. He grimaced and clutched his face, feeling a pounding on the inside of his skull and his world swirled out of focus. He placed a hand on the patterned wallpaper to steady himself and struggled along the hall towards his room. "Mother!" he called out weakly. "Mum!"

Darkness enveloped him for the second time in a few hours.

4.

The Past and Future King

"Are you sure?" asked a woman's voice.

"Yes. It is him," assured a male's voice filled with age. The two figures stood in the semi-gloom of a large cavern and examined a stone chalice, gazing into the watery depths of the vessel. The woman stood gripping the edges of the chalice with her semi-naked form and long blonde hair draped over her shoulder and hidden breasts. Her beauty shone like a beacon through the cavern, and she glanced up from the water at her companion. The man was older and dressed in long flowing robes of a tattered material. He stood leaning against a long staff and gazed into the pool rubbing his whitening beard. "He is the direct bloodline descendant."

"But is he ready?"

"Is anyone?" queried the old man.

"Why now, Merlin? After all of these years?"

"I can feel now, more than any other time the people of Briton need a protector." His words echoed through the cave as visions flashed over the surface of the water of people dying, explosions and violence in streets before the image returned to that of an unconscious Francis on the floor of his home with his mother kneeling beside his body.

"He is but a boy—"

"Who will prove himself when the time is right," assured Merlin. "As did Arthur." Merlin gazed at the woman for a moment before speaking. "Now return to the Isle. We shall talk again soon."

The woman nodded and draped a hand across his shoulder as she walked past. "You do realise that if he is a direct descendant to Arthur Pendragon and releases Excalibur, then she will awaken."

Her words hung in the air as he watched her while she walked along the passage to the entrance. He nodded sadly. "If Excalibur is awake then she shall know." He returned his attention to the pool of water and stared deep into its blackness at the image of the young man.

"Francis… Francis." His mother gently slapped his face as she knelt by his prone body. He could feel the sensation on his cheek but could do little about it. "Francis. You all right… come on, boy," she pleaded.

"Mother," he said meekly raising his head slightly.

"Oh! My boy," she cried and threw her arms around his head pulling her deep into her bosom.

"Mum," he whined. "I'm fine." Francis tried to push his mother's attention off him, but the woman's maternal instinct was overpowering.

"I say if you're fine or not," she reprimanded him as she held him tight in her grip.

"Please mother…" he said, pushing her off him. "I'm fine, I promise." He sat up on the floor of the hall and rubbed his head. "I've just been working too hard," he lied.

"This has happened before?" his mother asked.

"No… no," again he lied avoiding eye contact with her. "I've just had trouble sleeping."

"You need a rest," she declared. "Let me ring your work and tell them you won't be in."

"No, Mum."

"You can't go in. Not in that state," she chided. He shook his head and struggled to his feet and sagged against the wall. "That settles it! You get back to bed while I ring work for you."

Francis was too tired to argue with the woman and reluctantly accepted her help back to his room. She pushed the door open and looked into the mess laden bedroom. "And you can get this lot cleaned up and put away while your off!" she said.

Francis looked at her and saw a smile break across the woman's face as she chided him. "Mum…" he began uncomfortably. "I… well… what I said… you know… earlier." He shuffled in the doorway unsure how to broach the apology.

"Ssh… it's all right," she eased. "I know. Mummy always knows." She smiled and closed the door and Francis slumped onto the bed, allowing himself to become immersed in the pillow and he listened as his mother's voice echoed down the corridor singing as she walked.

He closed his eyes and struggled to understand the dreams and visions which were affecting him. They were getting stronger, especially the woman and as sleep overcame him a tiny part of his active mind worried that he was beginning to lose his sanity.

The door to the large bedroom was flung open and framed in the half-light of the flames from the torches in the corridor stood the king. His face matched the colour of his crimson robes and the light from the torch illuminated against the metal of his crown. "Where is he?" he roared. The room was still and the heat from an open fire burnt brightly in the hearth at the far end of the room which stifled the atmosphere.

"My Lord!" snapped the woman in the bed. "How dare you enter my chambers unannounced!" She sat in her bed fully clothed in a white night dress, lined with intricate frills and stitching. Her golden hair flowed down her back and strands snaked over her shoulder as she sat staring with hostility towards the king.

"No room in my castle is barred to me!" the king roared back. "Especially those of my wife!" He stood, with sword in hand casting his gaze across the room. "Now, I will not ask again," he demanded. "Where is that knave?"

"I do not know whom thee are speaking of," she replied and cast her gaze away from the doorway indignantly.

"Lancelot!" spat the king. "I know he is here!"

"There is nobody here but we two," she said still refusing to look at the king.

"Liar!" The king strode into the room and took a swipe at a hanging tapestry close to the door. "You lie! Harlot!" He glanced an accusing look at her and pulled at a second tapestry.

"My Lord," she begged casting a quick glance towards him. "You are my husband… and my life!"

A laugh from Arthur cut off her sentence. "My life!" he spat. "My life… Your infidelity is as clear as your lies. Once I catch the cur, I shall cut out his liver and feed it to the birds." The Queen glimpsed briefly downward, only for a moment, but her look was caught by the king. "I knew it," he roared dropping to his knees by the bed.

"No! Please, my Lord," begged the Queen. "Please…" she screamed as Arthur thrust the sword beneath the bed and swiped it wildly at the space. A figure scrambled from beneath the other side of the bed and pulled himself to his feet staring at his king.

"My Lord," he smiled as he spoke.

"Lancelot!" spat the king as he too pulled himself to his feet and leant on the bed. "Explain thy presence, Sir."

Lancelot spread his hands wide, before smoothing his black hair. "It is my duty to protect the Queen, my Lord," he said insincerely. "I simply entered her quarters to ascertain my Lady's safety in these times of unrest."

"You lie," accused Arthur and lunged forward across the covers of the bed with his sword. Lancelot jumped back from the bed, avoiding the thrust of the blade with ease.

He moved forward to the bed and sized up his opposition. "My Lord," he grinned. The king roared his disapproval at the knight and moved from his position by the bed around the foot of the bed. Lancelot dressed in a light plain white shirt and breaches leapt over the bedding and the Queen and ran for the doorway laughing as the king was left in his wake. Arthur swiped the sword at empty air as Lancelot made his escape for the corridor. Torches flickered as the knight ran down the stone lined hallways of the castle and flames jumped and licked at the heels of the disappearing Lancelot.

"Squire!" yelled Arthur angrily as he struggled out of the room fully adjourned in his ceremonial robes. "Squire!" he called as he gave chase down the corridor. "My horse!" The robes made the king more cumbersome than his fleet footed opponent, but nevertheless he continued the chase down the corridor. "You run, Lancelot," he called as the knight disappeared from view. "You run... for when I catch thee, I will fillet your gizzard."

Francis sat bolt upright in his bed and cast his gaze around his room. Nothing seemed different; the clothes were still scattered in indiscriminate piles across the floor. A small tide of rubbish cascaded over his bin and over the desk was an avalanche of paper and disks, but somehow, he could not shake the sensation that he was being watched. He ran his fingers through his hair and groaned as the pounding in his head drummed against the walls of his brain as he sank back down beneath the covers of his bed.

"Lancelot," he cursed quietly under his breath then frowned. Where the hell did that come from? he thought. He did not even know anyone of that name. He had lost count today how many times he had questioned his own sanity and attempted to rise from the bed. His body felt heavy, weighed down by an unsuspecting force presenting on his soul and pressing down against his body.

Francis attempted to pull himself out of bed, but again he felt an extreme pressure placed on his ribs and brought his arm up over the blankets and rested it on his naked chest. Breathing heavily for a moment he lay in quiet contemplation of just what exactly was happening to him.

"Come to me." The whisper was faint and came from the direction of the window.

Francis turned his head to the source of the noise and stared from his bed through the glass. A small bird perched on the sill and regarded Francis with curious eyes for a moment before flying off. For the briefest of moments Francis wished he were that bird, free to soar high above the Earth and through the darkening sky. Darkening sky? He frowned and turned his head towards his desk and strained under the light to make out the numbers dancing over the image presented by the small black clock resting on the surface. The red light seemed to swirl and buckle under his gaze, before settling down into a presentation of time. Four o'clock.

Francis closed his eyes for a moment. How the hell had he slept all day? he wondered to himself. Why hadn't his mother woken him? Questions surfaced in his mind and again he found an intense pressure push down on his chest stopping him from breathing. He could feel a panic rising through his body and forced into submission by the confusion in his head as the events of the day struggled to cross his memories. The dreams… the woman… Lancelot? Why that name again? What was happening?

He pushed at the blankets and allowed them to fall in a heap on the floor by his bed and threw a look down across his body. He lay prone on the bed, dressed in not his grey linen bottoms and plain white t-shirt, but instead in full body armour. The chest plate of the suit lay heavy on his chest and was bejewelled with a draped insignia cast in light material of a rampant yellow lion set before a field of brilliant red. His legs were encrusted with heavy armour, gleaming and shining in the fading light and his arms were covered in patches of chain mail.

He could feel himself losing control of his body and panic coursed through his veins. "Mum!" he yelled.

"My Liege." The man knelt on the floor before King Arthur as he sat regally staring out over the courtroom. The hall was empty, barring the two men and the king sat brooding over recent events which had led to the ultimate betrayal.

31

"Speak," he commanded in the quiet voice.

"It is Lancelot, my Lord." A fire sparked in King Arthur's eyes, and he glared at the kneeling knight who remained staring at the floor unable to meet his king's gaze. "I have news from Iseult, my Lord."

"I care not," lied Arthur as he sat with his fingers entwined for a moment, quietly seething under his own loathing.

The air was still in the room and the silence was deafening as the knight shuffled uncomfortably in his position and raised his head slightly to catch a glimpse of his king. Arthur looked tired. His eyes were ringed with eons of distress and edged with a bitter red hue. The pressure of the last few days had taken a toll on the king and the stories of Lancelot and Guinevere had spread throughout court like a plague and the ire of the king rose with each word. Riders had sped out through every part of the kingdom in search of the errant knight who had once been the favourite of the king as he fled. The love of the king towards his beloved Guinevere was unbridled by only his passion towards his position and his people.

"Well," spat the king. "I have not all day, speak!" he commanded.

"But, my Lord—" stammered the knight.

"I command thee to speak… or by God I will see that you never speak again," he roared.

"My Liege." A new voice came from the doorway and eased through the hall towards the pair.

"Lord Kay, this is of no concern to thee," spat the king.

"My Lord, your welfare is everyone's concern," he insisted. "We stand together against whatever threat beholds yourself and in turn the kingdom." He crossed the expanse of the hall as he spoke.

"You were one of my first knights," warned Arthur. "But be warned, Lord Kay, I shall not hesitate to dispatch you if I feel the need."

"My Lord, I have not come here looking for a fight, but instead to counsel thy good self."

"Then give me counsel."

"Merlin has sent me to broker a resolution surrounding this incident. He fears for thoust wellbeing."

"Then, where is he?" shouted Arthur casting his gaze around the hall. "If he is so concerned then why do I not see him in person?"

"He has other matters to attend, my Lord." Lord Kay spread his hands before him and bowed his head as he stood before the throne. "He fears for the future." He raised his head to look into the eyes of the king. "Thy *future."*

"My future," spat Arthur rising from the throne and crossing to the window. He looked over the cascading countryside and spoke over his shoulder. "The people depend on me, Kay," he spoke softly as he looked over the land. "They need a solid and strong leader. They need a powerful king whom they will follow. The actions of Lancelot have brought shame on me and my kingdom. My enemies will see this as a sign of weakness, Lord Kay, a weakness that they shall benefit from. I must act." He sighed and lowered his gaze to the floor before turning to look at Kay. He moved over to the knight and placed a hand on his shoulder and whispered, "If the people feel their king is weak then there is naught that can be done, perhaps my time is over."

"My Lord."

Arthur raised his hand to the knight. "Everything has its time, Lord Kay, and perhaps this is mine."

"No! My Liege, your people need you. You are a great and kind man."

"Thank you, but I am tired... I am tired of everything." He cast his eyesight around the hall. "The whole thing." He sighed and slumped into the throne and rested his head into the palm of his hand.

"No, my Lord, you are wrong. You are a strong leader and a better man than most of us. That is why you are betrothed as king and protector supreme." Lord Kay looked down at the errant knight still from his kneeling position on the floor. "At least, my Lord, hear what the man has to say."

Arthur nodded and gazed down at the knight. "Well, man! What have thee to say?" he commanded.

The knight kept his head towards the floor and spoke into the ground. "I have word from Iseult, that Lancelot has fled to France—" His words died in his throat as the king leapt from the throne.

"Lord Kay," he roared. "We ride this day for France!"

5.

Knightly Visions

The walls swam into view for what felt like the hundredth time that day and through sleep encrusted eyes, he stared around the room. A blurred figure sat at his table and Francis struggled to make out the person in the chair. He groaned as he attempted to sit, his hands fleeting over his body checking for signs of the armour which had caused his last 'panic attack'.

"Francis," cooed the soft voice from the chair.

"Mother?" he queried.

"Who else would it be? Stupid boy," she demanded before her tone softened. "Sorry, son, how are you feeling?"

His eyes wandered over his body and he tentatively, gently pulled back the blankets. The armour had gone and been replaced by his plain old grey bottoms and white shirt. He cast his gaze back to his mother and frowned as he glimpsed the clock on the table. "How long have I been asleep?" he asked.

"All day," she replied. "It's almost eight." She leant forward in her chair and placed her palm on his forehead and sighed. "You're feeling a little warm," she said.

"Mother," he complained half-heartedly as he brushed her hand away. "How long have you been sitting there?" he asked.

"Off and on all day," she admitted. "I've been worried about you." A concerned look fluttered over her face.

"Mum! I'm fine," he moaned and turned to face the wall pulling the blankets closer to his body.

"Don't you dare mum me!" she snapped. "I care for you, boy, and this is all the thanks I get! If your father were still here..." Her voice trailed off as she remembered her husband before he had walked out on them years previously. Francis turned back and sat up in bed and watched his mother for a moment with sadness. Although she never admitted it, he knew a day did not go by that she had not thought of his father and what had happened between them. "You're all I have left." She turned on her heels and made for the door.

"Mum…"

She absently wiped her eyes and turned her head away from him. "Dinners in the microwave," she said softly and smiled as she looked back at her son. She placed her hands together and her smile waned, and she regarded him solemnly. "Are you all right?" she asked again. Francis struggled to find an answer for her, in truth he did not fully understand what was happening himself. "Is it drugs? Is that it? Because if it is I can cope with that. I can help you."

"No!" snapped Francis before checking his speech. "Sorry, Mum, but no it isn't drugs." He swung his legs over the edge of the bed and gripped his mother's hands. "I promise, I've just been overdoing things at work lately. I probably just need a bit of a rest, that's all."

"All right then." She sighed. "If that's all it is." He nodded towards her but found it slightly disconcerting that she never returned his smile. He watched as she walked to the door and gently pulled at the entrance and paused in the door frame. "Who's Arthur?" she asked facing the wall of the hallway.

Arthur? Francis' head swam with the mention of the name, and he reached a hand for his head. "Pardon?" he asked weekly.

"I said," she reinforced turning to face her son. "Who is Arthur?"

"New bloke at work," he lied. "Giving the boss a bit of trouble, that's all, nothing else." He cast his gaze to the floor, and he pretended to search for his clothes amongst the piles of laundry cast around the room. The silence between the two of them was almost tangible and Francis sifted through a small pile of clean clothing, aware of his mother's presence.

"Not giving you any trouble, is he?" she said gazing at the top of his head. "Cause if he is, I'll go down to that garage of yours and have words with him, I will."

"No, Mum, don't." He looked up at her and could feel the panic rising in his stomach and the feeling that his lie had been seen straight through. He felt a twang of relief course through his body as he saw his mother standing in the door frame smiling in his direction.

"All right," she said eventually. "Do you want your dinner heated?" she asked as she stepped into the hall.

"In a minute. I will be there a moment. Let me get dressed first," he called at her retreating form as she stomped her way down the hallway. He sat alone in his room for a moment gazing around at the mess which littered his floor and shook his head. How the hell had he slept all day? He could not understand what was happening, the dreams… the visions. His head swam under the intensity of the day, and he placed his head in his hands.

"Come to me." That voice again. Francis lifted his head from his hands, half expecting to see the woman once again. He gazed around his room searching for the sound of the voice only to be met by silence.

"Where are you?" he asked the empty room.

"Come to me." There it was again. Soft and gentle but definitely there. He was sure of it. Was he going mad? he asked himself. Hearing voices. He had always doubted the plausibility of people who claimed they heard things, but now he was experiencing it himself.

The light of the moon spilled in through the window and cast shadows across the surface of the walls. He gazed from his bed out into the night sky and watched as the clouds floated aimlessly across the sky covering the small splattering of stars which shone and sparkled high above. He always thought there were more stars when he was small, and his memory was cast back as a child when he would stand with his father gazing at the Great Bear, Orion's Belt and the North Star. Where were they now? Things seemed much simpler when he had been a child. He stood, crossed to the window and stared down to the street below.

"Come to me."

He frowned as the light from a streetlight illuminated a small area of the road and beneath stood the form of a woman… no, *the* woman, still naked, and just… just standing there staring up towards his window. Francis could feel himself falling back away from the glass and was forced to steady himself on the edge of his desk.

"Come to me." The voice penetrated through the window and played at his hearing, teasing and tempting him.

With renewed effort, Francis forced himself back to the window and fumbled with the lock. His fingers felt heavy and clumsy as he struggled with the latch before pushing the pane wide open. "What do you want?" he shouted down into the street below. "Leave me alone!"

The woman gazed at the open window and smiled, beckoning upward towards the flat.

"Francis! Francis!" The sound of his mother's voice broke his concentration and he glanced towards the open door of his room.

"It's all right, mother," he called.

"What is all that shouting?" she called.

"I've got my window open! I think it's people outside arguing."

"Well, shut that damn window; it's cold and it's raining," she complained. "You're not the one who pays the bills."

"Yes, Mum." He looked out of the window again and frowned as the image of the woman had disappeared. He glanced around the room, searched briefly for some clothes and dressed hurriedly. He needed to do this, he thought as he pulled his jeans on over his bottoms and snatched his jacket thrusting his arms through the sleeves. "Mum," he stammered standing in the hall. His body was half framed by the sitting room door obstructing her view of him. He looked in the room at his mother sitting watching the television and waited for her to turn in her chair. "I'm just gonna go for a little walk to try to clear my head a bit."

She nodded. "Just you be careful," she warned, then called down the corridor as he walked for the front door. "Wear something warm and keep dry. Have you got your keys? I'm not waiting up."

"Yes, Mum, okay, Mum," he called back as his fingers wandered to his trouser pockets where the cold metal of the keys touched his skin. "Won't be long," he promised as he quietly pulled the door closed behind him and gazed down the hall towards the lift at the far end of the corridor.

The rain fell on his face as he stood on the threshold of the block and gazed over the car park towards a small patch of grass close to the main road. It felt cold against his skin as traces of water residue slid over his face and snaked over his features as the rain drenched his body. The world around him appeared to blur and fade from his view as he peered through the rain and over toward… the woman…

There she was just standing in the rain.

He frowned and wiped the rain from his face and stared at the woman. She stood under the light from the streetlamp oblivious to the rain around her, the water coursing over her naked body. The water soaked her blonde hair and cascaded over her head and shoulders before running down her chest following the curves of her breasts, then tracing the contours of her flat stomach and finally falling from her naked groin and legs.

Francis stepped out into the rain and walked slowly across the courtyard. His eyes never left the woman as his feet splashed in the puddles which lay scattered over the street. The cold bit at his skin through his heavy clothing and he pulled his jacket close around his body. He thrust his hands deep into his pockets as he forged a way out into the storm. He glanced around him as he walked through the rain at the empty street around him and eventually stood before the woman. She stood naked in the rain, staring out through deep mystic blue eyes and inclined her head slightly at his curiosity.

"Come to me," she whispered, her words floating to his ears through the wind.

His eyes flicked over her body, lingering on her breasts before wandering down her body, examining every aspect of her naked form and drawn towards her groin and legs before returning to her face.

"Who are you?" he asked. The woman said nothing just stood casting her gaze over his body. She tilted her head from side to side as she carefully observed his movements. "Well?" he demanded.

Francis glanced around him. He was sure he was being watched but even from his vantage point beneath the streetlight he could see no-one in the area apart from the two of them. The woman still stood in silence and Francis could feel frustration rising in the pit of his stomach and fought to remain calm. His eyes were once again drawn to her breasts, and he lingered over their form. He watched with a growing arousal as the water played over her breasts, running and flowing over the fleshy mounds and falling over her erect nipples.

"You are the Pendragon." It was more a statement than a question and were the first words he had heard from her since her demand.

"Pardon?" he asked.

"You are the Pendragon," she repeated blinking through the rain.

Francis examined her face as she spoke for the second time. The woman was extremely pretty, with eyes which shone and sparkled like pools of an azure liquid in the sunlight while her hair, although sodden by the rainfall was long and flowing with the cascading blonde locks falling over her slim shoulders.

She waited patiently for an answer as Francis stood shivering in the cold rain and he realised that despite the conditions she appeared not to notice the bitterness of the conditions. "He is not the one," she said again looking past Francis as she spoke.

Francis glanced behind him expecting a third person to be standing there, but again saw no-one. He watched and frowned as she appeared to be listening to something, someone…

The cave was dark and dank, and the woman stood gazing into the deep pool of the stone chalice. "He is not the one," she spoke into the water as she gazed into its depths. The image in the water shimmered under her scrutiny as the couple stood in the hostile conditions confronting each other. The young man stood in the ripples watching the naked female before him, unmoving. "He is confused," she stated.

"He is confused," spoke the woman. Francis pulled his hands from his jacket and spread them out by his sides.

"To right I am," he cursed. "What's going on? Who are you?" he demanded again.

The woman watched the scene unfold in the water. "He does not know. He is of no importance to us," she said.

"He will," the male voice broke the silence of the cave and caused the woman to look up from her vigil. "He is the one," came the old voice. "I can feel it." The man stepped into the light of the cave and crossed to the stone chalice and peered into the water. "Have faith," he said softly, and he eased into a position opposite her. Raising his head, he looked into the blue eyes of the woman and smiled through the ageing grey whiskers of his beard. "Have faith in me, if not him."

She looked at him for a moment and returned her gaze to the water as the young boy took a step towards the image before him.

"He does not know. He is of no importance to us," the woman said causing Francis to glance around him once again and not for the first time that day question his own sanity.

"Who are you talking to?" he demanded. He felt foolish as the silence between them grew as she stood gazing into the rain, past him into… into nothing. The rain was biting at her flesh and Francis felt a pang of guilt at her nakedness and took a step towards her pulling his jacket from his body.

The woman raised her hand out towards him and showed him the flat of her palm indicating for him to stop. "You're cold," he said meekly as his jacket hung limply in his hands. "Put this on."

"He has chivalry," commented the old man as the pair watched through the water.

The woman snapped, "That does not make him a hero or a king."

A look of anger flashed over her face as she spoke which caused the old man to smirk at her ire. "Trust me, the time is nigh!"

She sighed and returned to gaze to the water as he melded back into the shadows. She shook her head and allowed a small smile to play over her lips as she whispered to herself, "Merlin, you are a romantic fool," when he disappeared.

Francis found himself frozen as the woman held him at bay with her gesture. "That does not make him a hero or a king," she said as she looked through Francis as though she were talking to someone else. He could see her, but he felt she was talking to someone else. Was she a ghost?

"I never said it did," he said. "And I'm not either." He stood unsure what to do and pulled his jacket back over his body. Water drenched his body, and he could feel the rain trickling down his back and felt the cold biting at him even through his clothes. "Look," he admitted, "I don't know what's going on here or even what I'm doing or even if you're here or not, but I'm pretty sure that if we stay out here any longer, we'll catch our deaths."

The woman stood watching him and an amused smile fleeted across her face for a moment before she whispered almost inaudibly, "Merlin, you are a romantic fool."

Francis could feel his head spin with the name, and he staggered under his own weight. That name: it was so familiar, not just through modern culture and mythology, but a connection with the dreams he was having about Arthur and Lancelot and of course this woman. Were they connected? Merlin?

Francis sagged to his knees, and he gazed up through the rain at the naked woman before him as she cast her gaze down at his crumpled body. She took a step closer to him and he could feel the heat of her body close to his face as the woman peered down regally at him. Francis rested his hands on the pavement and water swamped his hands and ravaged his skin.

"You are the Pendragon," she stated simply from her vantage point over his body.

He raised his head allowing his vision to ease over her body only inches before him and sat back on his legs in the wet conditions. Her groin was close to his head, and he sighed deeply as a sob forced its way out of his body. He could feel himself losing his mind as events were spiralling out of control quickly. He did not understand what was happening. He knew at this distance from this naked woman he should be feeling highly aroused, but instead all he could think of was the increasing feeling of panic and fear coursing through his veins.

"Follow your heart," she said as she placed a hand on the top of his head. "Come to me." Those words again; they were haunting him. "Come to me," she purred as the image of the woman disappeared. "Come to me, follow your heart, come to me... your destiny..."

The feeling on his head eased as the vision of the woman faded before him and Francis found himself kneeling on the wet pavement, rain falling on his body. Alone. The woman had gone. He glanced around as he knelt on the ground and could see through his blurred eyesight a series of curious eyes and hidden whispers as couples walked past him.

He wondered how long they had been there and pulled himself to his feet glancing around. The woman was nowhere in sight. What had she said? Follow your heart. Perhaps that is what he needed. A holiday. Perhaps that is what his body was telling him, that he needed a break.

He pulled his jacket further over his body and made the short journey back to his home and shuddered as the cold wind combined with the biting rain pounded on his body. His mind whirled with thoughts of the encounter with the woman and the dreams which were haunting his sleep. He opened the door to his home, unsure how he had made it back and he frowned as he struggled to remember the short walk home. He looked down the hall towards the room where the light from the television spilled through the door.

"Mum," he called, "Mum." He waited for a response for a moment before continuing. "I'm going to go away for a few days. Is that okay?" His voice drifted down the hall and he stood in the hallway for a moment waiting for his mother's approval.

The door to the living room opened slightly and his mother poked her face through the gap. Shadows illuminated and played across her face and she looked on with concern towards her son. "Are you sure that's what you want?" she asked.

Francis nodded. "I think I've been overdoing things at work." He shrugged. "The break might do me good."

She smiled warmly at her son. "Where will you go?"

Francis blinked in the hallway. He hadn't thought of that, he realised, and his mind drifted back to the dreams and visions he had been experiencing. He was sure they were the key to his problems, and he struggled to remember the last dream. He closed his eyes and images of the king preparing to travel abroad swam into his mind. He opened his eyes and stared intently at his mother. "France," he said resolutely.

The woman straightened from her position over the stone chalice. She smiled in the shadows and spoke indiscriminately into the darkness. "It is done," she stated simply to the waiting shadows. "He will come."

From the back of the cavern a large shape detached itself from the wall and straightened to its full height. The image was still hidden from sight in the darkness, but its voice broke the revere of the cavern. "I am prepared." The gravelly tones shattered to the silence as the small glimmer of light touched on the shape's skin. The reflection from the figure's skin glistened in the semi-gloom and its eyes sparkled in the light as it settled back into its position against the dank cavern wall. "All is ready."

6.

Designs on the Throne

Sleep eluded Francis as he lay on his bed fully clothed and staring at the ceiling. His eyes wandered over to the hastily packed bag leaning against the wall in the corner of the room. The pack bulged under the weight of his clothing stuffed at random inside the backpack as it laid expectantly waiting, patiently for its impending journey. He clutched tightly at his small burgundy passport in his hands as they laid over his chest and he hazarded a quick nap allowing his eyes to close for a moment. Questions bounded into his head. Was he doing the right thing? he wondered or was he running away from his problems?

Most of the night he had spent convincing himself that he was doing the right thing. His tired mind begged for sleep, but his conscious mind reminded him that his visions crept into reality through his dreams, and he fought to keep himself awake. He sighed and swung his legs over the edge of the bed and stared through the darkness towards his clock on the table. The small red lights blinked at him and mocked his sleepless night. Four o'clock. Francis rubbed his tired eyes and sighed as he looked at the clock and its relentless march onward. There was no sound from outside his room and the quietness slightly unsettled him as he rose from the bed and crossed to the window, where he parted the curtains and gazed out onto the street below. His visions were beginning to leak into the waking house as the woman once again stood in her naked form beneath the streetlight and beckoned up towards him as he peered from behind the glass pane.

"Come to me," she whispered. Her voice wafted up through the early morning air and passed through his window caressing his ears. The sound of her whisper was barely audible, but still sent shivers along his spine. He backed away from the window and allowed the curtain to fall back into place hiding the street from view. "Come to me." He could still hear her voice as he collapsed down onto the bed.

Francis closed his eyes and hid the room as he crossed his arms over his head attempting to block out the sounds of her voice.

"*Sire!*" *The sound of Lord Kay's voice broke the revere of the king as he sat high in his saddle. He swept his gaze over the courtyard towards the plethora of knights awaiting his command before turning his attention to the knight at his side.*

"*Speak,*" *he replied simply before returning his attention once again to his charge between his legs. The dark brown charger swayed beneath his touch and stamped at its own impatience at the head of the precession.*

"*Is it wise to leave Mordred on the throne until our return, my Lord?*"

Arthur scanned his knight for a moment. "*You question my decision?*" *he asked.*

Lord Kay shifted under the king's scrutiny. "*No, my Lord, but...*"

"*But? Speak freely, Lord Kay,*" *replied Arthur.* "*I wish to hear your counsel.*"

"*Lord Mordred is known for his treachery, my Lord, and it is widely known that he covets the throne... as does his aunt.*"

King Arthur laughed at Kay's concerns and waved away his protests. "*Good knight, you question your king? You question my authority? Who would thoust place on the throne in my absence? Yourself, Lord Kay? Do thou covet my throne?*" *The king laughed as Kay held up his hands and shook his head.* "*You worry too much. Yes, I concede the ambitions of Mordred, but thy king has divine passage to the throne of Briton and Mordred would dare not wrestle that from these hands,*" *he held outstretched his armoured hands before him as he spoke.*

"*He seeks good favour, Lord Kay, and I have faith Merlin will keep that harpy Morgaine in check until our return. Now let us talk no more of deceit and instead ride to France to meet Iseult and deal with the treacherous Lancelot.*"

Kay nodded at his king and respectfully bowed his head before taking his place behind the king. Arthur cast a glance behind him and sat for a moment watching his knights settle into position and felt his heart swell with pride as the banners fluttered in the wind. Satisfied that all was well, he pulled his sword from its scabbard and raised it high above his head. "*Onward!*" *he roared and with a slight kick into the horse's ribs and line of knights spent forward into the morning air.*

From above the courtyard a figure detached itself from the window of the throne room and strode purposely across the hall to the expectant throne. His golden armour shimmered under the candlelight and a smirk played across his face as he settled into the large chair.

"Comfortable?" A female voice broke the silence of the Great Hall and caused the man to writhe uncomfortably in the throne for a moment.

"Good Morgaine," he purred as he turned to the source of the voice. He watched as the woman glided across the floor towards him. Her form was tall and slim, and she wore an elegant air of grace which matched her long flowing gown. Golden hair cascaded down her back and fell from beneath a simple jewelled golden crown which sat majestically on her head. Her blue eyes shone with a deadly intelligence as she regarded the figure in the chair. She smiled, running her hand across his chest as she slowly teased herself towards the back of the throne. Her beauty was as striking as it was deadly, and her silky tones played in his ear as she leant closely towards his head. She eased back his unruly black hair and breathed warmly into his ear, whispering softly.

"You covet what is not yours," she breathed seductively.

"What man does not," replied Mordred simply and turned to face her. "It is my desire which drives me, not the want of the people."

"That pleases me," she teased and allowed her hand to run down the front of his body until it reached his waistline. Mordred looked down at her hand but made no attempt to move it and instead allowed a smile to cross his face. "I offered Arthur everything," she continued as her hand played against the surface of his armour. Her eyes locked onto his; then, stood sharply and crossed to the window and watched as the last of the knights disappeared through the heavy gates of the castle. "But the fool rejected me in favour for that harlot Guinevere." She turned back to Mordred on the throne watching her with interest. "I offer thee the same." Her voice teased with intent as her gown fell to the stone floor. She stepped from the clothing and walked slowly towards the throne meeting his gaze. "Give yourself to me and I promise… you shall be king of England!"

7.

The Journey Begins

Francis awoke with a start and gazed across his room. He had not even realised he had fallen asleep, but the dreams had been so vivid – Arthur, Mordred and Morgaine. The clock told him he had slept for almost two hours and declared that it was almost 05:50. He rose from the bed and shook his head before crossing the expanse of the room where he bent and grasped at his bulging bag. He flung it over his shoulder and pulled at the handle. He cast a final glance at his room before stepping into the hall and with one final check of his pockets and bag, he opened the door to his flat and stepped into the dull grey corridor. He regretted leaving without saying goodbye to his mother, but he surmised it would be better this way.

The cold air bit into his skin through his heavy clothing as he stepped onto the street and casting a quick glance around him for any unusual signs, he pulled his jacket tighter around him before striding down the street towards the bus stop. He sat on the cold metal seat and glanced at the street around him. Signs of early morning activity was beginning to stir with the odd car motoring past the bus stop and heading off to unknown destinations further along the road and deep into the city.

Unknown destinations – the thought struck Francis like a rock. Where was he going? he thought to himself. Sure, the dreams were pointing towards France, but where in France? That was a question which he had not paid much heed to. He supposed he was just hoping that the voice in his head would be his guide. He sat and closed his eyes for a moment straining to hear the voice of the woman which had haunted him over the previous couple of days. Nothing, nothing at all. Could it all have been a dream, or even the first signs of stress? Maybe all he needed was a holiday and at a purely subconscious level his mind was driving him for an excuse to run away to another country or perhaps he was going mad.

"I don't think so, son." The voice of an elderly man broke his train of thought, and he opened his eyes and looked for the source of the sound.

Before him stood an elderly gentleman standing partially beneath the cover of the bus stand and partially out in the early morning drizzle. Francis blinked at the newcomer and allowed his eyes to examine the man who had spoken to him. He had an unruly grey mop on his head which ran down and draped over his shoulders where his hair met and intermingled with an untidy beard. He wore a simple tunic which appeared to encompass the entire length of his body and a bright golden necklace hung around his chest. The man looked down at the chain and raised an elderly hand to the circular locket hanging from the golden links.

"Madness is only a perception of the mind," he said continuing his response to Francis' thoughts.

"I'm sorry," Francis stammered. "I hadn't realised I had spoken out loud." He apologised meeting the old man's stare. His eyes looked old but bore a young shine to their appearance.

The old man chuckled at him. "Oh, my dear boy, no." He looked as the confusion cross over Francis' face. "You hadn't. But then in a way I'm not really here anyway."

Francis leant back as far as he could and felt his back press against the back of the shelter. He cast a quick glance around him and could see the look of puzzlement on the faces of the other passengers at the bus stop. They bore frowned expressions beneath heavy coats and umbrellas and many shifted uncomfortably under the gaze of Francis, pretending that the young man was not sitting with them at the stop.

Francis returned his gaze to the old man before him and frowned as his image disappeared. He allowed his head to sink into his hands and groaned audibly at his embarrassment. It was bad enough hearing a woman's voice, but now this old man and the dreams. France seemed a long way off. Francis wondered whether he should head for the nearest hospital and check into the first available ward.

"All is prepared, Master Merlin," the voice echoed through the cavern. Merlin stood from the stone chalice and peered at the woman through the gloom.

"The Fisher King?" he enquired.

The woman nodded. "He is ready." She walked slowly across the cavern floor as she spoke until finally stood by the form of Merlin at the chalice. "The boy?"

"He has begun his journey," Merlin stated simply. "You have done well."

"I simply extend the calling of Excalibur… nothing more."

"But, my dear," said Merlin reaching for her hand. "You are the keeper, its vessel if you will." He raised her hand to his mouth where he kissed the back of her hand, looking directly into her eyes as he spoke.

"With the calling," she replied. "It will awaken her."

Merlin nodded sadly and turned away from the woman. "This is unfortunate. We are but pawns in the designs of Excalibur. We can only do our bidding and aide the true king of England." His gaze returned to the vision in the water. The woman looked into the depths and watched as Francis hauled himself onto the bus.

"This is definitely the one?" she asked. Merlin nodded at her question.

"You doubt Excalibur?"

"I do," she admitted. "I have spoken to the boy. He has no idea of his true bloodline."

Merlin returned his attention to the naked woman and grasped both of her hands. "Have faith, my dear," he urged. "For the time will soon be upon us." He glanced into the chalice at the signs of the vehicle in the water moving down the road. "Prepare the sleepers and return to the Isle… for once he has arrived, expect the gates of hell to open."

8.

Destiny Bound

The remainder of the bus journey had seemed to pass without any further complication and Francis cast his gaze around the busy terminal at North Greenwich as he topped up his oyster card with another ten pounds worth of money. He could still hear the slight whisper in his ear, but the image of the old man had disappeared. He hoped this had been the product of an over-tired mind and nothing more. It was bad enough living with the relentless whisper of the woman without visions of old age pensioners haunting him. He glanced around at the queue growing behind him and quietly moved away from the machine. He moved in tandem with the crowd as the people around him swarmed onto the station platform. He paused in front of a large wall mounted map which hung in its rigid position close to the entrance of the station and mapped out his journey in his head. He knew to reach France he would need the Eurostar and mentally noted that he would need tickets to travel into France. They could be bought once he reached his final destination of St Pancras, he thought as his hand reached into his pocket and subconsciously closed around his wallet. His eyes followed the silver line as it snaked along the map and joined with the black line and meandered along the map of the Underground system. It looked easy enough, and Francis knew that although it looked far, the journey along the Jubilee and Northern line would go at a quick pace.

He stepped onto the escalator and watched the various advertising signs pass as he slowly descended beneath the streets of London. At the foot of the escalator, he allowed a throng of people to hurry pass as he once again checked the map on the wall and followed the line from North Greenwich along through Canary Wharf, Canada Water, Bermondsey until his destination at London Bridge. He sighed and hauled his bag up onto his back and stepped out onto the station floor and stared at the electronic clock on the wall. It slowly counted down its relentless march for the expected two minutes until the train arrived.

"Come to me," the voice echoed in his head. Even with the noise of the voices surrounding him the woman in his head sounded the loudest. The sound of the voice seemed to press against his skull, and he closed his eyes attempting to block out the noise around him. He never noticed the train stop at the station... or the doors open... or even his own movements as he boarded the train and took a seat. The faces around him seemed to blur as train sped through the long stretching tunnels. "Come to me."

Canary Wharf sped past as Francis struggled under the scrutiny of his fellow passengers as he grasped at his head as the voice continued its endless mantra. He absently thought of France as Canada Water sped past – where would he start once he arrived. Paris? Should he follow his instincts and travel where his heart wanted to go or where his head leads? He sat back in his seat and attempted to avoid the stares of his fellow passengers as more people boarded and disembarked at Bermondsey.

One more stop. The train pulled away from the station and forged a path through the darkness of the tunnel and Francis shuffled in his seat pulling his bag tightly around his body as the lights blurred around him.

He could hear the sound of hooves in his head... The roar of battle... The smells of dirt and blood invaded his nostrils... London Bridge... The colour of a dozen standards whirled through his head... What the hell was happening? Southwark... Where was he? Lancelot... Call to arms...

Francis stood to his feet and staggered under the sway of the train as it swept into Waterloo. He steadied himself against the side of the train and became aware of a voice beside him.

"Are you all right?" asked the concerned woman. He looked at her through the Perspex glass which separated them and stared into her ageing grey eyes and nodded dumbly. "Don't travel well? Poor lad," she said, nodding and smiling at him as he almost collapsed through the doors of the train and onto the platform of the station. Waterloo?

He frowned as the crowds pressed him against the wall and he grasped at his bag and pulled it into his chest and breathed deeply at the dank atmosphere of the tube system. He reached out and placed a hand against the tiled wall of the station to steady himself as dizziness threatened to overwhelm his senses and he stared blankly at the opposite wall. The large black letters 'WATERLOO' stared back and mocked him as he struggled to remember the last stages of his journey. The sounds... the smell... When had he passed London Bridge?

He placed his hand to his head and ran his fingers through his hair as the memories evaded him. He slowly picked his way through the crowds and stared at the map on the wall before him. He could still get the Northern line to St Pancras from Waterloo; it would just mean changing at Euston.

"Come to me."

"Shut the fuck up and leave me alone!" yelled Francis. He glanced around, embarrassed at his sudden outburst and pushed his way past several people as he followed the signs for the Northern line.

Passengers looked and stared as he forced his way impatiently past them, while others looked away embarrassed by his actions and worried in case, he spoke to them. The platform was just as busy as the one he had just left, and Francis became increasingly conscious of the number of eyes on him. Follow your heart – that would be the way to go once he reached France, he decided. Follow your heart and trust your instincts and hopefully these voices haunting his mind would disappear.

The doors of the waiting train stood open beckoning him into the bowel of the vehicle and Francis stumbled through the open gap and into the carriage. He stood watching the doors close behind him and watched as the tunnel blurred into darkness as the train thrust through the tunnel and onwards. Stations whirled past: Embankment, Charing Cross, Piccadilly Circus...

"Come to me," the voice continued and caused Francis to close his eyes at the sound of her voice.

"Leave me alone," he whispered. "I'm coming." His broken voice almost sobbed through her insistent urging.

Almost self-consciously, Francis opened his eyes and glanced around the carriage and almost audibly sighed as he noticed no-one was watching him. He stood by the doors and regarded the people mingling around him. There was nothing especially significant about anyone in the carriage. No sign of the old man, just several commuters probably heading into the city for work and students clutching heavy packs. A couple sat on the seats opposite whispering and giggling at unheard jokes while the floor was littered with bags, prams and bicycles. The train slowed and allowed several commuters to leave the train, while others stepped into the carriage. Oxford Circus came and went, and the train copied its actions at Regent's Park, then Baker Street.

Francis raised his head to study the map of the line above his head, but the glare from the subdued lighting blurred his vision. Marylebone… Edgware Road… Paddington. I am here, thought Francis and pushed his way out of the train and followed the herd of people as they cajoled and forced their way up the escalator towards sunlight.

Advertising hoardings for private clinics and theatre shows passed as he stared up towards the pinnacle of the moving stair with an expectancy growing within his body. This was it, he thought silently. He moved with the crowd through the station and stood silently staring at the ticket machine. His hands moved without thought over the screen as he punched in the information and placed his credit card into the thin slot on the machine. He blinked as the ticket slid from the device and retrieving his card, he stepped from the machine and scanned the boards high above his head and frowned as he struggled to see the board for the Eurostar service. Paddington. A tiny voice in his mind was screaming at him: Paddington, but the voice was unheard as Francis stood stock still, eyes falling across the boards.

Birmingham. Manchester. Leeds. Glasgow. Newquay. York. Where the hell was France? Newquay: his eyes were drawn back to the name on the board. France… no, Newquay. Platform nine.

He moved unconsciously towards the platform and crossed the vast hall of Paddington station. Faces and images blurred and swam before his face as he moved through the station. He handed the ticket to the stationmaster who allowed Francis access to the platform and he glided onto the station floor where he could see the train standing patiently as though it was awaiting his arrival. The door of the train beckoned towards him and drew Francis towards the carriage. He stepped over the threshold and placed himself roughly down on the plush red velvet seat. A quick glance around the carriage revealed an empty train and slightly relieved at the lack of company, Francis allowed sleep to overwhelm him. He smiled as he settled to sleep. France: the last word to cross his mind.

An old man stepped from the shadows of the platform and watched as the train pulled slowly from the station and began its long journey west.

"Soon, Francis, we will meet," he said softly before fading from view.

9.

Enemy of Briton

"My Liege, Mordred has laid waste to Camelot."

Arthur's face darkened in the sunlight as he faced the rider on horseback. "Explain," he demanded.

The knight lowered his head and spoke through the green visor of his helmet. "My lord, I sent riders ahead to Camelot to announce our imminent arrival. Upon their arrival they were taken prisoner, my Lord, by the castle guards and stripped and tortured." The knight raised his head to look at the king as he continued his tale. "One rider was freed and has spoken of the tyranny of Mordred and his abuse at his hands."

Arthur considered his words for a moment before speaking. "Good Gawain," he began searching his knight for any signs of emotion or deceit. "Such treachery, bring me rider!" he demanded. "So, I can question this knave myself!" Gawain nodded and pulled at the reins of his steed and headed towards the rear of the party. "Galahad. Percival," he said softly. "Your counsel."

Two horses extracted themselves from the column of knights and the trio separated themselves from the rest of the men. Arthur looked over the precession of troops at his disposal and attempted to hide his disappointment over the failure of the recent foray into France. Knights sat on horseback in a long column, flanked on both sides by foot soldiers carrying banners, pikes and weapons. Each man wore a demoralised look as they watched the conference at the head of the column.

"Do you trust Gawain?" asked the king.

"My Lord?" queried Galahad.

"With the news spent from Camelot regarding his brother, would you trust Lord Gawain?"

"He has shown devotion to your charge, my Liege," commented Percival.

"Ahh... but did not Mordred once?" Percival nodded at the logic to

Arthur's response.

"That is true, my Lord, but Lord Gawain's personal ambition has little in merit while..."

"Yes, Lord Percival?"

"Mordred has always had eyes for the throne."

"And Galahad, your thoughts?"

"I must agree with Lord Percival, my Liege. Lord Gawain has shown naught but utter devotion to your majesty. It would be my belief, Sire, that he would follow you into battle against any such foe, even a half-brother."

"He did follow to France," mused Arthur as he watched the return of Lord Gawain with a bedraggled figure, "and his counsel at Mons Badonicus did assist with our victory." His spoken thoughts trailed off as Gawain stopped his horse before the king and presented the rider. Arthur looked at the man, and through the cuts and bruises he could see a dejected and broken spirit. "Speak, man, speak to your king," he commanded.

The rider licked his mouth and spoke through cracked lips. His voice was strained and as he spoke, Arthur watched the cuts and abrasions on his face swell and turn with the man's facial movements. As he spoke the king's mind wandered to what other tortures he had endured in his name and instantly regretted his decision to enter the fool's errand to France. The search for Lancelot had proven fruitless and served nothing more than a long expense through the wilderness of France. Information gleamed by Iseult and Lord Kahedin had proved naught.

"My Liege... my life," the rider stammered. The king waved away his praise and urged the man on with his story. "Three of us rode to Camelot to announce our return and we were greeted by hostility from the castle guards."

"Are thoust sure," demanded the king, "they are loyal to the throne."

"Aye, my Lord, they still are, but it is a throne that Lord Mordred revels in." The king nodded his understanding.

"Proceed."

"We were seized as we rode through the gates and taken immediately to the throne room and paraded before Mordred." The rider almost spat his name as he spoke. "He demanded a reckoning with yourself and declared himself as the one true ruler of the kingdom."

"How dare he, I rule by divinity."

"My Lord." The rider lowered his head and coughed.

"You there!" shouted the king. "Get this man some water." He returned his gaze to the rider. "Proceed."

"We were stripped of our weapons and taken from the room and down to the dungeons. Our armour was stripped from our bodies, and we were beaten."

"To what end?"

"To denounce thy rule, my Lord." The rider drank heavily from the water vessel presented to him before continuing with his story. "I could feel bones crack under the pressure of the beating, the nails pulled from my hands – that was before the burning. They stripped us naked and placed hot pokers against our skin. I could smell the flesh cooking beneath the pressure as they burnt my body." He looked at his hands and from his position on horseback Arthur could just make out red marks running from the rider's sleeves across the back of his hands. "My arms… my back… my genitals… my legs… every part of my body was cut." He fought back tears as he spoke. "One of my colleagues died during the ordeal, but he remained obedient to you, my Lord, even in death."

"Then what?"

"Ordeal by fire and water. We were repeatedly burnt then doused in water. The two of us were dragged from the cells and forced into the courtyard of Camelot still completely naked and stoned by the common folk. They trampled us with beasts… horses and cattle and then hung us from our arms at the gateway." The rider paused as he struggled with his memories. "I am sorry, my Lord," he apologised. "I could stand no longer. They thrust swords and spears into our bodies as we hung, then lowered us. I watched as my comrade was decapitated and as pigs gorged on his body. I betrayed you, my Liege." He sobbed as he completed his story. The king sat in his saddle and watched the poor wretch before him. "I could take no more."

"That matters not. I think no-one in our company could blame you for your actions." Interjected Gawain as he moved to Arthur's side.

"Was all this the doing of Mordred?" asked Arthur.

"Yes, my Lord. Wait… there was one other in the hall when we arrived. The Lady Morgaine Le Fay."

"Damned that harpy!" spat Arthur. "I knew that fool Mordred had neither the mind nor the gall to usurp the throne." He clenched his fists in anger then turned sharply to the rider. "You man, why were you released?"

he asked suspiciously.

"On the orders of the Lady Morgaine, my Liege. I was instructed to present my story as a warning to thy personage."

"Hah! Then Mordred is a fool! The throne and the crown is mine by the right of God! Order the men, Lord Galahad, we ride for Camelot this day!"

"But my Lord—"

"Yes, what is it?" demanded Arthur impatiently.

"Your sister, my Lord... the Lady Gwenhwyfar. Mordred has her and has threatened her safety on your approach."

10.

Medieval Desires

"My brother shall kill thee," spat Gwenhwyfar.

Mordred laughed at her anger. "I think not, my dear," he sneered. He turned from the window and gazed across the hall towards her as she stood defiantly beside the throne. The beauty of Gwenhwyfar was striking. Her perfectly formed face was rounded by long flowing blonde hair which flowed down her back in a cascade of golden locks and hung tied with flowers and rimmed by delicate pink ribbons. Her eyes were the bluest that Mordred had ever seen he reflected as he watched the fire burn within their depths. Her small and delicate nose flared with hostility and her mouth twisted into a snarl as she watched him cross the hall towards her. "Once he realises, I have his precious sister hostage in the castle," he started as he crossed the floor from the window. He stood before her and regarded her slim form, then removed his glove and ran his hand across her soft cheek. "He won't dare move against me," he whispered softly in her ear.

Gwenhwyfar flinched under his touch and spat in his face. The tension between the couple was tangible as he wiped the fluid from his cheek with his hand. Then, with the other he grasped her chin roughly and trust her head in the direction of the window. "See!" he raged. "See, as your precious brother stands in the distance." He moved his head close to hers and circled around behind her pressing his body hard against hers as he spoke into her ear. His voice was sharp and full of menace and his words stung her. "He shall not dare move against the king."

"You are not the king." She writhed under his grip as she felt the hot breath against her face and recoiled in his grip.

Mordred moved his body against hers and smiled at her discomfort as she grimaced at his touch. "I am your king... and you are my servant," he sneered. His free hand snaked around her waist, and he slowly caressed her groin through the long material of her flowing gown. She closed her eyes, fighting the tears which were forming as the image of the sneering usurper fleeted before her eyes.

"You will never be king!" she gasped defiantly.

He grinned at her under his pressure and pushed his hand hard against her groin, revelling in her horror as she gasped at his touch. He released her face and brushed her long hair from her shoulder and planted a long hot kiss on her slender neck. "Your brother shall die at my hand, and I shall present you his head as a gift. I promise you this," he whispered pulling his head away from her, leaving a sliver of saliva running from his mouth and trailing down her neck. His other hand moved from her groin and slowly ran up the expanse of her body before he roughly grasped her breast in his hand. He cupped the fleshy mound in his grip and squeezed roughly, smiling as she gasped in pain.

"Mordred!" The shrill sound of his name forced him to release the young woman from his grip and he turned to face the woman in the doorway. She eyed the swelling bulge in his breeches and flushed with anger at his arousal. "Put aside thine lust and focus on the problem at your gates," she stormed.

"Morgaine," he fawned.

"Don't!" she warned and stalked towards the figure of Gwenhwyfar who had collapsed on the stone floor. She leant close to the woman's form and tenderly touched her face. "Arthur won't stop," she said softly.

"But I have his sister—"

"And he has the hand of God," she snapped interrupting Mordred and standing to her full height. "He believes in his own divinity and his birthright to the crown." She walked to the window and peered out onto the surrounding land around the castle. "Come," she urged Mordred. "Look." She pointed over the landscape at the waiting army in the distance and waited as he joined her side. "He shall be formulating a plan of attack and he knows every inch of Camelot."

"You promised, Morgan, you promised me the kingdom," he whined.

"And thy shall have it, once you defeat Arthur in battle."

"You never said that" he spat angrily and crossed to the throne and collapsed heavily onto the fur lined chair. "You promised me the throne!"

Morgan turned and regarded the petulant child-like Mordred sulking in the throne. His head rested on his hand as he stared into the darkness of the corridor beyond the hall. "I offered you the same as Arthur," she purred as she crossed to the throne and smiled down at the figure slumped in the chair. *"All I wish for is power… and I shall have that power through your will."*

She sank to her knees before the throne and pushed open his legs. He watched her as she ran her hands up the inside of his legs and grinned as her fingers hovered over his groin. His lustful gaze wandered over the prone figure of Gwenhwyfar as she watched the scene before her, then back to the attention of Morgaine. She raised herself onto his lap and purred in his ear as she rubbed fervently at his groin with her long delicate fingers.

He closed his eyes and gasped with pleasure, and she whispered seductively in his ear, "I promise you this, Mordred. Kill Arthur and thy shall have everything: the throne… the kingdom… me." She stopped and climbed from his lap and walked slowly towards the corridor, aware that his eyes followed the sway of her hips as she walked. Morgaine paused in the doorway and spoke over her shoulder, "Prepare your armies, Mordred. The fight is coming, and if you want this then thy shall have to fight."

A darkness crossed over Mordred following the words of Morgaine and his eyes lingered on the small damp patch which had formed over his breeches and his hand rested on the swollen groin. Lust and disappointment swelled over his body and consumed his heart as his eyes wandered over to Gwenhwyfar who had remained on the floor watching the events between himself and Morgan. "It would appear, my dear, that whatever I do I am compelled to fight your brother for the crown." He stood from the throne grasping his crotch and regarded her briefly. "But for now, I have an unfulfilled thirst that needs to be quenched."

"Oh, please, my Lord, no," Gwenhwyfar begged as she dragged herself back along the cold hard stone floor.

"I am sorry, I truly am, but my desire must be quelled for my own satisfaction." He grinned as he stalked her slowly still running his hand over his groin.

"Please, my Lord, I am begging you… don't." Gwenhwyfar hauled herself to her feet and backed towards the window.

Mordred lunged forward quickly and grasped at her hands and pushed his face into hers, pressing his lips roughly against her ruby red mouth. "Don't worry," he breathed hotly. "I shall tell your precious brother just how good you really were."

Gwenhwyfar struggled under his grasp, but his grip held fast as her tears streaked down her face, making stained rivers against her soft skin.

"Please," she sobbed. He sneered and pressed his head against her neck, running his tongue up her skin and over her chin. He stood before her and stared into her deep blue eyes and smiled as cruel intent crossed his features. She pulled back, horrified at the look on his face. "Please, my Lord, have pity," she begged.

Mordred grinned past her and cast his gaze onto the column of troops in the distance, then suddenly tore at the material of her robes which hung around her body. The material tore easily and fell across her torso and waist exposing her small, rounded breasts. Mordred gazed upon her naked torso hungrily and grasped one of her breasts roughly squeezing it in his rough grip. She grimaced and spat in his face, defiant in the face of fear.

He laughed at her futile attempt of defiance and savagely struck her across her face. The force of his gesture threw her to the floor. Her cheek swelled under the intensity of his thrust and tears formed in her eyes as he loomed over her. Mordred stood over her body and laughed looking down at her broken spirit and pulled at his breeches pulling them to the floor and standing over her, mocking her discomfort. She averted her eyes from his half-naked body and closed her eyes firmly shut. His groin swollen with lust and with desire burning in his eyes he lowered his body close to hers. His hands pulled at the last vestiges of the material surrounding her body as she struggled under his weight. Mordred pushed her back against the floor and grinned as he listened to her sobs as he forced himself upon her slim body, pushing his flesh into hers. Gwenhwyfar writhed under him as Mordred thrust himself deeper and deeper into her body, moving faster under his own rhythm.

From the window, a woman's cry echoed out over the land. The screams grew in noise and intensity and mingled with incoherent sobs of despair...

11.

Evil Awakens

Francis awoke with a start and stared over the rushing landscape that flew past the carriage. He frowned as trees and bushes hurried across the window at high speed and searched outside for signs of his location. It did not look much like France; he mused as he shook his head free of recent dreams… the dreams. He was surprised how vivid they had been and his memories of them. For some reason they had appeared stronger in their appearance as he travelled and had become a lot more graphic in nature. He questioned his own feelings and self-decency in the nature of his latest dream… the woman, Gwenhwyfar… the attack at the hands of Mordred. The visions had seemed so real… so… so… so… He struggled to find the words for the horror he felt. He glanced around the carriage for any signs of fellow travellers, but like the countryside around the train there was no signs of life.

He glanced at his watch and saw he had been asleep for at least four hours and returned his attention to the passing world outside the carriage as he tried to work out his location.

"Tickets please." The voice made Francis jump in his seat and a frown played over his face as he gazed up at the stern uniformed guard standing before him between the rows of seats in the aisle.

"I-I-I," stammered Francis. Surely the guard had not been there a moment ago, he thought.

"You aren't very articulate, are you, sir?" remarked the guard with a wry smile. "Ticket?" The guard held his hand outstretched in the direction of Francis who sat staring at the guard for a moment. "Have you got a ticket, sir?" he asked again impatiently. The question stirred Francis into action, and he grasped his bag and opened the zip.

"Yes. Sorry," he whispered as he pulled his small leather wallet from the bag and withdrew the small orange and green ticket from the wallet. "Is this France?" he asked as he handed the ticket over.

The guard laughed heartily as he accepted the ticket and inspected it, turning over the small card in his hand. "Oh, son," he exclaimed. "Have you made a mistake?" He handed the ticket back to Francis and laughed again. "We're nearly at Newquay, end of the line."

"Newquay!" exclaimed Francis. He accepted the ticket and collapsed into his seat. "But I'm supposed to be going to France," he said exasperated.

"Not according to your ticket," said the guard. Francis blinked and stared at the man as he watched Francis as though examining him as he did the ticket. He tried to ignore the presence of the guard as he inspected his own ticket, expecting to see the word France emblazoned across its surface. The dark black writing on the card did indeed say 'Newquay' across the ticket and Francis stared hard at the writing and a frown burrowed over his brow. How the hell did this happen? Newquay. Why the hell did he come here? How the hell had he bought a ticket for Newquay when he wanted to go to France?

He cast his mind back to the station. Paddington, he realised, not St Pancras. His head sagged into his hands as questions exploded in his brain. Had his heart overcome his mind and bought the ticket without him even knowing. He could see the first signs of life through the window rising out of the horizon as buildings began to replace trees. Houses and factories climbed from the ground emerging from the oncoming coastline like a goliath stirring from its slumber.

He glanced back at the guard... Where was he? He looked over the backs of the seats and down the train straining to watch the retreat of the guard but as before, the appearance of the guard had completely disappeared. Francis grabbed his bag and pulled it from the floor and onto his lap and gazed at the approaching town and sighed. Newquay. Best make the most of it, he thought as he waited patiently while the train neared the station.

Merlin stood alone in the cavern and watched Francis in the water of the stone chalice as he stood in the carriage and swayed in time with the motion of the train. "Soon," he whispered into the shadows and peered into their dark shroud.

Around the back of the cave stood seven stone pillars which ran from the floor of the cavern and rose until they touched the roof. The pillars were embedded into the wall of the cave and stood tall and proud overlooking a plain flat stone altar. Merlin left his position at the chalice and circled the altar until he rested by the pillars. He surveyed the monoliths and breathed deeply at the dank atmosphere and ran his hand over the roughly strewn rockface. Small stone chips fell away from the pillar which Merlin had touched and bounced over the water laced floor disappearing into the depths of a resting puddle. A hole appeared in the central pillar as further flakes of stone fell away from the rock onto the floor and gaped at the incessant darkness within the apparent hollow stone tubing.

"Galahad," whispered Merlin as he pressed his face against the stone pillar and pressed his ear hard against the rough surface. Three fingers snaked from the hole and writhed in the darkness, flexing and stretching from their sudden release from there solitary confinement.

The wind battered the ruins of the castle, which stood overlooking the sea as it sat perched on the edge of the cliff. The monument was a memory of its own fallen glory from a time gone by and as the wind whistled through open battlements and gaping holes in the walls of the crumbling structure, deep below the ground in the bowels of the main keep, movement broke the silence of the castle. The ground rose and fell as the earth beneath swelled and stirred and through the depths of the soil, hands pushed through the surface and thrust aside deep rivets of grass and mud. The long slender fingers pushed against the collapsing ground and separated the reams of earth pushing against the encompassing soil.

"Free," gasped a female voice as the hands clawed at the soil. The soft ground groaned under the strain placed upon it by the sudden force placed around the growing hole as hands placed flat on the edge of the precipice. Stained arms thrust out into the darkness of the yawning chasm and droplets of soil fell away as a head gently pulled itself free from the ground. The woman opened her eyes and blinked. She shook her head free of remnants of soil from her face and spat earth from her mouth and smiled in the darkness.

"Free," she repeated joyfully and pushed hard with her free hands on the soil around her. She contorted and writhed as soil fell away from around her as she pulled her way from the ground, releasing her slender body from her earthen prison. She remained on all fours for a moment panting heavily from exhaustion caused by the effort and strain of freeing herself from the ground.

She raised her head and listened to the wind as it passed through the castle ruins. "I hear you," she whispered pulling herself unsteadily to her feet. "Excalibur." Her eyes shone in the darkness as she cocked her head to one side, listening to the noises around her. "After all this time," she breathed flexing her hands and arms. "I'm free!" she screamed as a symphony of light burst from her hands and she danced around the confined space beneath the castle. "I hear you, Excalibur!" she cried towards the open sky. "I hear you," she laughed and spun in her position deep within the castle. "I live…" She abruptly stopped and stared through the darkness, scanning her surroundings. "After all this time," she whispered. "Morgaine Le Fay lives again."

12.

The Awakening

Morgaine Le Fay surveyed her surroundings as she stepped from her muddy 'grave' and over the rotting vegetation sprawled over the floor of the castle. She kicked out at a scuttling rodent as it ran from its burrow and regarded the woman curiously for the invasion into its domain. A shower of light emanated from Morgaine as she walked through the remains of the castle, casting off any lingering evidence of her ancient incarceration as her long robes sparkled and shimmered in the small vestiges of light which split in through the holes and gaps of the castle walls. She turned to gaze through the open roof and winced as the sun glared down on her. She stretched in the warmth of the sun for a moment before continuing her slow progress through the ruins. Picking her way over the uneven ground and stepping over discarded stones and rocks she cast glances at her surroundings at various intervals amongst the grass and shrubs growing throughout the site. She ran her hands over the ruins as she walked carefully searching the boulders for a specific site.

"Oh, my Arthur," she breathed as her hands ran over a small mound in the ground. She absently stroked the mound and allowed her fingers to flow through the grass as the patch beneath her touch glowed under the pressure of her fingers. "You were so beautiful," she said wistfully and to no-one in particular. "And we were so young." She smiled as memories returned to her as the ground began to part around her fingers.

Morgaine stood to her full height and watched as a thin column rose from the ground. It was tall and slim and built from the construct of the castle itself with four sharp points which ran from the floor and cradled a rounded glass sphere at its head. The column rose to waist height where it stopped, allowing Morgaine to stroke the circular top of the dome. She teased the glass, toying with the smooth surface of the dome as her thoughts strayed into the past.

"We could have had it all," she mused. A small light began to glow at the heart of the orb and its light radiated out into the confined space where she stood and illuminated the sad smile which had crossed her face. She stroked the glass and gazed into the depths of the crystal. "Show me Arthur," she asked quietly of the glass and stood as the orb darkened. A mist swirled across the surface of the globe. Several mounds across the sprawling courtyard caught her attention for a moment before she returned her attention back to the globe. She frowned at the mist inside the globe. "Where are you?" she urged as the mist swirled and darkened in the glass. "Where are you?"

The earth around the site began to move and shift beneath the pressure of the rising figures from the soil. Sun glinted and shimmered off the dullen steel armour which surrounded the bodies of the figures as the earth and soil fell away from the knights. "He must be near," cursed Morgaine. "I can feel the call of Excalibur pulling at my heart, I can hear her voice… but where is Arthur?" She peered deeper into the glass. "My love," she whispered almost silently as she searched the inky depths.

"My Lady." A knight stepped from his muddy grave and moved into position close to Morgaine.

"Agravain, my Knight Commander. Prepare the forces," she commanded still staring into the globe. "For if we have awoken, so must Arthur," she reasoned. "The time of reckoning is upon us again, good Agravain. We must prepare to do battle." She rested her hand on the top of the globe and faced the knight. She stared into the faceplate of the helmet. "Where is that fool Mordred?" she asked.

"I know not, my Lady."

"Then find him!" she shouted. "Idiot," she spat as Agravain nodded and turned to the small plethora of men at the rear of the courtyard.

She watched as the Knight Commander strode across the courtyard to his waiting men and indicated to the knights to follow his example and leave the area going out into the castle and the grounds beyond. Morgaine watched as the knights filed out of the courtyard and returned her attention back to the crystal ball. "Why do you hide from me?" she spoke through clenched teeth into the glass. Her own reflection stared back at her through the surface of the glass. She swept across the dirt on the floor, causing clouds of dust to fly and settle as she disturbed the ancient slumber of eons.

She crossed her hands behind her back as she paced the courtyard, anger flushing her finely tuned features as the orb remained dark, hiding its secrets.

"My Lord…"

Mordred turned from his position at the pinnacle of the outer wall of the castle. The wind swept his hair, and it played in the breeze as he gazed out over the sea and into the distance. "Look what has happened to my beloved Tintagel," he mused without turning.

"My Lord."

"I remember coming here as a boy," he continued, placing his hand on the hilt of his sword which lay holstered in its scabbard hanging from his waist. "I used to play down there," he said pointing to the cliff edge at a small, almost concealed path which led down to the beach from the cliff top. "When I was a boy, we would travel here… myself and Arthur and whilst he would play 'king', I would atone for my sins here." He indicated across the ruined site. "Now look at it, Agravain, in ruins."

"My Lord," replied Agravain bowing his head in respect.

"What is it?" he demanded.

"Your presence is sought."

Mordred sighed and ran a hand over his breastplate, examining the dents and abrasions in the metal. "And yet I live," he mused then leapt from his position and followed the Knight Commander into the castle.

"Still naught!" raged Morgaine as she returned to her position by the stone column. The globe still offered nothing more than dark mist swirling within the glass.

"Mother?" queried a voice from the edge of the courtyard.

"Mordred," spoke Morgaine quietly, refusing to turn at the sound of his voice.

Mordred walked briskly across the floor of the courtyard and knelt at her feet and took her hand. "Deathless Morgaine," he breathed as he kissed her hand. "Aunt." He gazed up into her green eyes as he spoke and lowered his head to her feet.

"Stand," she commanded. She gazed into the ether and sighed as Mordred stood by her side. "Arthur is hidden from me," she commented simply.

"Morgaine," he ventured as his hands ran along his armour. "I died," he said. She cast him a quick glance and regarded him briefly as he spoke but chose to ignore his statement. "I died... I can remember," he insisted. "The battle... I died and yet I live."

"Perhaps," she dismissed him absently.

"No... no, Morgaine, I died... I know I died at Camlann," he insisted. "The... the battle at Camlann, I died at the hands of Arthur after I had wounded him. I remember him plunging his sword into my chest. I can still feel the blade as it pierced my heart."

"Mordred," she said speaking into the glass. "I promised you that if you gave yourself to me, then I would give you the kingdom, did I not?"

"But... I do not understand," he admitted.

"Yours is the kingdom... even through death." She stalked him and gazed into his eyes and ran a hand over his chest. Her fingers stroked the dulled armour over his body and played across the expanse of his body as she circled him. She stood at his back and leant forward and whispered into his ear. "At the point of death, the essence of your body can be subdued into the ether of the netherworld and harvested," she breathed into his ear and despite his confusion, he found himself intoxicated by her words. "So, your last breath can be caught and subdued until a point where the physical constitution can be resurrected when the call is made." She released him from her grip and ran her fingers back over the globe and stroked the glass and leant close to the sphere. "Now is that time, the calling. Excalibur speaks."

Mordred looked into the sphere and frowned as images evaded him. "I see nothing," he admitted. "I hear nothing."

"But I cannot find him," she spat and stood from the orb. "What treachery stands before me?"   She spun and stared into the orb. "Merlin." She cursed the name into the globe. "Show me Merlin." The mist swirled and cleared as the shadows parted to reveal the old man deep within a cavern. Morgaine smiled as she watched the figure as he helped another from a stone cocoon hewn into the rockface. "See Mordred as he awakes."

"That is not Arthur," stated Mordred as he joined Morgan at the column. They watched for a moment as Merlin pulled at the last vestiges of the stone surrounding the knight.

Merlin reached out to the figure pushing its way from the cocoon. His dull silver armour glinted off the flame as he stepped into the dark cavern. "Merlin," he commented simply as he gazed around him.

"Sir Galahad," replied Merlin as the knight placed a hand on his shoulder.

"What place is this?" he asked as the vision of the cavern swam into view through the visor of his helmet. He pulled at the helmet and revealed long flowing brown hair which fell neatly around his neck. His brown eyes pierced the gloom and rested on the stone altar in the centre of the cavern. "Arthur?" he queried.

"Remains dead, Sir Galahad," replied Merlin coldly as he moved back to the stone chalice.

The knight lowered his head in remorse for a moment before staring at Merlin. "Then why are we resurrected?"

"This is the time of the calling," said Merlin. "Do you not hear the call of arms?"

"I do," admitted Galahad. "But with no king..."

"You are mistaken, my Lord. His bloodline continues." Merlin peered through the gloom towards Sir Galahad and beckoned the knight to join him at the stone chalice. The knight hesitated for the briefest of moments as though considering his options. "Please, my Lord, were you not the bravest and purest of all the knights of the round table?" prompted Merlin. "Did you not recover the Grail... thoust holiest of quests?"

"And did I not gain my own redemption?" snapped Galahad. "I chose my death as my reward. I earned my divinity. Let me rest in eternal sleep."

"You survived Camlann for a reason, my Lord," purred Merlin. "Your destiny is here and now... so it has been decreed."

"You talk in riddles, Merlin. You always did." Galahad eyed Merlin suspiciously with an air of contempt. "Your lies are no better than Morgaine's."

"You flatter me," lied Merlin as he bent low in a mock bow. "But I speak the truth." He paused and looked deep into the chalice and spoke over his shoulder. "The quest... what do thoust remember?"

Galahad paused and blinked in the darkness. His eyes clouded as he remembered the quest. "I... I... remember..." He closed his eyes and struggled with the memories. "I remember travelling alone, saving Lord Percival from twenty knights... I remember Sir Bors... I remember the death of Percival's sister... I remember the city of Sarras and the Holy Grail... I remember choosing my death and the rapture of my ascension to heaven." He rounded on Merlin angrily. "So why am I here?" he shouted.

His voice echoed throughout the cavern, rebounding off the walls and surrounding Merlin with vicious accusation.

"Arthur always regarded you as his bravest… the bravest of the brave, so it was pre-ordained by the Lady of the Lake that you would rise from his ashes to protect the king when he would need you most." He smiled at Galahad and bowed respectfully. "Now is the time of the calling." He indicated towards the water in the chalice. "The kingdom needs you," he whispered. "Look…"

Galahad stared into the water and watched as the young man in strange clothing stood before a building, looking back and forth up a metal road. "This is no king, he but a boy."

"But he can be," urged Merlin. "With our help, he can be great."

Galahad shook his head disconsolately. "I do not see."

"Excalibur is calling… and if Excalibur is calling then the forces of chaos will also be rising. Sir Galahad, it is our duty not just to protect the bloodline of the king, but the country itself." Galahad peered into the water and allowed his hand to drift to the hilt of his sword. "You are needed, my Lord… then your ascension can be attained."

13.

Terror Train

Morgaine felt a sudden rush of remorse flow though her body as she watched Merlin's conversation with Sir Galahad. "My Arthur," she said quietly.

"He is dead," cried Mordred. He threw back his head and laughed at the revelation.

"Silence," snapped Morgaine.

"Morgaine, oh deathless one, don't you see! With Arthur dead, I am the true king. I shall have Excalibur and the kingdom."

"Silence, idiot," snapped Morgaine. "You are half the man Arthur was." A tear rolled silently from her eyes and splashed onto the crystal globe in the centre of the stone column. "My Arthur was... beautiful," she said. Her voice was full of remorse, full of love. "I remember how his hair shone in the sunlight. I remember how we held hands; I can still see his smile and hear his laughter. We walked once through the lands around Camelot before things changed..." Her words drifted off into the distance as memories sparked her thoughts. She turned on Mordred savagely. "You will never be the man Arthur was," she spat. "But you can be great." Her fingers ran over the globe as she returned her attention back to the orb. "Knight Commander!" she called into the darkness.

"Madame." The knight emerged from the shadows and saluted Morgaine, waiting for his instructions.

"Is thoust and thy forces prepared?" she queried.

"They are amassing as we speak, my Lady."

"Good." She turned back to the globe and spoke into the glass. "Show me the boy," she commanded. The mists in the sphere swirled and parted revealing an image of the young man standing on the same platform that Merlin had shown Galahad only moments previously. "He is young," she mused as she examined him through the globe. "He has Arthur's eyes," she said wistfully as she watched and slowly stroked the glass. Her fingers ran around the circular cold device while a single tear ran down her cheek.

Francis stood on the station platform and stared down the tracks. He cast his gaze around the platform and noted his solitude was broken only by the sound of the occasional songbird. He stood alone on the platform and cast his eyes around the station and watched for a moment as a train thundered through the empty station. This was it then he thought, Newquay not France… if his heart brought him here then maybe he should let his subconscious mind allow him to continue his journey to…

He walked to the ticket office and stared at the information on the wall and let his eyes wander over the places displayed on the map. Tintagel… the name of the town rang in his mind like an alarm.

"Come to me." That voice again calling to him on the wings of the incoming breeze. "Come to me."

He looked around the station. He was still the only person in sight and although it had not bothered him, he was slightly disheartened by the quietness of the station. "Yes?" The sound of the voice disturbed his train of thought and brought him back to the station. He looked through the Perspex glass and into the eyes of a plump looking middle aged woman. "Can I help you?"

"Err… yes…" stammered Francis. "Return to Tintagel."

"You'll need the train for Bude which runs through Padstow… Tintagel—"

"That's fine," interrupted Francis and pushed a banknote beneath the glass. He glanced around again expecting someone to be standing close to him or at the very least on the platform, but still nothing. His eyes darted around reverently searching for someone… anyone. He did not know why but he had the strangest feeling that he was being watched.

"Thank you," said the woman behind the counter and pushed a small ticket under the glass with a handful of coins which Francis pocketed and hurried onto the platform. He stood nervously on the platform although he did not know why he felt this way. Again, his eyes were drawn to the station and he searched in vain for any sign of life. Nothing… so why did he have this feeling of dread.

A distant rumble and vibration through his feet alerted him to the approach of the coming locomotive and he took an involuntary step back from the edge of the platform and glanced up towards the electronic sign on the ceiling of the station. It told him all he needed to know about the train; it was his and with his bag firmly in his grasp he waited for the train to slow and stop at the station.

The locomotive slowed to a halt at the edge of the station and Francis checked the platform for further signs of passengers. Satisfied that he was still the only person on the platform he boarded the train and took his seat in the empty carriage. He peered over the back of the seat and down towards the front of the train, then repeated the action towards the rear of the carriage and frowned as once again the journey would be made alone. As the train slowly moved out of the station the movement and quietness of the train unnerved Francis and he peered along the aisle into the other carriages. The train was not particularly long and from his position Francis could see both front and back of the train from his seat. He had expected to see at least some people somewhere in the carriages, but the train was completely empty.

The ticket inspector walked out onto the platform of the station with a small ticket in her hand. "Sorry, sir, but the train to Bude has been delayed…" her voice trailed off as she looked along the platform for the young man, she had served only moments before. She searched through the crowded platform but struggled to see him through the throng of people. "Excuse me," she spoke softly to an elderly gentleman close to the door. "But has a young man just come out of here?" The old man squinted through his spectacles at her and shook his head, before returning his attention back to the newspaper. She scanned the crowd on the platform again before shrugging and pushed open the door to the ticket office and looking at the unwanted ticket to Bude in her hand. "Strange," she murmured and returned to work.

"Travelling alone?" The voice made him jump and Francis glanced into the seats on the other side of the train from his position. A man and a woman sat opposite. The man was staring out of the window as the landscape of Cornwall flashed past outside, while the woman… the woman was hypnotic. Her eyes stared right at Francis… no, not at him, but through him and straight into his soul. He could feel her intense stare as her eyes penetrated his mind and stripped his thoughts.

"I'm sorry," he stammered apologetically as his face flushed with feint embarrassment. "I didn't see you there. I thought I was travelling alone."

The woman smiled at him and could feel the awkwardness oozing out of Francis.

"You are," she purred and smiled at him. Her words struck Francis and he seemed to notice the couple's attire for the first time since she had spoken. The man still sat gazing out of the window, but he was dressed in heavy dull grey armour. From his position Francis could see a black fur trim running across the joints of the armour and running into an elaborate breastplate with an intricate floral design running over the dulled metal. He wore a black helmet, which had a long silver rim running along the crest of the helmet and 'fins' of a metallic grey sat at each side of the headpiece. The helmet had no visor and Francis could see the man's face reflected in the glass of the carriage as he continued to stare from the window. He had a cruel face, with small eyes and a sharp long beak of a nose thought Francis as he examined the man with interest. His neck was covered by a chain mail mesh which ran from the back of the helmet and down into the armour.

The woman in contrast sat staring at Francis, her face open and flushed with the look of contempt at the meeting. Her auburn hair fell around her naked shoulders and sprawled over her back. A small golden tiara was held in position on her head and crowned a dignified air which surrounded the woman's aurora. Her face was attractive and the word MILF drifted into the mind of Francis as he found her attractive. While she was older than the male her appearance was youthful with blemish free skin off-set by deep green eyes which sparkled in the sunlight reflected through the glass of the carriage. In contrast to the heavily armoured male, she wore little in the way of protection with a simple golden breastplate covering her flowing green and yellow robes which covered the entirety of her body. "So, you are the offspring of Arthur," she mused.

"No," said Francis resolutely. "My father was called Luther and my mother's name is Irene," he continued.

"But you are a Pendragon. I can sense his bloodline." She smiled in her victory.

"Who are you?" he asked.

"Oh, my dear, look closely you know who I am. I am deathless," she replied cryptically. Francis shook his head and found himself drawn into her gaze.

"This is foolish," spat the male. "Let us finish this here."

"Silence," laughed the woman. "Look at me," she teased. Francis could feel a word forming in his mind... no, not a word... a name. He looked hard at the woman, drawn in by her beauty. "Give yourself to my will in a way that Arthur did not."

"Morgaine Le Fay," whispered Francis. She threw her head back and laughed at the sound of his voice whispering her name.

She stood and gazed down at him in his seat. "See, I knew you would get it. Give yourself to me and join us, but I warn thee, oppose me and you will die. Surrender Excalibur and I will allow you to keep your life."

"I don't have it," he said. Morgaine brought her hand sharply across his cheek and he could feel the flare of the strike against his skin and the taste of blood in his mouth as rage crossed her face.

"You lie," she raged, her face flushing a deep crimson.

"No," cringed Francis, his hand resting on his cheek.

She regarded him for a moment before laughing again. "It matters not, you are nothing to me. Tell Merlin that I am coming," she turned to the male. "Mordred," she breathed and held her hand out towards him. He grasped her hand and the couple faded from view leaving Francis alone in the carriage.

"Wh-what just happened?" he questioned as he searched the carriage for signs of the couple. Morgaine Le Fay. Mordred. This was all too real for him and those names: Merlin and Arthur. This coupled with the naked woman and the voice in his head was bringing things to a head quicker than he could ever have realised. Excalibur. Was that what was drawing him towards Tintagel? The myth of King Arthur and the knights of the round table. It would explain a lot, but how much of it was a myth and how much was based in reality?

The carriage buckled under the constant sway of the train as it ran along the metal tracks. He cast a glance outside and watched the rushing landscape blur from view. Trees and bushes merged into one long green stream of colour. The train rocked again, violently on the track and Francis reached for the opposite seat to steady himself against falling into the aisle. The floor beneath his feet felt different from the hard flooring of the carriage that he had become use to, and he glanced towards the floor.

Along the surface of the carriage a soft clear gleam was covering the floor of the train and Francis placed his hand on the floor, running his hand over the glistening surface. It felt slightly rough beneath his touch and as Francis ran his fingers across the surface of the floor, he noted that the substance was warm and soft in texture.

The carriage buckled violently, throwing Francis to the ground. He lay face down and blew on the floor as the stench hit him and he rolled over onto his back to escape the rising odour as the floor of the carriage continue to writhe and contort beneath his body. He forced himself to his feet and the train lurched and buckled again throwing him off his feet and sprawling across the seats. A grimace grew across his face as an intense pain spread over his legs and as he looked down, the floor shimmered and changed before his eyes.

Colours mingled into view and a deep purple with bright yellow triangles blurred into his eyesight as he struggled to regain his footing. Desperately Francis grabbed for the handrails on the back of the seat and planted his feet on the softening floor as it rolled back and forth. His eyes strained to the light from the window and Francis forced his fingers into a growing gap at the top of the glass. He forced the window of the carriage down and allowed a sudden gush of wind to bellow through the train. The noise from outside the carriage deafened him as he forced his head through the open window.

He looked down the expanse of the train and reeled as the locomotive writhed and leapt from the track before his eyes. The engine twisted and turned, contorting into the unholy shape. The main body of the engine changed into a long thin snout; the window narrowed into large circular red eyes. A crack spread across the middle of the engine and opened revealing a set of sharp white teeth. Francis grasped onto the edge of the window and steadied himself against the vicious lurch of the creature that the train was slowly transforming into. He looked down at the track and recoiled in horror as it began to rise off the floor and into the air, turning slowly into large fronds which the main body of the creature moved across.

He could feel himself falling as the creature buckled under his body and he grasped desperately at the seats… the handrails… anything to brace the impact of him falling. His hands waved frantically in the air as they pushed through nothing. The creature lurched again and turned to face the falling Francis as he tumbled through the air high above the ground. The roar of the creature echoed in his ears and the sound of laughter filled the air around him as he slowly fell.

14.

Why... Vern

"The Wyvern will kill him," stated Mordred as he watched the train writhe and change into the creature. He licked his lips as Francis fell through the air and clung desperately onto the creatures back. The screams of the boy echoed through the courtyard and Mordred could feel the excitement rise in the pit of his stomach.

"Only if I wish," replied Morgaine casting Mordred a look of pure distain.

Francis clung desperately to the creatures back as it bucked and rolled across the track. The carriages had transformed from a long line of coaches. Fibre glass and metal combined into the soft malleable body which was covered in a ridge of thick scales. There, colour flicked at Francis as the creature turned and writhed beneath his grasp as he clung onto the back of the Wyvern with his fingernails digging into the fronds running along its back. The Wyvern rose into the air as two spiny arms pulled out from the body and reached into the evening sky, searching for the dwindling sun and feeling the warmth on its skin. Great leathery membranes unfolded from beneath the creature's arms and stretched and flexed, causing Francis to slide further down the body of the creature as it contorted under its new existence. A deafening roar emitted from its long snout, erupting through the air. Francis fought the urge to cover his ears and instead dug his hands further into the back of the creature. He looked over the darkening scales which ran along the surface of the creature and stared at the crest on the back of the Wyvern's head. It rose from the snout and climbed over the centre of the head in a mighty crescendo of frills and along the back of the creature to where Francis hung and along towards its tail. From beneath its body, it planted two large, clawed feet into the soft soil which had once housed the metal tracks and it forced itself up in the air, tasting the sunlight with a flick of its forked tongue.

Despite his fear Francis felt in awe of such a creature, and although a part of his brain told him that this creature was an impossibility, he still felt amazed by the ferocity and sheer force swelling beneath his body. He looked at the head once again, pulling his head from the body of the creature and watched as its keen yellow eyes searched from something…

The head flicked from side to side and caused a spasm which ran down the entire length of the body. Francis could feel it's every move as he forced his hands beneath its scales. He thrust his fingers under the hard exterior and into the soft flesh hidden from view. The creature roared and tilted its head back looking at the parasite which was currently clinging on to its back. It bared its teeth and Francis gasped and hid his face in the body of the beast as the light from the sun reflected off the pure white enamel. Francis knew the creature could not exist, but here it was and here he was clinging to its back… so what the hell as happening. Firstly, the naked woman, then Merlin and Morgaine Le Fay and now this… this dragon. He winced as he expected a plumage of flame to erupt from the creature's mouth and braced himself against the inevitable burn, then frowned as nothing happened. He opened his eyes and stared towards the head of the creature, which had once again lost interest in the parasite and was searching again for something in the distance.

Francis allowed his eyes to wander into the distance where, over the rising landscape, he could see the coastline and the faintest traces of the sea beyond the horizon. He once again hid his face as the creature roared and buckled as the taste of saltwater played on the creature's tongue. Francis struggled to hold on as it threw back its head and unfolded its vast wings, unfurling them in the sun and stood on its two legs. He slipped along the body as his hands desperately waved and grasped across the creatures back as he fell along the expanse of its body.

He stopped with a vicious thud and felt a searing pain course through his body as he crashed into a rising fin near its tail. Francis struggled as pain surged through his body. He felt the wind pushed from his lungs as the pain between his legs intensified and he desperately grasped the edge of fin of the creature and struggled to hold on to the creature as it moved. The tail was different from the rest of the body and Francis noticed that it felt colder than the body. The scales which ran along the creatures back were not as prominent across the tail and they were tighter and thinner than the larger ones higher up. The whole tail looked smooth and almost aerodynamic compared to the bulky body. The fins which ran off the sides and top of the creature were almost fish-like in appearance, thought Francis as he clung on desperately.

Fish-like.

The thought hit Francis like a ton of bricks, and he realised suddenly what the creature had been looking for... the sea. This was no dragon, he thought to himself, this was a sea dwelling creature, and it was looking for a way back to the ocean. His fingers struggled for a good grip as the creature surged forward and rose into the air as great gusts of wind thrust down the body of the dragon... no, the Wyvern. Francis recognised the creature from school trips to castles and realised the creature he was now on had been seen before on a shield and armour of British heraldry.

The Wyvern rose off the ground and Francis struggled against the rush of air against his body. Vast wind battered his senses and Francis lost his grip on the creature's tail. He grasped at thin air and watched as the creature flapped its great wings, disappearing into the distance as the ground rushed towards him.

Francis fell...

down...

down...

down...

Morgaine leant forward and watched with interest as Francis plummeted towards the ground. "Come on, Merlin," she urged. "Show thy hand."

Merlin turned away from the chalice in the cavern and stared down at the floor.

"Is thoust not to save him?" demanded Galahad.

The old man shook his head slowly and paced to the side of the cavern. "I cannot," he said sadly as he watched Francis fall.

15.

New World, New Days

The ground felt hard beneath his body and Francis pushed his hands against the floor and forced himself up. "Are you all right, son?" asked an old man who sat on a bench on the station platform.

Francis glanced around him confused and gently pulled himself into a sitting position on the cold hard floor of the station. He looked around at the gathering crowd and could see a mill of faces staring down at his embarrassment. "I-I don't understand," he stammered.

"You had a bit of a funny turn," said another voice kneeling by his body. Her face swam into view and he recognised the woman who had sold him a ticket earlier.

"Where am I?" he asked looking around the station floor.

"You're still at Newquay station. Don't worry, you'll be fine." She smiled sympathetically. "Here drink this." Francis looked at the glass of water and gratefully accepted it. He drank the cool liquid and traces of water escaped the glass and ran down his chin, settling on his jacket. "Can you remember what happened?" she asked kindly.

He shook his head avoiding eye contact as he took another long drink from the glass. "I can't remember," lied Francis as his memories of the Wyvern and Morgaine swam into his head. "I must have blacked out for a moment that's all." He smiled meekly at her and attempted to stand.

"Whoa! There youngster," shouted the old man. "You're in no fit state to move." He turned to the woman. "I think we should get an ambulance for him." The woman nodded in agreement and looked back at Francis, placing a hand on his shoulder.

"I'm all right," insisted Francis pushing her hand away. He almost immediately regretted the action and looked into the woman's eyes. "Promise," he said softly miming a cross over his heart.

Her frown was replaced by a smile and she stood and held her hand out for him to help him to his feet. "Whatever," she said smiling. "If you're sure," she added uncertainly.

Francis nodded. "I just need a bit of a break... That's why I'm here." He looked around the station and struggled to comprehend what was happening. Where was the Wyvern and how had he found himself back here on the floor of the station? "Overdoing it back home. Work," he added quickly following several suspicious glances from other commuters.

"Your ticket." The woman smiled at him and handed the small orange and green card. "You left it," she explained as he gratefully accepted the ticket and stood to his feet.

He felt his head swim as he stood and steadied himself with her help for a moment before glancing around the platform. Everything seemed normal, but he still could not shake the feeling that he was being watched. He could see the shape of the train in the distance and shuddered as the thought of his recent experience as the image of the Wyvern slipped back into his memory. The creature had seemed so real... so... so... immense. He waited as the train pulled into the station and slowed to a standstill at the platform and he cast his gaze along the tracks to the rear of the vehicle, then the front towards the engine.

"This is your train," said the woman as she ushered Francis towards the carriage. He stared at the open doors and stepped over threshold into the train and settled uncertainly into his seat.

"It didn't kill him," stated Mordred as he watched with disappointment from his vantage point.

"Obviously," commented Morgaine.

"Why not?" he demanded. "We could have taken Excalibur for ourselves."

"You fool," she spat turning on him harshly. "He does not have Excalibur yet and does not know of her whereabouts." She circled the column as she spoke and regarded Mordred coldly. "But she speaks to him. She calls him." She could feel herself losing patience with Mordred as confusion crossed his face. "We allow this boy to follow the calling until he finds the sword." She allowed her words to penetrate Mordred's skull for a moment before finishing her sentence, disappointed that he had not finished it for her. "And then we take it from him."

"We do not need this boy," hissed Mordred. "He is but a gnat."

"But it is to this gnat that Excalibur speaks!" She could feel herself losing control of her temper and briefly wondered what had drawn her to such an idiot. "As much as you cannot comprehend, you oaf, we need this boy as much as Merlin does." She clenched her fists at the sound of his name. "He is a direct descendant to Arthur's bloodline and as such he can hear the calling."

"But why now, deathless Morgaine?" Mordred asked. He looked about the ruined castle around them. "And why here?"

Morgaine laughed. "Here?" she queried. "Arthur's birthplace? I could think of no better place than here to secure his grave. I would believe that the Lady Viviane would secrete herself to this place, being close to the Isle of Apples and the holy lake of Avalon. Yes, I should think Excalibur would be near... as would Merlin. As for why now? This I cannot tell, Mordred," she peered into the ether of the mist as she spoke. "The future I cannot see," she admitted and turned to the knight. "But I can tell thee, Lord Mordred, you must be prepared to take to arms to win the seat of England."

Mordred nodded his understanding. "I did so once forth, my love. I am willing to do so again."

"And you lost... remember that, Mordred, remember." She turned from him humming and playfully ran her hand over the glass dome of the sphere. "Have a care, good Mordred, for your own mortality. For while I have resurrected you once, do not be sure that I can hold back your death again." She smiled and floated from the courtyard leaving Mordred alone with the stone column.

He watched her as she walked away from the stone altar. "Good Morgaine," he breathed. "I promise thee this: blood will be spilled on this land in my name." His hand rested on the hilt of his sword, and he pulled the heavy long blade from its scabbard and swung it through the air. The metal reverberated around the confined space and sparks flew off the rock as it fell to the floor as the sword sliced through the brick of the ruined castle. He panted through the sudden movement and mopped a pearl of sweat from his brow and he stalked to the crystal ball still locked in position at the pinnacle of the stone column. "Excalibur will be mine," he whispered into its depths.

Francis stepped from the train and gazed down the deserted platform. A shudder forced its way along his back as thoughts of the last time he believed he was alone, and memories of the Wyvern flashed through his mind once again. This was becoming far too real, he thought absently as he searched for the exit from the station. His eyes wandered towards the bridge which crossed the track and the road beyond the station, whilst close to him a small gate offered another way from the station, and he wavered unsure which path to take. The wind whistled around his feet, picking up absent items of rubbish and skirting them around his legs. He closed his eyes and strained his ears at the noises surrounding the station. He listened to the distant roar of the traffic and the crash of waves hitting the shoreline somewhere close, but out of sight. He tried desperately to hear the sound of the woman's voice, leading him, speaking to him… but nothing.

He sighed inwardly and moved silently to the bridge and stared up the metal steps and placed his foot on the bottom step before pausing and taking a final look around the empty station. He reasoned in his own mind that the main platform and ticket office would be closest to the town and with a final push forced himself up the steps, listening to his own footfalls as they echoed up the metal rungs.

"All is prepared?" asked Galahad. Merlin nodded in the darkness as he watched Francis walk slowly across the metal bridge towards the town. "This is a strange time," commented Galahad as he stared over Merlin's shoulder and into the water of the chalice. "Metal carriages pulled by noisy strange boxes along roads made of metal. I do not understand this world." Galahad shook his head and moved away from the chalice and ran his hands over the rock monoliths at the back of the cavern. "I do not trust this world."

"Then trust me, my Lord," said Merlin. The two men stood in awkward silence for a moment, their eyes meeting and locking, an obvious mistrust emanating between them.

"I admit I do not know who to trust yet," Galahad sighed. He moved rested his eyes on the rock before him and ran his hands over the surface of the rough rock. "Your words betray your desire, Merlin, they always did. You trade in mistrust and lies." He turned and looked straight at Merlin. "Was it not thy counsel that Arthur took to arms at Camlann? Was it not your words which drove him into battle? And your design which led to his death?" The accusations forced Merlin to stare deep into the water.

"I did not mean for his death," Merlin said simply.

"But it still happened!" raged Galahad bringing his fist down against the rocky walls.

"I loved Arthur like a son," snapped Merlin. "His death was not foreseen and could not have been prevented." Sadness descended over Merlin as he fought to repress the memories from centuries previous as they attempted to rise through the water and into the present. "He did what was ordained by a greater force than myself, but I could not stop his death." Merlin looked from the chalice and straight at Galahad. "Please, my Lord, help me redeem myself. Help me redeem his name."

"His name or thine, Merlin?" The silence was deafening between the two men as they stood staring at each other for a moment. "I will follow thee... for now," said Galahad simply. "But not for thee, for him... if he truly is the king." He indicated towards the chalice then turned and walked towards the small tunnel of light at the opposite side of the cavern. "I will be outside," he stated and stalked down the tunnel.

"Good Sir Agravain," purred Mordred as he walked out into the ruins of the castle. The knight turned and considered him for a moment before rising the visor and meeting his old friend with a smile.

"My Lord," he replied and knelt before Mordred.

Mordred removed his helmet and allowed the wind to sweep through his unkempt black hair. He shook his head in the breeze and threw his arms wide letting the wind to play around his body. "After so long, my friend. It feels good, does it not, to feel life once again?"

"Aye, it does, my Lord," Agravain looked about his person and whispered quietly to Mordred. "It is beyond my understanding why we are alive, my Lord. I do not trust thy kindred," he confided.

Mordred laughed at the knight's unease. "It is beyond thy comprehension, old friend, but be sure we shall succeed in our quest for the crown."

"Arthur lives still," asked Agravain astoundingly.

"No, my friend, but his bloodline continues in a child!" He laughed and placed his arm around the shoulder of Agravain. "Our victory is assured." He leant forward and spoke softly in his ear, "Once we have Excalibur, nothing can stop us..." He stopped mid-sentence and narrowed his eyes through the dwindling sunlight. A frown flashed across his face briefly before being replaced by a flush of crimson as anger replaced any other emotion. "Look!" he spat pointing down the cliff towards a small patch of trees. Agravain followed his eyesight and strained his eyes as he peered into

84

the distance.

"Is that?"

"Yes, Galahad," he said. He turned and clenched his fists in anger and regarded the land around him deep in thought. "Take two men and take an offensive position in the copse," he ordered.

"Morgaine," murmured Agravain.

"Damn, Morgaine!" raged Mordred. "I have given thee a direct order and thee will do what I say!"

Agravain nodded slowly. "My Lord," he commented and watched as his commander stood in the breeze staring down into the wooded area. His hands clenched in anger as he watched Galahad as he walked out into the wooded copse.

16.

Tintagel

The light was fading as Sir Galahad walked through the copse and absently snatched at the branches hanging from a nearby tree. "What world is this?" he asked himself as he walked. His eyes grew accustomed to the dimming light, and he could see the outskirts of the town in the distance. The lights from the houses shone like a thousand fireflies, sparkling and shining in the evening sky. "To be born again in this time," he mused as his fingers ran over the bark, flicking moss from the trees onto the grassy floor beneath his feet.

From the edge of the copse, eyes watched through the bushes through the visors on their helmets. Agravain glanced at his fellow knights and nodded a silent instruction towards the other two knights in his company. "Thy understand thee instructions?" The knights nodded their understanding and with hands firmly on the hilts of their swords the three knights moved into the wooded area.

Francis moved through the small town and glanced into the shop windows as he walked. He stopped outside one shop and peered through the glass at the small assortment of figurines standing on display on a variety of shelves inside the shop. His eyes wandered casually over the assortment. Statues of swords, knights, busts of who he presumed to be King Arthur and a variety of mythical beasts. He pulled his stare from the window and searched the street, casting his gaze around the town. Examples of the myth of King Arthur seemed to be scattered everywhere across the town, from street names to statues and the novelty items in the shop, wherever he looked there seemed to be an obsession over the myth.

"Come to me." The voice again. It had been so long since he heard it, he had completely forgotten what had brought him here in the first place. He cast he gaze around the street and hopefully the source of the voice, but again his vision could find no obvious source. "Come to me... you are close." His feet moved absently along the street in the direction of the coastline. "Come to me."

A sudden shrill noise broke his revere as he stepped from the edge of the street into the road. A car swerved violently in the road and from the window a series of profanities were emitted in the general direction of Francis. He shuddered at the thought of the near miss but allowed the voice to direct him forward along the road, being more careful where he was walking.

Darkness was falling and Francis suddenly became aware that he had nowhere to stay whilst here. He moved down the street close to the coast and looked out across the sea as the water slowly crept in over the sandy beach. In the horizon the sun slowly sank as darkness slipped over the town. Francis carried on his walk along the street, his eyes moving over the buildings and shops.

Despite the size of the town, it resembled many holiday seaside towns with its bright lights beaming from arcades and public houses. People moved in unison along the street in beautiful chaos as tourists and locals mingled in a variety of attractions from karaoke bars to miniature golf sites and cafes. He scanned several guest houses before settling on a tall prominent building sitting on the corner of the street. The sign displayed 'vacancies' inside and Francis stared at the name of the property set high above the door. The words stared down as though a beacon shining towards him like a radiant light broadcast from the town for Francis to follow.

"The sword in the Stone," mumbled Francis as he walked up the path to the front door, his hand wavering over the bell. He paused unsure whether to ring the bell or walk straight inside. Francis glanced around at the dwindling light and decided to push the door open and walk in.

Galahad spun around as a noise from the wood caught his attention. His lowered his visor and circled his position scanning the wood for signs of intrusion. "Who is there?" he called. "Show thyself." The wood remained silent, but Galahad stared through the darkness suspiciously. His hand moved to the hilt of his sword and withdrew the long blade from its scabbard. "Show thyself. I command thee," he called into the trees at the shadows. "I am Sir Galahad, noble of the round table, Conqueror of the Holy Grail, son of Sir Lancelot. Now, knave, show thy person!"

The bush parted and from its bowels stepped a singular knight. The last vestiges of light bounced off his armour and shone in the growing moonlight which fought its way through the tree line. He stood with his hand on the hilt of his sword and circled Galahad slowly, keeping his eyes fixed through his visor on the opposing figure.

"Identify thyself," demanded Galahad pointing his sword in the direction of the knight.

"My Lord."

Galahad turned his attention to the source of a new sound close to his right and watched as a second knight emerged from behind a tree. This knight stood taller than his comrade and his armour was more impressive. While the first knight wore a simple plain suit, with chain mail covering his arms and his legs, this knight stood proud and regal in his demeanour. The dulled armour was ringed with floral decorations around the breastplate. This knight's arms and legs were covered much the same as Galahad's, but the knee joints and arm joints were ranged by sharp obtrusive points. A singular feather rose from the helmet and spanned over the top of the helmet reaching the expanse of the metal. The knight moved his hand towards his visor and paused over his face before pulling the half visor open revealing his face. He smiled at Galahad and removed his sword from its scabbard and waved into the bushes for the third knight to move into the open.

"Agravain," breathed Galahad. "I have killed thee once before, and I shall have at thee again if needed."

"Camlann," sighed Agravain. "This time, Galahad, it appears I have the upper hand." He laughed as he indicated around him towards his comrades.

"These knaves shall not stop me from killing thee again if I have to."

"You stood on the wrong side, Sir Galahad," snapped Agravain.

"I stood with my king!" raged Galahad and thrust forward towards the nearest knight. The blade of his sword sank deep between his chest plate and the chain mail protecting his body and emerged from the knight's back soaked in a deep crimson. The sound of skin stretching and bone snapping as Galahad carefully pulled the blade from the knight's body echoed around the small area. They watched as blood erupted from the knight's mouth as his hands released their grip on the sword and snatched at the wound in the stomach. His hands moved desperately over the growing stain on his armour and a small eruption of blood gushed between his fingers. He looked despairingly towards Agravain as darkness swamped over his body and the knight slowly collapsed to his knees in a jet of blood. The knight pulled his hands away from his wound and looked down at the river of blood flowing over his hands and down his body towards his waist.

"I-I-I—" the knight stammered. Galahad raised his sword and swiftly brought it to arms, swinging it furiously through the air, metal connecting with flesh and bone. The headless body collapsed to the floor of the copse and stared out of his visor through lifeless eyes as the head bounced across the wood.

"I warn thee, Agravain, leave now and I will spare thy life," said Galahad ignoring the growing stain flowing from the suit of armour on the floor and staring into the eyes of Agravain.

"Have at thee, Galahad!" yelled Agravain and rushed the knight with his sword drawn and held aloft. The two clashed, their swords sparking in the moonlight as Galahad parried the savage attack of Agravain. They stood locked in a deathly embrace, pulled together by destiny. "I serve a greater service," murmured Agravain as locked swords. "Arthur is dead, thine is a false king."

"Who do thee serve?" asked Galahad through clenched teeth as he pushed Agravain from him. "That knave Mordred!" Agravain flinched at the sound of the name and raised his sword before his visor. "It is... he survived as we do," breathed Galahad incredulously. "And yet I saw him killed in battle."

"He lives as do I," raged Agravain as he rushed Galahad again. He swung the sword towards his side, where Galahad moved to block the attack. Agravain moved his attack to the other side of Galahad's body where the knight blocked him once again. Swords crashed together in a flurry of sparks as the two came together again, Agravain lunging forward in a wild attack. Galahad side-stepped the lunge and pulled his sword through the air slicing through the protecting chain mail on Agravain's arm. Blood rushed from the wound and poured over his arm turning the dull metal of the armour into the twisted parody of crimson as blood stained the wound. Agravain staggered back clutching his arm and turned savagely to his remaining comrade. "Get him, you fool!" he snapped.

The knight wavered uncertainly. "It seems your men are not so easily ordered, commander," laughed Galahad as he turned to face the other knight. "Do thee wish to die?" he asked, his arms spread wide in mock surprise.

The knight looked from Galahad to Agravain, then back again.

"Get him!" screamed Agravain.

The sound of the Knight Commander's voice sparked the knight into action, and he lunged forward towards Galahad. He stopped and stared at Galahad, his eyes widening as he searched the helmet of Galahad. His eyes slowly lowered down his body and mournfully gasped as the hilt of Galahad's sword protruded from his stomach, reaching up through his armour deep inside his chest. He could feel the rush of blood and every vessel within the body exploded and erupted in spools of crimson puddles coursing through his body. The knight could feel a numbness spread through his body as the cold steel forced its way through his vital organs and out into the cold night air. Words were trapped in his throat as he could feel something crawling up through his neck, something thick forcing its way through his mouth as thick reems of blood erupted over his tongue and through his lips.

Agravain roared in anger and pushed himself from the ground and towards the two men. Galahad struggled to withdraw his sword from the body of the knight and moved the man's body between himself of the onrush of Agravain who raised his sword and swung again and again. The sword dug into the back of the dead knight speared on Galahad's sword, cutting at the armour cast over his back.

Mordred licked his lips as he watched the images flash before him in the orb. A sickly smile crossed his face, and he clapped his hands as the force of Agravain's attack upon Galahad forced the knight backward.

"Where is the Knight Commander?" demanded Morgaine as she entered the courtyard. She eyed Mordred suspiciously as he stood abruptly from the column and moved into position to hide the images from her view. "What is happening?" She crossed the courtyard and pushed Mordred out of the way and peered into the orb. Her face flushed with anger as she watched the image as the two knight's clash. "I gave no instructions for this," she cried and stared down at Mordred accusingly.

"I gave the order—"

"You have no right!"

"I have every right; I am king elect."

Morgaine's hand flashed out and caught Mordred sharply on his cheek and forced him to stagger backward, stumbling on the uneven ground and crashing on the floor. "You are nothing," she raged. "Thee hast needlessly jeopardised my plans and for what? Thine own personal glory." She sneered at him as she peered back into the orb. The body of the dead knight had been discarded and Galahad stood on even footing with Agravain. She watched for a moment as their swords clash in the air of the wooded copse. "Knight Commander, hear me."

Agravain staggered back under the volley of lunges by Galahad and defended desperately under the growing momentum of the attack. He spied the bodies of his two dead comrades and sighed heavily as he caught his breath under the onslaught of blows. "You fight well, my Lord Agravain," commented Galahad as he lunged forward once again. The knight swung his sword to defend the attack and knocked the sword away before composing himself. He could feel his lungs swelling with the strain of battle and held his sword aloft, swinging it heavily downward where it was easily defended by Galahad's own sword.

A sensation tickled his ear, and he paused slightly allowing Galahad to deliver a vicious blow against his armour. The force of the blow rocked Agravain and forced him backward where he sagged under the attack, a small river of blood erupted from his mouth.

"Knight Commander, hear me," the voice was clear and the instruction simple.

"I hear you, my Morgaine," he panted breathlessly as he whispered her name.

"Return to me. Now is not the time."

Agravain nodded his understanding and glanced at Sir Galahad who stood before him smiling in the dwindling light. "'Tis not over," he warned, then turned and disappeared into the trees.

Galahad stood for a moment, tall and proud, smears of blood staining his armour and cascading down the blade of his sword. "Run!" he called into the darkness. "Run, thee coward!"

He stood and listened for sounds of movement for a moment before collapsing to his knees dropping his sword to the ground and his hand drifting to his side. He winced in pain as he pulled at his armour to reveal a deep gash in his side, a crimson smile growing across his body. He glanced around the wood and heaved himself to his feet using his sword. The pain from the wound seared and coursed through his body. He pulled the sword free from the deep gash of mud and staggered through the trees, heading back into the direction of the cavern. His head felt light, and he could feel his body succumbing to sleep as he struggled to walk through the ether.

"Merlin," he whispered as he sagged to the floor, his face buried deep into the sandy beach as he fell.

The bar appeared to fall into a deathly silence as Francis approached. He scanned the room and felt the weight of the stares as he leant on the bar and surveyed the pumps and bottles behind the counter. A young woman approached smiling and stood before him eyeing him as he waited nervously.

"Yes, love," she winked at him as she spoke.

"Err, lager please," he stammered softly and fumbled in his pocket for his loose change.

"Just arrived?" she asked as she pulled a glass from the counter beneath the bar and pushed it beneath a pump. She pulled at the handle and looked at him as he spoke… or rather nodded dumbly. "I won't bite." She giggled as she spoke and handed the drink over the counter, holding her hand out for the money. "At least not yet, if you're lucky," she whispered teasing him as her hand closed around his.

"Guinevere!" snapped a burly man from the other end of the bar. She flushed a slight shade of red and bounced towards the till with the handful of money, turning her head towards the man and sticking out her tongue in his direction before winking again at Francis. The man stood before Francis and folded his arms across his chest. "We don't want any trouble here, son, you got that?" It was more a statement than a question, thought Francis and he gazed into the frothy head of the drink on the counter. "You keep your hands to yourself," he warned.

"Dad," bemoaned the young woman, Guinevere. "I'm old enough to look after myself and I don't need you chaperoning every move I make."

"Just looking after my little girl, that's all, Gwen. These big city types…" He peered over the counter and leant closer to Francis. "I know what they come here for."

"I can only hope," she teased playfully and grinned at Francis. "Don't listen to him," cooed Gwen and smiled. "Where are you staying?" Francis blushed and looked around as she spoke. "You need a room?"

"Oh, no—"

"Dad! Stop! We need the business," she snapped and gestured for Francis to follow her to the other room. He picked his drink up off the counter and followed her into the adjacent room, pausing to turn and glance at the baleful stare of the landlord. "Don't mind him," she said as she walked. "Ever since Mum died, he's become this overprotective..." She trailed off as she waited for Francis to catch her as she moved from behind the bar and out into the room.

Francis watched her as she walked, his eyes drawn to the sway of her hips. She was speaking as she walked, but Francis never heard a single word as he felt hypnotised by her demeanour. His eyes wandered over her body as he walked slowly behind her, watching her every movement. Her body clung to her tight grey jeans. The contours of the material holding her long slim legs and tracing up towards a petite rounded buttock. Long ginger hair fell over her back in waves and cascaded across the blue material of her shirt.

She turned and spoke again breaking the spell cast over him. "Well?" she asked.

"I'm sorry," he blushed as he spoke.

She smiled and laughed slightly, knowing full well the effect that she had on men. "I said, how long are you staying for?" Her blue eyes shone beneath her glasses and radiated under her smile which lit her face as she spoke.

"About a week, maybe more. I'll see how it goes." He realised his face was turning a deeper crimson as he spoke, which fuelled her even more. She smiled and bent over the desk reaching for a large book behind the counter. Francis found his eyes wander to her waist again as the material over her rounded buttocks stretched tighter over her petite form. The shirt rose slightly revealing the slightest form of a black thong which sat just in view above her trouser line. She straightened and opened the book grinning broadly at Francis as she held the book open for him.

"I'll give you room twelve," she purred moving closer to him as he scribbled his name inside the pages. "Right at the top of the house... away from everyone else," she teased and bit at her bottom lip as she spoke. "No one can hear you up there." She winked and Francis could feel his loins stir with the suggestion and laid the pen in the centre of the book. He stared at her for a moment, lost in her eyes, falling under her beauty.

"Pendragon," the burly voice of her father snapped him back to the pub.

"Yes, sir," he stammered and looked towards him as the landlord eyed the book.

"You taking the piss or something?" he snapped.

"No."

"Do you know who Pendragon was?"

"Dad—"

"Don't, Guinevere," he warned. "Pendragon." He stood over Francis as he regarded him.

"I... I'm sorry, but no."

"King Arthur Pendragon." The landlord's eyes narrowed suspiciously at he stared down at Francis. "The greatest king of Britain."

"Yes, sir," said Francis dumbly.

"Is that all you can say?" he raged incredulously.

"Father—"

"Don't you Father me!" he snapped. Francis was aware that his anger was growing, and the growing interest from the bar was becoming tangible.

"You come here, the birthplace of Arthur, then to the Sword in the Stone and claim your name is Pendragon. Do you think us idiots?"

"But it is, sir," stammered Francis reaching into his bag searching desperately for his passport.

"You must think us all idiots!" The landlord stopped his tirade and grasped at the small purple book thrust towards him. He opened the page at the picture and stared at the image, then at Francis, then back again. "I'll let you off this time... but I'll be watching you," he warned as he handed the passport back to Francis and stalked back into the bar, taking his position behind the bar.

"So much for Cornish hospitality," murmured Francis as he stuffed the passport back into his bag.

"He means well," Guinevere said apologetically and held her hand out towards him. "Start again?" she ventured. Francis nodded and accepted her hand shaking and smiling at her. "I'm—"

"I know, Guinevere," he said smiling.

She pulled a face at the sound of her name. "Please call me Gwen; I hate Guinevere."

Francis nodded and looked back into the bar where her father was watching intently the exchange between the two of them. "Why is everyone around here so obsessed with the myth of King Arthur?"

"You're kidding," she giggled. "This is Tintagel, where King Arthur is supposed to have been born. Our whole town is built around the story; it's become a way of life."

"Even down to your name?" he teased.

Gwen laughed. "Yes, even down to my name." They stood staring at each other for a moment before Francis set down his drink and hoisted his bag over his back.

"If you don't mind." He indicated towards the stair.

"Oh, yes of course," she said smiling. Francis turned and began to walk up the stair towards the upper floors and his room. While his mind turned to a shower, he could not help himself smiling as the thought of Gwen crossed his mind. He stopped at the first-floor landing and glanced down the stairs and saw Gwen standing leaning on the banister up at him. "You never know," she called up, "who might turn up tonight." She winked, smiled and skipped back into the bar leaving Francis flushing with embarrassment on the landing.

Outside a flash of lightning distracted Francis from the young woman and caused him to stare outside the small boarding house. He gazed from the small window out into the street. Under the light stood the naked woman who had plagued his dreams for the last few nights. She pointed up towards the window as the storm drew in overhead, lightning flashing across the sky. "Come to me," she breathed. Francis turned from the window and continued his climb up the stair, choosing to ignore the temptation of leaving the house and confronting her again. He was here and that was enough. "Come to me," the voice urged. "You must come to me."

"Leave me alone!" he shouted as he stopped and stared out of the second-floor window. The rain fell across the pavement under the streetlight, and he could see the water crossing her body.

"Come to me," she urged. "Beware…"

17.

Battlefield

Morgaine looked at the bedraggled form of Agravain standing before her. His armour bore the wounds of battle and the air had the bitter twang of iron from the blood staining the knight's body. He stood with his head bowed before Morgaine as she circled him, like a predator stalking its prey. She stood before him and stared down on his body and frowned.

"Madame. Forgive me," he begged as he kept his view firmly on the ground beneath his feet.

"You idiot!" she snapped. She placed the palm of her hand on the back of his head and grip his hair as she spoke. "Thy actions today will have alerted our enemies to our presence." Her voice rose into a crescendo as she spoke and glanced in the direction of Mordred who cowered from her intense stare in the shadows of the courtyard.

"I meant nothing, my Lady," stammered Agravain.

"Silence!" she snapped as her fingers curled around his hair and pulled his head sharply back, until his eyes met hers. He winced as he met her gaze and could see the anger flashing in her eyes. She held Agravain fast in her grip as she changed the focus of her gaze from the knight to Mordred. "Think very carefully before answering, Knight Commander. Who instructed you to attack the position of Sir Galahad?" Her eyes met those of Mordred as she stared accusingly towards him.

"My Lady... I thought..."

"You lie, dolt!" Morgaine pushed his head savagely downward and continued to meet the stare of Mordred. "You are incompetent of independent thought. You are a Commander of men, a follower of orders! Do not think me an idiot, Agravain, you acted on whose orders?" Agravain said nothing as he pulled himself off the floor of the courtyard and cast a quick glance into the shadows where Mordred sank further deeper into the embrace of darkness. "And there we have it," she said still focusing on Mordred. "Did thoust think I would not find out?" she snapped. "Do thee think me a fool?" She stood over the prone knight but spoke directly into the shadows and the direction of Lord Mordred. He lowered his gaze in shame under her stare and his hand wandered to the hilt of his sword. "Stand!" Morgaine snapped. "Stand and face me," she ordered again turning her attention back to the Knight Commander. He stood slowly straightening and stood to attention before Morgaine. He stood tall and proud before her, his armour stained with the blood of the battle, but also showing glimmer of the light from the moon.

"My Lady," he breathed as he raised his head proud before her scrutiny.

Morgaine regarded him for a moment, casting her gaze across his body and up and down his armour. She turned her back on the knight and stared at the crystal ball, cradled in the stone column. "We must not be discovered," she mused as she peered into the glass. "And yet here we are."

Her hands spread over the orb and traced the edges of the sphere as the dark ether within the globe reacted to her touch. She spun quickly and savagely brought her hand into contact across his face. The suddenness and ferocity of the attack forced the knight to the floor, his hand tracing the intense pain flowing through his cheek as the flesh began to swell under his touch and a sliver of blood trickled from his mouth caressing his skin as it wandered down his chin.

He wiped the blood from his mouth and stared hatefully at Morgaine and lowered his head, full of resentment. Morgaine bent down to the knight and whispered in his ear, "Thy is mine to command, Lord Agravain, remember I own you." She stood and stalked into the shadows close to Mordred. "You have dishonoured our cause, Mordred," she snapped pausing on the edge of the courtyard. Mordred lowered his head casting his gaze towards the floor away from her stare. "To take to battle before honouring the fallen dead," she spoke quietly as she regarded the darkness. "Have a care, Lord Mordred," she warned. "For I do not need thee, if thee cannot follow my instructions." She shook her head sadly and moved from the courtyard. "Knight Commander," she snapped as the errant knight scuttled after her from the courtyard and into the night.

Mordred stared venomously into the darkness. "Have a care, Morgaine," he breathed into the darkness.

Francis looked around the room as he pushed open the door and stepped over the threshold. The room he stood in was plain and simple, with a single bed lying in the centre of the room with a dressing table and a set of drawers. A door set off to his side revealed a simple bathroom with a shower cubicle with a sink and toilet. Francis pulled the door shut and stabbed his finger at the small switch on the wall and waited briefly as the light from the ceiling blinked into existence illuminating the room. He noticed the room had no television, and only a small radio and kettle sitting on the set of drawers, and he almost regretted leaving his drink downstairs. He sighed heavily and sat on the edge of the bed before dropping his bag by his feet. Shaking his head, he pulled his arms from his jacket and threw this across the room into a small pile on the floor in the corner. He could feel his eyes getting heavy under the strain of the journey and struggled to undress as sleep threatened to overwhelm him. His jacket was joined by his jumper, then t-shirt, then trainers, socks and finally jeans. He dropped backwards onto the bed, dressed only in his boxer shorts and allowed sleep to consume his senses. The covers of the bed closed in on him as he sank down onto the soft layer on the bed and he fell into an uneasy sleep.

King Arthur sat in the saddle of his mount and stared out over the army before him. He steadied the beast between his legs and pulled on the reigns of his horse as the creature fidgeted under his control. "'Tis a good day to get back the throne," he shouted smiling at his comrades at his side.

The figure on the horse looked back at him and frowned. "My Liege, this is not a folly."

"No, good Galahad. 'Tis England!" He reached over and slapped his comrade on the shoulder, then fell back into the saddle and stared out over the field. The army stretched out before him, a mixture of mounted knights and common foot soldiers. Each one held their weapons before them in a macabre dance with the opposing army. Arthur gazed over the army and sighed. "'Tis good to be back home," he said eventually, "and once I have the throne again..."

"My Liege," Arthur turned in the saddle to face another knight at his side. The large brown horse cantered towards the pair and the knight raised his visor to address his king. "The preparations are complete." He began meeting his king's gaze. "Our army is ready for your command."

"My thanks, Lord Tristan," said Arthur. He turned back to face the swelling ranks of men stretching away in the fields below. He gently kicked at his mount's ribs and the horse slowly moved forward away from the

knights. *Arthur pulled himself high into the saddle and looked over the expectant faces of the soldiers gazing in his direction. He struggled to find the words to rally them, how could he? Tell them that they were about to lay down their lives for their king? Arthur knew most if not all may fall in battle, and this saddened him. So many deaths in his name. But, if the blight of Mordred were not halted now how many more would fall beneath his reign of terror?*

"Men!" he called over the expectant throng. "We have gathered here on the fields of Camlann to face the hordes of Mordred and the Lady Morgaine to stand in the face of darkness to regain the rights of Briton. We fight not for ourselves, but that of us all and our families and as we honour and respect those who have already fallen, we must stand against this blight cast over our land. Stand with me and follow me into battle men! For Briton… for your king!" He could feel his heart swell with pride as the congregation of men raised their swords and staffs in their hands and cheered their agreement into the air.

The horse struggled and buckled beneath the roar of the horde and Arthur steadied himself, turning the animal to his comrades and smiled before lowering the visor of his helmet. "You see, my friends, we have God on our side!" he cried confidently. He turned and pulled Excalibur from the scabbard around his waist and raised it high above his head. He dug his feet into the horse's ribs and drove the animal forward and cried, "Onward… for Briton!" He surged forward with the cry of battle in his mouth.

The resounding cry of attack from Arthur's army, sparked the forces of Morgaine into battle. The two opposing sides clashed with ferocity in the fields of Camlann, marking a stain across the land and tainting the river with the blood of a hundred men. Swords swung and clashed with a resounding thud as metal contacted with metal and slashed at soft limbs. The field was swamped with a mass of people as the countryside writhed beneath the onslaught of the opposing armies. Bodies lay where they fell, trampled into the mud and buried beneath the dead as metal broke through protective suits and sliced deep into crevices of the living. Swords sliced through the skin and bone, cracking and breaking ribs as men fell in the name of honour.

Merlin stood over the field, gazing down from his high vantage point above the fight. "How goes the day?" The question seemed slightly out of the ordinary, even for her, thought Merlin as Morgaine's voice broke the sound of war from below.

"All this death," he breathed sadly.

Morgaine sniffed at the air and stood beside Merlin as he watched the carnage below. "You can smell the blood in the wind," she commented. She watched his movements with feint amusement.

"What do you want, Morgaine?" he snapped.

"I wish to end this… this slaughter," she confided.

"Then instruct Mordred to surrender."

"You know I can't do that," she said softly. The two stood in silence as the sounds of death reached them through the air. "Do you remember when we were younger?" she asked suddenly. He turned to face her frowning at her remark. "I can," she continued. "I can remember the fields of Camlann." She gazed down below as the grass ran red with death. "They were so pretty… the flowers, they were a blaze of yellow," she smiled as she spoke. "Now look at them." Morgaine turned her head from the sight of death.

"Morgaine, please it is not too late."

"It is," she said simply.

"No… no, it isn't," insisted Merlin. "Call off Mordred. Arthur will forgive you… he always did."

"No, Merlin. Thoust is wrong, it is too late." She waved down into the valley below. "Look at the deaths… all those innocent men. All the deaths at our hands. It is too late."

"Arthur—"

"Damnation to Arthur!" she cursed. "Arthur will not forgive me, not after this. No, Merlin, old friend… we have come too far. Now is the time of reckoning."

"Please, Morgaine," he begged.

"Some will survive," she said looking at the old man. "But ultimately we are all doomed to die in a river of our own blood." She turned and walked away, calling over her shoulder one final time before disappearing. "We will meet again, Merlin… remember this."

The horse had died. Arthur waded through the mud and the dead scattered around him. He would swing out occasionally with Excalibur and watch sadly as another faceless soldier fell into the mire at his feet. The sounds of battle were resounding and through the blood and haze he could see man after man fall under a volley of blows with sword or pike. "Mordred," he breathed as a figure loomed out of the darkness before him.

Mordred looked bedraggled in his armour, as blood stained his black polished metal giving it an uneven, tired complexion. The wings on the sides of his helmet gave off his instantly recognizable armour and he stared with hatred and contemplation at his rival on the field. "Arthur." He nodded and pulled his sword before him. "Only one of us shall be destined to die here today." He smirked under the mud smeared across his face.

"For my crown," breathed Arthur as he surged forward with Excalibur held aloft over his head. The blade swung down and halted sharply as Mordred blocked the attack with his own blade. He grimaced under the attack of Arthur and sagged under the pressure of the swing, sinking to one knee under the brutal volley of blows. The two men clashed as the sound of battle erupted around them marred only by the noise of metal striking metal. Sparks from the swords illuminated the armour of the two men as Arthur lunged into the body of Mordred, who in turn swept away yet another attack from his adversary.

"Thee tire, Mordred," mocked Arthur as he surged forward, Excalibur high in his grip. Mordred grimaced as he pushed away the force of the attack and swept through with his own thrust of the sword. The speed of the attack caught Arthur by surprise and the momentum of his defence pushed him to his knees. His armour hit heavy in the soft mud of the field of Camlann, and a small spray of dark brown cast over his armour. He cast a quick glance upward and rolled as Mordred brought his heavy sword crashing into the mud. Mordred watched as Arthur desperately struggled in the mud and brought his sword down again on the prone king. Arthur pulled Excalibur before his chest and pushed away the attack of Mordred. He could feel the tide of the battle change as Mordred became spurred on by his own success and grew in confidence. He swung wildly as Arthur pulled himself to his feet and caught his blade deep into the shoulder of the king.

He smiled as Arthur cried in pain as the blade broke through the joint by his shoulder and bit into the soft flesh beneath the metal. Mordred stepped back and regained his own composure and inspected the blade of his sword, smiling through his own helmet at the sight of deep crimson *toying with the mud on the metal. "First blood," he breathed as he lunged forward again.*

Arthur countered the movement and defended the attack with ease, pulling the knight close to him. He could feel the hot breath of Mordred against his armour as the two men stood nose to nose. A burning sensation coursed through his shoulder as blood ran its way along his arm. "A minor victory, my Lord," he whispered as he pushed Mordred away.

The two men circled each other in the mud for a moment, each surveying the other scanning and analysing any weakness in the other's armour. The fight continued around them, with the sound of death overcoming all other sensations. They circled for a moment as time passed before Arthur lunged, his sword barring down upon Mordred in a swarm of brutal attacks. He could feel his shoulder burn with every thrust; he could feel the pain seer through his body as the reverberation of Mordred's defence shattered his nerves. Mordred reeled under the pressure and moved back out of reach of the swing of Excalibur and could feel his lungs burst under the strain of battle.

He slipped as the mud beneath his feet gave way in a puddle of soft earth and as he struggled to regain his footing, his concentration of defending against Arthur's attacks became compromised and as Excalibur struck his chest plate he fell backward. Arthur watched as Mordred sagged and stumbled under the hazardous conditions and swung his sword savagely, catching Mordred square in the chest for a second time. He pulled back and watched Mordred fall to his knees, his sword falling momentarily by his side as his hand drifted to his chest plate.

Mordred looked down at the thick mark on his chest plate and ginned, reaching for the hilt of his sword. Excalibur had badly dented the armour, but apart from the visible damage, no penetration had been made by the sword. Arthur made forward, lunging past Mordred as he struggled to his feet. As Mordred moved aside, Arthur's thrust and momentum took him past the knight, leaving his midriff open to attack. Mordred grimaced as he swung viciously, striking the king deep into the side of Arthur's armour. The blade cut deep into the side of the king, causing Arthur to winch in pain as Mordred pulled his sword along the side of his body. He collapsed into the mud as he grasped at his side. Agony and pain surged through his body, and he could feel the life drain as blood flowed across his armour. He looked up at Mordred who stood over his weakened body smirking at his imminent victory.

"I am better than you. I always was," he mocked as he grasped his own sword in his hand as he watched Arthur flail in the mud. "The crown is rightfully mine in battle!"

Arthur winced under the volley of words and struggled along the floor, reaching for the hilt of Excalibur which lay in the mud just out of reach. "Thee shall never be king," replied Arthur weakly.

"Thee are wrong," crowed Mordred. "I had thine sister, now I shall have thy crown."

"What?" Arthur's eyes narrowed as he whispered at Mordred's boasting.

Mordred bent forward and smirked in Arthur's face. "Thy sister," he mocked blood smearing his teeth and his rancid breath invading Arthur's nostrils. Arthur could feel the hilt of his sword as he listened to Mordred mocking him. "She cried for mercy," he laughed and stood at full height, rising his sword over his head. "She begged me to stop!" he cried as he positioned his sword over the king. "I enjoyed taking her again and again, almost as much as killing you." He looked down at the prone knight and smiled. "Now thee shall die as in the knowledge that she begged for thee over and over, even as I took her... she cried thy name." Mordred stood for a moment, a grimace frozen over his face and a look of horror crossing his features. His eyes bulged and blood trickled from his mouth as a sharp pain suddenly erupted through his mid-rift. He lowered his head as the pain coursed through his body and stared uncomprehending at the end of the sword protruding from his body.

Blood forced its way up through his throat and over his tongue as his sword fell heavily to the floor. His hands wandered to the blade thrust between the plates in his armour. Mordred grasped at the sharp blade of Excalibur and pressed the flow of blood erupting from his stomach. He fell to his knees and faced Arthur, meeting his eyeline, and could see the pure hatred burn in the king's eyes as mist clouded his vision. Arthur watched as Mordred feebly grasped at the blade of Excalibur as the blood flowed down the blade, staining his own gloves with the blood of his enemy.

"I am king," he breathed quietly as he pulled Excalibur from the body of Mordred, who collapsed in a bloody mess on the muddy ground. Arthur knelt in the mud and cast his head around the battlefield. He could see seven survivors from the battle... only seven, he thought, out of so many, and for

what? He pulled the crown from the head of Mordred and looked into the golden depths. He staggered and stumbled in the mud with the crown in his hand and fell to his knees. He looked at the crown in his hand and dwelt briefly on the gold and jewels which were smeared in the blood of hundreds... no... thousands. "It is over," he whispered as the first of the knights came through the mist and allowed himself a smile. "Galahad..."

Sir Galahad waded through the death. Bodies were littered before him as he stepped over corpse after corpse. His eyes had become accustomed to death as he searched for signs of survivors. He could see his comrades, Tristan, Bors, Gawain and Bedivere walking through the mud and further still in the distance the forms of another three knights. Friend or foe? At this distance and in these conditions, he could not tell but...

A figure caught his eye, prone in the mud and weak from battle. On the verge of death and reaching out to him as he approached. "My Liege," he breathed and dropped his sword picking up his pace into a trot over the ground. He stopped short at the sight before him, Arthur knelt in the mud with Excalibur at his side, while Mordred lay in a pool of his own blood at his feet.

"Galahad." His eyes fluttered open slightly as the knight approached. "I am injured," he said simply pulling his hand away from the gash on his side. Galahad watched for a moment aghast at the severity of the wound. He could see the flow of blood from the wound ebb over his armour and another smaller wound on the king's shoulder, partially covered in mud.

"My Liege," he said simply and knelt by the king's side as Arthur fell into the ground. He lowered his head and gently pushed his hands under his body, before forcing the last vestiges of his strength to stand taking the king up in his arms. Lord Kay and Lord Tristan stopped short of the two men and watched dumbly as Galahad stepped over the corpse of Mordred and looked over towards his comrades and shook his head.

"It is over," whispered Arthur as blood trickled from the side of his mouth. He smiled up at the knight who held him in his arms. "I am king." Arthur could feel darkness closing on him as he spoke.

"My Liege, I... I..."

"Silence, good Galahad... take me to Merlin." Galahad looked over at the remaining knights and shook his head as Arthur closed his eyes and quietly slipped away.

"The king is dead," said Galahad simply.

18.

Knight of Passion

A sharp noise awoke Francis from his uneasy slumber, and he lay for a moment in a pool of sweat on the top of the bed struggling to locate the source of the noise. The dream… the death of the king. Was the noise in his head? he wondered as he sat rubbing his temples. The noise erupted once again, and his eyes were drawn to the door of the hotel room. After everything that had been happening to him lately, he was unsure whether to open it or not. Three knocks… but then the apparitions had not knocked before, had they? he reasoned. He forced himself off the bed and glanced at the clock as he walked slowly across the cold hard floor of the bedroom. Five minutes past one. Who the hell could be knocking on his door at this time in the morning? His thoughts drifted back to his dream for a moment. The death of the king… the battle and then there was the calling of the woman leading him to this point, but for some reason he did not feel his journey was over. His hand waivered over the metal handle for a moment before tightening around the knob, he paused before opening the door slightly and peered through the small crack between wood and frame.

"My Lord Galahad," the voice whispered through the darkness as Sir Galahad staggered through the copse, emerging onto the beach.

The knight gazed up and stared through blurred vision at the new voice. "Tristan," he said softly. "Is that really thee?" he asked. The newcomer placed his arm around the knight and helped him to his feet.

"Me thinks it is, old friend," laughed Tristan. "It seems that Merlin has brought us back from the dead for some reason. Thoust is hurt," he added suddenly noticing the gash of colour spread at his side.

"'Tis naught. The king is rising… Excalibur," gasped Galahad.

"Don't talk," said Tristan. "Let's get thee back into the cave." His arm snaked around his colleague, and he placed his body beneath Galahad's body allowing the knight to rest his weight against him. "I know. Not all but bits of it anyway. The bits that Merlin has decided to tell me. I don't think he's telling me everything though," he admitted as they made their way back to the cavern over the beach. Their feet sank into the soft ground as they walked through the darkness and as they walked Tristan continued to talk. "The king is dead," he said dropping his voice to a whisper. "I remember that." His eyes struggled in the dark to locate the cavern as he pulled Galahad across the beach. "We laid him to rest."

"'Tis not the king," whispered Galahad. "It is Excalibur that calls." Tristan paused briefly with this new information.

"Excalibur… then where is Arthur?"

"He is still dead," said Galahad, simply. "We are resurrect for a child—"

"Not just some child! Thy king," the voice came through the darkness stern and harsh.

"Merlin. I did not see thee."

"That much is obvious, my Lord." Merlin strode through the darkness towards the two knights. "Whom did this to thee?" he demanded staring at Galahad's wounds.

"'Twas Agravain—"

"Forces are arising against us," said Merlin glancing suspiciously around. "Come, come." He beckoned them forward. "We must hurry, he is awakening."

"Merlin, wait," stammered Galahad. "Mordred lives."

Merlin paused in the mouth of the cave and looked deep into the darkness beyond. "Mordred," he whispered. "'Tis not important. It changes naught." He watched as the two knights passed him and moved slowly along the tunnel to the cavern. "Morgaine," he whispered into the darkness and allowed a slight smile to spark over his face.

"Are you going to let me in?" asked Gwen as she peered through the door. She was standing in the hall, still dressed in her flimsy blue shirt and grey jeans. He blinked at her through the crack in the door and frowned. "Come on," she said smiling glancing behind her. "You gonna let a girl stand here all night?" she teased and pushed the door open and forced her way into the room. She eyed him standing in the door frame in only his boxer shorts and smiled, before turning and bouncing further into the room. Francis flushed a deep crimson and his hands wandered over his groin before shutting the door quickly.

"What did you want?" he whispered as he pressed his hands against the wooden door.

She laughed dropping onto the bed and kicked off her shoes allowing them to fall in the corner of the room. She stood and walked into the bathroom, placing her small bag on the side of the sink. Francis followed her, his hands still covering the front of his body. He watched her as she stood before the enamel basin, his eyes playing over her breasts hidden beneath the flimsy blue top. She grinned at him and winked, turning to face the mirror. She bent over the sink and watched him as his eyes strayed to her tight jeans. "I've come to check out your plumbing, make sure you know your tubes are working fine," she teased smiling into the mirror as she examined her reflection.

Francis moved into the bathroom from his position in the door frame and stood behind her watching her every move. He could feel a swelling in his groin as he stood watching her hips sway from side to side as she bent over the sink.

"Come closer," she purred into the mirror. "Look at this."

Francis did as he was instructed and moved close to her, peering over her shoulder and watching her fingers play around the metal taps. He watched entrapped as her finger slid into the nozzle and emerged only to run around the rim of the metal, then back inside the tap again. He glanced at her reflection and met with her eyes as she smiled through the mirrored surface on the wall. He placed his hand on the lower part of her back, his fingers sliding beneath her shirt and touching her soft skin. She smiled and closed her eyes slightly at his touch and pushed her hips against his groin, allowing his growing organ to rest against her buttocks. Her fingers rested on the edge of the tap and she played with the faucet.

"Hmm," she murmured smiling. "Something feels a bit stiff." She giggled.

Francis allowed his hands to work under her top, feeling and pressing against her soft skin moving slowly over her body and massaging her back as her hips swayed playfully pressing against his waist. Francis closed his eyes as he allowed her body to writhe against his own and his hands wandered down her body until they rested on her swaying hips. A giggle from her forced him to open his eyes and look at her reflection in the mirror.

She was looking at him, smiling at his pleasure and pushed hard backward against his groin. "Maybe a bit of lubrication will ease things. Make it nice and moist. Almost slippy," she said playfully as one hand snaked into her bag where it disappeared inside before withdrawing a small cylindrical tube. He eyed the small bottle and took it as she passed it to him. Francis flicked open the lid and squirted a swab of oil into his hands, the clear liquid rolling in his palms before placing it over her body… her perfect body. His hands ran easily with the moisture beneath her shirt. The cold of the liquid caused her to start slightly under the pressure and she grinned as his hands moved further up under her shirt working the oil into her skin.

Slowly she pulled at the buttons of her shirt as his hands worked feverously beneath the soft cotton, oil staining the material as he forced his hands up her back towards her shoulders. He leant forward and brushed her ginger hair from her neck as she pulled off her shirt. He planted a long lingering kiss of the nape of her neck as lust filled his veins. She threw her head back under the hot touch of his lips and gyrated her hips towards his groin, allowing a small lingering groan to pierce her ruby red lips.

As one hand moved slowly down her back, Francis moved his other to the front of her body. His fingers played with the black cup of her bra, tracing the line of the wire before delving into the lace and cupping the soft mound of her breast. His handmade small circular movements under the material for a moment allowing the oil to cover her skin, before pulling her breast free from the cup. She gripped the edge of the sink as his fingers worked over the contours of her breast before flicking at her small nipple, erect and free from its moorings.

His other hand moved across her lower back and slipped into the top of her grey trousers, moving over the edge of her black thong. He could feel his own passion rising to almost boiling point as the movement of her body and the oil infused in a mixture of lust and sexual tension. He reached around her waist and pulled desperately with his free hand at the buttons on her jeans as his other hand played around her tender nipple. Fingers gripped and pulled hard against little resistance as the buttons fell away from their moorings and opened easily.

He reluctantly moved his hand away from her naked breast and stood upright, staring down at her loose trousers before pushing down at the material and forcing the jeans to fall to the bathroom floor and looked down lustfully at the small strip of material covering her waist. The black thong offered no resistance as his hands moved slowly down her body and gripped at her soft tender buttock. He placed another kiss against the top of her neck as he leant forward over her body, before his fingers curled around the small bottle of oil. He squeezed hard on the bottle, watching as the contents fell over her waist and ran down her buttocks towards her legs. Then he moved close to her pressing his own body against hers and rubbed the oil across her skin, moving from her thighs and up along her spine towards her neck.

She pressed her hips against his and breathed softly. "Now," she whispered as her circling movements intensified their already heightened stimulus.

His hands pushed down at the oil-stained shorts which covered his waist and stood with his hands resting on her waist for a moment looking at her small, rounded hips pressing against his. He placed his hand against her hip and grasped at his swelling excitement with the other, moving closer so their bodies pressed against each other.

"Do it," she urged, grasping the edge of the sink. "Do me now."

Francis closed his eyes and moaned as he thrust forward, stabbing at her tenderness. An overwhelming feeling of pleasure and lust flowed through his body heightened by the noise of her as he pushed forward deep inside her.

The sounds of the bodies entwined echoed through the room as the slow passage of time marched relentlessly onward.

19.

Tease and Fury

When Francis woke the next morning, the bed he lay in was empty apart from his sweaty body and the stained sheets from the oil from the passion of the previous night. He struggled to sit and gazed through blurred vision around the room. There was no sign of his female companion from the previous night, and nothing remained apart from muscle tension in the top of his thighs and the stained bedding which revealed their shame.

He stood from the bed naked, allowing the blankets to collapse on the floor around his feet. Slowly and tenderly, Francis stalked into the bathroom where he stared at his reflection for a moment and allowed himself a wry smile at his prowess as he looked at his naked body in the surface of the glass. The figure in the mirror copied his every movement as Francis placed his hands on his hips and examined his body carefully. He could not shake the effects of the night and the effect that Gwen had on him and he smiled as he reached for the shower controls. The steam from the jet of water flushed the confined space and hot water connected with the cool air of the bathroom and condensation fogged over the reflective glass.

Francis stepped into the cubicle and closed his eyes as the water cascaded down his body, flowing and cleansing every part of his physique. His hands rubbed at his body, smearing soap over his chest, arms and legs before a layer of thick foam covered his groin and trickled down his legs into the swirl of water escaping down the gaping plug hole. He smiled as he thought of Gwen and the night before; visions flashed in his head of her naked body. As he remembered the positions of their passion, he could feel himself becoming aroused under the combination of thought, water and his own activities. He rubbed his groin as the foam lathered further under the flurry of pressure from his working hand, while he steadied himself against the wall with his free hand. The water from the showerhead intensified and poured over his head as he stood with his eyes closed, remembering and rubbing faster and faster until...

"Come to me." The voice. No, not the voice... a different one.

The shock of the voice forced him to stop his 'washing', and he staggered back against the wall of the cubicle, opening his eyes expecting to see the naked form of the woman before him. His naked buttocks pressed against the cold glass of the cubicle as he scanned the steam filled space searching for the source of the voice.

"Come to me." Laughter filled the bathroom and through the steam, Francis could see the regal form of an older woman. The woman from the train. She was standing in the bathroom dressed in full clothing, one hand pressed down against the sink, the other raised in front of her as she examined her fingernails. "Don't stop on my account," she laughed as she eyed the naked Francis. "I understand a man has needs." She stepped forward towards the shower and leant close to the glass. "And so does a woman," she teased.

She abruptly turned away and returned to the sink where she spoke into the mirror staring at her reflection. "I ache," she said staring at her reflection. Her hand drifted between her legs as she continued to stare at her image. She stood and closed her eyes as her hand rubbed herself between her groin then slowly snaked its way along her stomach and over her chest plate, where her fingers followed the contours of her golden armour.

"But the difference is I ache for something more than that of flesh." She turned to look directly at Francis. "Excalibur," she whispered. Francis reached for the towel hanging close to the open cubicle and pulled it over his body, which forced a feign smile to cross her lips. "Oh, come now. Don't be shy," she teased as he pulled the towel around his waist. "It isn't something I haven't seen before," she laughed and approached Francis. She stopped before him, and he could feel her hot breath against his face. Her hand reached beneath his towel, and he could feel her fingers wrap slowly around his shaft. "Where is Excalibur?" she whispered as she looked down towards his groin. Francis stood dumbstruck at the sight of this woman standing in the bathroom, with her hand gripped firmly on him. "Tell me and I can take you to places where you have never been before," she whispered as her hand slowly moved beneath the towel, stroking his growing bulge. Morgaine smiled. "This I can promise."

Despite himself Francis closed his eyes as he could feel the sensation of her touch. "I… I… don't know," he stammered through his pleasure. Her grip became weak, and Francis opened his eyes and stared at his own reflection in the mirror. The towel he wore hung limply around his waist and the bulge beneath rose to attention, but the woman was nowhere to be seen. He shook his head free of the vision and gazed around the small room whilst he rubbed the towel over his body. He felt dirty from this encounter and rubbed harder with the towel, attempting to remove any evidence of the presence of the woman. He peered out of the bathroom and into the room and satisfied that there was no-one in there, he moved, sat on the bed and buried his head deep in his hands.

"The forces of Morgaine will be moving," stated Merlin as he stood before the stone chalice. He cast his gaze around the seven figures standing before the altar. One of the knights ran his armoured hand across the roughly strewn rock.

"Why, Merlin? I do not understand," he stated simply.

"Nor do I, Lord Kay, at least not yet" admitted Merlin, "but I do know 'tis our duty to protect the king."

"The king is dead!" snapped Galahad from the edge of the cavern. He stood with part of his armour cast on the floor while Tristan stabbed at his wounds with a small damp cloth.

"Why does thee insist on this course?"

"We all saw, Merlin," insisted Galahad angrily. "He fell at Camlann. 'Twas I that lifted the lifeless body of the king and carried him yon, over the moorlands to this place." There was a murmur of agreement from his fellow knights as Galahad continued, "Now you ask us to follow blindly this… this child! He is but a boy, an infant in arms."

"He is hardly a child, my Lord; he is the direct descendent of the king."

"Your words mean nothing to me!" roared Galahad as he stood, pushing away the concerns of Tristan. "Thee play in lies, Merlin. Thee are a master of false glib; thy always were." He stood before the old man and stared down at the frail old body of the magician. "You play your own games, for your own position," he accused. "I do not trust thee, my Lord Merlin. Whilst I stand for the king, whom do thee stand for?"

"I stand for God," said Merlin simply. "I stand for the crown of England, and I stand for right. Are these not enough?" He stood for a moment meeting the accusation of Galahad and matching his glare.

"How do we know this is the true descendant?" a new voice pitched through the darkness. A knight pulled himself away from the wall, his golden armour shining off the dim light of the flaming torches hanging from the cavern walls. He removed his tall thin helmet and shook his long golden hair free from its confinement and stepped between the two men. He stood for a moment; his golden armoured gauntlets pressed against the bodies of them. The cavern was filled with tension and mistrust as the accusations thrown by Galahad had drawn serious doubts over the plausibility of the bloodline of the king.

"Bedivere?" queried Merlin.

The knight stood glancing between the two men; his arms outstretched holding each in check from their words. His armour shone through the cavern like a beacon and revealed a thin grey mesh covering a red and yellow fabric tunic beneath the large chest plate. "This boy…" Bedivere indicated towards the water filled chalice. "How doth thee know he is the one? The true king."

"We don't," replied Merlin simply. Galahad snorted his derision and stalked away to the back of the cavern, where Tristan eased him back into a sitting position and replaced the cloth to the cut on his shoulder. "If we are awake, then Excalibur has made the calling," he continued looking at the knights in turn until his view rested on Galahad. "We must have trust, otherwise are we not lost? Have we not hoped? We would be no better than those we are inclined to protect against." He waved away Bedivere and returned to the chalice and gazed into the water and spoke into the shimmering pool as he watched Francis dress. "'Tis not our place to judge, my Lords. He is coming. He will decide."

Galahad rose from his position and thrust forward. "You can't mean…"

Merlin nodded sagely. "He was charged with its protection."

"Merlin—"

"'Tis too late, my Lord Galahad, if we are here then the calling would have awoken him."

"May God have mercy on us all," whispered Galahad as he stared into the depths of the tunnel. He frowned through the darkness, expecting the shapes to move and contort under his scrutiny. He closed his eyes and as his hand wandered to the cross around his neck, he whispered quietly to himself, "Fisher King."

20.

Admission of Madness

Francis walked into the foyer of the guest house and looked around the expanse of space before him. He stood unsure where he should go or what he should do. His hand fingered the large red book which he had signed the previous night and his eyes drifted over the empty pages and he noted that his signature was prominent and conspicuous by its loneliness on the page. He studied the wooden lined walls until finally fell on a small wooden stand with a plethora of pamphlets advertising various locations across the area. Gaudy images and letters designed to entice the reader beckoned towards him and offered trips to Lands' End and Newquay as well as offers of shopping in Bude and the picturesque Dartmoor, but as his eyes scanned over the leaflets, they rested on a particular pamphlet displaying an image of a half-ruined castle sitting amongst green scenery, overlooking the sea. Slowly he pulled the leaflet from the wooden stand and fingered the paper, looking over the images as pictures flashed through his mind. He could see the ruined building staring out of the paper in his hand, while in his head he could see images of flags flying from the turrets and ramparts. He could see figures dressed in armour riding horses in and out of the castle; he could see lords and ladies strolling through the grounds surrounding the castle.

"The castle is beautiful this time of year." The words broke his daydream and he focused on the source of the voice. He blinked as Gwen walked through the sunlight streaming through the window from the other room and he could feel the start of a smile trace over his face.

"Morning," he whispered as he leant forward to kiss her as she approached.

"Whoa, whoa, whoa, tiger," she said hurriedly placing her hands upon his chest and gently pushed him away.

"What?" he commented confused over her actions. "I thought…" he stammered as he looked at her. "Last night…"

"Look, honey," she smiled as she spoke. "Last was fun," she said refusing to meet his gaze. "But that's all it was… fun. It meant nothing." She finally looked at him and smiled. "I have a boyfriend, okay? Last night was good. Don't get me wrong, I enjoyed it… God, I enjoyed it, but that's all it was; a piece of fun nothing more nothing less. Just fun."

"Then why?" Francis spread his arms and shook his head in desperation.

"I don't know," she admitted. "It was something I wanted." She ran her hand across his body tracing his chest down to his stomach and finally his groin. "And I usually get what I want." He could feel a stirring in his groin as her hand rested over the front of his trousers and she whispered hotly into his ear before she planted a kiss on his cheek and flounced away into the adjoining room. She giggled slightly and paused in the doorway and looked back at him. "You want some breakfast, lover?" she cooed. "You might need to keep your strength up, just in case."

She winked and disappeared through the door leaving Francis alone in the foyer of the building. He stood for a moment conscious that the bulge in his trousers was evident and straightened his clothing before following her into the larger room.

The room was empty as he stepped through the doorway and his eyes searched the room for evidence of Gwen. He could smell her perfume lingering in the centre of the room as he stood looking around the small ring of tables scattered across the floor. He walked across the lounge, picking his way through the tables until he came to a stop at the large stone fireplace standing at the end of the room. He stared at the scabbard hanging over the fireplace and his fingers reached out for the object, tracing the brass adornments that ran along the spine of the antique. He allowed his fingers to run along the swirls and legends which decorated the black leather casing.

"It's beautiful, isn't it?" Francis turned to face the landlord of the public house and nodded dumbly as the larger man walked across the floor with a menu tucked firmly under his arm. "It's only a replica, of course, but I like it." Francis could see the man's eyes glaze over as he stared at the object hanging from its moorings over the fireplace.

"It's very good," breathed Francis returning his gaze to the scabbard.

"No, it's more than good; it's magnificent," replied the landlord passing a menu to the younger man. "Breakfast?" he asked and for the first time since his arrival, he smiled at Francis and he continued to stare at the scabbard. "Son."

"What? Oh, sorry," stammered Francis. "I was lost in its…" He struggled to find the words as he spoke.

"I know what you mean," the landlord said kindly. "It draws you in… it's this place." He waved around as he spoke, "I don't mean the pub, the whole town. It has a magic." He turned and walked into the kitchen. "Gwen will be out in a moment to take your order," he called as he walked away.

Francis stood alone in the room staring into his reflection distorted through the brass of the scabbard, lost in his own thoughts. "It's exact," he whispered to himself as he stared at the object hanging from the wall and immediately wondered how he knew.

"Come to me." He spun around and faced the woman from his dreams standing in the centre of the room amidst the tables. She raised her hands towards him, and small traces of water dripped from her arms. "You must come to me," she urged through moist lips.

"I don't understand," he called back. "What do you want?"

The woman stood staring at him for a moment, water seeping from her body and spreading forming a damp space where she stood. "Come to me," she said again.

"I'm here," he whimpered. "I've done what you wanted. I followed your voice here. Now what?"

"You must come to me." Her eyes danced past Francis and stared into the scabbard as she spoke. Francis turned to look at the replica as he followed her eyeline.

"Is this it?" he asked. "Is this what you want?" he yelled, turning back to an empty room. The woman had gone, only a wet puddle lay on the carpet to show she had ever been there. He stood for a moment feeling foolish at his outburst and placed his hands on each side of his head and pushed at his skull as the itch of her voice remained inside his mind.

"Come to me." The whisper echoed through his brain and reverberated through his soul, and he could feel the beginning of tears well up in his eyes. He glanced around the empty room and ran through the tables towards the exit of the public house and out into the street beyond, allowing the fresh morning air to sweep over his body. He gulped hungrily at the air and took great swathes into his lungs as the voice still echoed through his mind. "Come to me." It was relentless in its persistence. "Come to me."

Gwen watched as Francis sped out of the pub and stood by the kitchen door staring at the main door of the pub at his departure. She frowned as the door slammed shut behind him and sighed inwardly. Perhaps last night was not such a good idea after all, if this were how he would react, she thought to herself. Her eyes strayed over the empty tables, and she frowned as they rested on a dark patch in the centre of the room. Slowly Gwen picked her way forward through the maze of tables until she stood over the blemish on the carpet. She gazed at the patch and lowered herself to the floor, where she reached out and placed her hand on the carpet. "Wet," she murmured as her hand played over the damp patch swelling on the floor and she glanced towards the closed door of the pub. "Dad!" she called. "I'm just popping out for a moment. Back soon." She stood and followed the path taken by Francis only moments before and stood on the threshold of the pub and scanned the street for traces of their young visitor.

She looked down the road and found Francis sitting on a bench by the edge of the pavement, staring out over the expansive beach and into the distance where the waves rolled over the edge of the sand and crashed onto the beach. "Hey!" she called but found herself shouting at shadows as he ignored her calls. "Hey!" she tried again walking along the road towards the wooden bench on the promenade. She sighed and could feel the frustration rising within her as he sat staring across the expansive beach. "Hey, ignorant," she said as she lowered herself roughly next to him on the wooden bench.

He turned and looked at her. "Sorry," he said slowly, "I didn't hear."

She could see his eyes were blurred and reddened from the marks of tears which stained his face. "If this is about last night—" she started.

"It's nothing to do with you!" he snapped, immediately regretting his words. "Sorry, I didn't mean to snap," he apologised. "I just have some shit going on that I need to work out."

"Great," she exclaimed throwing her hands up in the air. "I pick a nutcase." She smiled and nudged him for a response, but Francis remained silent. She looked at him for a moment before speaking. "Why did you leave like that?" she asked. "I mean, that quickly." Francis shrugged at her question and turned to face the ocean once again. Gwen sighed loudly allowing Francis to hear her frustration. "If it's about the carpet." He looked at her sharply. "It's easily cleaned."

"It's not the carpet!"

"Dad won't be angry. Accidents happen."

"I said it's not about the carpet!" he snapped again.

"Whatever you spilled—"

"Look, it's not the fucking carpet!" his voice grated her as he shouted over the distant sounds of the waves.

She raised her hands in mock defence. "Look, I was just saying," she said.

"I'm sorry."

"Again."

"Yes." He smiled as he spoke. "Again."

"That's better," she said softly. "You have a beautiful smile. Don't hide it." Francis blushed as she spoke and looked down towards his feet, looking at his marked trainers. She smiled at his discomfort and placed a hand on his. Francis looked at her hand and returned her smile, then gazed off into the distance once again. "Penny for them?" she enquired.

"What?"

"Your thoughts… penny for them."

He looked at her for a moment and found himself lost in her eyes, his mind briefly drifting back to the night before: the hotel room, the encounter. "I didn't mean to come here," he admitted as he looked into her eyes.

"Didn't think so," she said. "You don't look the sort." A confused look flashed over his face which caused her to laugh out loud at the look of bemusement which flirted with his emotions. "The only people to come here are usually history enthusiasts and usually with an obsession with the myth." She indicated to the castle in the distance.

"King Arthur," he murmured.

"Yeah, good old King Arthur! Dilly dilly," she mocked. "Tintagel Castle, his birthplace!" She slapped her hand against her leg and laughed. "Fucking rubbish!"

"Why?"

She looked at him and smiled. "You don't believe in this shit, do you?" she asked and looked at him as he sat there dumbly staring back at her. "You do!" She giggled. "Oh, my fucking God, you do. You believe in all of this… you actually buy into this rubbish."

"How do you know it's rubbish?" His question struck her for a moment as though she had never considered it before, and she thought.

"It has to be, doesn't it?" she said eventually. "I mean… an ancient

118

king, born to lead the Britons who will one day rise again when Britain needs him. Come on." She laughed again and gazed over the beach into the distance. "It's only a fairy tale."

"What about the romance of it?"

"How much do you know about the story?" she asked.

Francis shrugged. "Only what I've seen in films," he admitted.

"Only what you've seen in films," she mocked. "I've been brought up on this shit all my life," she said. "How Arthur led the Britons into battle against God only knows what and the tales of Mordred and the rest of it." She waved around her expansively. "Dad's obsessed with the bloody story." She laughed with sadness toying at her heart. "Christ, he even named me Guinevere."

"But what if it were real? What if something made you believe?" he asked looking in her eyes. She turned away and remained silent as she watched the horizon. They sat for a moment in silence as they stared into the distance, each one fighting their own demons. "I was called here," Francis said eventually. Gwen looked at him and he matched her gaze. "I was called here," he repeated to her unspoken question.

"By whom?" she asked.

"I don't know," he admitted. "I was called here by someone... I don't know who and I don't know why but I was called to this place." His gaze tracked away from her and eventually rested on the castle perched on the cliff tops in the distance.

"Go on," she said softly watching his movements and following his vision to the castle.

"I kept hearing a voice... in my head," he said gazing through the tree line. "A woman's voice. She kept telling me to come here... to this place." He glanced at her and smiled as she returned his gaze. "Over and over, she would call to me telling me to come here. Then I would have the dreams. The visions: knights and battles, Arthur and Mordred, Merlin and a woman, Morgaine." He struggled as he fought back the fears of his admission. "All the time they were calling me here." Gwen watched as tears were welling in his eyes as he spoke, and she could see the pain in his face and with a sudden realization she understood his pain and his commitment to his story. "The water in the pub... it was her, she was there," he said. "Calling to me, calling me there." Francis pointed into the distance towards the castle. "Camelot."

119

21.

Protectors of the Forest

She laughed at him nervously. "That's not Camelot," she said. "It's Tintagel."

"But it could be," he urged. Then appeared to change his mind as he looked at her. "No... you're right... it couldn't." He seemed distant in his thoughts. "Tristan said Camelot is to the north of here."

"Who's Tristan? Your friend?" she asked kindly.

Francis blinked at her for a moment confused. "Who?" he asked.

"Tristan."

Francis shook his head. "I'm sorry. I don't know anyone called Tristan," he admitted.

Gwen sighed in frustration. "But you said Tristan said Camelot was north of here."

"Did I?"

"Yes, you did!" she snapped. She could feel her frustration boiling at his attitude. "Like talking to a child, or a nutjob!" she said.

"Tristan." The name lingered on the lips of Francis for a moment, and he slowly shook his head. "Sorry, but I don't know a Tristan..." His words trailed away into the distance as his eyes marked the castle. "Knight of Cornwall," he whispered.

"Shit!" snapped Gwen. The suddenness of her outburst brought the meandering mind of Francis back to reality and he looked at her. She was looking further down the promenade at the figure of a man walking briskly towards them. His heavy-set frame swung as he walked, and his jacket cast open as he stared defiantly at the couple on the bench. "It's Lance," she whispered.

"Lance?" queried Francis his attention wavering on the man's clenched fists. A look of anger and jealousy flushed over his features as he neared the pair.

"My boyfriend," she explained in a hurried whisper.

"Lance," he said again. "As in Lancelot?"

She nodded. "I told you, everyone around here is obsessed with the legend."

A shadow crossed over the bench as Lance stopped just short of the pair and gazed towards Francis. "Guinevere," he said his deep voice cutting the atmosphere.

"Lance—" she began.

"Who's this?" he demanded.

"Please, Lance."

"Come on, Gwen, baby," he mocked. "I only asked who your friend here is?" He stood over the form of Francis who remained on the bench staring uncomfortably out towards the castle in the distance.

"Lance, he's just a tourist, that's all. He's staying at the hotel… wants to know the way to the castle…"

"Yeah, well as long as that's all he's after," he said menacingly. He sat down between Francis and Gwen and pushed his body against her as he stared down at Francis. "She's mine," he said placing his arm around her shoulders. "And if you come near her…" The warning was tangible and hung in the air between them for a moment.

Francis looked Lance up and down and could see the bulk of his body beneath his clothing. The newcomer dwarfed Francis in both size and stature as he leaned over his body attempting to intimidate him. "Look, mate," said Francis. "I'm not looking for any trouble, I'm just here to see the sights."

"Yeah well," sneered Lance. "She ain't one of them, you got that?"

Francis nodded his understanding and stood from the bench. "Anyway, as I was saying," started Gwen. "If you follow that road there," she said pointing. "It will lead you straight to the castle… or you could cut through the woods. It's longer, but it makes for a nicer walk."

Francis nodded in her direction and set off down the road, casting a final glance behind him as he set off. Lance sneered at him as he walked and leant closer to Gwen, whispering in her ear. She feigned a laugh and waved towards Francis as he turned and stared up the road towards the castle. He briefly considered the walk along the road before looking into the woods. A signpost indicated towards a small path which offered directions through the wood towards the castle. He looked at both paths and thought about the options before shrugging and resigned for a long walk, he plunged into the wooded area.

"He is coming," breathed Merlin as he watched Francis in the depths of the chalice as he plunged from view into the wood.

"He is heading for the castle," stated Galahad simply as he peered over the old man's shoulder into the chalice.

"But he will come," insisted Merlin. "Is all prepared?" Galahad moved away from his side and Merlin cast his gaze over the seven knights and allowed a small smile to pierce his face.

"What about Morgaine?" asked Bedivere. "Her forces will be alert to his movements also."

"She will not dare move against us till Excalibur is secure," Merlin said. "By that time, it will be too late."

"Thy still have not told us why we are resurrect," said Galahad from the shadows.

"At present I do not know, my Lord," admitted Merlin. "But once Excalibur has been recovered all should be revealed to us." Merlin turned to Tristan who stood silently by the wall. "My Lord," he started. "Thee know this area better than anyone; will thee assist the young king to safety?"

Tristan nodded and pushed himself off the wall he was leaning against. "My home, Cornwall, has changed a plenty since I roamed its country," he said sadly. "But it still is my home. I will endeavour to protect my Liege."

"What of us?" asked a large knight masked in the shadows.

"Lord Kay?" enquired Merlin.

"Are we expected to stand around baying to the orders of one such as thee?" he queried rudely. "I am a knight of the round table not a babysitter to a false king or his magical sage," he spat the words. "If Morgaine is here then we should do battle with her forthwith instead of hiding in the shadows like rats. Nay even rats have more honour than... than this!" he snapped and threw down a stone on the floor at Merlin's feet.

"My Lord Kay, please. Until the boy passes the test of the Fisher King then our quest remains for naught," said Merlin.

"Fisher King, Fisher King... always his name."

"Do not speak his name in haste, my Lord," warned Merlin. "He will verify the destiny of the boy and lead us to Excalibur. Until then we must be patient."

"I shall not skulk in the shadows like some weak-minded peasant!"

122

snapped Kay as he pushed his way close to Merlin.

"Did thee not miss most of the battle of Camlann, Kay?" scoffed Galahad as he moved between the two men. "Take your angst out on those who are worthy of thy venom."

"Take care, Galahad, your purity shall be thine death."

"As your arrogance, my Lord, shall be yours."

"Please, my Lords," urged Merlin. "Have a care… you seven are the final survivors of Camlann," he said casting his gaze over the knights. "We stand together as protectors of the crown and the kingdom of Briton. It is our duty to protect the bloodline as is our oath. You, my lords, are the noblest and bravest of all the knights of the round table. So, act that way!" he snapped. "Please, my Lord, join Lord Tristan and protect the young king."

Lord Kay snorted and moved close to Tristan who placed his hand on the larger knight's shoulder. "My friend." Tristan smiled as he spoke softly to Kay and turned to face the entrance of the tunnel. The larger knight shrugged off the hand which laid on his shoulder and stalked away down the tunnel towards the sunlight cast through the distant opening.

"Good luck," commented Galahad towards Tristan as he moved to join his comrade in the tunnel and watched in silence as the two knights walked away disappearing into the gloomy dank conditions.

Francis glanced around him as he walked along the dirty wooded track which led from the road and up towards the castle. Small streams of light shone through the branches and played across the leaves as they danced in the slight breeze. Around his feet lay a carpet of tiny blue flowers, each bulb swaying and waving as he passed, his feet pressing down in the soft ground beneath the pressure of his shoe. He stopped and paused in a clearing and glanced back in the direction he had walked. The road was completely covered by the tendrils of the trees as they reached through the wood, clawing and grasping at the penetrating rays of sunlight. He strained his eyes upward towards the sky and squinted as the sun forced its way through the blanket of leaves which spread its way over the top of the forest. He frowned as he watched darkness force its way over the blue sky and fall over the landscape around him. Under the blanket of darkness, the wood took on a different feel… a sinister feel. He shivered and felt as though he should not be in this place. He felt as though he was intruding somewhere he should not have gone. Francis checked the time, pulling the cuff of his jacket over his arm to reveal a small digital watch. The red numbers shone out from the face of the small black square and revealed he had only been walking through the woods for twenty minutes, and only two hours since he had awoken in his hotel room.

He cast his gaze around him once again, listening to the sounds of the wood as it settled in the breeze. He couldn't understand how it had become so dark so quickly and moved deeper into the wood, following the rough dirt trail. The ground crunched under foot as branches and bracken were forced from its slumber and kicked up as Francis pushed his way through the darkness. He could see in the distance ahead of him a pair of bright shining lights, small and intense but nevertheless bright and full of fire and wisdom. The sound of movement from the trees disturbed him for a moment and when he glanced back towards the source of the light he frowned through the darkness as they appeared to have been swamped under the blanket of blackness. More noises surrounded and circled Francis as he stood, stock still and unsure of his surroundings and presence. "Is there anybody here?" he stammered into the dark, awaiting an unheard reply. Another noise to his right caused him to start and he peered through the darkness into the dark expanse of the bushes to the side of the path. He crouched staring intently through the leaves and into the depths of nothing, nothing but darkness, nothing but a deathly black.

A pair of yellow orbs broke the surface of the darkness and met his stare. They remained before him unwavering and unmoving, the pupil in the centre of the orb dilating to the vision of Francis in the clearing. A thick growl broke the tension of the glade, and the source of the orbs slowly pushed its way from the bush and circled Francis, meeting his stare with its own. The grey fur of the large animal bristled and shone in the darkness, as slight glimmers of light fought its way through the blanket covering the glade and how Francis wished it had not. The creature circled Francis, its teeth bared into a fixed grimace as it stared through burning eyes fixed on the soft flesh of Francis.

"Don't worry," whispered a female's voice. "They won't hurt, not unless I wish them to." Francis turned sharply and watched as the tall regal woman pushed her way elegantly through the bracken and the thorny undergrowth. The thorns and stems seemed to bounce off her golden armour and were swept beneath a mass of glistening chainmail which formed a skirt around her waistline. Flecks of golden hair streaked down her back and cascaded over her shoulders and over the gleaming gold metal as it fell from a petite golden crown perched on top of her head. She smiled at Francis as she walked unharmed through the dense bushes. The forest apparently spreading and unfolding before her as she took one step after another. He eyed the large creature before him and glanced to a second walking by the woman's side and gulped at the air of intimidation they held.

Francis recognised her from yesterday, he realised. The train, this was the same woman from the train and the same one from that very morning. The woman threw her head back at laughed as though she had read his every thought, before she suddenly fell silent casting her gaze around the glade as they stood opposite each other.

"When I was a young girl," she started staring into the past. "I would play in these woods." Her hand drifted above her head and he watched as her hand entwined around an overhanging branch and pulled it down to her line of vision. "Of course," she explained, "the wood was a lot younger in those days and so was I." She smiled as she spoke as the memories surface in her mind. "Oh, it was beautiful then, none of this… this… rubbish," she snapped as she waved her hand around the ground at the signs of debris left by absent ramblers and tourists.

She released the branch and placed her hand flat on the grey fur of the large beast by her side. "The forest was alive then," she said wistfully. "Their packs would roam the forests hunting for prey. Hundreds of them as I remember." She bent down and tickled the wolf beneath its chin and smiled. The wolf closed its eyes and lifted its powerful head to allow her greater leverage as her hand ran through its coarse thick fur. "Now look at it!" she snapped. "Nothing but decay… even my friends here," she said sadly looking down at the two creatures circling her as she spoke.

"There are no wolves in the forest," insisted Francis as he watched the animals snap and growl in his direction.

"Exactly!" she said triumphantly. "There are no wolves in the forest," she repeated then looked straight at Francis, "except these." She smiled with true menace, her teeth matching those of the wolves as they circled his legs.

"They're not real," he shouted as they moved slowly around him occasionally brushing against his legs as they moved. He looked at the woman in defiance. "They don't exist!" he shouted. "They can't… there are no wild wolves in England."

"There aren't," she agreed. "At least not anymore."

"Then what are those?" asked Francis.

"A folly," she teased before her face clouded with anger. "Give me Excalibur!" she raged.

"I don't have it!"

"But you will!" she shouted her anger turning into a fire. "And thee shall give it to me, for I am Morgaine le Fay!" She laughed hysterically as she threw her hands in the air. "I am your destiny!"

"I don't know where Excalibur is," begged Francis looking straight towards her. "And even if I did, I know I would never give it to you!"

"Then thou shall die," she snapped her fingers in the direction of the two waiting beasts.

Francis stared in horror as the wolves moved quickly in a blur of activity. Grey fur melded with the rush of air and fusion of fury. The sound of gnashing teeth filled the air as saliva and blood mixed in a symphony of design and nature. Blood, fur, teeth and claws raked at the air as the wolves moved in unison towards Francis, who stood frozen in terror within the wooded glade as the beasts lunged forward for their prey.

22.

Confrontation

Lord Kay crashed through the undergrowth of the forest at the sight of the wolf lunging towards the young boy in the open glade. He watched as the boy held up his arms in mock surrender as he wrestled with his own sword in its scabbard. The metal gleamed as it bore free of its holster and shone in the slight sunlight cast through the thick canopy of leaves above their heads. He drove himself forward, his sword thrust out before him and collided into the boy, forcing him backward to the ground and held his sword aloft before the plunging it into the beast. Blood and sinew erupted in a cavalcade of crimson as the wolf skewered itself on the end of Lord Kay's sword and writhed in pain and agony as it slid down the blade before reaching the hilt of the weapon. Kay sagged under the weight of the animal and staggered back, dropping onto one knee and straddling the boy as the last vestiges of life ebbed from the creature impaled on his weapon. The wolf rolled its eyes in its head and snapped hopelessly at the knight as it felt the final embers of life sweeping from its body. A grimace passed over Lord Kay's face as the sudden bout of energy and the loss the life by his hands mingled and entwined together as one, then just as quickly subsided.

Francis closed his eyes as the creature lunged towards him. He could feel its hot breath against his face. The rub of its thick grey fur against his body and the sharp touch of its claws scratch against his shoulders. In his mind's eye he could see the beast open its mouth, saliva cascading over its savage maw and sink its teeth deep into his throat. He could see it holding on as the blood seeped across its matted fur and the life drained away from his body. He could feel a heavy weight force him roughly to the floor as bodies collided, and the rush of air against his cheek as he fell heavily backward against the cold hard floor of the wood. This is it, he thought and as he lay imagining the oncoming end, his thoughts strayed to his home… his mother. He had not even told her that he loved her…

Francis lay there awaiting his certain death at the creature's bite. Then he felt the pressure of the large weight lift from his body followed by a gruff complaint. "Move, boy!" snapped the voice.

Francis hazarded opening his eyes and almost wept at the sight above him. The wolf was sprawled almost motionless on the blade of a sword and standing, almost kneeling over him was a large thick-set man dressed in elegant knight's armour. His armour partially draped in exquisite robes of yellow as they fell away over the knight's breastplate and down past his legs. A black creature which resembled the imagery of a dragon sat proudly on the material and fluttered under the movements of the owner as he knelt under the weight of the creature.

"Come on, hurry, dolt," he cursed. Francis sparked himself into action and crawled from beneath the knight's weight and moved backward as the second wolf padded across the clearing impatiently eyeing the knight with his fallen comrade. "Tristan!" the knight shouted as he pulled himself to his full height and lowered his sword to the floor, allowing he wolf to slide from the blade.

Francis watched in a morbid fascination as the flesh of the creature pulled at the sword as it slid along the cold metal, smearing a crimson stain as it slowly journeyed to the floor. He stood transfixed by the sight of the wolf as it lay on the floor, a dark smear spreading and staining the glade beneath its body.

"Boy!" came the hoarse whisper from the bushes as a second knight stepped from the undergrowth. This one was smaller in appearance and gone was the armour worn by the first, instead replaced by simple clothing made of fabric and animal skin. He stood signalling to him in a blue tunic with the hide of an animal fashioned into a designed long panel which stretched over one shoulder and trailed down to his waist where it was secure by a thick leather belt. He wore simple red hose around his legs which stretched down to a pair of leather boots on his feet. A heavy scabbard hung limply around his waist and from its leather strapping. A thick sword had been drawn and was currently being held by the knight as he stepped forward between Francis and the second wolf. The two men stood facing the woman as she quietly seethed at the death of the animal in the clearing.

"My Lords, it doth appear that we meet once more," she whispered quietly towards the knights as they stood side by side, the first knight dwarfing the second.

"Morgaine," said the smaller knight as he watched the slow tracking of the second wolf. "'Tis an honour." He smirked as he bent low at her feet, but his eyes never left her as he bowed.

"Do not fear me," she said. "For I have no argument with thee, my Lord. I am here only for the boy."

"Then let us past," commented Tristan.

"You think me simple," spat Morgaine. "I know why thee are in the forest." She looked at Francis cowering behind the first knight as she spoke. "You seek the same prize as I."

"Then thee will know, we cannot succumb to your wishes, good Lady," replied Tristan politely. "We are here to see the boy comes to no harm."

Morgaine spied the blood on Kay's sword and stepped back with the second wolf close in tow. "'Tis not my wish to enter the fray at a disadvantage, my Lords, but be warned there shall be a reckoning." She pointed at Francis as she moved backwards into the trees, the wolf circling her as she glided through the wood.

"That was good fortune, my Lord Kay," remarked Tristan as Morgaine disappeared through the woods.

"Ay, that it was," agreed the larger knight as his gaze turned back to the fallen corpse of the wolf at their feet. He looked sadly at the animal. "'Tis not right," he complained. "The creature was helpless in its actions."

"'Twas not your fault," commented Tristan as he rested a hand on the other knight's arm.

"The creature was dumb in its actions… and you are right, Tristan, it was not my fault." He rounded on Francis savagely and spat his words with venom towards him. "'Twas yours."

The force of the words took Francis back and he recoiled under the intensity. The weight of the burden of the creature's death weighing heavy in the accusation. "What? No, it wasn't," he stammered.

"If thee had not been foolish enough to walk abroad then thine creature would not have fallen foul to the dementia of Morgaine. Do thee not understand the perils of the forest!" Kay demanded.

"Yes… no… yes… I mean… I don't know any more." Francis felt flustered under the stare of the two knights. "This is England," he offered meekly. "We don't have wild animals like wolves roaming the woods."

"These woods are rife with creatures such as this," scoffed Kay kicking the carcass of the dead animal.

"Not anymore," insisted Francis. "There might have been in your day but…" His words died in his throat as Lord Kay stared down at him.

"The boy could be right," offered Tristan placing a hand on his arm. "I grew up in these woods and I have seen hide nor hair of any beast. No deer, no wolves, no boar, I see and hear nothing." He looked at Kay sadly. "It would appear that the child is correct. Times have changed, my old friend; the country is naught how we knew it."

Kay looked up at the sky through the canopy and spied the darkening clouds gathering above their heads. "Aye, perhaps thee are correct, my Lord, but I do know that there is evil abroad in these parts." He looked at Francis. "If thoust truly are who Merlin says thee are, then we must make haste. The woods are not the place to be caught in a downpour." He sheathed his mighty sword, wiping the blade clean of blood and turned back to the undergrowth and peered through the dense covering. "The path has disappeared," he mused as vine and branch stretched out reaching for the clearing.

"The plants," whispered Francis.

"Aye, I see, they are moving," breathed Kay as he watched the slow progression of vegetation as it spread across the ground towards their feet.

"What witchcraft is this?" asked Tristan as he backed into his larger comrade, sword in hand and pointing out into the forest.

"Morgaine," whispered Kay withdrawing his sword once again.

Francis peered silently above their heads into the branches of the trees and watched in morbid fascination as they grew before his eyes extending over the skyline and blotting out the rays of the sun. Around his feet creepers stretched and pulled across the dirty brown floor, flowers craned their stems to stare venomously at the three men in the clearing, their heads glaring at them while thorns reached and grasped at their clothing. The three men backed slowly into the centre of the glade; their backs pressed hard against each other's as the relentless march of the plant life continued. Vine, creeper, thorns, all reaching out with murderous intent.

Francis lifted his feet to avoid the sprawling mass of roots snaking its way across the ground and watched as thorns grew and protruded from the vegetation searching for the men. He felt a brush against his arm and cast a glance downward, recoiling in horror as ivy wrapped and coiled around his wrist, before twisting up his arm. The vine tightened as it crawled and reached over his chest confining his movement and pulling tight over his body. He could see similar situations happening to his comrades.

130

Vines and trails of creeper and ivy snaked up the legs of the two knights holding them transfixed to the spot and leaves and flowers erupted as a symphony of pollen clouded the atmosphere around them. He could see Kay pull hard against the roots which held him and twisted around his torso, restricting his breathing and pulling him slowly to the ground. Tristan swiped with his sword and great leaves sprouted from the ground and pressed against his body, surrounding and covering his neat clothing. His face contorted with fear as the leaves swamped over his body and engulfed him in a twisted parody of a closing bulb. The sword struggled to penetrate the hide of the plants as it covered his body.

Francis could feel the sharp stab at his arms and hands as the thorns spread from the roots and dug deep into his skin, opening his pours and delivering a thick red liquid over the vines. His face stung with the bittersweet taste of his tears as his vision blurred with the fragrance of the forest and he felt his legs sag under the intense pressure of the entwining vines. He could feel his lungs burning as the air was slowly squeezed from his body and darkness threatened to engulf him.

23.

Strange England

Mordred stood on the grass surveying the monument before him. He turned his head to Agravain who stood respectfully with his head bowed at a short distance behind his comrade. "'Tis a shrine," he commented returning his attention back to the monument and knelt close to the polished stone surface of the large stone obelisk set high on a marbleised plinth. He ran his fingers over the metal plaque on the front of the monument and spoke over his shoulder. "A memorial," he continued. "To the fallen dead of this world." His eyes followed the line of letters as they spelt out name after name of soldiers fallen in the line of duty.

Agravain gazed around him as he stood on the wet grass and flattened the strands beneath his feet. He placed his hand on the hilt of his sword for security. He nodded as an elderly couple passed the wall of the church and stared over the heavy-set stonework. "How goes the day?" he called as the couple paused then lowered their heads and moved hurriedly along the winding road. He shrugged and turned back to face the back of his colleague. "What is this place?" he asked as he looked around.

The church was prominent in the centre of the ground, its heavy stones holding eons of untold stories, and the gathered prayers of legions of believers throughout the ages. Stone crypts lay abandoned around the perimeter, each with a forgotten cargo within. Moss and grime transversed the stone and invaded the condition of the casket, forcing through slight cracks in the stone. Rows of headstones protruded from the ground, each hiding from view a hidden chamber holding silent occupants and staring out into the graveyard in a bitter reminded of mortality.

"'Tis a graveyard, nothing more," said Mordred simply standing from his inspection and looking around at the accusing stones. "There is naught 'ere for us to fear."

"No… my Lord. Not the graveyard," insisted Agravain reaching out a hand to place on his friend's arm. "Everywhere." He looked past the church into the road and out into the distant town.

"Why, my Lord Agravain, there is naught there but England. Our birthright, my heritage." He breathed deeply and listened to the sound of the silence chorus from the graves below.

"The smells," said Agravain breathing deeply. "It does not smell like England, my Lord." He continued glancing around him as he spoke, "It smells of the devil's work."

Mordred considered for a moment and breathed the air heavily in. Indeed, there was a residue in the atmosphere which displeased him, but nevertheless this was England. He could smell a heavy tang in the air and taste the bitter atmosphere of Sulphur and Brimstone from the very pits of depravity. The noises which surrounded them invaded and offended his hearing. "We have been asleep for many years, good Agravain, we cannot expect England to have remained the same," he said simply.

A new noise from the skies above their heads broke the conversation and caused the two men the glance upward. A plane smashed through the cloud coverage and climbed through the sky and out of sight. "But, Mordred, this place, these creatures of metal." He looked into the sky as he spoke. "'Tis unholy. 'Tis not England, my Lord, 'tis a nightmare."

"Hold! Good Agravain, once we have Excalibur, we can restore order to this society. We can return our world onto this." He waved around as he spoke. His face broke into a wide grin as he spoke, and a flash of pure madness danced in his eyes. "Destiny belongs to us and once we have the sword, we can dispatch that harpy Morgaine," he whispered. "And rule this land."

"Thee speak against Morgaine," gasped Agravain.

"Aye, I do," smiled Mordred as he threw his arm around the shoulders of Agravain and led him down the overgrown path towards the rusted iron gate set in the stone wall. "Politics are fought on the battlefield, old friend… not by those plotting in the chambers and galleries in their ivory towers," he whispered and pointed across the road and smiled. "We will take the sword and the throne with or without the help of Lady Morgaine. Now, I see a tavern down yonder. Let us partake a beverage or two before combat." He slapped Agravain hard on the shoulder and laughed. "Dismiss the men. I shall meet you in yon Inn!" Mordred pushed open the iron gate and listened as the hinges protested under his influence as the metal frame swung outward into the road.

Agravain turned and strode up the path towards the church and towards the small congregation of knights who stood stock still and to attention before the stone monument. Each one held his sword aloft before his face in silent respect to the fallen.

"Troops," snapped Agravain. "Dismiss. Return to the castle and await further orders." He turned to watch his commander walk away from the church. "And prepare for battle… and may God have mercy on our souls." The sentence drew out into a barely audible whisper as he watched his troops parade from the church yard and head towards the coastline and ultimately the castle.

The heavy sword swept across the air and cut through the heavy roots which entwined around his body. Lord Kay pulled and heaved his frame out of the grip of the vines which held him placed in the glade. "Take heed," he yelled as his hand brought down the heavy blade and connected with vegetation and shards of bark and leaf fell as the sword cut through the creeper and vine forcing the plant to release its grip on the large knight. Kay brought his sword down again and again as the blade chipped and cut wood, small tendrils snaking out desperately to stop the relentless pressure of the sharp implement as blows rained down through the forest. "Tristan!" he called as he fought the bramble.

The large leaf which encased the other knight bulged and swelled as it held the form of the smaller knight as he struggled inside the plant. The point of a sword forced its way through the thick sinew of the green leaf and thrust out into the dying sunlight. The blade grew as it charged into the air, then forced its way down the massive leaf cutting the heavy plant and creating a gaping maw to the cocoon. Tristan collapsed into the glade, a thick glutinous gel covering his body which forced him to cough. violently. He lay on the floor for a moment and spat out lungsful of oil as he gasped desperately against the air.

He rolled onto his back and kicked out at the plant as it collapsed in on itself and forced himself to his feet, slashing the dying vegetation with the blade of his sword whilst gasping for breath. He stopped and surveyed the fallen mess of the plant which lay in a messy pool of glutinous gel around his feet and leant heavily on his sword. He buried the tip of the sword into the soft ground of the clearing as he caught his breath. His legs sagged briefly, and he sank to one knee, leaning against the blade and pressing the hilt against his face.

"I never thought I would hit out at a blessed plant in anger," he whispered hoarsely catching his breath. He looked around the glade and could see a tangle of vines and thorns bulging and writhing in a mass of green and brown tentacles, while Kay fought back several other roots rising and falling beneath the pressure of his blade. "The boy," he whispered forcing himself to his feet.

Tristan staggered to the writhing mass of thorn and brought his sword down onto the thick mass, cutting into the roots. He could see the boy on the brink of death beneath the mass of vegetation which swelled over his body. "Kay!" he called desperately. "Help me!"

Kay risked a quick glance in his direction as he brought his sword down the branches again. "Fend for thyself!" he yelled as a root rose high above his head before sprouting off several smaller buds and delivering a mist of poisonous intent. Kay covered his mouth with his free hand and brought down his sword into the thick branch above his head. "Get the boy and pull back to the cave!" he called pulling the sword from the wood and thrusting it into the bramble.

"I cannot," complained Tristan.

"Just do it!" snapped Kay.

Tristan sighed and forced his sword into the scabbard around his waist and thrust his hands deep into the bramble. As the sharp spines bit into his skin, he immediately wished that he wore the thick heavy armour which covered his comrade. Thorns and bramble cut at his bare arms as he reached through the dense undergrowth and grasped at the body of the young man hidden from view.

Francis could feel his head swim under the intense pain of the thorns as they bit into his skin. His blood mixed with his tears as darkness swept over his conscious mind. He felt two hands grasp at his shoulders and pull him roughly through the undergrowth. He felt dizzy as the sudden inrush of air hit him forcibly and he could hear distant voices as the light from the sun blanked out as his body was pushed through the wood where he eventually succumbed to the sweet embrace of sleep.

Morgaine emerged from the wood and cast her gaze around the road. Her eyes fell upon the distant sea and she wished for a serenity which she could never have. The troop of knights were disappearing into the distance and the faintest trace of a smile cast over her mouth as she allowed for the taste of oncoming victory. "Soon, all will be mine," she whispered as the sun battered against her golden armour. She frowned in the sunlight and examined the precession in the distance and the absence of Mordred and Agravain from its head.

At that same moment, the two knights stood before the old wood lined building of the public house. Mordred looked at the sign which swung from its frame above the door and smiled. "Look, my friend, a sign of providence." He laughed pointing at the ageing wooden board which swung in the slight breeze.

"The Sword in the Stone," mused Agravain as he examined the image of a sword protruding from a large boulder in gaudy colours from the hoarding.

"'Tis a sign," laughed Mordred again and spread his arms wide spinning to face his comrade. "We drink," he shouted. "For tomorrow we cast this country in the blood of our enemies!" He turned and pushed at the wooden door of the pub and crossed the threshold into the old house and stood in the amidst of a range of tables. "Inn-keep!" he called pushing aside the furniture and striding confidently through the tables towards the bar with Agravain close behind. The door to the kitchen behind the bar opened and Gwen stepped through into the room. "You," snapped Mordred. "Serving wench!"

Gwen looked behind her in mock surprise, then pointed to herself. "You talking to me?" she asked incredulously.

"Insolent girl, does thee not know who I am?" he demanded banging his fist down against the wooden top of the bar.

"I know you could do with a course in manners!" she snapped back.

"How dare you?" raged Mordred raising his hand.

"What seems to be the problem?" came a heavy voice from the adjoining room.

"Ah!" breathed Mordred. "Is thoust the proprietor of this establishment?" he said waving a hand around the room.

"I am," said the newcomer cautiously.

"Dad—"

"She is thy daughter?" asked Mordred and watched as the landlord nodded. "She has fire in the pit of her stomach! I like that!" He laughed and slapped his hand against the countertop.

"Can I help you?"

"Aye, my good man, I wish refreshment," he said looking over the various pumps behind the bar. "Thee serve beverage?" Again, the landlord nodded and recoiled as Mordred laughed and moved close to him placing a hand on his shoulder. "Then I wish to drink... thyself and my friend," Mordred said heartedly and sat at a table. "Thine finest Inn-keep, I wish to be entertained!"

"Gwen," said the landlord softly and nodded towards his daughter cautiously eyeing the two men in armour as they sat at the table close to the fireplace. He turned to the men as Gwen began to pour ale into two glass vessels. The brown liquid clung to the edge of the glass as a swelling white head swarmed across the top of the glass. "What brings you here?" he asked as he perched himself on a stool close to the bar.

Mordred regarded him for a moment before talking. "Why, my good sir, to take the sword Excalibur and flood this land in blood." He laughed as he spoke, and both the landlord and Gwen felt a chill cross over the room.

24.

Court of Knights

Tristan lowered the unconscious body of Francis on the damp floor of the cavern and took a step back and gazed down at the form of the young boy. His body lay in tatters as he sprawled across the dirty ground, cuts had torn through his clothing and small abrasions littered his arms and legs while bruises started to rise and form on his face and a swelling beneath his right eye took on a bloated appeal.

"Explain what happened," asked Merlin as he looked down at the broken body.

"Will he live?" asked Percival from across the cavern peering through the dank conditions.

Merlin nodded sagely and inspected the wounds on the body. "The injuries are only superficial, nothing life threatening," he stated simply then rose and looked straight at Lord Kay and Lord Tristan. "Thee were instructed with his safety," he snapped. "And yet thee bring him to me in this condition. The consequences of thy actions could have led to his death."

"Be wary of your accusations, old man," warned Kay. "If it had not been for us, thine youth would be dead by now." He glowered at Merlin through the darkness.

"Do thee not realise that he is the reason we are here," said Merlin pointing at the body of Francis laying on the floor. "It is not of our design, but that of Excalibur."

"We have not yet decided that" injected Galahad from his position at the edge of the cavern. "That is but thy assumption."

Merlin nodded in his direction but continued, "If he had died then all of this…" He waved about the cavern dramatically as he spoke, "Would be for naught."

"The child stirs," commented Bedivere; his eyes never wavered from his body as he spoke. Merlin turned to face the boy as he struggled to open his eyes.

"Who are they?" demanded Gwen as she returned from the table with a tray of empty glasses.

"I don't know," admitted her father. "But their money is as good as anyone else's," he said casting a quick glance over her shoulder towards the two men in full body armour at the table. Mordred laughed and threw his head back as he drank heavily at the brown liquid in the glass. He slapped his comrade on the shoulder and let out another loud laugh as his liquid spilled over the table. "I suppose they could be part of an actor's group or some kind of medieval society here to re-enact some kind of battle," he said watching the knights.

"Their money is as good as anyone's," quoted Gwen. "Does that mean they've paid?"

"Well, no... not yet."

"Don't you think they should start," she said spying the cavalcade of empty glasses lining up along the counter of the bar.

"Yes, yes... in a minute," he said reluctantly watching as Mordred lit up the room once again with his laughter. Gwen sighed and pulled at another two empty glasses from beneath the bar and pushed the first beneath a stiff white pump.

"Well, if they carry on in this manner, they will have drunk us dry by the end of the day."

Francis pulled himself into a sitting position on the floor of the cave. His eyesight blurred as he opened his eyes and looked around the roughly strewn cavern. He could feel a damp patch spreading across his trousers and briefly wondered whether he had lost control of his bowels before realizing that he was sitting in a puddle. His arms stung from the scratches which littered his body, and he rubbed them feeling slightly sorry for himself. "Where am I?" he asked looking over the puddles which surrounded him.

"Look at me," said Merlin standing over him. Francis remained seated looking across his battered and bruised body. "Boy!" snapped Merlin.

"My name is Francis!" he snapped back finally looking into the eyes of the old man.

"Ah," he breathed triumphantly. "At last." Merlin bowed his head low and spoke through the darkness. "Forgive me, my Liege," he purred.

"Look," said Francis. "I don't know who you think I am... well, I have a pretty good idea, but I'm not," he said resolutely.

"We know thee are not Arthur," said Merlin waving around the cavern at the other figures in the cave. "But thy art his descendant… by divine right."

"No, I'm not," insisted Francis. "I'm just a regular guy. Nothing special, just a normal guy."

"See how modest he is," whispered Percival to Bedivere behind him.

Francis shot him a venomous glance then looked over the other figures. He recognised the figures from the forest, but the others he had not seen before. He cast his eyes over the various forms of armour and clothing everyone wore ranging from heavy thick silver armour to the sleeker green body armour adorned by Bedivere, then the simple material worn by the knight from the forest and the black and white tunic worn by the person who had just spoken. Each one looked powerful in their own right, either in nature or stature while Merlin, or at least who he assumed the old man to be, stood dressed in a long flowing cloak which covered a dull grey habit. His ancient eyes bore into Francis and he could feel his mind being stripped away of the centuries which divided him from… where? Somewhere else… if not here then where was his mind wandering. He could see these knights; he could see eternal death; he could see a sword and then a voice… a female voice.

"Come to me. You are almost at the end of your quest," she purred in his mind. Francis closed his eyes and strained to block the whispering of the knights around him.

"Look at the boy," whispered Bedivere.

"He is scrawny," said the large knight from the forest.

"As was Arthur when he first came into your father's care," said another.

"Aye, that he was." An uproarious laughter echoed around the cavern as the knights laughed.

"'Tis not decided he is Arthur's kindred," snapped another.

"That is agreed," said a softer voice… the small one from the clearing.
"I am not satisfied."

Francis kept his eyes closed as he strained his hearing… listening…

"Your quest shall lead you to me," said the women's voice.

"Where are you?" he asked into the darkness.

"Who does he talk to?" came one voice.

"There is but no-one here but us," said another.

"Is this madness?"

"Merlin?"

Francis remained focused despite the questions ranging around him. "I can hear you," he said. "But why can't I see you?" he asked.

"Use your mind to see," the voice urged. "Open your eyes and you will see."

Francis obeyed his instructions and looked around the cavern at the knights still in heated debate around the cavern. Only Merlin seemed quiet, almost distant from the others. He watched the old man as he glanced behind him and stepped back as a woman emerged from the shadows and smiled.

"He is here," she said.

"Yes," agreed Merlin. "As I said he would."

"You heard the call?" She directed her question directly to Francis who nodded dumbly in her direction. "Is he mute?" she asked Merlin.

The old sage shook his head and smiled. "Only puzzled... as am I," he said as his expression turned into a frown. "Why has Excalibur woken?"

"This I cannot tell thee," the woman said, a look of concern flirting over her face. "At least not until he has proven himself." She looked over at Francis who remained in dumb silence in his seated position on the floor. The woman stepped forward into the dim light of the cavern, water glistening in the light broadcast from the torches adorning the walls of the cavern. Francis blushed frantically at her naked form as she moved close to him and she smiled as his face lit up a deep crimson. She circled him for a moment as he sat in the shallow water on the cavern floor. "Stand," she instructed simply.

Francis stood, his eyes never leaving the woman's naked form and despite his best efforts he found his eyes wandering over her body. He followed the line of her long flowing hair, which ran down the course of her back and ebbing over her shoulders. He blushed as his eyesight lingered over her breasts and watched as small droplets of water played over the small pert mounds then fell from her erect nipples onto the rough ground at her feet. He allowed his eyes to cross her flat stomach and down over the slender hips and played across her groin as the small patch of hair glistened with an intense moisture in the flickering light of the flame. Her legs fell from her slender hips, and he traced their expanse as they ran towards the floor, then as she turned, he raised his gaze and stared lustfully at her round hips and tightly formed bottom.

"Come to me," she said seductively.

Thoughts of an immoral nature crossed his mind and stirred in his loins and reluctantly he shook his head free of the lust and sexual images which danced through his mind. "I have and I am here," he insisted.

"But you have not proven yourself worthy," she said slowly turning to face him again as she stood at Merlin's side.

Francis looked over her small, but well-formed bosom. "What must I do?" he asked into the shadows as she slowly dissolved into the darkness.

"Nothing," she whispered.

"Wait!" he shouted into the cave. The echo of his voice bounced off across the walls back to him. "I don't understand." He could feel the frustration welling over him. "Please," he begged. "Come back."

"Come to me." The whisper of her voice tinged the cavern as her naked body disappeared from view.

"Is thoust mad?"

"Is thoust ill?"

"What madness is this, Merlin?"

The voices of the knights smashed him back into reality and he found himself almost embarrassed by the realization that they had not seen or heard the exchange.

"There is no madness," insisted Merlin who spoke turning to Francis. "You saw?" he said.

Francis nodded. "Yes, but I still don't understand," he admitted.

"All will become clear," promised Merlin and stepped forward close to the chalice and took the hand of Francis. "You might want to cover that up," said the old man smirking as he pointed down towards Francis' groin. Francis followed the line of his finger and blushed once again as the lump in his crotch pointed out into the cavern beneath his blue jeans. He thrust his hands towards the front of his trousers and adjusted himself as laughter from the knights echoed through the cave. "That was Nimue."

"The Lady," whispered Bedivere. Merlin shot him a glance, then peered into the depths of the chalice.

"Yes, the Lady," he confirmed.

"Who is Nimue?" asked Francis.

"My love," said Merlin wistfully looking into the water and trailing a hand across the surface of the liquid.

25.

Coming of the King

"But who is Nimue?" said Francis slightly embarrassed by his own lustful intention towards this man's... what? He did not quite know who she was and what she was to Merlin.

"Nimue is an Enchantress," began Merlin. "A harpy." He looked into the water of the chalice and smiled sadly as the image swirled in the liquid. "She was my lover," he admitted sadly as an image of a woman standing naked in the middle of a large lake appeared in the water. "She beguiled me with false tales and promises." He smiled as he watched her sink beneath the water and whispered into the chalice, "My love."

"I... I'm sorry," said Francis struggling to find the words. "But what does this have to do with me?" His question hung in the air for a moment, and he wondered whether he should leave the old man to his thoughts.

"Nimue is the mistress of the Lake," he said eventually. He slowly turned to address Francis. "It was she that betroth Excalibur to Arthur upon his ascension to the throne."

Francis frowned. "But I thought Excalibur was pulled from the stone... that was what deemed Arthur fit to rule."

"Only partially correct, my young friend," said Merlin smiling. "The sword set into the stone was indeed a test placed there by divine right to the true successor of the throne. It was on this test of character and purity that Arthur was chosen by divinity to rule as king, but it was Nimue who presented the enchanted sword to the king upon his ascension," he explained.

"Aye," agreed Kay from the shadows. "And if I hadn't injured my shoulder jousting—"

"Thee'd still be there now pulling on the wretched stone!" laughed Galahad. Kay snarled at the joke and the laughter which surrounded him.

Merlin chose to ignore the interruption and continued with his story. "Upon his death, the sword was returned to whence it came." He cast a glance towards Bedivere who lowered his head as he spoke, "And after three attempts, 'twas finally returned."

"But I still don't understand," insisted Francis. "What has this got to do me?"

"Thine boy is truly the king's kindred," laughed Kay tapping the side of his skull.

Tristan frowned before joining Kay's laughter. "Not too bright, is he?" he agreed.

"Are we to believe this to be the heir to the throne?" snapped Galahad.

"Please!" snapped Merlin. "Legend states that Excalibur will awaken in time of need," he explained. "It appears that time is now."

"Inn-keep!" shouted Mordred. "More ale," he ordered slamming the empty glass on the table.

"Father," whispered Gwen over the bar towards her father who sat watching the antics of the two knights. He looked at his daughter and nodded standing from his chair and slowly picked his way through the maze of tables which lay before them.

"Excuse me, sir," he began as he stood over the table, his eyes straying across the empty glasses on the wooden surface of the table.

"Ah, good Inn-keep," said Mordred. "What is thine name?"

"Leo," said the landlord softly.

"Then, good Leo, drink with us," he said laughing and thrust the chair next to him out from beneath the table. "Sit, sit," he urged.

"I'm sorry," stammered the landlord weakly. "But I must ask, how you intend to pay for this?" He indicated across the table at the empty vessels strewn over the table.

"What does thoust mean?" snapped Mordred. "Come, man, spit it out!"

"My Lord," injected Agravain. "He seeks retribution for his wares," he explained.

"Ah, I understand," laughed Mordred. "My tally!" He looked at Leo and smiled. "Thoust wish compensation for thine wares," he stated staring at… no through the landlord. Leo nodded and fiddled with his fingers as he watched the smile fade form Mordred's face. "Do thee not knowest who I am!" he snapped and thrust his hand across the table scattering the glasses across the floor, where they smashed into a thousand tiny shards. He stood from his seat and slapped his hand across his black polished armour. "I am Mordred, rightful king of England!" He lowered his hands to grip the edge of the table and looked directly at Agravain as he spoke. "And if it wasn't for that accursed Arthur, I would still be king," he spat.

"That may be," said Leo defiantly. "But thoust… sorry, you," he corrected himself as he spoke. "Must still pay for these drinks."

"Thy dare defy me!" shouted Mordred straightening and staring into the eyes of the Landlord. "I shall smite thee where thy stand. Now get me more drinks before thou shall feel the edge of my blade!"

"Now… now, sir," stammered Leo. "There is no need—"

Mordred brought his hand across his cheek, sending the landlord sprawling across the floor. "Insolent dog!" he spat.

Leo could taste the bitter iron tinge of his own blood swell in his mouth as he struggled to a sitting position on the floor. His hand strayed to his mouth, and he could feel through the tenderness, a slight bulge as his skin swelled beneath his touch. "Gwen, call the police," he said as Mordred stood over him, his hand playing over the hilt of his sword as he glowered down at the landlord.

Gwen ran the length of the bar and pulled at the phone, lifting the receiver to her ear. The buzz of the phone echoed in her ear as her fingers stabbed at the numbers: 9… 9… a sudden click diverted her attention from dialling, and she looked at the phone hanging on the wall. A long, elegant finger streaked over the cold plastic and pressed firmly down on the receiver.

"Please, my dear," purred the woman who smiled as she spoke. "I think my nephew's temper has got the better of him, don't you?" she said hypnotically. Gwen found herself nodding as she stared at her older woman's striking beauty. "Please," she said softly and took the phone from Gwen's hand and replaced it in its cradle. She looked down at the landlord and smiled. "Thee will be duly compensated for your custom," she purred. "If you could…" She indicated towards the table of Mordred and Agravain.

Leo nodded and pulled himself to his feet under the gaze of the newcomer and moved quietly to the bar. Morgaine turned to Mordred who returned to his seat and stared shamefaced into the last remaining dregs of his drink. "I might have known I'd find thy in the nearest hostelry," she said softly and moved gracefully towards the table where she stood over the two men and gazed down at the remnants of glass around the floor. "Imbeciles!" she spat. She brought her hand swiftly across Mordred's face.

"I like her," commented Gwen as she watched the woman from the bar as Morgaine stood aloft over the two men.

"Why now?" asked Francis. "And why me?"

"We still don't know if thee are indeed of the king," said the large knight at the rear of the group.

"Please, my Lord Galahad," eased Merlin. "We shall know soon enough."

"He does have a point," said Francis. "I mean, I'm not so sure myself."

"See!"

Merlin shot Galahad a glance which settled the burly knight's revere. "He knows of thy arrival," said Merlin cryptically. "And he will decide thy divinity… or not." He paused and looked at Francis. "As to why now… I do not know," he admitted.

Francis nodded, still unsure of his surroundings. "What is this place and who are they?" he asked.

"Surely, my Lord Merlin, if he truly were Arthur then he would know these questions," insisted Galahad.

"What is your problem?" snapped Francis. "I keep telling you that I'm not Arthur and who the hell do you think you are?"

"I am Lord Galahad, holy knight of the round table and sworn protector of the Grail."

"My Lord," said Merlin softly. "Thee recovered the Grail; thee are not the protector."

"But mine is the divine right!" snapped Galahad. "If thee are truly the king then thee shall have my life at your command… until then, I must reserve my right to doubt." Francis nodded his understanding and looked back at Merlin.

"As I said, my Lord," insisted Merlin. "Thee are not the protector," he said looking past the congregation of knights and down the tunnel beyond. "He is," he breathed quietly as he spoke. His eyes diverted into the gloom of the tunnel where the light was swallowed by the darkness.

In the distance of the tunnel a form moved through the darkness, followed by a dragging sound as something large pulled its way across the roughly sewn rocks and up the tunnel towards the cavern.

26.

The Fisher King

The smell struck Francis before the image of the creature appeared silhouetted in the light from the end of the tunnel. He looked down the long passage in abject horror as the shadow peeled away from the wall and slowly progressed along the tunnel towards the group in the main cavern. "What is it?" he whispered transfixed by the image.

"Not what... who," whispered Tristan in his ear. Francis looked at him through the darkness of the cavern and could see his own expression mirrored in the knight's face.

"What do you mean who?"

"'Tis the Fisher King," Tristan stated simply as though that explained everything he needed to know.

Francis glanced back briefly down the tunnel as the shadow continued to move along the corridor of darkness towards them and looked back at Tristan who was moving back to the group of knights at a respectful distance. Francis could see at the back of the group, almost hiding from the creature (no man) the form of one of the smaller knights cowering from the impending arrival of the Fisher King.

"Percival," indicated Merlin nodding in his general direction. "Had the opportunity to heal the wounds of the Fisher King, but failed to perform the correct incantation," he explained. "That is why he hides."

"His wounds?" Francis enquired returning his gaze down the tunnel.

"The Fisher King is cursed to protect the Grail," Merlin said following the gaze of Francis. "His wounds prevent him from travelling away from his kingdom."

"How did he get his wounds?" asked Francis.

"We do not know... and we dare not ask," chided Merlin. "The Fisher King may be impotent, but he has his pride, and he is powerful. Be careful, child, do not upset the Fisher King."

Francis could feel a chill descend over the cavern as the shadow neared and from this distance, he noticed that the creature appeared to drag a heavy weight behind him as he walked. He felt an ultimate sense of foreboding enter the cavern as the Fisher King neared and recoiled at the stench of death which followed.

The shadow appeared to stop in the mouth of the cavern and raised itself to its full height as it spoke into the cave. "Merlin." The voice was loud and deafening as it echoed over the walls of the cave.

"I am here," Merlin replied stepping from behind the chalice.

"Old friend." The voice softened slightly as Merlin approached. "He is here?"

"Yes."

"Where?" Merlin turned and pointed towards the chalice where Francis stood almost self-consciously of his own mortality. "He knows why he is here?" asked the Fisher King still bathed in shadow.

"Only partially," admitted Merlin.

"He knows the procedure?"

"No."

"He knows he will be tested?"

"Yes."

"He knows the consequence?"

"No."

"It is better that he does not." The Fisher King stepped from the shadows and bathed in the light from the flickering torches on the walls. Francis recoiled at the horror of the behemoth before him and involuntarily took a step back. "Does my form scare you?" asked the Fisher King, the faintest of smiles crossing his deformed face. He stretched in the cavern to his full height and towered above both Merlin and the knights of the round table and stepped closer to Francis who found himself cowering behind the stone chalice and close to the altar. "Do not fear me… you only need to fear, fear itself. I shall not harm you if you are the true successor."

"And what if I'm not?" asked Francis meekly, his voice quavering under the scrutiny of the Fisher King.

"Then you die," stated the Fisher King simply.

Morgaine ran her fingers across the cold hard plastic flowers which adorned the fake scabbard that hung over the fireplace in the public house. "The boy does not have Excalibur," she mused as she traced the line of the replica as it hung distracted from the rigors of finery. Her fingers gently stroked the object and wistfully spoke. "He will not part with it when he finds it."

"Then we take it," scoffed Mordred as he took a deep gulp of ale. "His forces are but small," he offered resting the glass on the table and wiping the froth from his mouth with the sleeve of his tunic. He slapped the front of his black chest plate and laughed, throwing his arms wide. "We are strong. We can take Excalibur by force if we wish!" he boasted.

"Silence, fool!" snapped Morgan still toying with the scabbard. "Thee forget our forces at Camlann were large and yet…" Her voice trailed off as her thoughts spun back over the events millennia ago.

"But that force was led by Arthur," said Mordred. "'Tis but a boy that leads them now."

"And that boy has Excalibur… or will have," she mused as her hand came down heavily on the plastic scabbard angrily. "We must find a way for the boy to give us the sword of his own free will." She turned her back to the scabbard and the fireplace and gazed over the room. Tables lay scattered throughout the room sitting amidst the debris of broken glass shattered in a multitude of pieces, sparkling and gleaming from the floor.

"I still say we take it by force."

"Then thee are a fool, Mordred," snapped Morgaine with disdain. "What I ever saw in thee…" She shook her head as she spoke and looked over the bedraggled figure at the table.

"Thee saw greatness," he offered grinning.

"I saw weakness, which I could use to my own ends," she replied, smiling at his discomfort. "I offered thee certain favours, in reward for the crown and all I got was…" She flung her arms in the air. "This!"

Mordred brought his glass down heavy on the table, anger clouding his mind. "You! Girl, more drinks," he snapped directing his anger at the slender form of Gwen who watched with interest from the bar.

Morgan returned her attention back to the scabbard and ran her fingers over the plastic, deep in thought. "He has been here," she mused. "I can sense it. I can feel it." She closed her eyes and her head spun as she recoiled under her own ferocity. "I can taste it," she whispered. Gwen carefully lowered the tray to the table and cast her eyes towards Morgaine as she swayed under her own hypnotic trance. She placed three glasses, each laden with a thick brown liquid on the table and watched entranced at the bewitchment that encompassed Morgaine as she stood before the scabbard.

"The boy was here," she whispered.

"Francis?" Gwen almost winced as she blurted out his name and turned from the table. She heard a slight click of fingers from behind her, then the sudden pain burning through her wrist as a heavy thick hand grabbed at her slender wrist. "Let go," she begged as she turned and looked down at Mordred gazing up at her from his seat.

"Wench!" he spat through his stained teeth.

"I knew he had been here," whispered Morgaine as she moved towards Gwen, her eyes intense with fire. She stood over the girl and took a deep breath and smiled as she ran her nose over the girl's hair. "The boy has been here," she whispered cruelly as she leant close to Gwen's ear. With a sudden movement of speed defying her age, Morgaine flashed out with her hand and grasped at the chin of the young girl and smiled as her face contorted with pain under her grasp. She held her firm and strong in place, while stroking her hair with her free hand and moving it away from her ear, smiling as she whispered. "He was here, wasn't he, girl?" she goaded.

"Gwen!" the male voice resounded from the kitchen as the door opened and the landlord stepped through into the bar. He moved through the tables but slowed under the harsh gaze of Morgaine.

"He was here," snapped Morgaine still holding Gwen firmly around her delicate chin. She smiled at her sweetly, looking into her eyes then she forcibly thrust her other hand between her legs grasping at Gwen's groin. Morgaine smiled as she looked the girl in the eyes as she slowly moved her hand around her groin. "Or should I say he was here." She laughed and thrust her hand deeper between her legs and slowly ran her fingers in small circular movements, causing Gwen to close her eyes under the sudden attention and finding desire rising through her body at Morgaine's touch and a dampness in her groin.

"Gwen... I," stammered her father.

"Oh, my dear," goaded Morgaine. "Least I forget, thine payment." She released her grip on Gwen and allowed her to fall on the floor at Mordred's feet in sexual frustration. Morgaine strode confidently towards the landlord who stopped dead in his tracks, transfixed to the floor and frozen on the spot. "My nephew, he drank well?" she said looking around her at the mess littered across the floor. "I see he did." Her tone was pleasant, but her words betrayed a bitter threat. "I must offer his tally," she spoke quietly and rested the back of her hand against his forehead and closed her eyes, raising her head to the ceiling, laughing.

Gwen screamed as Mordred pulled her to her feet and forced her to watch as the life began to drain from her father's body under the touch of Morgaine. His skin withered and became brittle as signs of ageing snaked across his face. Deep lines furrowed through his brow as his skin dried and lightened in colour; his cheeks sank beneath the weight of age while his hair thinned and withered from a dark black to a fine sliver of white before dissipating over the skull. His body shrank and withered beneath his clothing as his frame shrunk under the intense touch of Morgaine, her hand still planted firmly on his ageing forehead. His legs sagged and buckled beneath the weight of his body as brittle bones struggled to cope with the harsh ravages of time as years passed in seconds.

Leo gazed out through now bulging eyes as his cheeks and face withered around his pleading brown eyes and he reached towards his daughter, who was held watching by Mordred. He raised his arms outstretched towards her almost pleading to hold her for one final time, his fingers bent as his skin tightened and constricted over his hands. "Gwen," he whispered almost inaudibly as his voice drifted through chipped and cracked lips.

Bones cracked and snapped as his body slowly mummified and sank lower to the floor with his skin finally stretching and straining against the skeleton beneath. Morgaine finally released her grip and smiled as the body collapsed to the floor with a sickening thud and turned to the door, walking gracefully through the tables.

"Did thee enjoy the show?" sneered Mordred in Gwen's ear.

"Bitch!" spat Gwen as Mordred held her arms behind her back and flinched as the knight laughed down her ear.

"By the saints," declared Mordred. "I like this one." He laughed as he ran his hand through her long flowing locks and sniffed heavily at her hair.

"Dad." Gwen sobbed as she watched the lifeless form of her father sprawled, bent and twisted amidst the debris of the room. Tears welled in her eyes and drifted down her cheeks, masking rivers which etched over her ivory skin. Her vision blurred and through the tears she saw the image of Mordred as he released his grip over her arms and moved before her, staring into her face… smiling, taunting. She sneered through her tears and spat into his face. She had a warm satisfaction as she watched her saliva slowly crossed over his face. Mordred laughed and wiped away her fluid with the

151

back of his hand, his eyes never flinching from hers.

Mordred slowly raised his hand to his face and looked at the signs of her spit on his palm and a smile broke his face. His hand whipped out and grasped at her slender neck, and using his body weight he lifted her body and thrust her backward against the wall of the pub. She gasped as her legs were lifted off the floor and her back thrust against the roughly sewn brickwork of the wall. The pressure on her neck and the hot breath of Mordred against her face repulsed her, but she could not move from his grasp.

"You have fire," he whispered as he placed a hand beneath her buttocks and raised her hips to his own, her legs draped around his waist, and he pushed his groin close to hers. "It has been so long since I tasted flesh," he sneered through clenched teeth and looked down her towards her heaving chest. Gwen struggled beneath his touch and could feel his body swelling against her own through the material of her clothes. "Even that of a cheap whore as yourself."

He laughed and hoisted her from the wall and brought her roughly down onto a table. Her back crashed hard against the wooden surface of the furniture and the air was pushed out of her body. Mordred grasped at her hand and forced it down the front of his clothing, where her fingers played around his genitals against her own will. He closed his eyes as her fingers struggled to pull away from his bulging organ and the excitement overwhelmed him as he roughly grasped her breast through her blue long-sleeved shirt. He smiled as she struggled in vain against his pressure and turned her over on the table. Mordred pushed her face against the beer-stained wood. Her hands gripped the edge of the table, tears streaking across her face. Mordred moved behind her looking lustfully at her rounded buttocks through Gwen's tight white jodhpurs as they stretched and strained over her body.

He leant forward over her body, pressing his body weight against her pinning down on the table and whispered deep into her ear. "I will make you weep, whore," he promised.

Gwen could feel the pressure of his groin pressing hard through her clothing, and the clawing of his hand as it grasped firmly at her buttock. He pressed his body down upon hers and held her head firmly in position with his other arm. Mordred laughed as he held her flesh in his grip and he looked over her body, pulling her hair hard and forcing her head back as she gripped the table harder fearing what was to come. He snatched at her jodhpurs and pulled them roughly down, exposing her buttocks and small black thong.

"My prize," he whispered and smiled cruelly as a sliver of drool dribbled over his lips as he stared down at her half-clothed body. His hand traced over her hips and streaked down her buttocks until it rested between her legs. "Still damp," he sneered. "I will enjoy this more than thee," he whispered as he pressed his body against hers. "Of this I promise thee."

27.

The Test

"Mordred!" The sound of his name distracted his lust for a moment, and he glanced around at the sound of the voice. "Enough!" Mordred remained in place over the body of Gwen as she lay sobbing on the table still gripping the edge, braced against the horror behind her.

"Leave me, Morgaine!" he warned as he returned his attention to the girl on the table at his mercy.

"Mordred!" she snapped again.

"I told thee, Morgaine, leave me. I have business to attend." He looked down on the quivering form of Gwen and sneered as he released his own clothing.

"As I remember it would not take much time," she chided.

"Have a care, witch!" he snapped his lust rising through his body as he pushed his breeches to the floor. He smiled as he gripped his genitals and rubbed it against her skin. Gwen flinched as a sticky mass smeared her leg, leaving a trail like a snail.

"Leave her. We have much to do," she commanded.

"I said leave me!"

"No, Mordred, thee will not touch the girl," she commented. "We need her."

"As do I," roared Mordred. "I shall have my fun!" he snapped.

"I warn thee!" shouted Morgaine from across the room. "Release the girl." Mordred lay on top of her pressing his body against hers for a moment then stood, raising his hands above his head as he straightened and turned to face her. "Thee show wisdom for once," she said smiling as she looked over his naked waist. "I do not remember it so small." She laughed and turned away from him. "Now, bring her, we have much to plan before we take Excalibur."

Mordred nodded to Agravain who had stood watching silently. "Bring her," he ordered the Knight Commander who allowed the girl to pull her clothing back up over her waist before lifting her gently in his arms.

Gwen sobbed as his hands covered her and lifted her over his shoulder. "I am sorry. This is not honourable," he whispered as he hoisted the girl and followed Morgaine from the building.

As they passed Mordred, he sneered. "I shall have my sport with thee, girl," he promised, then lifted an empty glass from an adjoining table and threw it savagely against the wall.

As the glass scattered into a thousand pieces, light glistened through the tiny shards as they came to rest across the floor close to the lifeless corpse of the landlord who lay staring out through unstaring eyes.

"Whoa!" yelled Francis raising his hands up before his chest slowly backing away. "What do you mean I will die?"

The Fisher King paced slowly forward, stalking Francis as he moved around the cavern. "If thoust are pure of thought and mind thy will survive."

"Pure of thought and mind... What's that supposed to mean?"

"The bloodline must be pure," whispered the Fisher King as he reached out.

"No, no, no," complained Francis. "I'm not prepared to do this."

"Thee do not have a choice," proclaimed the Fisher King. "Thee answered the call of Excalibur. Thee must undertake the test."

"No," said Francis resolutely.

"Thee do not have a choice; thee answered the call," said the Fisher King as he continued his slow approach.

"I refuse," snapped Francis.

The Fisher King moved with lightning-fast reflexes and grasped at Francis' wrist pulling him close to his hulking body. Francis recoiled as the stench of rotting flesh struck his senses and struggled against the grip of the giant. "Thee cannot. 'Tis ordained."

"I won't," he complained as he writhed beneath his grip pushing desperately as the Fisher King dragged him protesting towards the stone chalice.

"The choice has been made," the Fisher King stated simply and reached out a long scrawny hand towards the chalice and placed his hand into the depths of the dark water within.

"You cannot make me!" shouted Francis.

"'Tis done."

The water in the chalice bubbled under the touch of the Fisher King as small strands of steam rose from the liquid and spilled through the cavern. The knights pressed themselves against the back of the cavern, while Merlin watched fascinated by the effects of the water from the touch of the Fisher King. Mist spilled over the edges of the chalice and crawled across the floor, touching and caressing the walls and climbing the rock, forcing its way to the ceiling. Flashes of light danced between the clouds as streaks of colour stained the dull patches which now threatened to consume the entire cavern.

"Merlin!" called Galahad.

"Be calm," instructed Merlin and waved away his concerns as the cloud thickened and images began to appear around the cavern.

The Fisher King released his grip on Francis' wrist and placed the palm of his rotting deformed hand on the top of his head. Francis could feel the bony sinew of its fingers as they lay softly across his hair and felt a sharp sensation penetrating his mind and the tendrils of the Fisher King's mind entered and searched the recessed of his brain which slept.

"Show me," he whispered, closing his eyes and raising his head to the ceiling. "Ancient mystics," he urged. "Show me the truth… show me what I need to know… Is the boy pure… Is the blood tainted?" The clouds thickened further as images intensified and spread across the cavern. "Show me," urged the Fisher King as Francis screamed as the tendrils of thought invaded his mind.

An image rose from the chalice and stood erect and regal within the mist, his armour a rich silver with golden trim sporting the edges of breast plate which ran over the front of the armour. The helmet held a large red plume of finery from its peak, which ran over the crest and fell towards the back of the helmet. Rich red velvet covered his arms from a partially hidden tunic, and heavy brown breeches covered thick powerful legs. His hand rested on the hilt of a powerful looking sword which hung from a scabbard tied tightly around his waist as the figure stood ghostly silent as the mist around offered further imagery.

"'Tis him," declared Galahad. "Arthur," he breathed.

Around the cavern the expanse of land beyond spread over the walls and cast an illusion of a vast moorland, with rolls of banks and mud cast out as far as the eye could see. Lord Bedivere nudged Tristan and indicated to the changing scenery which cast around the walls. "Aye, he is right, 'tis Arthur," he whispered. "But see." Tristan followed his eyes and nodded as chaos began to run through the cavern. "Camlann," he whispered almost silently.

28.

Arthur Rises

Tristan blinked at the sight before him and nodded his agreement at Bedivere's comments. "'Tis how I recall," he said sadly. "The death…"

"'Tis magnificent!" roared Kay from behind them and slapped them both hard on the shoulder.

"How would thee know?" laughed Galahad. "I seem to recall thee missed most of the battle!"

"Aye, my Lord, didn't thee oversleep?" Percival laughed as he spoke interjecting his own memories. A symphony a laughter broke the deepening tension which was steadily growing around the cave.

"Have at thee!" snapped Kay resting his hand on the hilt of his sword. "I fought with honour that day!" He could feel his anger grow as the laughter continued at his expense.

"Aye, with yon bedsheets!" roared Gawain.

"Enough!" roared the Fisher King, turning his head towards the errant knights. "Cease thy mindless prattling!" he snapped as the clouds thickened and darkened through the cavern. "Ancient mystics… Show me thine destiny… Show me what I need," he urged.

Francis struggled beneath his grip and sagged under the pressure of the Fisher King's touch. Small traces of blood seeped through the giant's fingers and tinged his hair with a sickening crimson, as streaks snaked down his forehead. His eyes rolled in his head and a river of blood flowed quietly and absently from his nose while his mouth opened in a silent scream.

"Ye child will die," whispered Bedivere as the knights watched.

"'Tis not the true king," commented Galahad as blood cemented the boy's hair.

"We cannot allow this," whispered Gawain.

Galahad placed a hand over his fellow knight's chest and shook his head. "We cannot interfere," he warned.

Tristan leant close to Gawain and placed a hand on his arm and smiled.

"We must let this play… I have faith in the boy." Gawain nodded and stood amidst the knights watching the images as they cast through the clouds.

"The king," whispered Kay peering through the darkness.

The silence in the cavern was deafening as the images danced over the walls and solidified around them. Arthur stood atop a small mound in the centre of the field, his mouth yelling quiet commands to the army scattered around the cave. The ghosts of the past moved through the walls and cast their unseeing gaze around the wilderness which spread out before them. Two sides, one battlefield, a single goal, a single outcome, one final resolution.

The two armies clashed as the memories laid dormant in the mind of Francis spilled out across the cavern. The smell of battle and the odour of blood invaded the senses, then almost inaudible at first before rising into the fury of sound the noise of battle. The shouts, the clash of swords against metal… bone, the noise of a thousand feet running through the muddy wasteland. The sound of screams echoed through the cavern bouncing off the walls and rebounding from the ceiling. They watched as Arthur ran forward, wielding Excalibur before him, slicing and hacking soldiers before he stood frozen briefly to the spot.

"Mordred!" His voice echoed through the cavern above the sound of fighting and carried over the expanse of the field. A figure bathed in dark armour turned and sneered at his rival and sliced viciously at a peasant dressed in simple rags. He fell away as Mordred stepped over his lifeless carcass and faced Arthur.

"My king," he sneered as Arthur stood before him. "'Tis been a long time."

"Prepare, my Lord." Arthur smiled as he raised Excalibur close to his face. His twisted smile reflected in the gleaming polished silver of the blade.

The two men ran towards each other, weapons held out in vicious confrontation as metal struck metal. Their bodies brought close as they tangled in a mass of raw power. The knights watched the devastation as the two lords swung and blocked each other's attacks, both evenly matched and neither gaining any advantage. Mordred swung his heavy sword violently at Arthur who brought up Excalibur to block the blow, then pushed the cold steel down towards the floor.

"Thee fight well," he breathed as he stepped back watching Mordred's

movement and panting heavily through the exertion.

"As do thee," acknowledged Mordred bowing low. "But I shall have your blood today." He rushed forward, sword thrust before him and swung at Arthur's body. The king blocked the attack and brought the hilt of his own sword down on the exposed neck of Mordred, sending the knight reeling into the mud.

Arthur laughed as he watched his opponent sprawl and slide in the mud. "'Tis fitting," laughed Arthur as he pointed Excalibur towards Mordred's head.

"Dispatch me or I swear I shall have thy head," warned Mordred.

"There is little honour in killing a downed opponent," stated Arthur and he stepped back allowing Mordred to regain his footing.

Mordred pulled himself to his feet, using his sword for leverage in the soft mud. "Then thoust are a fool," he spat.

Both men stood stock still for a moment, each weighing and sizing their opponent for signs of weakness. They stood on opposing sides yet wanting and fighting for the same goal: the crown. Mordred looked bedraggled in his armour, as blood stained his black polished metal giving it an uneven tired complexion. The wings on the sides of his helmet gave off his instantly recognizable armour and he stared with hatred and contempt at his rival on the field.

"Arthur." He nodded and pulled his sword before him. "Only one shall be destined to die." He smirked under the mud smeared across his face.

"For my crown," breathed Arthur as he surged forward once again, Excalibur held aloft over his head.

The blade swung down and halted sharply as Mordred blocked the attack with his own blade and forced the thrust of the attack away. He grimaced under the attack of Arthur and sagged under the pressure of the swing, sinking to one knee under the brutal volley of blows. The two men clashed as the sound of battle erupted around them, marred only by the noise of metal striking metal. Sparks from the metal illuminated the armour of the two men as Arthur lunged into the body of Mordred, who in turn swept away yet another attack from his adversary. Arthur looked at his opposition and smiled, flecks of mud smearing his features.

"Thee tire, Mordred," mocked Arthur as he surged forward Excalibur high in his grip.

Mordred grimaced as he pushed away the force of the attack and swept

159

through the air with the thrust his own sword. The speed of the attack caught Arthur by surprise and the momentum of his defence pushed him to his knees. His armour hit heavy in the soft mud of the field of Camlann, and small spray of dark brown cast over his armour. He cast a quick glance upward and rolled as Mordred brought his heavy sword crashing into the mud. Mordred watched as Arthur desperately struggled in the mud and brought his sword down again on the prone king.

"Thee have no honour in thy heart," panted Arthur under the relentless volley of blows.

Arthur pulled Excalibur before his chest and pushed away the attack of Mordred. He could feel the tide of the battle change as Mordred became spurred on by his own success and grew in confidence. He swung wildly as Arthur pulled himself to his feet and caught his blade deep into the shoulder of the king.

He smiled as Arthur cried in pain as the blade broke through the joint by his shoulder and bit into the soft flesh beneath the metal and gushing a red smear over the armour.

Mordred stepped back and regained his own composure and inspected the blade of his sword, smiling through his own helmet at the sight of deep crimson toying with the mud on the metal. "First blood," he breathed as he lunged forward again growing with a resumed eagerness and confidence.

Arthur countered the movement and defended the attack with ease, pulling the knight close to him. He could feel the hot breath of Mordred against his armour as the two men stood nose to nose. A burning sensation coursed through his shoulder as blood ran its way along his arm. "'Tis naught but a minor victory, my Lord," he whispered as he pushed Mordred away.

The two men circled each other in the mud for a moment, each surveying the other scanning and analysing any weakness in the other's armour. The fight continued around them, with the sound of death overcoming all other sounds. They circled for a moment as time passed before Arthur lunged, his sword barring down upon Mordred in a swarm of brutal attacks. He could feel his shoulder burn with every thrust; he could feel the pain seer through his body as the reverberation of Mordred's defence shattered his nerves and grated his senses. Mordred reeled under the pressure and moved back out of reach of the swing of Excalibur and could feel his lungs burst under the strain of battle.

He slipped as the mud beneath his feet gave way in a puddle of soft earth and as he struggled to regain his footing; his concentration of defending against Arthur's attacks became compromised and as Excalibur struck his chest plate he fell backward. Arthur watched as Mordred sagged and stumbled under the hazardous conditions and swung his sword savagely, catching Mordred square in the chest. He pulled back and watched Mordred fall to his knees, his sword falling momentarily by his side as his hand drifted to his chest plate.

Mordred looked down at the thick mark on his chest plate and grinned, reaching for the hilt of his sword. Excalibur had badly dented the armour, but apart from the visible damage no penetration had been made by the sword.

Arthur made forward, lunging past Mordred as he struggled to his feet. As Mordred moved aside, Arthur's thrust and momentum took him past the knight, leaving his midriff open to attack. Mordred grimaced as he swung viciously, striking the king deep into the side of Arthur's armour. The blade cut deep into the side of the king, causing Arthur to wince in pain as Mordred pulled his sword along the side of his body. He collapsed into the mud, dropping Excalibur as he grasped at the gaping wound in his side. Agony and pain surged through is body and he could feel the life drain as blood flowed across his armour. He looked up at Mordred who stood over his weakened body smirking at his imminent victory.

"I am better than thee," he mocked as he grasped his own sword in his arm as he watched Arthur flail in the mud, desperately crawling towards Excalibur. "The crown is rightfully mine by battle!"

Arthur winced under the volley of words and struggled along the floor, reaching for the hilt of Excalibur which lay in the mud just out of reach. "Thee shall never be king!" replied Arthur weakly as he clawed the discarded remains of battle. Staffs, banners and armour lay as remnants of death around his sprawling body.

"Thee are wrong," crowed Mordred. "I had thy sister, now I shall have thy crown."

"What?" Arthur's eyes narrowed as he whispered at Mordred's boasting.

Mordred bent forward and smirked in Arthur's face. "Thy sister," he mocked, blood smearing his teeth and his rancid breath invading Arthur's nostrils. Arthur could feel the pressure of a hard-cylindrical shape fall into his hand and he slowly closed his fingers, grasping at the cold dirty metal as he listened to Mordred mocking him. "She cried for mercy," he laughed and stood at full height raising his sword over his head. "She begged me to stop! Oh, how she screamed as I took her again and again," he cried as he positioned his sword over the king. "I enjoyed taking her, almost as much as I shall enjoy killing thee." He looked down at the prone knight and smiled. "Now thee shall die in the knowledge that she begged for thee, over and over, even as I took her... she cried thy name."

Mordred stood for a moment, a grimace frozen over his face and a look of horror crossing his features. His eyes bulged and blood trickled from his mouth as a sharp pain suddenly erupted through his mid-rift. He lowered his head as the pain coursed through his body and stared uncomprehending at the end of a large spear which protruding from a widening hole spreading across his torso. He followed the expanse of the steel and metal and stared into the eyes of Arthur who stared up from the mud, spear held aloft in his hands skewering the knight.

Blood forced its way up his throat and over his tongue as his sword fell heavily to the floor, his hands wandering to the spear thrust between the plates in his armour. Mordred grasped at the sharp blade attached to the wooden shaft and pressed the flow of blood erupting from his stomach. He fell to his knees and faced Arthur, meeting his eyeline and could see the pure hatred burn in the king's eyes as mist clouded his vision.

Arthur watched as Mordred feebly grasped at the spear as the blood flowed down the wood, staining his own gloves with the blood of his enemy. "I be king," he breathed quietly as Mordred slid slowly down the expanse of wood until he lay heavily on the prone body of the king. "'Tis over," he whispered into Mordred's ear and as the knight lay on top of him Arthur could feel the life die in Mordred's heart.

The knight gazed at him through dying eyes and spat into his face, a tinged reddening patch of saliva coursing over Arthur's face and spoke through blood-stained teeth. "Thoust shall not be king," he whispered as he pulled a small blade from his waistline and thrust it deep into the king's neck.

Arthur cast Mordred from his body and knelt in the mud, blood seeping from the wound in his neck. He could see seven survivors from the battle... only seven, he thought, out of so many, and for what? He looked at the crown in his hand and dwelt briefly on the gold and jewels which were *smear in the blood of hundreds… no… thousands.*

*   "'Tis over," he whispered as the first of the knights came through the mist and allowed himself a smile. "Galahad."*

Francis screamed and collapsed to the floor as the eyes of King Arthur closed and the life drained from his body. The clouds disappeared and the ghosts faded from view as the Fisher King released Francis from his icy grip. "'Tis over," he said sadly and looked down at the image of the boy crumpled in a huddled bundle on the floor. Francis lay amidst the water, barely breathing as the efforts overwhelmed his body as through the eons of time, he could feel the death of the king.

    Sir Galahad stepped forward and picked up the boy from the floor and laid him onto the stone altar and looked across the body. "The king is dead," he declared as Francis lay unmoving on the rough cold stone.

29.

Fight Knight

The other knights joined him at the altar and looked over the body of the boy as he lay still on the hard rock. The scene evoked memories of a time long past as the seven knights surrounded the altar as Merlin stood over the body and stared down at Francis examining the traces of blood which stained his forehead with his eyes.

"'Tis over," rasped the Fisher King.

Merlin turned to look at the giant and lowered his head. "Then we have failed," he said.

"No… the boy will live," he stated simply and pressed his hand down over the chest of Francis. "His heart is weak, but he lives."

"Then he is the one," declared Merlin triumphantly and watched as the Fisher King bowed slightly in his direction. He turned to the knights and smiled, spreading his arms out towards the waiting party. "He has passed the test," he confirmed. "He is the one." A feeling of relief swept through the cavern and all eyes once again fell onto the rock where Francis' chest rose slightly under his tattered jacket. A small exertion of air forced its way from between his lips and slowly his eyes fluttered open as he struggled to pull himself off the stone altar.

"The king is dead!" shouted Galahad above the silence punching the air. "Long live the king." Francis pulled himself into a sitting position as a chorus of "long live the king" echoed throughout the cavern.

Morgaine stepped from the public house and staggered as the cold air hit her. She leant heavily on the handrail which led up the stone steps to the pub and looked around at the empty street. Mordred placed a hand on her shoulder and knelt by her side, his faced masked with false concern at her sudden collapse.

"Morgaine, what ails thee?" he asked.

"I felt…" She frowned as she struggled to find the words to express her sudden bout of weakness. "I felt… something," she admitted shaking her head. "'Twas like… like… something stepped over my grave."

"I do not understand thy words."

"'Twas like something had stirred in the past… a vision." She pushed herself to her full height using the handrail and stared off through the ether. "I could feel a presence… a stirring as though something had disturbed the past."

"Thoust does not make sense, Morgaine!"

"Do thee not feel it?" snapped Morgaine as she watched a figure appear in the distance. She glanced at Mordred. "I could feel Arthur…"

"Then he lives."

"No, but I could feel…" She searched for the words and looked straight at him. "Camlann…" Her words trailed off as her mind cast back to the battle.

"How?" Mordred took her hand and led her down the stone steps onto the road as Agravain stepped from the pub, Gwen draped over his shoulder.

"The Fisher King," said Morgaine. "He is the only one whom has that kind of power."

"But thyself—"

"Nay, Mordred. Indeed, both myself and Merlin are equal in many ways, but we have our restrictions to our abilities. But the Fisher King, he can bend the will of time itself to his command." She breathed heavily as she spoke, her chest rising and falling as an excitement coursed through her body.

"What does this mean?" asked Mordred.

"It means that we do not have much time!" snapped Morgaine pushing Mordred from her. "Get the girl back to the castle and prepare our forces."

Agravain nodded and stepped into the road looking past both Morgaine and Mordred. "My Lady," he commented.

She stared at the figure now running towards the small group and turned to Mordred. "Thee want thy sport," she commented smiling. "Have at thee."

"With pleasure, my Lady," grinned Mordred pulling his sword from its scabbard around his waist.

"Dispatch the peasant and meet us back at the castle." With her instructions Morgaine turned back to Agravain. "Let us leave at once; we have much to prepare." She strode past the Knight Commander and smiled as she heard his obedient footsteps on the road behind her.

Gwen struggled in his grip as she lay across his shoulder, trapped within his thick mighty hold and she looked up as Mordred withdrew his sword and held it stretched out before him, pointing it towards the figure running towards them. She forced her head up and struggled as she recognised the figure as he neared at speed. "Lance!" she called. "Lance!" The figure paused for a moment then, head down ran forward towards them once again. She looked on aghast at his progress and called desperately at him. "No, Lance, no!" she screamed. "Turn around! Run, run," she urged as Agravain tightened his grip on her.

Mordred laughed as the youth skid to an ungainly stop, yards short of the group and met the knight's stare with fear in his eyes. "Lance," he mocked. "Could this be Lancelot?" Mordred laughed at his own humour. "I think not... yon boy is naught but a coward. See how he stops before my might," he scoffed calling back over his shoulder.

"Run, Lance, just fucking run!" called Gwen desperately.

"Shut her up!" yelled Mordred glancing over his shoulder. "Well, boy, are thee a man?" Mordred returned his gaze towards the boy in front of him. His sword outstretched pointing directly at the boy's chest. "What say thee, Lance?" he mocked laughing again.

Lance hovered unsure what to do; he wavered as the woman and man walked briskly along the road and out of sight, whilst this other man dressed in black armour and off-set with a winged black helmet stood before him brandishing a heavy thick sword. He turned and began a swift retreat calling back over his shoulder as he ran. "I'd be pretty stupid to fight a fucking nutter like you, wouldn't I?" he called as he ran.

"I knew thee to be a coward!" called Mordred.

Lance paused and looked back. "Hardly, you have a fucking sword and all I have are these." He raised his fists and showed them to Mordred.

The knight laughed. "By my soul, I like thee boy," he scoffed and threw his sword down on the floor beside him. "Thee think thoust can best me?" he asked almost incredulously. Lance looked the knight up and down for a moment and nodded, causing another rapturous laugh from Mordred. "Then so be it, come to me, boy. If thoust win I shall award you handsomely."

"What with?" queried Lance.

"Gold... silver... riches beyond your wildest dreams," boasted Mordred. "And then their art the women," he teased.

"The women?"

"Yes, boy, the women. Not that cheap whore," he said nodding over his shoulder towards the pub referencing to Gwen. "Real women of noble birth. You would have status, boy," he promised as Lance took a step towards Mordred, his fists raised before him.

"Your funeral," sneered Lance as he lunged quickly forward, catching Mordred off guard. The punch landed on the knight's chin knocking him backward and cutting his lip in the process. "Just for starters," said Lance as he lunged forward again swinging with his fist, connecting with his right fist against the chin of Mordred, followed by the left which struck the knight square on the nose. "And see that blonde bit you were with," sneered Lance as he stood over Mordred. "She'll be the first."

Mordred laughed. "Ha! She would eat thoust alive, boy."

"I'm counting on it," countered Lance and brought his fist deep into the midriff of the knight.

Mordred bent double and gasped as his fist connected just beneath his chest plate and took the air out of his body. He knelt on the ground on one knee and spat a patch of blood onto the street beside the feet of Lance. He placed his hands on the shoulders of the knight and hauled him roughly to his feet and spat into his face as Mordred stood face to face with the young man. Their eyes met for the briefest of moments before Lance brought his fist down into Mordred's midriff once again. The knight staggered back under the attack and watched as Lance stepped forward, his fists raised and watched as the boy's fist swung down catching him over his left eye.

"Ain't no-one in this town who can take me," boasted Lance as he watched Mordred sag back again.

"Mordred!" the voice echoed around his head. "Hear me."

He raised his head and spoke into the sky. "I hear thee, Morgaine," he called into the atmosphere.

"You going fucking mad," snapped Lance smiling as another blow caught Mordred full on the chin.

"Do not delay; make haste forthwith."

Mordred nodded and stood to his full height before Lance and smiled. "Thee have shown spirit, boy," he commented. "I can commend that."

"Yeah, well fucking commend this," snapped Lance as he swung with his fist again connecting with the knight's chin. His fist connected with a sickening thud, but the knight barely moved under the attack. Lance stepped back unsure what to do, then moved forward again swinging his right fist catching the knight on the cheek, followed by a swift left beneath the chin.

Mordred stood and threw his head back releasing a hearty laugh. "Go ahead, boy. I'll give thee one final blow," he said and placed his hands firmly on his hips as Lance wavered confused by the sudden turn of events. He pointed to his chin and laughed. "Go on… thy best shot," he mocked and stepped closer to him. Lance clenched his fist and raised them before his face and nodded, taking several deep breaths before thrusting his fist forward into the face of Mordred. Blood exploded from the knight's nose, but little else happened much to the dismay of Lance who stood facing Mordred. "By all that is holy!" exclaimed Mordred clapping his hands together. "'Tis fun!"

He struck Lance hard in the face and watched with a satisfied grin as the boy staggered back, his face instantly swelling from the impact of the strike. He laughed as the area around his left eye began to rise and cover the young man's brow, then admiring his work Mordred's smile vanished and he swung his left fist catching Lance across the cheek. As Lance felt the force of the impact, blood erupted from his mouth and spat in a geyser effect across the pavement as he fell back. He staggered desperately trying to remain on his feet and raised his head as a third fist swung down savagely against his already bulging face. Air and blood escaped his lungs as his body sagged under its own weight and he rested his heavy hands upon his knees as he struggled with the gravity around him.

He felt a large arm snake around his neck and pull his body close to his face as Mordred held him fast in a tightening headlock. Lance stared down at the cold hard grey concrete on the street beneath his feet and watched as blood fell onto the ground smearing the floor and spreading outward in a splattered pattern. Pain coursed through his body from the impact of just three blows from the knight as his legs struggled to cope with the pressure placed from the exertion. Unconsciousness threatened to swim into his mind as his thoughts were clouded by visions of darkness and crimson.

Mordred's face was deadly serious as he grasped Lance around the neck and pulled him close to his body in a vicious grasp. He tightened his grip, restricting the passage of air to the young boy's lungs, then swiftly brought his fist into the boy's face three times before letting go and watched him sink to the floor. Blood smeared the knight's hand from the impact of the strikes and the sickening sound of bone splintering echoed in the air as the third blow struck. Blood spewed freely over the pavement as Lance was released from the grip of Mordred and collapsed onto all fours on the pavement coughing violently and spitting out great swathes of blood as his insides vomited and constricted. Lance could feel his heart pounding against his rib cage from the beating, and desperately sought an end to the prolonged agony. Mordred looked down at the figure on his hands and knees before him and spat down on the back of his head in utter disgust. He circled the boy and grinned through his own blood-stained teeth, then kicked Lance viciously in the stomach, laughing at the sound of bone breaking as his feet connected with the boy's ribs.

Lance felt his insides scream as bone broke beneath the kick of the knight, and he rolled onto his side from the force of the attack. He struggled against the darkness which swam around him and curled himself into a fetal position, clutching his legs and pulling them close to his chest from protection.

"Snivelling dog! Stand! Stand and face me," spat Mordred as he brought his foot into contact with the lower back of Lance, bringing an indiscriminate groan of pain from the young boy. "Thee actually thought that a peasant as thine could best a knight of noble birth," mocked Mordred as he stood over the body of the boy.

Lance felt his kidneys explode inside his body as a second kick connected with his body, in the unending nightmare which surrounded him. He could feel the blood seep from his body and the fire burning through his insides as another kick rocked through his body. He could feel nothing but pain as the knight bent forward laughing at the boy's pain and felt the pressure of a hand running through his hair.

Mordred allowed his fingers to run through Lance's hair for a moment before closing them tight around the follicles and hauled the boy to his feet. Lance could find no energy to struggle against the strength of the knight and allowed himself to be pulled to his feet where he staggered under the strain of conscious thought. His legs buckled and he felt the pressure placed on his head through his hair as the knight held him fast and pulled him once again to his full height. He released his hair and placed a thick hand on the back of his neck, bringing his own face close to Lance's and resting on his forehead. Lance could feel the hot breath of Mordred on his face, and they stood in a deadly embrace.

"I like thee," whispered the knight as he pressed his forehead against Lance's. "I really do." He smiled as he spoke, and Lance attempted to see him through swollen eyes. His face was a bloodied mess of pulp as his flesh swelled over the whole of his head. Mordred laughed and planted a kiss on the lips of Lance and smiled as he withdrew. "It therefore pains me when I have to do this," he apologised as he flicked a small blade from his armoured gauntlet and plunged it deep into Lance's neck.

The scream died in his throat as blood seeped through in an avalanche of red and stained his clothing. He could not find the words as the life drained from his body as he listened to Mordred as he boasted whilst holding Lance upright in his standing position allowing the boy's blood to seep over his armour.

"'Tis how I injured Arthur at Camlann," he said softly. "Oh, how thee should have seen his face." He released his grip on the boy and allowed him to drop to his knees on the street at his feet. Slowly Mordred pushed the blade back into the concealed pocket in the gauntlet as he spoke. "The surprise," he said wistfully. "'Twas the last thing I ever saw…" His voice trailed off as he turned and stared into the distance at the castle perched high on the hill beyond the line of tress and overlooking the sea. "So how am I here?" he asked himself.

He brought his attention back to the boy who lay writhing in pain on the street and sighed. "'Twas fun," he said quietly as he walked towards his discarded sword and picked it up weighing it in his hands and walking back to where Lance lay on the road staring through a reddening vision towards the sky. "Rest boy," said Mordred softly and thrust the sword into the boy's chest, thrusting the blade deep beneath the ribcage and up into the cavity which housed his heart.

Lance convulsed for a final time, gripping at the blade as the life left his body and collapsed into a grateful and eternal sleep, as the blood ran across the road staining the floor and playing across the cracks in the street. Mordred watched as the boy died at his feet and looked up at the castle wistfully before disappearing in the trees.

30.

The Last Pendragon

"Forgive me, my Liege," said Galahad softly as he knelt before the stone altar, his sword pressing down with the point of the blade digging into the rock. He leant against the blade and spoke directly towards the ground as he rested his forehead against the hilt of the sword. "My life is thine to command."

Francis struggled into a sitting position and swung his legs over the edge of the rock. "What happened?" he asked as he gazed around the cavern, his eyesight clearing as the haze inside his head cleared slowly. He could feel a pressure behind his eyes and a throbbing from his mind as his head clouded and dizziness threatened to overwhelm him.

"Thee have proven thyself," the Fisher King spoke in a low rumble and his voice echoed through the cave. "Thee truly are the last Pendragon," he stated simply.

"What does that mean?" asked Francis. "I am sorry, but I don't understand."

"Aye," laughed Lord Kay. "He definitely has Arthur's quick wit!" The other knights laughed, and Francis knew the comment had not been complimentary.

He frowned at Kay and spoke directly to Merlin. "Please," he said. "You seem to understand what is going on. Please, tell me," he asked softly.

Merlin sighed. "Thee are just like the young Arthur, full of questions and inexperience. Expecting the world to fall at your feet," he said smiling. "Thee are definitely a Pendragon."

"Yes, yes, I got that, but what does he mean? What does all this mean?" he snapped.

It was the Fisher King who spoke, his voice clouding the cavern. "Thee are the last in the direct bloodline to King Arthur of the Britons," he explained. "'Tis thy divine right to hold Excalibur and protect the country in its greatest need."

"And that is now?" The Fisher King stood silently watching as Francis pulled himself off the stone altar and staggered slightly, placing a hand back on the cold rock to steady himself. "Well?"

The Fisher King turned and walked slowly down the tunnel from whence he had travelled, his figure silhouetted in the light spilling from the entrance. "The Lady will tell thee more. I simply define whether thee are who thy claim to be."

"What... and that is Arthur?" He watched as the Fisher King continued to drag its form down the corridor. "Wait, wait," Francis called. "I need more answers!" he called.

"I will meet thee at the appointed place... Follow the voice and she shall guide thy quest."

"Then it isn't over," Francis shouted down the tunnel, then turned to the congregation of knights who bowed their heads as he looked over the group.

"My Liege—" began Galahad.

"Don't start that again," snapped Francis. "I'm not a king. I'm not a hero, I'm a nobody. I'm not important. I'm just me!"

Merlin placed a hand on his arm and spoke softly. "There be no such thing," he said. "Everybody is important... at least to someone. I have never met anybody yet in my life who I have not thought was important. I have watched as empires have risen and fallen. I have watched births and deaths, and in all that time there has never been anyone who has been unimportant. Life and death run hand in hand as constant companions and for some death is the greatest gift." Francis frowned at the comment as Merlin spoke. "Thee are the last Pendragon and while the world has gone on and thee may not be of royal descent, thee are the last of the Holy line of pre-ordained kings. It is thy duty as the last of thy bloodline to retrieve Excalibur and do its bidding."

Francis sighed. "But how do you know all this?" he asked. "How do you know I am who you think I am?"

"The Fisher King," Merlin stated simply.

"Yes, yes, the Fisher King," Francis replied throwing his hands in the air. "Always the Fisher King, but how do you know?" Merlin paused with his answer and stared at him for a moment as though considering his response. "I mean, if I am Arthur's descendant, shouldn't I be pulling Excalibur from the stone or something?" Francis was met with a blank stare from the old sage. "You know," insisted Francis. "Pull the sword from the stone, that kind of stuff. He who pulls the sword from the stone shall be king of England!"

"That was but a legend—"

"Exactly, this whole thing was but a legend!" laughed Francis. "None of this was real... sorry, is real. Arthur didn't live; it was a myth, a story designed to unite the country against... whatever."

"Excalibur was not the sword."

"What?" snapped Francis turning to look at the knights who had been quiet to this point staring at the exchange between Francis and Merlin.

A large man stepped forward. His clothes were simple, but elegant with golden trim running down the centre of his chest plate forming into a rampant lion on the polished metal. Yellowing robes clung to his body over the armour and chainmail and swelled across the rotund stomach which strained beneath the armour. His ginger beard fell across the top of the chest plate, in a bedraggled state and ginger hair swept down his back from an unkempt forehead. Francis could see a scar snake its way down his forehead as it ran deep and bore witness to a sadness hidden within the man. He spoke again softly through the crowd. "The sword in the stone was not Excalibur," he explained. "The sword was a simple blade placed there as a test of true divinity. The sword Excalibur was presented to the king by the Lady upon his ascension following the test."

"That's just it!" exclaimed Francis. "I haven't done any test." He walked around the altar to face the seven knights. "I haven't done anything..." He trailed off as he thought his life over. "I haven't done anything," he said softly. The knights shuffled uncomfortably as Francis continued to speak mainly to himself. "Eat, sleep, work... I haven't done anything, just existed," he said and hauled himself back onto the stone altar. "I've done nothing," he said softly. "Haven't been anywhere or seen anything. I've wasted my time."

"Then what better time to start living," said Bedivere walking from the crowd and placing a hand on his shoulder. "We should all have a starting point for our journey," he said. "This could be thine." He smiled at Francis as he spoke.

"And we are thine to command," said Galahad. "We are aligned to the throne."

"We will accompany thee on thy journey," said Bedivere.

"But how do you know I am Arthur… or at least his descendant?"

"The Fisher King showed us," explained Merlin. "Your mind holds latent images of a bygone age. A time past, but linear in its respect for thee… thyself as a person. Thee are the last Pendragon; thee are from Arthur's loins. Your mind holds family memories of Camlann and his death. Thee remember…" Merlin grasped his arms as he spoke directly to Francis. "Thee heard the voice."

"And this proves who I am?"

"No," said Merlin smiling. "Thee are alive," he said smiling. "If thee had died, then thee would have been a false king." The knights around them broke into rapturous laughter as he spoke, much to the horror of Francis as the thought about Merlin's words and the magnitude of the test finally sank in.

"Well then," said Francis. "If I am who you say I am… and I'm still not convinced, then you had better introduce me…" He waved towards the line of knights who stood lined against the wall of the cavern.

31.

Introductions

"Galahad," said the knight simply as Francis stood before him. The large burly man knelt low as he spoke and rested on the hilt of his sword. "My life at thy command."

"The doubter," commented Francis as he spied the knight on one knee before him.

"Please forgive my doubts, my Liege—"

"It is not his fault," snapped Merlin. "Please do not find fault with those who serve thee loyally." He moved gracefully and quickly around the stone altar to where Galahad knelt and placed a hand on the back of the knight's head. "His concerns echoed all of ours. Only he had the voice to speak them," he chided Francis with his words and his eyes shot daggers of contempt as he spoke. "Thine is not the only life in question," Merlin said looking around at the nobles in the cavern.

"I'm sorry," stammered Francis taken back by the suddenness of Merlin's outburst. "I didn't think."

"Thy fate is naught," continued Merlin. "But thy destiny is linked with that of our own. If thee are indeed the kin of Arthur, then Excalibur shall call thee further until thy art reunited with the sword."

"Then what?"

Merlin shrugged. "Take heed, my Lord, Morgaine seeks the sword, and if she seeks Excalibur then not only our lives are in danger but the whole of reality."

"What do you mean, the whole of reality?"

"With Excalibur, Morgaine can use the enchantments to shape will itself to her command. She courts dark forces," said Merlin sadly. "And may stop at naught to retrieve the sword for her own design. This is why my Lord Galahad was cautious with his favour."

Francis nodded and smiled down at the knight who remained in his kneeling position as the two men spoke above him. "Please, Galahad." The knight raised his head at the sound of his name. "If you could?" Francis waved before him towards the remaining knights and nodded in their general direction.

The knight stood and slid his sword into its scabbard and moved to the side of Francis. "My Liege," he started. "May I present the remaining knights of the round table," he said proudly placing a hand on Francis' back and waving towards his comrades. Each knight bowed their heads in respect as Galahad moved from one to another introducing each knight in turn. "Bedivere." The knight nodded as Francis looked at him. "Marshall to Arthur, brother to Sir Lucan. It was he whom returned Excalibur to the Lake," he explained then leant close to Francis's ear and whispered with a grin spreading across his face. "Just don't mention that it took him three times to complete the task." Bedivere blushed at the remark but remained silent in courteous respect.

Galahad continued, "Gawain, the Maiden's Knight, brother to Agravain and one of the greatest knights to be seated at the table." Francis nodded at the knight and could not help being impressed by his polished green armour with its raised black Griffin embossed in the centre of the chest plate. He held a large green helmet beneath his arm, which had a large black Griffin similar in design to the one on his armour perched on the crest of the heavy metal, running over its peak and down the back of the helmet. Galahad continued to move along the line of knights. "Lord Kay—"

"We've met," interjected Francis.

"Aye, in the forest," confirmed Galahad as he cast a quick glance towards the young boy. "Stepbrother to the king and the first of the knights of the table." Kay nodded and glanced up at Francis as he past and smiled broadly at the boy. Despite his brutish nature, Francis could not help warming to the heavy-set knight. "Lord Tristan, Knight of Cornwall," continued Galahad referring to the other knight from the clearing. "Son of Blancheflor and suitor to Iseult."

The knight nodded. "My Liege," he purred softly keeping his head firmly down.

"Lord Percival." He frowned at the knight as he lowered his head. "Old friend." Percival raised his head and smiled at Galahad. "Bravest of knights and seeker of the Grail with myself."

Percival nodded towards Galahad and rested on the hilt of his sword. "I am at thy command," he whispered through the darkness towards

Francis.

"Just don't let him carry any of yon magical incantations for you." Kay laughed loud at his remark and slapped Tristan on the back as Percival grimaced at the statement.

"'Twas a mistake anyone could have made," he stuttered glancing towards the tunnel and the disappearing shadow in the distance.

"Who is the large man?" whispered Francis in the ear of Galahad through the laughter echoing around the cavern. Galahad followed his gaze to the large bulk of the knight who unlike the others stood to his full height and stared at the slow progression of the two as they continued through the cavern.

Galahad extended his hand to the knight, who accepted it firmly and shook his whole arm in greeting. "My Lord Bors," said Galahad warmly.

"My Lord," smiled Bors. "It feels good to be alive, does it not?" he asked staring at Francis. "To be aligned to yon youth on the Holy quest once again."

"Aye, old friend," he agreed and turned to talk to Francis still holding the grip of the larger knight. "Bors journeyed with me and Percival for the Holy Grail, which the Fisher King now holds," he explained. "He is the most noble and courteous of knights, granted divinity through his vow of chastity and chosen by the Lord himself."

"Please, my Lord," urged Merlin. "The Fisher King." He indicated down the corridor.

Francis looked at Merlin and smiled. "Don't worry," he insisted gently as he strode around the cavern. "I have been ordained as king, I think… what could possibly go wrong?"

"My Lord forgets Morgaine walks abroad." His eyes darted about the chamber as he spoke, "If she knows our moves, then she could court our defeat."

"How would she know?"

"She has powers almost as strong as my own, but hers are devout in darkness," explained Merlin. "She courts with demons and twists the truth to her own meaning." He placed a hand on Francis' back and gently eased him into the mouth of the tunnel. "Thee must go, for reality could be fashioned around us as we speak."

"Thee worry too much, old man," laughed Kay as he moved to follow Francis down the tunnel.

"Least ye forget the forest, my Lord," warned Merlin. He turned to Francis and spoke directly to him. "Or thine metal carriage."

A shiver ran up the back of Francis as he remembered his own experience. "You know about that?"

"I watched it," he said indicating towards the stone chalice which still stood silently close to the stone altar. "Morgaine has great powers; do not mistake her will as a weakness. She will do what she must to obtain Excalibur. She will use anything or anyone to get what she desires."

"Gwen," whispered Francis.

"I beg thee pardon?"

"Sorry... you said she would use anyone."

"Aye, my Lord. If Morgaine can use a person to obtain Excalibur, then she will do so." Merlin paused and eyed Francis as he spoke. "Thoust came here alone?" he queried.

"Yes, but..."

"What is it?"

"Well, there was a girl..."

Lord Kay laughed loudly through the cavern and slapped the young man on the back. Francis stumbled forward under the pressure of his strike. "Is there not always?" He laughed.

"Explain," demanded Merlin.

"When I arrived, there was a girl."

"Continue."

"Well, we kind of did things," he stammered embarrassed by his own admission. "You know... things."

"He means sex, my Lord," whispered Gawain in Merlin's ear.

"I know what he means!" snapped Merlin. "This could be bad. If Morgaine knows of this, then she could use the girl as a weapon against thee."

"What should we do?" asked Francis.

"Thoust must travel with the Fisher King."

"But Gwen."

"Thoust are the king, we shall follow thy orders," stated Galahad stepping forward.

"Okay, okay," he breathed heavily taking in the damp atmosphere of the cavern. "I don't know what to do," he admitted looking around the cavern desperately. His eyes flicked over the seven expectant faces in the

178

cavern of the knights, then stared at the smiling face of Merlin.

"Thee will do what is right. I have faith," the old sage whispered.

"Come to me," a female voice whispered in the wind and played around his ear. "You must come to me." Francis sighed. What had Galahad said earlier: Maiden's Knight, chivalry, chastity…

"Right." He started looking around the knights. "Galahad, Kay and Bedivere, you come with me," he said as confidently as he could. "Percival and Tristan, you go with Bors to collect and protect Gwen. Gawain, you will stay here with Merlin in case of trouble." He smiled as best he could and walked along the tunnel, disappearing down the tunnel, followed by the small procession of knights.

"Well done," whispered Merlin. He turned and moved towards the stone chalice and gazed into the depths of the water within. He smiled into his own reflection and spoke into the water as a female face flirted across the surface tension of the liquid within. "He is the one," he breathed softly as the face disappeared then glanced down the tunnel briefly allowing his eyes to paused over the form of Gawain before staring into the light at the end of the tunnel. "He comes," he whispered into the darkness and turned his attention back to the water where the images began to swirl into life.

32.

Warning of the Future

Gwen was pushed roughly into a vast open space within the ruins of the old castle. "Watch it!" she snapped as she stumbled onto the ground and sat looking around her rubbing her arm.

"She has fire," exclaimed Morgaine as she strode around the site her eyes darting to the orb which sat in its stone berth in the centre of the clearing. Gwen looked on as the woman before her stood before the orb and stared into its depths. "Show me," she urged.

Gwen strained her eyes as she peered through the diminishing light of the mist-filled sphere, but struggled to see anything from this distance, instead choosing to examine the immediate area. She had been to the ruins many times before, but never like this. These people were mad, she had already decided and spied Agravain who stood barring her retreat.

Stone lay about the ground, scattered through the ravages of time and the once proud towers which had risen majestically over the years staring out over the sea now stood hunched in disrepair. The toll of time and the weather had withered the once mighty building.

"Damn you!" Gwen's attention was snapped back to the woman who slapped her hands roughly against the sides of the sphere. She could see anger rising in her as she placed both hands on each side of the orb. "Show me," she shouted into the glass and once again turned from the sphere, her face reddening with anger. "Agravain!" she snapped, and the Knight Commander briskly left his post by the main entry point to the ruins and stood close to Morgaine.

"My Lady," he said obediently, bowing his head slightly.

Gwen glanced towards the opening and thoughts of escape played over her mind. She shifted slightly and tensed as she thought her options through whilst always keeping one eye on the pair.

Morgaine roared with anger and her hand flashed through the air, catching Agravain flush on the cheek in a completely unprovoked attack.

Gwen recoiled at the ferocity of the strike and her muscles relaxed as she decided against flight from the castle. Her mind argued against the actions in the oncoming darkness, coupled with the madness of the people around her. The knight stood his ground as his head was forced back from the slap, his cheek showing off a reddening mark which swelled slightly beneath the pressure.

"My loyal Commander," Morgaine purred as she gently rested her palm against his swollen cheek. "Loyal to the end." She smiled as she looked into his eyes. "If only." Her hand trailed from his cheek and down the front of his body along his breastplate. "The time is nigh," she said as her hand continued its slow descent downward towards his waist, her eyes meeting his as she spoke. "Soon, good Agravain, all this will be mine," she breathed and smiled warmly, leaning close to the Knight Commander's face and whispered softly as her hand rested on his groin, her fingers cloying at the rough breeches he wore.

Gwen sat in an uncomfortable fascination as she watched this dance unfold before her and despite her best efforts, she could feel a tingle of arousal within her own groin.

"Once I have Excalibur," she breathed softly, rubbing the outline of his genitals beneath his clothing whilst still staring into his eyes, not missing a beat as the soldier stood to attention. "The world will bend to my will." Morgaine abruptly stopped and turned to face the girl, still sprawled on the floor and gazed down at her form. The knight stood uncomfortably still awaiting his instructions, standing to attention in sensual frustration. "And you, girl, will be the key," Morgaine said softly walking towards her, slowly masking her feelings and smiling towards Gwen as she stalked her. "Stand," she commanded and waited patiently as Gwen obeyed the instruction and stood before her. "Once the boy has the sword, he will give us Excalibur in return for thee." She jabbed her in the chest as she spoke then turned back to the orb and spoke into the glass. "But where are they?" she snapped. "They are hidden from us. It must be that damned Fisher King!"

"You're mad," whispered Gwen.

Morgaine threw her head back and laughed. "Never more have I been saner," she said.

"Excalibur doesn't exist; it's just a myth!" snapped Gwen.

"Oh, but it does, sweet child, it doth exist as much as thee or I," purred Morgan as she indicated for Agravain to move back to his position. "And once I have it… I, Morgaine Le Fay, shall have dominion over reality itself."

"Thyself Aunt?" the voice of the newcomer came from behind Agravain and even at this distance and through the darkness Gwen could see the form of the third person from the public house.

"Mordred, thy face," she said.

Mordred's hand snaked up to his marked face, where cuts and bruises played with dirt. "'Tis nothing, good Lady," he said spying Gwen. "Yon child gave a good account of himself," he said smiling. "But 'twas not a fight, more a sport!" He laughed as he thrust a handout before him indicating a death blow with his sword.

"You're all mad," spat Gwen through the tears which swelled in her eyes. She struggled against her own feelings, desperate not to let these people see her grief.

"Where be the boy?" asked Mordred looking past Morgaine towards the orb.

"I know not," Morgaine admitted. "The Fisher King will not let me see." She clenched her fists in frustration as she spoke, "But the boy will have the sword soon enough and once he does." She looked straight at Gwen as she spoke, "He will come to us."

"Boy?" blinked Gwen as she spoke. "Francis?" Her voice trailed off as she looked at Morgaine, then Mordred. "Am I mad?" she asked herself as they laughed at her confusion.

"He will come and give us the sword of his own free will," purred Morgaine. She indicated towards Agravain who stepped forward at her bidding. "Take the whore to the dungeons," she ordered. "But Agravain, be sure that not one hair on her head is harmed," she said switching her gaze to meet that of Mordred. "The girl is not to be harmed or abused in any way. She must remain pure."

Francis watched as the three knights walked along the beach in the opposite direction from his own journey. He glanced at the sky. He had not realised that the night had closed in on them and wondered whether the risk of travelling through the night would be worth it. The clouds overhead closed around the evening sky and wandered meaninglessly across the heavens as he closed his eyes and struggled to listen to the voice ringing in his ears. "Come to me," the woman spoke softly in his ear and despite the constant reminder of his own fragile sanity, he was beginning to find the presence of the voice reassuring as the madness of the world surrounded him.

"I hear you," he spoke softly into the air. "Where are you?"

The knights watched on frowning as Francis spoke to the unseen woman which spoke to him. "Come to me," she said softly again. "You are close."

Francis opened his eyes and sighed; he knew his journey would soon be at an end and glanced along the beach to where the Fisher King stood. Great grooves had been dug deep into the soft sand as the creature had dragged its crippled legs along the expanse of beach to a small outcrop of rocks which sat on the edge of the sea. The waves playfully caressed the roughly sewn boulders before retreating across the beach. He cast a glance the other way towards the town and wondered the reaction of Gwen and her father if he strode in with the three knights at their pub. He smiled as he thought of the landlord being confronted by a real knight and he briefly wished he would be there to witness the confrontation.

"My Lord," said Galahad softly. "The Fisher King awaits." He pointed along the beach. "What are thine wishes?"

"We go on," he said confidently looking down the beach.

Merlin stood by the stone chalice gazing into the watery depths and watched as Francis set off down the beach, his footsteps masked his journey as they sank deep into the soft moist ground. "He is coming," he whispered into the water briefly looking towards Gawain who stalked around the cavern in brooding contemplation.

"He is pure of thought," said the voice from the water.

"Be still," warned Merlin raising a hand.

"Merlin?" Gawain frowned as he looked towards Merlin as the voice of the sage reached him through the emptiness. He stepped forward and felt the air around him thicken, his legs growing heavy and time around him slowed to a standstill. Merlin hurried to the frozen form of Gawain and moved around the body, jabbing and probing the knight with his hand as he was caught in a temporal freeze.

"Lady," breathed Merlin turning back to the chalice. "He is still."

The water in the chalice swelled and rose over the edges of the basin and spilled across the floor in a large puddle. It swam and moved under the intense gaze of Merlin as it formed slowly into a shape which rose higher in an undefined mass of swirling liquid before hardening and taking on a form. "He is coming." The female voice echoed Merlin's first words as he had spoken into the chalice. "That is to be expected. He is the one."

"His journey shall soon be at an end," stated Merlin and he reached for the woman's hand. "As shall our own."

"Soon, my love," she breathed. The woman stood staring into the darkness, water falling from her naked body. "But take heed there is danger ahead," she warned. "I see death…"

33.

Blue Guards of Cornwall

Bors pushed his way from the undergrowth which separated the forest to the road and stepped onto the hard pavement and glanced about the street. "For whence we came," he said pointing back through the forest as his two comrades pulled themselves free of the vegetation and swung around pointing up the street. "Thereforth hence we must travel yonder," he declared.

"My Lord Bors," said Percival cautiously. "What be yonder lights?"

The three knights stared along the road to the source of the light where a small congregation of people huddled around a yellow cordon, straining to see past the rope and through the hastily constructed white tent which stood on the hot tarmac.

"I know not," admitted Bors. "'Tis a strange world indeed."

"Aye," said Tristan sadly looking around at the small town which had grown up around the castle. "Much has changed to my beloved Cornwall since our time."

"But 'tis still thy home," said Bors encouragingly.

"To a sort... just not... if thoust doth understand my meaning." Bors nodded and placed a hand on his shoulder and smiled looking the knight directly in his eyes. "'Twas my home," continued Tristan. "I can still see the land rising and falling in my mind." He sniffed. "The land still smells like Cornwall, yet doth not. It is tinged with... a presence."

"My Lord," said Percival. "Should it be wise that we dwell?"

"No," admitted Tristan. "We had better move onward."

"Aye, prudence shall be our valour this day," said Bors looking over the heads of his comrades. The three knights walked slowly up the road, their clothing and manner gaining little interest from the growing spectators around the tent. As they neared, the blue light flashed on and off and they could see a swarm of people, mostly men dressed in an official blue uniform standing behind the yellow line. "I say, good sir," said Bors loudly as they neared the rear of the crowd. "What goes on yonder?"

An elderly gentleman turned and spied the knight suspiciously for a moment then spoke through narrowed eyes. "You here for the castle or something?" he asked. "Your clothes," he added nodding down at the armour and tunics worn by the knights.

"Aye, aye, thoust is correct," said Percival hastily as he leant forward. "We come for the pageant." He winked at the man as he spoke.

"Pageant you say… yeah… well… bit early for that, ain't you?" said the old man.

"Best be early than late," laughed Bors.

"What goes on?" asked Percival, gazing past the man to the yellow tape and beyond.

"Don't rightly know," the man admitted. "But the word is someone's been killed… stabbed to death," he whispered leaning close to Percival. "Old Doris reckons some guy stabbed him with a sword…" He trailed off as his eyes wandered down to the scabbard around the waist of Percival, then back to Percival's face. "Ere, you're not…"

"No, no, no, good sir," said Tristan at his side. "These art not real, but mockeries."

"Oh," said the old man. "Like plastic fakes or something."

"Aye, 'tis right," agreed Tristan frowning. "Now, Doris?" he urged.

"That's about it. She reckons these guys had an argument on the road, fought and…" He thrust his hand out before him. "Dead," he said finally.

"Does ye wise woman know who?" asked Percival craning his neck past the crowd. "'Tis man or woman?"

"Eh? Wise woman? I don't know," said the old man. "Asks a lot of questions your pal, don't he?" he said turning to Tristan.

"'Tis the best way to learn," said Tristan smiling warmly.

"Reckon your pal doesn't think so," he said nodding through the crowd towards Bors, who was pushing his large body through the melee of people.

"Bors!" shouted Tristan. "Bors!"

If the large knight had heard him, then he had chosen to ignore him and continued his journey to the edge of the yellow perimeter. His fingers ran along the edge of the tape and he looked about the other people who all stood in a strange fashion behind the boundary. He frowned; he did not understand the custom and took the plastic in his hands examining the item.

It ran around several large poles around a large white tent and had strange black markings running in diagonal lines at intermittent intervals across the tape. He frowned and released the line and looked at his hands, then reached out gingerly for the tape once again, pressing the edges of the tape gently before moving his hands away for a second time. He examined the tips of his fingers and pressed them together, watching as the skin stuck together gently as he opened and closed his digits. He pressed his fingers around the sticky tape once again; he frowned as he lifted the tape high and gazed at the markings running along the line of the tape. He recognised that the markings were letters, but such things were for men of learning, he thought, and not for the likes of him, then swiftly ducked beneath the cordon and walked briskly across the road towards the tent.

"Excuse me, sir!" the voice was tinged with panic as it struck his back. Bors turned and watched puzzled as a small man dressed in the same blue uniform as the other men ran across the road towards him waving.

"My good man!" Bors greeted him as he slowed to a stop before him.

"I'm sorry, sir, but you can't enter here," said the policeman.

"Why?" the question seemed simple enough to Bors as he asked it and smiled heartedly at the man.

"It clearly says do not cross."

"Ah," exclaimed Bors. "My apologies, but alas I cannot read."

"I'm sorry, but the area has been cordoned off." He indicated towards the yellow tape as he spoke. "This is a crime scene," he explained, "you are not allowed in here."

"Your words," said Bors slowly. "I do not understand their content."

"You're not allowed in here, sir," said the policeman politely.

"But why?" asked Bors again. "'Tis not a free country." The man seemed puzzled for a moment and Bors continued, "Am I not permitted to wander where I wish?"

"Not here, sir," insisted the policeman. "This is a crime scene. A serious crime has been committed and your presence may contaminate the scene."

"Your words still make naught sense to me," said Bors shaking his head.

"I am sorry, sir, but I am going to have to ask you to leave."

"Are thee threatening me?" asked Bors, his hand resting on the hilt of the sword.

"No, sir," said the policeman. "Please, if you could…" He indicated towards the yellow cordon.

"What is thine purpose?" demanded Bors.

"I beg your pardon?"

"Ye heard me!" roared Bors. "What is thine purpose?"

"I am here, sir, to keep people like you out!"

"Ah, I see now," laughed Bors. "Thoust is a guard!"

"Yeah, well... sort of... now if you could..."

Bors spied his comrades waving to him from the crowd, who had turned and were watching the exchange between the police officer and the knight with interest and reluctantly the large knight moved back behind the cordon and joined his comrades. "Yon blue guard has ushered me away," he complained.

"'Tis good that he did," whispered Tristan, clutching at his arm and pulling him through the crowd towards the rear of the congregation of people.

"Has thee lost thine nerve, old friend?" snapped Bors frowning.

"No, my Lord," snapped Tristan. "Yon blue guard is an official of the new crown; their presence is most lawful."

"They are akin to a sheriff," added Percival.

"I understand," said Bors nodding as he looked over the crowd towards the police officer who was standing talking to a comrade looking into the crowd.

"Their presence is most severe," insisted Tristan in hushed tones. "It would appear that one such as ourselves may have slain a youth."

"Mordred," breathed Bors. Tristan nodded. "Then what should our recourse be?"

"We need to withdraw to think our actions," said Tristan.

Bors spied the public house beyond the cordon and pointed past the tent. "Yonder ale house," he said softly. "'Tis our goal. I suggest we continue with our quest and not let these matters interfere with our goal."

"Aye, my Lord, but the two could be connected—"

"Is thoust art saying we should proceed with utmost caution?" Tristan nodded at the statement and moved slightly behind the larger knight causing Bors to laugh. "Thoust is too careful." He pushed his comrade before him and ushered him towards the building. "There is naught to be scared of in yonder building except for the strength of the ale inside," he laughed and pushed Tristan forward.

The knight spied the same tape which had sealed off the road behind them and cast a glance towards Percival, who answered with a shrug and followed the two up the steps. "There does not seem any of ye blue guards," he remarked as they stood outside the building, casting a wary eye around them. A sound from overhead broke their chain of thought and the three knights averted their gaze upward where a helicopter hovered over the tree line for a moment before moving across the town. "What is yon whirlybird?" asked Percival covering his eyes as the glare from the setting sun masked his eyesight.

"Some vile creature," ventured Bors.

"I think not," said Tristan with his hand covering his forehead. "'Tis metal of nature," he said. "I believe it could be a carriage."

"That flies like a bird!" laughed Bors. "Thoust has been in the hostelry already!"

"Nay, my Lord, but I have seen many strange things since we have awoken," he confided softly. "Many of these carriages; both in the air like a bird and on the ground."

"I do not comprehend such things," said Bors.

"'Tis true," insisted Tristan. "Yonder carriages," he said pointing towards a line of parked cars. "Run without horses."

Bors stared at him for a moment, then laughed and pushed his bulky frame beneath the yellow tape. "Thoust jest, old friend," he said and with one final glance along the street he pushed at the door of the pub.

Tristan looked at Percival and sighed, following the knight inside the pub. "'Tis a world of nightmares," remarked Percival before he too ducked beneath the tape and disappeared inside the building.

The scene which greeted them was of pure chaos. Glass littered the floor and strewn across the room were the remnants of tables and chairs which lay discarded throughout the room. "I would hazard a guess that Morgaine has paid a visit," said Tristan as he followed his comrades gaze around the room. Bors was lifting tables to their feet and replacing chairs beneath the wooden structures. His feet crunched the glass into the carpet as he moved across the floor, the tiny shards whispering their terrible secrets as they shone in the dwindling light within the bar.

"Aye, it would seem so," remarked Bors as he lifted one of the few remaining glasses that had not broken from the floor and held the vessel to his nose, sniffing hard at the contents. "And it would seem that she was not alone," he commented.

"Mordred?" queried Tristan as he moved further into the room.

Bors nodded and placed the glass on the table and straightened from his crouching position. He nodded over to a figure covered by a long white cloth close to the fireplace. "Be it the girl?" he asked cautiously.

Percival pushed his way into the room and moved briskly through the debris strewn floor to the body and lifted the cloth slightly revealing the corpse of a withered man beneath. He gingerly touched the skin and withdrew his hand quickly as the leathery brown flesh felt dry and brittle beneath the pressure of his fingers. "Nay, it would appear to be a man," he said moving his head from side to side as he surveyed the body. "He be dead," he said simply stating the obvious. "Morgaine," he whispered and replaced the cloth and stood gazing around the bar. "There doth seem no further person."

"Then we must assume that Morgaine has the girl," said Bors.

"What is our recourse?"

"Why that be simple," declared Bors as he strode towards the bar lifting the hatch and walking behind the counter. His hand pulled at a glass from beneath the bar and he placed it beneath a long white pump which stood proudly on the bar and tugging at the handle and laughed. "We raid the castle and rescue the fair maiden from the clutches of Morgaine Le Fay!"

Bors raised the glass to his lips and let the brown ale float past his lips and the white froth cast a covering over his moustache, while his comrades looked towards each other, both feeling an ever-growing sense of dread prevailing over the pair.

34.

Wonder of the Modern Age

Francis stood on the soft sand and gazed over the sea and watched as the waves crashed against the beach. He was becoming increasingly concerned, not over the condition of the sea but rather the dwindling light as the sun gently set on the horizon. He felt the looming presence of the Fisher King by his side and felt the soft touch of his decaying hand as it pressed down against his shoulder. "Follow the voice," he said softly to Francis' unspoken words.

"How did you…" His words trailed off as the Fisher King pressed a finger against his own parched lips then moved it up to the side of his head where he tapped gently. Francis turned back to the sea and continued to gaze out into the surf.

"My Lord." The voice at his side broke his silent meanderings and he turned his attention to Galahad who had joined him at the edge of the water. "Tell me," the knight began uncertainly. "Is this the time of restitution?" he asked.

"I'm sorry?" blinked Francis.

"'Tis a strange time and a strange land is true. But is this truly the time?" His eyes looked sadly at Francis through his heavy visor, almost pleadingly.

"I don't know," admitted Francis unsure of his answer. "What time?"

"The time," urged Galahad. "The time of the calling, when Excalibur calls for Arthur, King of the Britons." Galahad struggled with his words as the other two figures watched with keen interest at the answer.

Francis realised this whole thing had not just affected him personally, but also had torn these knights… no, not knights, but people from their own time and into a world not of their own making. He had not considered anybody else's feelings or thoughts during this, but now here he was with their future in his hands as well as his own. The thought made him glance down at the palms of his hands and he sadly shook his head as a sudden wave of guilt swept over him. All this time he had been feeling sorry for himself, and yet here were these people, pulled from their own time and own lives and placed here in a world completely alien to them as their world was to him.

"The weight of responsibility is a burden, young Francis," whispered the Fisher King.

Francis gazed up at his ancient eyes. "I never realised that they were looking for me, or rather depending on me," he said.

"They simply seek restitution, and they hope that is what thee can deliver them. Forgive them for their actions, as they are set in their ways; 'tis not of their making."

"But what is this restitution, and can I help them?"

"The restitution is the call of Excalibur," explained the Fisher King. "The time for Arthur to rise from the ashes and lead the Britons in war."

"That's not me," said Francis sadly averting his eyes to the sandy floor beneath his feet, almost feeling a wave of ashamed embarrassment wash over his body.

"Nobody said it was, young Francis," said the Fisher King. "But thee shall do what is expected when the time is nigh," he said cryptically.

"I don't understand," said Francis. "Shit! I don't understand much of anything that is going on!"

"The Lady will explain."

"Yes, you've said that, but how do I find her?" He followed the line of the Fisher King's arm as the giant raised his decaying limb and pointed along the beach towards a small boat moored on the sand. "You've got to be kidding!" exclaimed Francis. "We'll never find her in this light."

The Fisher King moved his hand to his waist, where he pulled at the scabbard which hung around a belt. He held it aloft before him and presented it to Francis. "Thee will need this," he said simply.

Francis gingerly reached out for the object and took it and pressed it against his body. It was simple in appearance with small indentations running along the shaft of the leather-bound sheave. Silver metal trim ran around the top and the bottom of the scabbard and Francis traced his fingers along the length of the object tracing the line of the pattern until finally touching the cold metal tip.

"The scabbard," he breathed and looked up at the Fisher King who nodded towards Francis. "Will this lead me to the Lady?" he asked.

192

"Thoust does not need to find her; she will find thee." The Fisher King turned and stalked slowly away, dragging his legs behind him as he pulled himself up the beach. "Follow the voice, young Francis."

"Wait! One more thing!" shouted Francis. The Fisher King paused and turned his head slightly smiling down at the boy. "Do you know?" he asked. "What will happen?"

The Fisher King lowered his head and turned away, speaking into the night air as he continued to pull himself up the beach. "I see a choice... a terrible choice... decisions must be made." He stopped and paused before speaking a final time. "Follow the voice," he said and disappeared into the night.

"Night is nigh," commented Percival as he gazed through the netting over the window of the pub and out onto the street. "We should make haste."

"Less haste," urged Bors as he pulled at the pump once again and stood watching the brown liquid flow into his glass. "We can use the cover of darkness to our advantage."

"I do not like it," insisted Percival.

"Thee would be scared of thine shadow!" laughed Bors as he drained the contents of his glass and wiped his mouth free of the white froth. "The night will mask our flight through yon forest."

"Aye and conceal a number of things ready to attack our personage."

"Thy caution is almost as bitter as this ale," snapped Bors and slammed the glass heavily onto the wooden counter of the bar. The glass shattered in his hand and tiny shards cut into his skin and dug deep into his fingers. The tension between the two men grew over the accusations thrown into the room and it was Tristan who moved between the comrades.

"Hold thy selves!" he snapped. "We argue like washer women in the marketplace." He glanced from Bors, who stood nursing the small cuts on his hands and Percival who stared at him from his position at the window. "Thee both talk with wisdom, but we cannot hazard caution or haste where a life is in danger." The two knights cast their gaze away from Tristan as shame descended over the pub. "Bors, pour thyself another drink and thee Percival take guard over yon window. We shall make haste forthwith, but we must take care of the blue guard," he warned and moved to the fireplace and stared up at the scabbard which hung over the long dead fire. He listened as the other two knights moved away, their feet crunching on the

193

glass covered floor before running his fingers over the object on the wall.

"'Tis not the scabbard," commented Bors from his position behind the bar as he pulled on the long white handle. He glanced towards the window briefly towards Percival as he directed his comment to Tristan.

"Nay," agreed Tristan who lifted the scabbard from the wall and weighed it in his hands. "'Tis a strange feel to it," he said as he moved his hands up and down. "It has a coldness across the body of the shaft and has a sheen." He brought it up to his eye line and stared down the body of the scabbard. "'Tis hard, but not of metal; 'tis soft but not of leather. 'Tis a strange substance."

Percival moved from the window to join Tristan at the fireplace and took the scabbard from his hands. "I cannot see the blue guards," he said simply as he stared at the object in his hands. "What kind of fakery is this?" he asked as he looked at Tristan. He held the plastic scabbard out towards Bors who had moved into the main body of the room with his full glass of ale.

He moved through the tables, catching the edges as he moved. "There is much strange in this place," he commented as he stopped next to a large box like device by the wall. He peered inside the device through the clear Perspex covering and placed his palm flat on the cool covering. "'Tis not glass," he stated as he moved his face closer to the cover. "What is yon box?" he asked himself as Tristan moved to his side and peered inside.

"'Tis for food," he stated as he too looked through the Perspex covering.

"How does thee know that?" demanded Bors.

"There." Tristan jabbed his finger against the cover. "Small plates," he said.

"I do not see," complained Bors.

"There," insisted Tristan. "Look deep, rows of tiny silver plates."

"Hah!" exclaimed Bors. "What manner of eating is that? Those plates would not fill a gnat's body let alone my own," he said slapping his hand against his rotund frame. He continued to peer through the Perspex glass covering the top of the box. "I see no food," he mused.

"It must be within," said Tristan.

Bors drained the remnants of his glass and threw it down on the floor where it shattered and mingled with the shards of others drinking vessels. "I see not how to obtain yon food," he complained and placed his hands on either side of the box and shook the device. The box tremored in his hands for a moment before one of the silver discs slowly fell from its place and lay flat on the surface of the inside. Bors laughed and shook the device again as he watched the disc light up and spin persistently in place.

"When I see your face, there's not a thing that I would change, 'cause you're amazing. Just the way you are..." The words erupted from the speakers mounted on the wall as the dulcet tone of Bruno Mars sparked from the jukebox.

The three knights jumped at the sudden burst of music. They drew their swords and glanced around the room in confusion. "Music!" snapped Bors. "Yet, I see no minstrel." Their eyes flicked over the bar and out into the small foyer, their swords waving before them as the sound of music continued the play in the air.

"She's so beautiful, and I tell her every day," the sound of music continued as the knights struggled to comprehend to source of the music.

"I understand not," complained Bors. "I see no minstrel." He waved his sword before him swinging wildly at air.

"Wait!" exclaimed Tristan as he leant nearer to the box pressing his hands against the cool Perspex as it vibrated beneath his fingers, he glanced upward towards a small box mounted on the wall above their heads. The raised his hand and placed his palm flat on the black mesh at the front of the speaker. It vibrated beneath his touch, and he frowned. "Yon music seems to emanate from this chest," he said as the music continued to play. He pointed towards the jukebox and spoke carefully. "The music seems to start from this point." His fingers traced an invisible line from the jukebox to the speaker. "And end here."

"What magic is this?" queried Bors.

"'Tis a strange contraption indeed."

"The whole world stops and stares for a while, 'cause you're amazing. Just the way you are!" The words continued from the speaker and Bors found himself smiling at the wall mounted speaker.

"'Tis a marvel," he said softly shaking his head. "'Tis becoming—"

"Take heed!" snapped Percival from the window glancing back into the room. "Blue guards' approach." He peered through the netted curtains which covered the windows and stared out into the street where two uniformed police officers had stopped their patrol of the cordoned area and were now walking towards the pub where the sounds of music spilled into the street.

"He is right," remarked Tristan peering past Percival into the street beyond the window. "Bors!" he snapped. "Cease that prattling."

Bors looked about desperately unsure of what to do. He raised his hands to the jukebox and brought them down onto the Perspex, which only made the track jump a groove and begin once again in an endless chant. "It will not cease," he complained hitting the device once again.

"They are near," urged Percival.

Tristan moved towards the jukebox and pushed Bors out of the way and stood for a moment staring at the device. "Go and guard the entrance," he spoke softly but forcefully enough for Bors to comply with his request. He watched briefly as Bors pushed his way past the tables towards the main door and thought if the music had not attracted the guards, then the noise made by Bors would surely have done so. He returned his attention back to the music chest and examined it carefully, tracing the wires which ran from the back of the device into the wall. "How near?" he shouted over his shoulder.

"They are on the threshold," whispered Percival ducking low beneath the window. Tristan nodded and glanced towards Bors, who had drawn his sword from its scabbard and stood erect by the main door. He shook his head and placed a finger against his lips, then pointed towards the door. His attention returned to the wires and he gripped them firmly in his hands and pulled hard. The black cord paid no resistance to his efforts and fell away from the wall sending the room into a deafening silence. Light spilled into the bar from the crack in the door as the wooden barrier to the outside opened slightly.

"I tell you," came the voice outside. "I heard music."

"You're sure? There's nothing now," came a second voice.

The knights hid in the semi-gloom of the darkening room as the voices invaded the silence. Tristan signalled towards Bors who moved silently through the room to the edge of the bar, close to the door.

"I think we should take a look," commented the first voice. The door was pushed open, and the first of two police officers stepped through into the bar. He cast a torch around the room and moved forward as his colleague followed cautiously behind. "Is there anybody here?" he asked into the room. Tristan ducked down low behind the jukebox as the light from the torch swept across the room; he glanced towards Percival who was kneeling beneath the window, his face set into a determined look and his hand resting on the hilt of his sword. "Anybody here?" he said. "Show yourself, it's the police." The officer moved further into the room, followed by his comrade and Tristan watched as Bors moved from the shadows behind the policemen.

Slowly he stood from his position. "Raise your hands where I can see them!" ordered the officer. Tristan pulled his arms slowly in the air, whilst paying attention to Bors as he stalked the officers from behind.

"I mean thee no harm," commented Tristan as he stepped forward.

"That may be but keep your hands in the air where I can see them," ordered the first officer. "Now then, why don't you tell me exactly what you're doing here?" he asked.

"Waiting for me!" laughed Bors as he grabbed both officers' heads at the same time and brought them crashing against each other. The knights watched in unison as the policemen fell to the ground in an unconscious heap.

"Well done," commented Tristan as he stepped over the bodies.

"Be they dead?" asked Percival as he moved from the window looking down at the officers.

"Nay, but they will sleep for hours," laughed Bors slapping him on the back as he stopped by the large knight. "Let us make haste," he said and glanced through the still open door into the darkening street.

"Aye, thoust is right. We should go," agreed Tristan. "For the castle."

35.

Beached

Francis stood on the beach with his colleagues and closed his eyes allowing the evening air to sweep through his air and cleanse his mind. A whispering voice nagged inside his ear as it carried on the breeze as it swept in across the sea. He looked along the expanse of the beach and the quietness of the entire area. Only he stood on the edge of the water, with his three comrades standing behind him as silent observers, just waiting expectantly for his instructions. His mind wandered to their fate and their roles and realised that their lives had been linked to his by this haunting voice which had called him to the point. Whatever choice he made now would tie them to him forever and despite his best efforts he could feel his chest bursting with pride.

"Come to me." The voice still drifted across the tide and toyed with Francis.

"Where are you?" he whispered quietly to himself as he stared out over the sun towards the setting sun in the distance.

"Come to me."

"I can hear you; I just can't see you."

"Come to me."

Francis closed his eyes and allowed his senses to listen and feel the voice. "I hear you," he whispered.

"What is the youth doing?" whispered Bedivere as he stood watching from his sandy position.

"He has lost his mind," commented Kay. "It has snapped."

"Nay, hold," said Galahad, "he listens."

The other two knights cast their gaze towards Francis who cocked his head to one side as he stood stock still.

"'Tis the pressure of leadership," continued Kay. "He cannot cope with the responsibility. Look he speaks to himself; 'tis a sign of madness."

"Do not mistake madness with greatness, my Lord," replied Galahad,

198

"even the most bent of minds can be driven by greatness. I have faith—"

"Thoust didn't though," snapped Kay.

"But he has been proven," said Galahad, "and I am loyal to my Liege. Whatever form he takes."

"Be still," snapped Bedivere. "See how he moves." He indicated towards Francis who was glancing down the beach, still with his eyes closed. "He is searching—"

"Searching?" queried Kay. "Thoust is as mad as yon king."

"Nay, he searches, look how he moves."

"Indeed," agreed Galahad, "but what or who does he search?"

"Come to me." The voice was insistent in its attitude as Francis turned his head listening to the breeze, his eyes tightly closed as he attempted to blot out all his other senses.

"I hear you, but I cannot see you," he mused. "I know you are near."

"Come to me."

He let the air caress his face and play over his senses... then he turned and frowned looking at his comrades on the beach. "Can you smell that?" he asked and watched in dismay as each knight shook his head. "Sweet like apples," he insisted.

"'Tis the Isle," commented Bedivere.

"What?"

"The Isle," explained Bedivere. "'Tis where the Lady resides." He stepped forward to the edge of the sea and gazed out over the ocean. "When I cast Excalibur into the lake, I journeyed to the fabled Isle of Apples, where a small lake sat in the centre of the Isle. I remember the fragrance..." His words belied his own feelings as Francis could see a pain to his words as he thought back through the centuries. "The sweetness in the air, the aroma of apples and flowers which played with thy senses," he said wistfully. "I remember throwing the sword far across the water, where it was caught by the Lady." He shook his head and looked at Francis. "If thoust can smell apples, then it must be the Lady."

"I can hear her in my head," he confided to the knight, glancing briefly towards the other two. "And I can smell the scent of apple."

"Then follow your senses," urged Bedivere.

"But... there is nothing there."

"The Isle lays across the water," remembered Bedivere. "We must travel by sea." He pointed out across the water. "You lead us, and we will follow."

"But what if I cannot do it?" asked Francis. "What if I'm leading you all to your deaths?"

"Death holds no fear or barrier for us, young Lord," commented Bedivere kindly. "If we die, then we die for a noble cause." He looked towards Galahad and smiled. "He has faith in you young Lord, as do I. You will make the right choice… I know you will."

"You haven't answered my question," whispered Francis. "What if I'm leading you to your death?"

"As I have said, death holds no fear for any of us. We were born to serve; we follow the noblest of quests and know of the consequence of our actions. There is not one man among us who would not lay down our life for our king, or our belief. I choose to follow thee, as do we all." He smiled at Francis as he spoke. "We have all died before," he commented, "and are cursed to die again. Do not fear for us, young Francis. Our life is yours to command," he said proudly. "Now what is your choice."

Francis closed his eyes and listened hard to the voice in the air. "Come to me." It urged persistently on the breeze. "Come to me."

He looked over the waves and pointed out into the bay. "It is there," he said softly to Bedivere. "I can feel it."

"Then that is where we go."

"How do we travel?" asked Francis looking at Bedivere.

"You are king elect, that must be your choice."

"I can't even see the Isle…" His words were lost in the breeze as he glanced along the beach.

"If you can hear her voice, then you can follow it," whispered Bedivere softly as the other knights joined them at the water's edge.

"Where do we go from here?" demanded Kay. "We waste time standing looking at the sea like forlorn lovers."

"We go…" Francis pointed out over the sea. "There."

36.

Sea... King

"Thoust is mad!" exclaimed Kay. "Did I not say he was mad!" He slapped Galahad on the arm as he spoke.

"If he says that is where we must travel, then so be it," said Galahad.

"Look!" snapped Kay. "The darkness swallows the sun."

"Have at thee!" countered Galahad. "Your fear betrays thine own senses."

"I fear nothing!" snapped Kay angrily, resting his hand on the hilt of his sword.

"Stop it!" shouted Francis. "Stop it now! We have a problem," he continued. "We must travel out to sea and it is getting darker. If we do not leave now, we will not make land."

"And how do we travel?" retorted Kay. "Swim?"

Francis considered the sarcasm of Kay's words for a moment and smiled. "Thank you for your counsel, but I do not think it would be safe."

Galahad laughed at the look which crossed Kay's face and slapped him on the back. "My Liege jests," he roared through his laughter. "We sail." He pointed up the beach towards the dunes where a small rowing boat lay discarded amongst the sand and the beach grass. Its wooden frame was partially hidden by the fronds which submerged the small vessel as it peered out over the landscape.

"Fortuitous," remarked Bedivere and he walked up the dune to inspect the boat.

"'Tis a sign," breathed Galahad and looked upward towards the sky.

"Whatever it is," said Francis, "we need to make sure it is seaworthy before we set foot in that thing."

"Show me the boy!" snapped Morgaine as she stood before the crystal sphere in its stone mounting. The images swirled and cast a divine darkness within the confines of the ball as her reflection stared back through the glass.

"My Lady," Agravain spoke softly as he moved through the courtyard close to where Morgaine stood. She turned her attention to him, her face flashing with rage at her futile attempts to see the youth. "The female," he said hesitantly, "she is secure."

"At least something has gone well," she snapped viciously.

"My Lady is perplexed."

"Yes, Knight Commander. I am perplexed. I cannot find the location of that young knave," she spat and turned away from the sphere in frustration. "How am I to rule this obsolete world, if I cannot control the simplest of fashions?" She clenched her fists and approached Agravain, who flinched upon her as she glided through the ruins. "Be still," she purred. "I shall not harm thee," she insisted. "At least not yet," she teased as she smiled at the knight. She moved behind him and gazed through the open archway and sighed. "It is beautiful, is it not?" she asked and waited for Agravain to stand by her. "My nephew does not appreciate the world around him," she explained. "He does not see the colours; he does not see the patterns in the air or along the ground. He just feels for war and conquest; he is still young and impatient. He knows not the ways of the world."

"My Lady," said Agravain politely.

"There is more to the world than conquest," she said softly. "Look abroad…" The couple walked through the arch and up the ancient ruins into the night air and stared for a moment into the night sky. "Look, good Agravain, the night sky."

She waited for a moment as his eyes were drawn skyward and as he looked into the darkness; he could see the tiny sprinkle of light cast from a variety of stars which stared down from their heavenly position onto the landscape below. "The sky is not black," she said. "There is so much more, blue dances with black and sparkles of brilliance play in the sky." She sighed heavily as she spoke wistfully. "This is the beauty of reality, not the world we live in. Not the death of all those around us, this is the true divinity."

She waved out before her as she spoke, a soft smile cast across her lips, "This is the world that commands us… and with Excalibur, I shall rule it, Agravain. I shall twist nature to my design." She clenched her fist and raised it to the sky, a madness descending over her eyes. "My rule shall be complete dominance, not over the peoples of this land, nor the world, but over the very fabric of nature itself. We stand on the cusp of greatness, good Agravain; destiny is ours!" She smiled triumphantly as she spoke and flashed him an insane glare. "Gather your men and send them abroad into the land. I want the forest and the beaches around the castle searched. I want that sword, Agravain!" The palm of her hand connected with his unprotected cheek, leaving a vicious red mark. "Otherwise, you shall feel my wrath."

Bors pushed his way through the undergrowth and separated the plants for his comrades to step beyond into a small clearing. "Is thoust sure this is the way?" he queried.

"This is my homeland," remarked Tristan. "I know this country." He paused in the clearing waiting for Percival to push his way past Bors and into the clearing.

"Which way?" asked Percival glancing around the clearing, looking into the growing shrubs and making images of the trees and they stand tall and proud in the forest.

Deep grooves bore a mark in the sand and ran down the beach towards the edge of the water. Francis stood in the centre of the boat as it rested on the uneven sand and gently bobbed up and down testing the endurance of the wooden structure.

"We waste time," complained Kay as he watched the charade play out before him. "We should be travelling to the Isle."

"It's no good if the boat sinks," said Francis looking at the boards beneath his feet as he bounced. "We need to get there in one piece, dry hopefully," he added smirking.

"Aye, my old friend. The boy is right," commented Galahad then turned to Francis, "but to the same virtue my Lord Kay is also correct."

"I understand that," replied Francis, "but I have no intention of swimming to the Isle."

"Ha! The boy has mirth," laughed Kay and slapped Bedivere on the back, who turned and frowned at his comrade.

"The sea looks calm," Bedivere remarked as he turned his attention from Lord Kay and back out towards the ocean. Francis followed his gaze, the sea looked calm as the moon shine down and cast a shadow off its reflective surface and sat down in the boat. Bedivere briefly glanced at the sitting form of Francis. "Is thine boat worthy?" he asked.

"Yes," he stated simply. "Can't see any problems."

"Then we begin," said Bedivere softly and placed his hands on the rear of the boat and began to push the boat towards the water, where his two fellow knights joined him in his efforts to move the vessel into the sea. Francis rocked from side to side as the boat travelled along the remaining few feet of sand as the water lapped up against the bow.

On the beach, two figures moved through the sand grass, their eyes fleeting along the beach and out into the sea beyond. Their silver polished metal of the armour they wore shone in the light of the moon, which bore down as witness to their progress through the sand. Their eyes flirted with the light of the moon as they stalked the beach in search of prey, their bodies moved like predators as they used the shadows which danced the shoreline to hide themselves from view. They stopped in unison on the banks of the beach and gazed out through the night air and stared into the distance, staring at the small boat with its four-person cargo over slowly into the wash of the edge of the water.

"Return to the castle," spoke the first figure as he stretched to his full height, his armoured body silhouette by the moon. "Tell Morgaine... they are found."

37.

Time and Tide

The boat rocked to the rhythm of the waves as it pressed its way through the water and into the darkness. Francis sat at the head of the boat and stared out over the sea and watched as the water stretched out before them. The light from the moon shimmered and glistened in the reflective surface as the ripples from the boat cascaded off the paddles as they struck the tension of the water and expanded over the rolling waves, growing as they moved away from the boat. He closed his eyes and listened to the slight whisper in the air, focusing on the voice which still hung in his mind, slowly talking and beckoning him closer... closer to what he was believing was his destiny. He turned and sat with his back against the bow and watched his companions as they worked against the tide, pushing hard against the wooden struts which held the paddles in place. Even from his position, in this growing darkness he could see the bulging muscles of Lord Galahad and Lord Kay straining against their chain mail and see their chest heave beneath the heavy thick armour as they exerted themselves, thrusting the paddles through the water.

He glanced at the smaller knight – Bedivere, who sat at the rear of the boat, his hand gripped on the rudder as he moved the mechanism slightly to the gestures made by Francis as he listened to the voice inside his head. He watched Francis intently, matching his stare as he sat resolute, his eyes narrowing beneath his visor. "Penny for them?" he asked Bedivere.

Bedivere was brought out of his silent revere and blinked hard at Francis and frowned. "I know not what thee mean?" he asked.

"Penny for them," insisted Francis.

"I heard what thee said; I do not understand thine meaning."

"Your thoughts."

"I know not what thee mean?" repeated the knight.

"What are you thinking?"

"He is worried," commented Galahad.

"About what?"

"The Lady…"

"Explain," commanded Francis and almost blushed with embarrassment with the curtness of his talk.

"Yon Bedivere!" laughed Kay. "Couldn't throw thine sword back into the lake for thy Lady." He craned his head back towards Bedivere and smirked. "Three times, thy tried."

"Be still," snapped Bedivere.

"Once is a mistake, but twice!" Kay laughed and returned his full efforts to the paddle, channelling his strength into his movements.

"At least I fought at Camlann with honour."

Lord Kay narrowed his eyes as he pushed roughly through the waves. "I survived the battle," he said softly.

"Aye, but did thoust not arrive late?" chided Bedivere.

"Cease!" snapped Galahad. "You forget, we are knights of the round table." He paused in his rowing and glanced at both his companions. "We are the noblest and bravest of our age and here we are squabbling like children. Lest ye forget who we are, and act like it." His temper rose through the night, and he settled back into his task. "My Liege, which way?" he asked returning his attention to Francis who closed his eyes and listened to the voice, then pointed forward almost embarrassed by the sudden outburst of Lord Galahad. "Then I suggest we use our guile to effort our own journey."

The boat pushed on through the waves in silence and Francis sat at the head of the boat in quiet contemplation of the argument. He could understand the growing tension that was growing between the knights, and he hoped that once they had Excalibur, they could get answers. His foot played against a large thick rope and he bent forward and picked at the object holding it in his hands, his eyes wandering over the twine, turning it over in his hands. The rope was thick and long, and Francis struggled to close his hand over the expanse of its girth as he traced it towards the end, where a large, rusted metal hook was tied untidily to the end. Flakes of oxide fell from the old artefact as he pushed his fingers along the curve of the hook, tracing the large barb on the top of the hook. He shuddered and cast a gaze out into the water and briefly wondered what kind of creature a hook of this size had been used for.

"My Lady." Agravain's voice carried into the courtyard and reached Morgaine who was pacing around the stone pillar. He came rushing in and stopped before her, struggling to catch his breath under her scrutiny.

"Agravain," she breathed and calmly waited for his response.

"I have a report from my men," he panted.

"Excalibur?" she queried.

Agravain shook his head. "Nay, my Lady, but they have found the boy."

"'Tis not the news I had hoped, but it will suffice," she said and glanced around the ruins. "Mordred!" she shouted into the old walls and listened as her voice echoed around the ruin. She looked at Agravain and waited for his report, her arms folded across her chest as he spoke.

"My men have witnessed a small boat being put to sea off the coast, my Lady," he started.

"So, what of it!" commented Mordred as he strode into the courtyard.

"Where have thoust been?" asked Morgaine as she eyed Mordred up and down. "I warned thee about tormenting yon maiden."

"Do not worry, Aunt," laughed Mordred, "I have not lain a finger, or anything else upon the girl. At least yet," he said menacingly, "but have at thee, I shall have my sport with her once we have Excalibur." He adjusted the front of his breeches as he spoke. "I wish to taste her wares." He laughed.

"Then where—"

"Resting!" he snapped and turned back to Agravain. "What of thine boat?"

"My men have reported that four men have entered the water and have spent time journeying into the sea."

"Four men?"

"Aye, my Lord, it is believed that the young boy is with them."

"That is indeed good fortune," commented Morgaine as she strode towards the crystal sphere and gazed into the depths. "Show me the sea," she said softly into the glass and watched patiently as the mist inside the glass swirled into view.

Mordred joined her and peered over her shoulder. "I see nothing," he complained and turned away angrily.

"Be patient!" she snapped, casting a quick glance over her shoulder to the knight and shook her head at his impatience.

"He is there, My Lady. Of that I am sure... my men—"

"I understand your loyalty, Knight Commander," she said as she gazed into the orb, "and I believe what thee have said. Now I must concentrate." She frowned as she peered into the glass. "Where art thoust?" she urged. The waves crashed over the surf as the sea rolled in through the night onto the beach as Morgaine watched as the image scrolled slowly across the beach. Mist swirled and covered the image as she rubbed her fingers across the cold glass surface of the sphere. "Thoust must be here," she said softly into the glass as the image moved along the beach, then stretched over the sea. In the distance a small object rocked gently on the surface of the water and Morgaine leant forward frowning into the sphere. "There!" she exclaimed.

Mordred hurried to her side and peered into the glass. "I see him!" he laughed and pressed his hand against the surface of the sphere. "Galahad, Kay and Bedivere," he whispered clenching his fist at the sight of the three knights.

"Be still, Mordred," she chided placing a hand on his arm. She waved a hand over the top of the sphere and smiled as the mist gathered within the glass, covering the image inside the orb.

"'Tis a thick mist," complained Kay as he peered through the mist which had descended over the water.

"There feels a coldness," remarked Bedivere who shivered.

"I don't understand," said Francis peering through the mist.

"'Tis simple enough," rebuked Kay. "'Tis common that mist lies upon the water."

"No, I don't mean that."

"Aye, 'tis not natural." They turned to Galahad who was looking out over the side of the boat into the fog. "It feels strange... Unholy."

"I mean," urged Francis, "the way it came in." He struggled to find the words as he spoke, "It was clear a minute ago, with not a cloud in the sky... and now this." He waved about the boat indicating towards the thick mist which surrounded the boat.

"Magic," whispered Galahad.

"Morgaine." Galahad looked at Bedivere and nodded.

"We must take heed," he warned. The men looked about the boat and into the thick mist and scanned the calm water which surrounded them.

"You're right," said Francis looking at Bedivere, "it has got colder." A chill ran up his spine as he looked out over the water, running his eyes over the still water.

"No waves," whispered Kay as he followed the gaze of Francis across the water.

"No ripples," commented Francis.

Galahad looked up into the air and frowned. "No wind," he said.

"We had better keep moving," said Francis whispering hoarsely over the silence. He closed his eyes and strained to listen to the voice in his head. "I can't hear," he said softly.

"My Liege?"

"The voice. I can't hear it," snapped Francis, fear sweeping into his voice.

"Be calm," urged Bedivere, "from whence did the voice come?" Francis closed his eyes and struggled to hear the voice… still nothing, which way had it come, he had no idea, he realised; he had just been following her sound. "My Lord," urged Bedivere. Francis frowned; follow your feelings, he thought and raised his hand, pointing off into the mist. "Is thoust sure?"

"As sure as I can be." The knights looked around and pushed the oars through the water. Francis watched as the oars plunged into the calm water and stared as the impact caused by the wood striking the water made no sound or ripples.

Morgaine laughed as she walked from the sphere and into the ruins, where she stood before a large boulder which lay in its side on the grass. She brushed the moss from the rock and stared into a large crater of water which lay in the recess of the boulder. She waved her hand over the puddle and sat on the edge of the stone and laughed as she stared into the water as a thick cloud of mist swamped the small boat. Her fingers dipped into the water and trailed through the puddle stirring up small tidal waves as her fingers circled the water.

"'Tis a storm!" called Galahad as the boat rocked under the sudden influx of water pressure. He gripped the side of the boat and struggled to maintain his grip on the wooden oar in his hand. The actions of Kay and Bedivere mirrored his own as they struggled to retain their grip on the small boat as it was thrown across the waves. Francis fell onto the floor of the boat and grasped desperately at the seat which ran across the bottom of the boat.

"It isn't!" he shouted over the sudden rush of sound and the swell of the waves. "The sea was calm!" His voice was almost lost on the air as the boat rolled over the waves. "This storm isn't natural," he shouted as the words were snatched from his mouth and carried off over the turbulence.

Water cascaded over the sides of the boat as the small craft rocked violently on the surface of the water, thrown from wave to wave. The knights struggled under the pressure placed upon the boat and fell into each other as they desperately clung onto their oar. Water sprayed into the faces as a steady wash of water covered the floor of the boat.

"We are in fear of sinking," shouted Kay above the squall of the storm.

"We must be calm!" yelled Bedivere.

Waves hit the boat and water rolled over the sides into the vessel. Francis desperately struggled to stem the tide as the boat slowly buckled and filled from the growing monsoon.

"'Tis Morgaine!" shouted Galahad, his beard covered with water and the salty water flowing across his already gleaming armour.

Morgaine laughed as her finger circled the stone basin, rising a tidal wave of water within the boulder. She stood and surveyed the scene broadcast within the water and an insane smirk flashed across her cracked lips. "Feel my wrath, Arthur!" She laughed and plunged her hands into the depths of the puddle. Her manic laughter echoed throughout the castle as she stood by the ruined boulder, her hands thrust deep onto the cold surface of the rock beneath the surface of the stone.

The boat buckled and rocked as the waves grew stronger and less tolerant of the tiny craft which violated its body. "Hold on!" yelled Lord Kay as he struggled to maintain his position on his seat. The oar slipped from his grasp and fell over the side of the boat, sinking into the depths of the water which surrounded the boat. Laughter surrounded the boat as the sea buckled up, rising high into the air and throwing the vessel into a violent lurch which threw Francis across the seats and into the back of the boat, into Bedivere. The boat spun as the sea quietened and settled into a calm revere before swelling into a watery mound before the vessel.

"This is it!" yelled Francis as the sea rose into a mighty wall before the small wooden vessel.

Before the boat two watery humps grew in the wash and stretched out into the air, reaching and grasping through the mist for the sky above the water. The columns of water sprayed the occupants of the boat as the geyser of water forced its way upward… ever upward, then it sprayed outward, changing, forming into something else. Francis looked on with fear growing in his heart as the two columns of water slowly transformed before his eyes and five digits stretched and elongated from each geyser. The apparition before the boat swayed in the raging wind for a moment, flexing and bending as they felt the air around them. Francis could only watch with a horrified fascination as the columns slowly changed into a pair of massive watery hands which ebbed and flowed in the wind. Droplets of water fell from the fingers, and the spray reached out over the boat as the hands turned with a renewed vigour and energy.

"'Tis black arts," shouted Bedivere.

"'Tis Morgaine!" shouted Kay over the noise of the storm.

They watched as the hands flexed its fingers, before they stopped and turned so their palms faced the small boat. The first hand came crashing down on the water by the boat, throwing the vessel high in the air. The knights clung onto the wood of the boat desperately fighting against the sudden swell. The second hand crashed into the water throwing a large wall of water which crashed close to the boat, flinging the vessel high into the air.

Sir Galahad drew his sword as he clung onto the edge of the boat and swung his sword over the side and into the column of water which was now close to the boat. The arm reacted savagely and tossed the boat up into the air. Galahad buckled under the sudden force of the water and collapsed hard against the floor of the boat, the water crashing over his armour. His hand gripped at the thick rope which rolled across the surface of the boat and he tugged it close to his body, then forced himself up onto his hands and knees, steadying himself against another rise in water from outside the boat.

Another crash of wave brought Kay tumbling onto the floor of the boat by Galahad. "We are doomed to a watery grave," he whispered through gritted teeth.

"We have survived worse," commented Galahad.

"Not much," complained Kay as another sudden wave pushed him to the back of the boat, where Bedivere clung desperately held onto the rudder, water crashing over his body and drowning him in a relentless tidal wave of water.

"My Liege," started Galahad as he struggled to his feet, the rope held tightly in his hands.

"Don't," whispered Francis as another lurch forced him beneath the seat further.

"'Tis my duty to serve and protect," he said sadly as he stood staring into the dark sky, filled with cloud and mist. The watery hands rose high over the boat and reached through the mist as they stretched over the storm. Galahad placed one foot before the other and stared skyward, the rope in his hands and he began to swing the heavy hook, slowly at first, then as it grew in momentum, he raised it slowly over his head. "It has been a honour!" he yelled as he released the heavy hook high into the air towards the column of water. The hook spun and caught the geyser, wrapping around the first wrist and spinning through the air catching the second wrist, pulling the hands together in tight bondage.

"Galahad!" shouted Francis as he watched the rope pull against the water and pull the two hands close to each.

Galahad pulled hard on the rope, a grimace crossing his face as water sprayed across the boat. The hands crashed down into the sea throwing the boat into the air, riding high on a crest as the tidal wave of water from the impact savagely rocked the occupants. The water columns submerged into the water, dragging Galahad off balance and throwing him against the side of the boat. Blood forced its way through his clenched mouth and small rivers of crimson merged with the salt water as he struggled to pull against the rising pressure.

"For Excalibur!" he shouted above the noise. "For Briton!" He looked at Francis and smiled, relaxing his grip on the rope. "For Arthur," he said quietly. The hands lurched and pulled violently against the constraints and dived deep into the depths of the salty water. "My Liege," he whispered finally and closed his eyes as the hands pulled on final time, submerging completely beneath the surface of the ocean and pulling Sir Galahad overboard.

Francis pulled himself from his watery seat and leant over the edge of the boat. "Galahad!" he yelled at the water. "Galahad! Galahad!"

38.

The Rescuers

Bors broke into a clearing on the edge of the castle and looked over the ancient remains. A noise behind him disturbed his thoughts and he turned his head to watch his two companions push through the undergrowth. "Tintagel," he whispered, his voice dripping with sadness at the site of the ruined castle.

"My home," said Tristan as he pushed past the large knight and stood over the castle, looking into the remnants of the site from his cliff top vantage point. "What has happened?"

"Time has not been kind," offered Percival gently.

"Time be cursed," spat Tristan. "This not time; this is wanton carnage." He turned from the castle and placed a hand across his eyes. "'Tis neglect," he said sadly.

Bors placed a hand on Tristan's shoulder. "'Tis sad, but hold... we have a life to save," he said softly.

Tristan nodded sagely and turned back to the castle and stood overlooking the castle for a moment, his heart heavy with regret and sadness tainting his soul. "Yonder path will lead us to the castle," he said sadly.

"We are not to go through the front door," exclaimed Percival.

"Nay, the path leads to the rear," he countered, pointing around the main body of the castle. "There lays an escape passage constructed for my family in times of siege," he explained as he began his slow descent down the path. "Few know of it, and it will offer us safe passage within the castle."

The three knights walked slowly down the path, picking their way through the shrubs and undergrowth growing across the path, partially covering the small narrow path.

The shrubs parted behind them, and a knight stepped out and signalled to an unseen figure behind him, hidden by the thick bramble. "Go forth," he said quietly, watching the retreating knights. "Inform Lord Agravain we have visitors."

Mordred peered over Morgaine's shoulder into the water and licked his lips in excited fever. "Is he dead?" His question hung in the air for a moment and Morgaine chose to ignore her nephew as she continued to stare into the water. She straightened and returned to her sphere which was still and clouded, the image within the ball was blurred and still offered the image of Francis peering over the edge of the boat, screaming into the water. "Morgaine," whispered Mordred, "is he dead?"

"Be still, Mordred!" snapped Morgaine. "He is not important."

"He is to me!" retorted Mordred. "Is he dead?" He fervently grasped at Morgaine's arms and shook her as he questioned her.

"I warn thee," snapped Morgaine. "My patience runs thin."

Movement at the edge of the courtyard brokered the confrontation between the two main antagonists as a knight entered and whispered into the ear of Agravain. He listened to the report and moved respectfully into the centre of the yard. "My Lady," he said slowly, bowing towards her.

"Speak."

"We have visitors, My Lady."

"Explain?"

"Three trespassers have been spotted travelling towards the castle on the westerly road."

Morgaine turned to the crystal ball and spoke into the glass. "Show me!" she commanded. The image of Francis blurred and changed, showing a vegetation covered path winding down towards the rear of the castle and three knights picking their way through the heavy bramble. "It would so appear we have company." She smiled.

"Does thoust want them bringing here?" asked Agravain.

"No, not yet" she purred and looked at Mordred. "We know their destination. We shall let them continue to their goal, then we shall take them."

"Their goal?" queried Mordred.

"Idiot!" spat Morgaine. "The girl." She turned on Mordred. "Is it not obvious?" she said. "They have been sent to save the girl." She looked at the Knight Commander and barked her orders towards him. "Observe their progress, but do not engage... yet. We shall let them reach their objective before we engage." She turned back to Mordred. "Does thoust think thee can manage that?"

Mordred pulled his sword from its scabbard and ran his hand along the expanse of the blade. "It will be a pleasure, Aunt," he purred, flashing a twisted wry smile.

Tristan pulled at the undergrowth which was growing up the side of the castle wall. His heavy armoured gloves pulled at the thorny barbs and tiny fangs dug into his exposed skin on his arm as he pulled and moved the vines. "'Tis a passage around here," he said as he worked.

Bors and Percival stood with their backs to their comrade and stared out over the extending landscape. "Hurry," urged Percival. "I feel we are being watched," he complained.

"Thoust are letting your imaginations to cloud your mind," remarked Bors. "There is naught here, except us; we are undetected."

"I do not feel so…" Percival held his sword aloft as his eyes flicked over the trees and shrubs. "'Tis perfect cover," he complained. "Does thoust not feel it in the air?" he asked and waited for Bors to shake his head. "There is something here."

"Thoust is too cautious," he complained.

"Thine reckless nature shall be your death!" snapped Percival, then his nature softened slightly. "I am sorry, old friend, but I do not like this." He indicated towards the trees.

"I like it not either, Percival," admitted Bors, "but are we not divine in our quest and true of heart. Have faith, my Lord."

"It is here!" exclaimed Tristan and pulled at a large prickly burst of bramble. He pulled his sword from its scabbard and chopped savagely at the thick undergrowth, letting large swathes of branch and thorn to fall away from the gaping hole in the wall. "This should lead into the bowels of thine castle," he explained, "close to the dungeons."

"What of the ruined building?" asked Percival. "Is this not a risk?"

"We must take the risk," said Tristan. "'Tis a maiden's life at risk if we do not."

"Nay, I mean, the building," Percival explained. "If the building is in ruins, is it not possible that the tunnel is also decayed?"

"Come, young Percival," laughed Bors pushing past both knights and into the mouth of the tunnel, "we push forward."

"Wait!" whispered Tristan. "We must proceed, but Lord Percival… if thoust could remain here."

"Nay, I go with thee," complained Percival. "Do not mistake my caution for cowardice. My blade thirsts for blood and glory as much as thine."

"Your honour is not in question," remarked Tristan, "but our safety is."

"What does thoust mean?"

"Our retreat must be guarded to ensure we can escape with yon maiden."

Percival nodded. "Why me?"

"This is my home," explained Tristan. "I know the castle better than anyone, and Bors is larger and stronger than us both together. Thoust has stealth and cunning which can conceal our retreat. If thoust can remain on guard to protect our retreat and ensure our safe passage. We may need a fleet return."

"I understand," said Percival nodding. "May God be with thee," he said and offered his hand towards Tristan.

"And thee," he whispered and ducked into the tunnel, swallowed by the darkness.

"Be careful," whispered Bors as he hovered for a moment at the mouth of the tunnel before he too allowed the darkness to swallow him.

"And thee," whispered Percival as he watched them go. He stood for a moment looking at the mouth of the tunnel and contemplated following for a moment, before sheaving his sword and leaning against the wall of the castle glancing around into the darkness.

The bushes moved slightly, causing Percival to start and he pulled his sword from its scabbard almost immediately and stepped forward towards the bush. He swung his sword into the vegetation and watched as a small rodent ran from its confines. He smiled and watched it run across his feet and escape down the tunnel beyond.

"Go yonder vermin," he said softly as its tail disappeared into the darkness and pushed his sword back into its scabbard at his waist. He stood facing the yawning gap in the wall and moved forward, with his hand on the hilt of his sword. The bushes moved again behind him, and he barely offered another glance as they parted and from the confines of the thorns three knights burst from the bramble and rushed towards Percival, two grasping at his arms whilst the third stood before the knight grinning in his face. "Mordred!" spat Percival. "It would appear not all rats are sleek in nature," he mocked.

Mordred swung the back of his hand across the face of Percival, drawing a thin sliver of saliva to explode from his mouth as his head was thrust back. "Me thinks thoust should show some respect," he countered as he circled the knight. "Thy have grown ignorant over the years."

"Release me and I would still best thyself."

Mordred laughed heartily. "Do you think me a fool?" he said as he walked over the tunnel mouth, resting his hand on the top of the tunnel and peering in through the darkness. "Where does this lead?" he asked.

"I know not," admitted Percival.

"Thee lie!"

"I know not," repeated Percival.

"Who art thou with?" Mordred turned to face Percival as he asked the question. He waited for a moment in silence before swinging his fist deep into the knight's stomach. "Thoust shall tell me," he insisted as Percival doubled over, a sudden pain coursing through his body. "I shall repeat… who art thoust with?"

"I journey alone."

"You lie!" he yelled and brought his hand sharply across his face drawing blood from his mouth. "I know you are accompanied!"

"I journey alone," insisted Percival.

Mordred clenched his fist and brought it to bare once again in the stomach of the knight and watched as Percival sagged beneath the blow. The two knights holding Percival strained against his weight as his knees sagged beneath the weight of his body weakening from the blow to his stomach. "Take him away," ordered Mordred, returning his attention to the tunnel. "Inform the Knight Commander that I shall meet him inside." He watched as the knights bowed slightly whilst holding the heavy form of Percival in their arms, then as they crashed through the surrounding undergrowth he moved into the darkness of the tunnel.

Tristan pushed at the roots which poked through the stonework from the ceiling. His fingers pressed against the edge of the wall and watched as parts crumbled beneath his touch. "We should be beneath the main castle wall," he commented as he forged his path through the darkness.

"I hear noise from behind," whispered Bors.

"There is naught," said Tristan, his eyes flirting with the darkness.

"I can hear—"

"There is naught!" snapped Tristan. "Our goal is close, and Lord Percival guards our rear." He pushed at more roots as they covered his face. "We must focus."

"Indeed," agreed Bors, "but let prudence be our word and caution our companion."

"If Morgaine has the maiden," said Tristan, "she will have placed her in the dungeon if they still exist."

"The walls are confined," complained Bors as they moved slowly along the tunnel. "If we are attacked—"

"Then we will defend ourselves, now be still." Tristan pushed forward, his temper rising as the extent of the ruins became more apparent. He stepped over rocks and bricks which lay discarded over the floor of the tunnel and shook his head sadly. He could see a small wooden door in the darkened passage, small cracks of light pushed through the rotting planks. "There," he whispered, "ahead." Bors looked past his shoulder and could see the small door at the end of tunnel and followed Tristan to it. "'Tis locked," said Tristan quietly.

"Out of my way," commanded Bors, "I shall remove the barrier."

"Nay, we must be silent," warned Tristan as he put his shoulder against the door. "Assist me," he said as he pushed firmly against the rooting wood. Bors moved into position and placed his shoulder against the door and pushed his extreme body mass against the wooden barrier. The rotting door shifted slightly under the pressure of the two knights and gave way, offering access to the ruined echelons of the castle. Tristan stepped into the open space beyond the door, forcing the overgrown creepers as they hid the door from view. Parts of wood scattered over the floor and the door gave way and metal feet sank into the moss lined flooring. He knelt and ran his fingers over the floor and looked up at the exposed sky, through the open roof top. He sighed heavily and could feel remorse sweep through his body as memories past through his mind; Blancheflor and Rivalen, his father and mother and his uncle King Mark of Cornwall before his mind wandered to his dear sweet Iseult… all dead. He felt a hand placed on his shoulder and he looked up into the soft brown eyes of Bors and smiled sadly. "They are lost," he remarked.

"Aye, time has been harsh," agreed Bors, "but let us mourn later. There is one life which is alive now."

Tristan nodded and stood, gazing along the ruined walls of the castle. "From my recollections, the dungeons should be this way." He pointed down stone lined corridor which ran along a moss lined passage. Bors followed his eyes casting around as they walked slowly through the ruined building.

Behind them the creepers covering the tunnel parted and Mordred peered through the ivy and watched their progress down the passage and smiled cruelly, before pulling himself free of the tunnel and pressing himself against the wall of the castle, following… moving slowly and carefully picking his way through the debris.

Gwen sat on the floor; she felt cold against the open roof and shivered as the wind whistled through the open rafters. She brought her legs up against her chest and pulled her arms around herself as she felt her cold arms press against her hands. Her plain white t-shirt giving no protection against the savage cold; she tucked her head into her knees she sobbed into her brown, tight fitting jodhpurs. Tears stained her legs, as a flurry of water ebbed from her eyes and masked slight rivers across the face, staining her ivory skin. Cold, hard chain bit into her wrists and ankles as her shackles restricted her to the small, confined room. Puddles lay across the floor, and light streamed in through the open roof, where once great beams would have masked the line of stars which hung mournfully in the night sky staring balefully down on her. Large bales of hay sat in the corner of the room, and fragments of straw scattered across the floor as small insects and rodents ran across the strewn dirty floor. Fear had been replaced with despair and her sobs masked her terror at the present position, alone and cold in a nightmare world.

A noise from the door alerted her to company and she braced herself against another nightmare. She pressed her legs further into her body and watched as the door opened slightly, and a helmet slowly moved into the room. "Go to hell!" she spat as the knight moved into the confined space.

"Be thy not scared, my Lady," said the knight softly. "I am Lord Tristan of Cornwall." He smiled and pulled his helmet from his head and moved into the room. "I have been sent by my Lord Francis to set thee free."

"Francis," she whispered, a smile breaking out over her face. Tristan could see the marks of her dismay across her face as scars of tears mixed with the mucus and tinged her beauty.

"Aye, my Lady, he awaits," he said softly and moved closer to her, his hand raised before him.

"I can't move," she said, a sob escaping from her mouth as she spoke. She raised her hands, and the sound of the chains shook the room slightly as the echoed tinged the air.

"Be still," said Tristan as he knelt by the girl. His hands touched the metal of the links, and he ran his fingers across the thick chain. He could feel her tense as his fingers inspected the chain and his touch brushed against her skin. "I will not hurt thee," he insisted, looking into her eyes. She shook her head and looked past him, her body tensing and moving under his presence. Tristan looked behind him and could see Bors framed in the doorway, the light silhouette behind his large frame. "Be not afraid," he said, "he is a friend." He waved Bors into the room and the large knight move quietly inside, his feet moving silently across the debris in the dungeon.

"I am Bors," he said softly and bowed towards her, his face breaking into a smile. She could see the light play over his large bulk and even through the darkness which surrounded her could make out the scar which ran over his forehead. "You are safe, my Lady." He smiled as he spoke.

For the first time in hours, she felt safe. Her thoughts guiltily went to her father, and Lance and despite herself found herself smiling. She glanced at Tristan who had pulled his sword from its scabbard and had placed it between two links on the chain, then her eyes went back to Bors, framed in the doorway.

His smile froze and his eyes bulged in the light as he stood watching his comrade. Gwen frowned at his expression and watched as the front of his chest began to bulge beneath his armoured chest plate. His body contorted and writhed forward as the bulge grew outward and slowly a point forced its way through the metal armour, rising into the air, slowly and methodically. His fingers stretched outward on his hands as his arms tremored beneath the extreme pain coursing through his body, his eyes bulged upward and rolled in his head. His smile turned into a grimace as blood forced its way through the open orifice and tinged his ginger beard. A final thrust forced the end of the sword through the last part of the armour and a scream was muffled by blood as Bors sagged, skewered on the end of a long blade.

Gwen watched with horror as the giant of a man sagged beneath his body weight and sunk to his knees, blood flowing freely down his chest and staining his armour, while crimson tinged his beard as his mouth froze open in a quiet scream. Mordred stepped from behind the knight and smiled as he held his sword, deep in the back of Bors and smiled into the room.

Gwen screamed.

39.

Sounds of Sirens

"Galahad!" yelled Francis, his hands forcing their way through the still water on the sea. Francis stared into the water and yelled into the dark inky depths, his hands working hard to part the waves and forge a path deep below. "Galahad." His yells died on the surface of the water as he desperately clawed further and further, leaning over the edge of the boat. He felt two large hands on his shoulders and offered no resistance as the hands pulled. "Galahad," he whispered softly, the breeze taking the words from his mouth as remorse mixed with guilt and played over his senses.

"He is gone," commented Lord Kay, who placed himself opposite Francis and stared into his eyes. "We can mourn later, for now we have a quest to complete."

"We can't... I mean... I can't," stammered Francis. "We can't do it."

"Of course, we can!" snapped Kay.

"No, no, we can't." Francis looked over the edge of the boat. "I never asked him to come, but he did anyway. He gave his life for us... for me."

"As would we all, my Lord," said Kay and placed his large hands over Francis'. "None of us chose to follow you, but we do so. This is our duty... our destiny. We are knights of noble birth and noble of heart. We are bound by duty, our duty to our king. There is not one man of us that would not lay down our life for thee."

"But I'm not the king," cried Francis. "I'm nobody."

"Nay," said Bedivere, who had remained silent up until this point staring out across the water as the small boat floated aimlessly. "You are the last Pendragon and as such, thee are a direct descendant to Arthur and by rights of divinity, we are yours to command."

"But I can't ask you—"

"We know the risks!" snapped Kay. "Now cease this prattling and leave it for washerwomen!" He looked at Lord Bedivere and nodded. "We have a duty to perform, now I suggest we continue."

"I agree," said Bedivere. "We must continue to the Isle." They both looked at Francis who was still staring down at his hands on his wooden seat, water splashing around his feet. He rubbed his face and looked at the two knights and nodded solemnly. "Let us swap places," said Bedivere as he sidled forward onto the seat next to Kay.

Francis stood carefully and picked his way between the two knights and sat at the back of the boat, leaning mournfully against the wooden rudder and sighing heavily. He gazed out across the sea, and realised the mist was clearing as the small boat rocked on the waves. A slight breeze picked up and pushed the boat forward on the water. He sat and looked mournfully as the knights sat in silence on the bench, their hands draped over the side clawing at the water and pushing great amounts of spray to cast up over the side as they worked in unison pulling the boat through the sea.

The wind picked up and caused Francis to stare up at the sky. His eyes picked at the stars as the cloudless sky stared down mocking their journey and he feared a repeat of recent events. He cast his gaze back towards the shoreline and realised that his vision was blurred from land. Guilt swept over him as the disappearance of Galahad played heavily on his mind, and he looked towards Kay and Bedivere and wondered what they were thinking. The words cast by both knights had done little to placate his own feelings that his actions had led them to his death... there that word... death, so final, so pronounced. It seemed so final, so complete. He struggled to accept the death and glanced back to the water, hoping against hope that he would see a flurry of bubbles broker the surface, followed by an explosion of water heralding Sir Galahad from his watery prison... but nothing. No bubbles. No heroic escape.

"Come to me." The voice again. It played with him as it hung around his ears.

"I hear you," he said softly, glancing at the knights.

"Do nothing," the voice came back soft, but firm in its instructions.

"What do you mean?" he asked a little too loudly, causing Bedivere to glance at his position. He gave the knight a wide berth as he stared at Francis and listened to the voice carried on the breeze.

"Do nothing," it repeated. "The breeze will bring thy to me."

Francis sat in the boat for a moment, staring out to sea doing nothing. He looked at the two knights still paddling, forcing their hands through the water. "Stop!" he instructed.

"My Lord?" asked Bedivere.

Francis held a hand high in the air and showed his palm to Bedivere. "Be quiet," he whispered. Bedivere looked at Kay and shrugged, sitting back on his seat and straightening. "Can you hear that?"

Bedivere listened for a moment and frowned. "I hear naught," he said eventually.

"No, no, listen," urged Francis as he strained against the breeze.

"The boy is tinged with madness," commented Kay. "It spreads like plague." He nudged Bedivere in the ribs as he spoke and smirked. Bedivere frowned and shot Kay a glance to silence him.

"What can you hear?" asked Bedivere.

"Singing," said Francis softly.

"The Isle," Kay whispered almost inaudibly and looked out over the edge of the boat. "We must be close."

Francis strained his hearing as he struggled to pick up on the melody which haunted him across the breeze. It teased at his senses and pulled him forward. "It's beautiful," he breathed.

"Be careful, my Lord," warned Bedivere. "There are many temptations both on land and sea."

"I can hear..." Francis seemed intoxicated by the sound of the singing which enticed him forward. "There," he said finally pointing to his left. "Start paddling," he ordered.

"But, my Lord, thoust told us—"

"I don't care what I told you... paddle!" he snapped back.

"Do nothing," whispered the voice. "The breeze will carry you to me." The singing blocked out his senses and pulled at his loins as the melody teased and fulfilled his desire. "Come to me." The voice was insistent, but the sound of singing was too much of a distraction, too much of a lure.

"My Lord, I must advise—"

"You shall obey your king!" snapped Francis as he listened to the singing in his head. His hand wandered to his crotch almost subconsciously as the singing became more frantic and erotic in nature; it fuelled his desire and fulfilled his needing of love and sex. "I hear you," he whispered into the breeze.

"His mind is addled," whispered Kay.

"Nay, I fear he has heard the siren."

"That is just a tale," remarked Kay. "Surely… to scare the unwary."

"Perhaps but are we all not stories in the end."

"I hear nothing," commented Kay as he watched Francis rubbing the front of his trousers as he stared into the sea. "Are we not safe?"

"Nay, if yon lad can hear thee siren, then all our lives are in danger."

Lord Kay looked over the edge of the boat as the water was disturbed by a splash. He caught a glimpse of a tail as it broke the tension of the water, then just as quickly disappeared.

40.

Painkiller

"What is thine nature?" asked Mordred as he stood before the chained figure of Lord Percival. Percival smiled at Mordred through his blood-stained teeth and spat in his face, smirking as the red tinged saliva slid down his cheek. Mordred wiped the fluid away with the back of his hand as brought it savagely across Percival's face. "I shall ask thee one final time!" he shouted in his face. "What is thine nature?"

"I shall not betray my king," said Percival hoarsely through cracked lips.

"He is not your king," laughed Mordred, moving into the centre of the room. "He is but a boy." He stopped before a large cauldron and surveyed its contents before turning his head back to Percival. "He cares not of you nor your kindred."

"Thee lie," said Percival, his eyes never leaving Mordred as he spoke.

"His motives are purely his own," chided Mordred.

"As are thee," spat Percival coughing as he spoke.

"Quiet," said Mordred softly. He turned his attention back to the cauldron, with its bubbling fluid within. Steam rose and fell as the fire burnt beneath the pot, scolding the dark black metal and bubbles rose and burst on the surface of the water. Mordred pulled at a metal rod close to the fire and placed the end beneath the pot and stood watching as the tip glared a vicious yellow as the fire played over the metal. "Thoust has a nice body," remarked Mordred staring into the flame. "Easily burnt," he teased.

Percival pulled at his constraints as they bit into his skin; his arms stretched high above his head and the armour stripped from his naked torso. Small cuts and abrasions scattered across his body and traces of bruises stained his skin from the relentless onslaught of Mordred's attention. His body felt weak as he hung limply struggling to maintain his posture in his harness. Through his swollen eye he could make out the form of Tristan laying on a harsh wooden frame, his hands and feet bound by shackles and pulled hard by thick heavy chains which ran through large metal spindles at each leg of the bed. Like Percival, Tristan had been stripped to the waist, and cuts and bruises littered his body with patches of dried blood layered over his torso.

Percival glanced back at Mordred who was toying with the long metal pole which sat idly in the fire, tempted by the flame and glowing with the increasing heat. He watched in morbid fascination as Mordred pulled the poker from the flame and held it close to his face, grinning and pulled a hideous smirk in the shadow of the flame.

"Now let me ask thee again," he said carefully walking slowly towards Percival, metal pole gripped tightly in his hand. He stood before the weakened form of Percival and placed the poker close to his face. Percival could feel the heat from the metal warm his cheek as it hovered close to his skin. Mordred leant close to Percival and whispered, holding the pole menacingly close. "What is thine nature?" he whispered.

"I know not," said Percival defiantly.

"Pity," mused Mordred teasing the red-hot metal. "My friend," he said, indicating towards the metal pole, "desires to taste bare skin." He laughed and moved over to the prone body of Tristan and moved the heavy pole over his body. "Now I ask thee again, what is thine nature?"

Percival clamped his mouth shut tightly and turned his head from the sight as Mordred smiled and lowered the poker close to the skin of his comrade. Screams raged through the castle ruins and the metal touched bare skin and burnt at the rich tender flesh of the knight. He pulled the poker from his body to reveal a deep red groove in Tristan's skin and stood menacingly close to the knight once again with the metal pole held out over his chest. Mordred cast a glance towards Percival and smiled, before lowering the poker against the chest of his friend. Tristan screamed as the red-hot metal singed his flesh; his body contorted with pain as the poker thrust down and ran over his chest. He could feel tears of pain and anger surge through his body, but despite himself remained quiet.

Mordred smirked and walked back to the fire, placing the metal back under the boiling cauldron and turned to survey Percival. "Now," he said softly, "imagine how the metal would cut through the flesh of…" He trailed off in thought for a moment before flashing Percival an evil grin. "A young girl." He laughed as a look of horror danced over the knight's face. "Or maybe a nice quiet bath," he said, looking into the bubbling pot. "I would imagine a pretty young maiden such as she would make good sport." He laughed.

"Thoust mind is twisted," spat Percival.

"Thoust shall tell me what I wish to know," stated Mordred simply. He pulled the poker from the fire once again and stared into the blazing white-hot metal and moved silently towards the prone body of Tristan. He stood over the scarred and bloodied knight and ran the tip of the poker along his torso, tracing the line of his breastbone. The knight reacted to the light touch of the hot metal and writhed under its touch. "Thoust could end this," he teased looking up at Percival.

"I shall not betray my king," Percival said quietly and looked away from his friend.

"Then so be it!" snapped Mordred and thrust the end of the metal into the side of Tristan. Screams filled the air as the poker punctured the flesh of the knight and sunk deep into his body and echoed off the walls rebounding and filling the room with the sound of pain and torment. "Tell me!" shouted Mordred over the screaming. "Tell me!" He turned the poker in the wound and the flesh twisted under the pressure of the metal as blood seeped from the wound. He looked straight at Percival, anger flashing in his eyes. "Tell me!" he shouted manically.

Percival closed his eyes and attempted to block out the screams of his friend. "I am sorry, but I cannot," he whispered softly.

"Look at me!" raged Mordred. "Look at what thine stupidity is doing to your friend." He turned the poker in Tristan's body again and caused yet another scream of pain. "Tell me and I swear this ends." Percival shook his head and looked at Tristan, tears swelling in his eyes.

Tristan matched his gaze and smiled slightly before an intense tearing of pain raged through his body as Mordred moved the metal further into his body, then pulled it out. Blood smeared the wound and cast a shadow over his torso, and he could feel consciousness slipping away. Was this the end? he asked himself as darkness swept over his body.

Mordred stared down at the wound and placed the poker across the open scar, searing the flesh and a smell of burning filled their nostrils, while the echo of scream strangled their ears. "Bring me the girl!" snapped Mordred, his anger reaching a peak. "Then we will see how quickly thee sing," he sneered.

41.

Sea of Pity

Gwen sat on the bale of hay in the corner of the small dungeon and pulled her legs tightly into her body. She pulled at the thin fabric of her brown jodhpurs, her hands trembling under the slight pressure. Her eyes were tinged with a redness through the excess of tears, and her hair was filthy and bedraggled. She stared at the form of the knight laying on the floor close to the door. His eyes bulged as they stared out, his mouth contorted into a frozen silent scream as patches of blood smeared and covered his beard and clothing. Gwen had not known her 'saviour' and briefly recalled the sudden sensation of joy upon his arrival, then to have it snatched from her. She felt guilty at her own position and stared at Bors as he watched her through his dead eyes. Gwen wanted to cry; she could feel the sensation growing within her, her muscles tightening and contorting with every second, but no tears came. She wanted to scream, her stomach tightened, and fear gripped her, but no sounds came. Instead, she buried her head deep into her knees and closed her eyes from the nightmare around her. She did not know nor understand what was happening or why, but she wished it would end soon.

"'Twas a fish," commented Kay as he stared into the water. "Of that, I am sure."

"It cannot be," said Bedivere following his gaze. "There are no fish of that size in these waters."

"How can thee be sure?" asked Kay. "The world has changed from our time."

Bedivere nodded. Kay's logic seemed sound; times had indeed changed since their time. The roads were filled with metal carriages which ran along hard flat tracks apparently of their own accord, while the air was filled with obnoxious smells and sounds. He glanced back at Francis who was gazing out over the side of the boat, his legs spread wide and while one hand was placed firmly on the rudder, his other was resting between his legs. "It would seem our Lord Francis is bewitched."

"Aye," agreed Kay. "It would seem so." He followed Francis' gaze out into the water. "We had best be on guard," he said. A splash from the side of the boat disturbed his thinking and he placed his hand on the hilt of his sword. "There is trickery afoot."

"Come to me," the voice urged in his head, but Francis shook the thought clear.

"I can't," he whispered. "That sound." He craned his head in the opposite direction and stared out through starry eyes into the night.

"You must come to me."

"No, the singing." He struggled between the two voices. "It wants me." His voice was tinged with lust and longing as the singing grew stronger in his mind. "I must answer."

"No!" snapped the voice. "You must come to me."

Francis stared out over the water at the two voices in his head. Both luring him; one he knew would lead to his destiny… the other… his thoughts were clouded by the allure of the singing. His passion rose and his thoughts were driven by the altercation with Gwen the previous night. He thought of her body beneath her tightly fitting clothing, the rise of her breasts and the swell of her arse as the material of her clothing struggled to contain her frame. He could feel his excitement rising through his own clothing and his trousers felt tight around his groin as the anticipation grew. The singing was an arousal in itself but coupled with the thought of Gwen and her body was overwhelming his every thought. The whole reason for being here, everything he had strove for.

"Come to me," the woman urged him, but Francis ignored the calling consumed with lust and wanting for the sound of singing in his head.

He turned and looked over the edge of the boat and stared deep into the water. He could see a figure forming beneath the surface of the still water and watched as it cleared in his head. The woman swam up towards the boat, her hair flailing in the depths, extending and reaching through the water. She was beautiful, perfect, from her expansive ginger hair to her petite face, her elfin features staring back at him through the water. Her eyes shone like pools of opal in the midnight sky, while her smile irradiated the darkness and shone like a beacon… calling to him, alluring him. "I want you," she mouthed through the water, and giggled, biting her lips seductively.

Francis reached for the water. "I want you," he whispered as his hand dragged across the surface of the water. He could see her naked breasts heaving beneath the water, the swell of the waves playing against her nipples and could feel his excitement rising further.

Kay and Bedivere glanced around them as the sounds of water lapping against the side of the boat disturbed their focus. The swipe of tail against the surface of the water and gentle tap against the wood of the boat distracted them from Francis. "'Tis witchcraft," breathed Kay.

"Morgaine," whispered Bedivere.

Morgaine watched in the sphere as the two shapes swam around the boat, while Francis leant over the side of the small wooden vessel reaching into the water. Slowly a hand rose from the sea, its arm covered in scales and a fin ran down its length towards its elbow. She threw her head back as she kept her hands firmly over the crystal ball. "Typical male!" she laughed. "Driven by their own sexual needs!" She gazed into the sphere and laughed again. "Thine desire shall be thine death!" she cried.

Francis could feel the warmth of the woman's fingers as she reached from the water; he watched as traces of the sea ran down her arm, across the wrist and down towards the elbow. His eyes were transfixed on her eyes, only fliting to near naked bosom as a slight respite from the beauty of her face. She smiled at him and everything seemed perfect; all his worries, all his fears and concerns seemed to drain as she smiled and pulled his senses into her. Just one look… that is all it took for him to feel all right. Her beauty was intoxicating; he realised that he did not care about her figure… it was her looks. He did not care about the sword… He did not care about Gwen… He did not care about the knights – Kay or Bedivere or even Galahad. He did not care about his mother. Francis frowned. Why had he suddenly thought about his mother? He did care… His thoughts went out to her as she probably sat at home watching Emmerdale alone. He did care.

A hiss from the water disturbed his thoughts and he gazed back into the depths at the vision of… what… what was he looking at? The slender hand which he held was replaced by a slimy arm, filled with scales and tough tendons; fins ran along the expanse of the arm as it gripped Francis. But it was her face… gone were the exquisite looks and bewitching smile that had enticed him, now in its place was a vision of hatred. Her creature spat at him as it stared through malicious eyes, thin spiteful eyes which narrowed in the moonlight. The once beguiling mouth which had held him captive now were filled with rows of sharp pointed teeth, gnashing and growling as it pulled on his arm.

"Help me," he whispered, glancing over his shoulder.

Lord Kay leapt forward and reached for his legs as he struggled against the side of the boat. The water by the boat exploded upward in a geyser of water as a creature climbed onto the edge of the boat knocking Kay off his feet and sent him sprawling into the bowels of the boat. He lay from a moment struggling against the rope at the bottom of the vessel gazing upward at the apparition climbing into the boat. It was slender in form, but powerful muscles ran across its torso and down its body to a long slender grey tail. It lunged towards Lord Kay, its talons clawing at his face, and its teeth gnawing for his throat.

"What be this creature!" he gasped as it lunged for him, landing on top of the knight. Kay struggled holding the creature's hands in place, keeping its long talons away from his throat whilst pulling his head back avoiding the gnashing teeth.

He could feel a swipe of air and the sudden release of the creature's grip was followed by a geyser of thick glutinous blood poured over his face as the creature's head bounced onto the floor of the boat. Kay stared up and smiled at the form of Bedivere standing over his body, his sword firmly gripped in his hand and his other hand reaching out for his friend. "Perhaps you need my help." He smiled as he hauled his comrade to his feet. "Take heed to thy warning," said Bedivere, sword aloft gazing around the boat at the circling figures in the water. "There be more of them."

"I am ready," said Kay resolutely and stared into the black inky depths of the sea. "Yon blackhearts!" he called defiantly. "I smite at thee!" He looked at Francis who sat at their feet, scratches running up his arm. "The boy?"

"He is fine," said Bedivere, casting a quick glance downward. "I cut off the creature's arm to save him." Kay looked back at Francis and could indeed see the remains of the creature's arm as the boy sat huddled in the boat.

"What art thoust creatures?" he asked.

"I do not know," admitted Bedivere, streams of water falling from his hair. "'Tis madness for sure," he said.

"They are sirens," muttered Francis from his position at their feet.

"Explain."

"Sirens lure weak minded sailors to their deaths by singing to them," Francis said ashamed that he had been the only one to hear the singing.

"Such creatures do not exist," spat Kay. "Only in thine mind."

The boat lurched as one of the creatures slammed against the side of the vessel, rocking the two standing knights. "Be still!" warned Bedivere as he struggled to remain standing, sword still in hand. The water broke as a tail flash through the surface and dived back under the water, followed by an intense hissing sensation which echoed through the air. "What madness…" murmured Bedivere again, his eyes following the trail left in the water.

Kay watched as a tail broke the water, then thrust his sword deep into the water ahead of the stream. "'Tis not madness!" he shouted over the sudden scream of the creature beneath the surface of the water. A thick red liquid sprayed onto the surface of the water and spread around the expanse of the boat. "'Tis England!" Kay roared as he pulled the sword from the back of the creature and watched as the siren sank below the surface.

The knights fell backward as a taloned hand grasped the back of the boat and pulled the vessel downward. It pulled itself up onto the boat and stared with hatred at the occupants of the boat as they sprawled over the water drowned bottom of the boat. It hissed and hauled itself forward, clawing at Francis with its one remaining hand. Kay and Bedivere struggled under the weight of their own armour and the creature pulled itself into the vessel, its bony hands reaching for Francis.

He could feel the touch of the creature against his legs as it clawed at him; he could feel the hot breath of the creature as it sprawled itself on the top of his body. He struggled to push the creature from his body and felt the weight press down against him, forcing his body onto the floor of the boat. He could feel the water beneath his body and the pressure of the creature's claw against his throat, the sharpness of the creature's nails pressing against his skin.

42.

Dominion over Flesh

Francis winced as he felt the cold embrace of the siren stroke his neck and the pressure against his neck increased. Her talons pressed hard against his skin, and he could feel the sharp clawing at his head as she ran her fingers through his head and grasped at his head, pulling it back and exposing his soft naked neck. He could hear shouts and rustling from the other end of the boat and the two knights struggled under the weight of their own armour and he closed his eyes and turned his head under her weighty pressure. The image of her teeth sinking into his exposed flesh dominated his thoughts as she bore down on his neck, her warm breath fleeting across the surface of his skin as coldness embraced.

"My Lady!" snapped Agravain.
"Not now!" she said testily.
"But my Lady," insisted Agravain. "It is Mordred."
"What has thoust imbecile done now!" she raged and took her eyes away from the crystal ball.

Francis felt a sudden release in the creature's grip, and he felt a wave of relief wash over him. He hazarded a quick glance and saw Lord Kay standing astride the creature, one hand firmly in the siren's hair pulling it up off the boy, while his other handheld firmly the hilt of his sword, which swung through the air connecting with the creature. The siren twisted and writhed for a moment as the body fell onto the floor of the boat, blood pouring from the open wound on its body. Lord Kay stood panting, legs akin either side of the writhing body and the head dangling from his hand, blood seeping from the severed neck and onto the floor of the boat. Francis could see pearls of perspiration on his forehead and forced a smile at the knight. Kay frowned at the boy and threw the head over the side of the boat and turned to Bedivere and thrust out a hand to his fellow knight.

"We have lost much time," he said gravely as he leant forward to grasp the body. Bedivere copied his actions and grabbed at the corpse, hauling the creature over the side and into the water. "We have lost more than time," remarked Bedivere sadly gazing into the water as the creature disappeared beneath the waves, sinking from view.

"We can mourn for our loss later," commented Kay and looked disapprovingly towards Francis. "Thine foolishness almost cost all our lives," he said harshly. "Thoust has a responsibility not just to yourself or us, but to England. It is time thou lived up to it." Francis watched as the knight sat in his seat and stared out across the sea into the distance.

He stared at the back of Kay for a moment and looked at his feet covered in water and blood and sighed. "I'm sorry," he whispered as he hauled himself onto his small seat and gripped the rudder as the boat turned under its own pressure.

"Damnation!" snapped Morgaine as she glanced back into the sphere and brought her fist down onto the cold stone by the plinth.

"My Lady?" asked Agravain.

"It matters not," said Morgaine softly. "What of Mordred? What has the idiot done now?"

"It is the two knights, Lord Percival and Lord Tristan."

"What of them?"

"He questions them at this moment."

"To what end?"

"The purpose of their expedition."

"Oh, the idiot!" snapped Morgaine. "But we know why they are here," she said looking at Agravain, who said nothing. "Am I surrounded by idiots!" she raged. "The girl! They have come for the girl."

"My Lady." Agravain bowed and he could feel the suspicious glare of her eyes bore into the back of his skull.

"Tell me, my dear Agravain," she purred as she approached the Knight Commander and ran her fingers through the back of his hair. "What has my idiot of a nephew done now?"

"It is his intent to torture the girl before the Lords," Agravain whispered quietly, almost flinching in anticipation to her reaction. It came as almost as suddenly as his reaction as she pulled him up by the hair and slapped him hard against his face. He recoiled to her touch as the bitter sting of her hand played in his cheek.

"And thoust thought nothing of it!" she screamed in his face. "Have at thee!" she fumed and swung her hand at his face again, catching him across the eye and turning his head with the momentum of her vicious thrust. "Come with me!" she instructed and stormed from the courtyard, Agravain hurrying at her heels, a burning sensation swelling in his face and bitter seething growing in his soul.

Gwen felt the coolness of the stone flagstones as she fell heavily onto the ground. Her face was buried in soil as she lay face down from the rough treatment of her arrival. Only moments ago, she had been quietly mourning her position in her cell, then any hope of escape or rescue had been robbed and exposed as a travesty as the door to her cell had been flung open and two burly guards had pounded into her room and pulled her from the confined cell and out into this... this nightmare.

"My dear girl," purred Mordred as he stood over, his hands on his hips and his legs either side of her body giving off a sense of power and domination over his captive. "So glad you could make it."

Gwen looked up from her position and clawed at the dirt beneath her body, her fingers digging into the soft ground. "Go to hell, you bastard!" she spat.

"Your words are strange," said Mordred amused by her actions. "But I understand the meaning," he said laughing. He knelt close to her face as she looked up and smiled softly at her. "You are after all the main attraction," he said softly.

Gwen pulled a face and spat into his face, smiling in quiet satisfaction at his change in demeanour. His sickly smile faded as the saliva ran down his cheek and towards his chin and he brought his hand to bear savagely against her face. "Whore!" he spat and pulled her hair, hauling her to her feet. His grip was tight as he turned with her, and he pulled her face close to his. "Look!" he ordered, then when she refused, closing her eyes tightly he shook her head and yelled in her ear. "Look, whore," he raged. "Look at what a wanton slag like thee has brought." Her hands desperately pressed against his as his hand entwined in her hair and shook her head further. "Look at thine saviours," he cooed as she opened her eyes and gazed across the darkened room at the two knights, bound and chained to varying degrees of objects. "Thine debauchery has brought them to this!" he sneered and licked her ear, running his tongue around her organ, then down her neck. He pressed his body against her back and with his free hand grasped at her breast roughly. She gasped and winced in pain as the savagery of his touch pulled at her flesh beneath her tightly fitting t-shirt.

"Leave her be," whispered Percival meekly from his chained position on the wall.

"Thoust does not care for it," remarked Mordred glancing towards the knight.

Gwen could see the hatred in Percival's eyes even from this distance, but it was his body that made her recoil. She could see burn marks scattered across his chest, with the redness and swelling accompanied from a beating. His torso was swollen, and discoloured bruises littered his face and body, while his wrist was bloodied from his incarceration. His legs were limp and struggled to maintain his weight against the constant pull of gravity and she briefly wondered how he was still standing.

"I promised thee girl, in the hostelry that I would have my fun." He glared at her through vengeful lustful eyes and pulled at her hair, forcing her into the corner of the room. Mordred glanced towards Percival and grinned sickly at him. "Thoust has the pleasure to witness her taking." He smiled and brought the back of his hand viciously against her face. The sound of the slap resounded across the chamber and caught the echo off the wall. Gwen bit her lip, determined not to scream or cry as she felt her face swell from his touch.

Mordred pounced on her and used his body to pin her hips to the dirty stone floor. She writhed and struggled beneath his frame, kicking and punching at his body, before a second strike connected with her face. Her head recoiled as he clenched his fist and struck for a third time, and she felt the rush of blood flowing from her nose, and the release of a sob from her throat. Her body fell limp from the third blow and the energy she had displayed suddenly ebbed away in utter defeat.

"Thoust is a fire hearted vixen," laughed Mordred, as his hands clawed at her shirt, pulling the material over her head and revealing a small white simple bra. "I shall enjoy taming thee." He laughed and pushed the clothing up over her breasts and exposing her bosom. Mordred smiled as he gazed down on her naked chest and grasped at her already erect nipples, squeezing them hard and revelling at her moan of pain. "I shall have thee, again and again," he said lustfully as he burrowed his head into the chest, his tongue flicking at her nipples and across the expanse of her small cleavage while his hand snaked down her body, across her waist and beneath the elastic line of her jodhpurs.

Gwen tensed as his hand slid beneath her knickers and a tear escaped from her eye as he smirked at her, gazing into her face. He pressed down with his body against her slender frame and pressed both hands down towards her trousers, pulling at the material and forcing them further down her thighs. His hands worked at his own crotch, and she could feel an ever-increasing bulge growing as he lay on top of her, expectant of his pleasure and his heart filled with lust.

"Please," she begged softly.

Mordred laughed as he pulled at his own clothing. "See how she begs for me!" he laughed. "See how the whore wants me to take her."

He leant over her for a moment and surveyed her half naked body as he forced his own breeches down his legs, exposing himself fully to her and lunged forward, laughing as she screamed at his touch.

43.

Dishonour of Honour

"Land," whispered Francis as the boat rocked up on the shoreline. He looked back and across the water and felt a tinge of guilt over his actions coupled with the remorse of their fallen comrade. The rest of the journey had been tense with none of the occupants of the boat speaking and Francis knew his actions over the sirens had led to this. His weakness had endangered all their lives and Francis sighed inwardly, resound in the promise largely to himself that he would not place anyone in danger again. He watched in silence as Lord Kay leapt from the front of the boat into the sea. Water splashed up against his armoured legs and he thrust his way through the shallow water, his hands gripping firmly on the front of the boat as he hauled it through the waves and up onto land. He stared over the land as Bedivere stood upon the shoreline looking over the rolling dunes and up onto land.

"What does thoust see?" called Kay as he hauled the boat upon the sand bank.

"Nothing but mist," said Bedivere softly as he peered over the landscape. Lord Kay discarded the boat and walked over the beach to join Bedivere amidst the sand grass.

"Do we trust the boy?" asked Kay glancing back over his shoulder towards Francis who was struggling to climb out of the boat.

"He has much to prove and a long path to travel," said Bedivere following his gaze. He placed a hand on his comrade's shoulder and smiled waving down the beach as Francis stumbled in the water. "Remember how Arthur was when he took the throne."

Kay laughed. "Aye, your counsel is sound as always, my Lord," he said. "Arthur was an idiot, was he not?" He laughed again.

"He too lacked the wisdom of age when he took to the throne, as does the boy." He looked down at Francis who was climbing up the dunes towards them. "It is our duty as Knight Royal to guide the boy to greatness."

"Which way, boy?" demanded Kay as Francis stopped before them.

Francis narrowed his eyes; he could not blame Lord Kay for his attitude towards him he considered. He had just seen his friend die before them, then he had led them almost to their own deaths, so why shouldn't he act this way. Francis surmised that he would probably have reacted in much the same way. He listened to the voice in his mind as it played on the breeze and turned his head inland. "This way," he said softly, pointing towards a small crop of trees.

"Then lead us and we shall follow thee," said Kay, resigned to his fate.

"Mordred!" snapped Morgaine as she stormed into the dungeon area of the castle.

"Leave me," he whispered softly as he stood half naked above Gwen.

"Mordred, leave the girl," she said, her tone softening.

"I told thee, Morgaine, that I would have my fun. Now leave me to my pleasure." His voice was quiet, but full of menace towards her.

"If that girl has been harmed or touched in any way." She stalked forward into the chamber, watching Mordred's naked buttocks intently.

"I have not touched her yet, but if thine leave I will soon remedy that fact," he said, pushing her legs open and moving slowly between her thighs, stroking the inside of her legs with his hand. "She will enjoy my pleasure," he purred, "or die in my ecstasy, but I shall taste her." He licked his lips and moved his hands over her breasts, squeezing her fleshy mounds tightly in his sweaty paws.

Morgaine moved close to him and gazed over his shoulder, looking down towards his groin. "M' thinks thoust is smaller than I remember. Perhaps thoust is cold?" she teased smiling.

"Be thee gone!" snapped Mordred. "I have business to attend."

Morgaine ran her fingers through Mordred's hair and tightened her grip on his black mane. "I told thee, the girl must not be harmed," she whispered in his ear and with her free hand she reached around his waist and firmly grasped his testicles, her fingers toying with the tender objects in her hand. She squeezed and smiled as he doubled over with the sudden sharp pain running through his groin and sending an intense agony up through his body. "If thoust does harm her in any way, I shall be sure to rip these from thine body and feed them to yon crows," she whispered through smiling teeth. "I have had your pleasure before, remember, and I do not recall it

240

being a pleasant experience." She released her grip and watched him drop to the floor gripping at his groin as a fire welled up through his groin. "Full of sweating and noise as I recall, and over within minutes." She smiled and stepped over Mordred's writhing body and reached forward towards Gwen, offering her hand for the girl to take. "Do not flatter thine ability to pleasure a woman," she said over her shoulder, "for thine own inadequacy."

Gwen stared at her hand and attempted to cover her semi-naked body from the gaze of the older woman.

"Is thoust hurt?" Morgan asked. Gwen shook her head as she lay amidst the hay, her hands covering her groin and breasts. "Whilst thee are under this roof, thee are under my protection," Morgan said softly. "Now dress thyself. The cold bites and the eyes of those here are offensive." Gwen pulled at her knickers and jodhpurs pulling them up over her knees and around her waist, then pulled her bra down before reaching for her top and pulling it over her head she listened as Morgaine spoke. "Your clothing is strange," she commented. "The fabric is harsh and ungainly, but I sense they are comfortable are they not?" Gwen nodded and wiped her nose and mouth with the back of her hand. "Have thee lost thine tongue?" said Morgaine, amused at the girl's refusal to speak. "Do not fear me; you need only fear, fear itself… and there is naught be too scared of within these walls." Gwen glanced at Mordred who was pulling himself up onto his hands and knees and Morgaine followed her gaze and laughed. "Do not fear Mordred," she said. "He shall not harm thee, will thee, Nephew?"

Mordred shook his head slowly. "Nay," he whispered softly as he adjusted his own clothing.

Morgaine held her hand out towards Gwen and smiled warmly at the girl. "Now then," she started, "what madness is this?" Her eyes flicked over towards Percival and Tristan, battered and close to death from their wounds.

"We sought to discover their goal," said Mordred. "Loosen their tongue to make them squeal."

"And thee would do that by half killing them, then taking thy own pleasure?" she chided him. "We know why they are here, I thought that would be obvious, even to one such as yourself." The force of the insult towards Mordred was not lost on the knight, nor anyone else in the room. "They are here for her." Morgaine's eyes strayed back to the girl who still hovered by the wall, her arms wrapped closely around her chest. "They are under orders to protect and save her." She laughed and looked at the two knights. "Thoust have done a good service to your king!" she goaded. "Now, girl!" she snapped staring at Gwen. "Take my hand. I wish to walk in the moonlight."

Gwen reached out and tentatively took the older woman's hand and allowed herself to be led from the darkened room. She glanced back into the room as she left and her eyes strayed to the figure of Mordred who stood stock still in the centre of the room, his hand still hovering over his groin and a look of pure hate and seething cross his face.

44.

The Isle of Apples

"Can anyone else smell apples?" asked Francis as they walked through the trees.

"'Tis known as the Isle of Apples," said Kay as he strode a short distance behind Francis.

Francis paused and looked back at him and frowned. "Pardon?"

"The Isle of Apples," said Bedivere, "is said to be the dwelling of the Lady Nimue, the lady of the lake," he explained as he walked past Francis. "We must continue to move if we are to reach our objective," he urged.

"Yes, yes," agreed Francis. "Can you tell me more about this lady?"

"It is said that she dwells on this fabled isle and holds Excalibur sacred. Her power to deceive is greater than Merlin himself and her will is absolute." He walked alongside Francis as he spoke and occasionally glanced in his direction as the strands of grass whipped up against his legs. "Her deceit lasted into a lustful unity with Merlin and brought Arthur to the point of restitution. Upon his death, it was Arthur's instructions that Excalibur should be returned to the Lady."

"But why?" queried Francis. "I don't understand any of this." He waved around the trees as they pushed their way through the wood. "If the sword was returned then why all of this? And why now?"

"It would appear thoust questions may soon be answered, my Lord," said Bedivere softly as he stopped and stared before them.

A large oak tree stood alone in the centre of a large clearing, its branches reached out over the smaller trees into the forest as it stood tall and proud towering over the rest of the vegetation around it. Its branches were covered in white and pink blossom, which fell slowly to the floor of the forest, covering the floor in a blanket of petals and bloom. The centre of the tree was hollow and through the chiselled bark stepped a woman bathed in a shower of golden rays.

Francis gazed at her beauty through the cavalcade of colour and looked at the figure beside him. Bedivere was knelt on one knee at his side, with his head bowed low to the floor in respectful pose towards the approaching woman. He cast a glance behind towards Kay who was in the same pose as Bedivere and looked back at the woman. She was as beautiful in person as she was in his dreams as she floated towards him on an apparent cloud of air. He could see the shadow of water coasting across her body and behind her lay small pools of water as she slid over the ground. Her hair glistened in the small light from the sky, as the sun shone down within the clearing. Francis frowned and cast his gaze into the sky and could see a beacon of light shining like a column through the trees and over the Lady. Small pearls of water clung to her hair and small rivers of water ran along her arms and fell from the ends of her fingers.

"You are here." She smiled softly as she spoke and gazed at him.

"Well, yes," said Francis uncertainly. He looked at her unsure what he was doing.

"You are here because you followed the call," she whispered softly. He frowned as she spoke. "I know what you are feeling. Your mind is my mind in many ways and different in other ways. We are connected through your birthright."

"My birthright? You mean through King Arthur?" The Lady nodded and smiled kindly at him as he shook his head. "Look, I don't mean to sound stupid or anything, but how can I be connected to King Arthur? The King Arthur... of the Britons! I mean it is not like I have not heard of him or anything, but I mean... me. I can't be."

"You can and you are," she said softly as she walked forward away from the tree. She gently took Francis by the arm and led him away from the tree and further into the woods. He blushed at her touch and his eyes were distracted by her naked body beneath her flowing white robes. "Does my form embarrass you?" she asked innocently.

"No, no," stammered Francis, "it's just... I mean... well..."

She laughed and placed her head on his shoulder as they walked through the flowers arm in arm. "Be still," she commanded. Francis obeyed her instructions and remained quiet as they walked. The light seemed to follow them through the forest and the flowers sprouted underfoot as they moved from clearing to clearing, his eyes darting about for any signs of danger. "You are safe here," she commented, pausing briefly to look at him.

"How did you... I mean that's the second time."

"As I said we are connected." She looked behind them as they continued through the forest. "Your comrades are brave men," she said, looking at the trailing Bedivere and Kay. "Do not take them for granted." Her smile faded as she searched the forest for someone. "You are missing someone," she commented.

"Sir Galahad," said Francis gazing at the floor.

"Ah yes, the first to fall."

"There will be others?" gasped Francis.

"Another has gone already," the Lady remarked casually as she picked her way through the bluebells and daffodils. "Be sure their deaths are not in vain."

"Can you explain what this is?" Francis looked around them. "How can you be sure we are safe?"

"This is the Isle of Apples," she explained. "My home. It is enchanted and while I am here it does not exist... and yet it exists everywhere."

"I don't understand."

"I would not expect you to." She smiled cryptically. "Do not worry; while you are on the Isle you are safe."

Francis nodded. "Can you at least tell me about my connection with King Arthur then?"

The Lady smiled. "The boy Arthur was chosen by divinity not by blood right to lead and protect the Britons by Holy powers against the Saxon hoards. His communion was divine, and his chastity proven by the holiest of ascension his acts were devout and pure and as such he was given the holy blade of Excalibur." She took his arm and continued to walk through the expanding forest of flowers as she talked. "He led the Britons to glory," she said smiling, "and prosperity came to the land, then a serpent soiled the garden and tainted the pure of heart."

"Mordred," whispered Francis.

The Lady shook her head. "Guinevere," she said sadly. "She tempted Arthur with the ways of the flesh and corrupted him through her body. Then came Mordred and his kindred, Morgaine. Their machinations of the throne and usage of Lancelot to seduce the Lady Guinevere served to usurp power and the crown." She sighed and stopped, looking at her feet. "Then came Camlann."

"That's where he died," Francis said triumphantly. "I know all of this, well most of it, but why me?"

"I am getting to that," she admonished. "The battle was bloody and vicious and there were but seven survivors…" Her voice trailed away to the knights who bore witness to the battle. "The seven took the body and laid the king in an eternal sleep to heal his wounds. But his wounds were fatal. The knights never knew and left the king wounded and alone, returning the sword to myself and the scabbard to the Fisher King."

"But where do I fit in?" said Francis impatiently.

She waved him away and moved by herself through the grass and the flowers and Francis watched as streams of pollen rose from the blooms as she glided across the carpet of colour. "The knights continued their lives, all separate and yet all combined by a single tie… Camlann. The three observers, I, Merlin and Morgaine, were not permitted by the rules of battle to participate through our magical knowledge, lest we influence the tide of war. But Morgaine was… is mad with power, and she made a pact with darker forces beyond our control for the crown. It is because of this we are here." She beckoned Francis forward, holding her hand out to him. "Over the centuries that tie us, people were born, and people died and through it all the bloodline remained strong… and yet." She stopped and searched him with her eyes. "You are the last."

"The last?"

The Lady nodded. "The last of the line Pendragon. You have no heirs?" Francis shook his head. "And no kin?" Again, he shook his head.

"No, just me and Mum," he admitted.

"Then it is you," she breathed and smiled. "You are the last in the line of Pendragon. The last of Arthur's loin." She reached forward with her hand and grasped his. Francis could feel a glow run through his body as she looked at him. "It must be you."

"Yes, but for what?" he insisted.

"You must save us all." She smiled and released his hands, turning and walking through the flowers.

45.

Lies of Seduction

"Let me apologise for my nephew," purred Morgaine as she held Gwen's hand and led her through the castle ruins. "He is a man," she said as Gwen attempted to force a smile at her. "He is ruled by his genitals." She laughed at her own comment and stood breathing in the night air. They stood on the pinnacle of the castle and overlooked the ruins and out into the sea. "It is beautiful, is it not?" she commented looking over the sea. The moon shimmered in the calm waters of the bay, and few stars shone and sparkled above their heads.

Gwen nodded. "Yes," she said softly.

"You grew up here?" asked Morgaine.

Gwen nodded, her mouth turning slightly at the scene before her, then all the pent-up emotion of the last few hours exploded from her. Tears fought with sobs as tracks of water ebbed and flowed freely across her skin. Morgaine placed her arms around the girl for a moment and rested her head against Gwen's, kissing her temple and burying her lips against her soft hair. "I'm sorry," apologised Gwen, pushing the older woman away.

"Do not apologise," whispered Morgaine and gently stroked the girl's cheek, wiping away the rivers of tears.

"I'm sorry, but I can't do this," said Gwen, flinching under her touch.

"I do not understand thy meaning."

"I mean… this…" Gwen waved around them. "Come here with… with… you!"

"Please, I mean you no harm."

"So, you keep saying, but I watched you murder my father. Then your madman of a nephew tried to rape me… twice! And you expect me to discuss where I was born and do all this."

"My dear, your father was unfortunate I will admit, but thy must understand while I seek Excalibur thy are under my protection," Morgan said simply.

"Why?" demanded Gwen. "What makes me so special?"

"You had a connection to the boy."

"Francis?" Gwen said incredulously. "But we don't even know each other."

"Well, enough me thinks," stated Morgaine, glancing towards her groin and smiling. "The glamour of carnage gives a strong appeal." Morgan laughed as Gwen blushed.

"Look," said Gwen staring at Morgaine, "I don't know what you think you know… and yes I will admit that we did have sex, but I have a boyfriend."

"But thoust does not love him," Morgaine said flatly.

"You don't know how I feel!" snapped Gwen.

"I don't, my dear," said Morgaine, taking Gwen's hand in her own and looking out towards the sea. "I see the pain in thy eyes, the feeling of entrapment. Thoust do not love yon youth, but thy fears admitting the truth." She smiled as she watched the sun rise above the horizon in the distance. "The first step to true happiness is the admission of thy heart." She looked at Gwen. "Thy true love is not the one you are with." Gwen could feel her heart swell and burst within her as Morgaine's words struck a resonance. While she did love Lance, she knew her heart did not belong to him, and tears welled in her eyes as the pair gazed out over the water. "Beautiful, is it not?" Morgaine said smiling.

"I did have feelings for Lance once," Gwen admitted. "I still do… but not like they were. I mean our relationship, it's comfortable but nothing else. He is not the one… I used to think he was, but not any more." She looked away from the rising sun and to the ground sadly. "We argue more and more, and his moods… God, his moods drive me crazy. But I'm scared of losing everything that is…" She struggled to find the words to express herself.

"Safe," offered Morgaine. Gwen nodded sagely and turned from the cliff and looked over the ruined castle. "The boy is no more," Morgaine stated simply.

"What?"

"The boy… Lance. He is dead," Morgaine spoke in a matter-of-fact tone.

Gwen struggled to comprehend her own feelings; she knew she should be filled with remorse but somehow could not connect with her grief. "I don't believe this," she said eventually.

"Explain?"

"Well, look," Gwen started, "yesterday I was happily in a relationship in my own little world and now… look at me. Here I am standing on the edge of a cliff, watching the sun rise on the horizon chatting to the woman who has just killed my father and probably my boyfriend about a world that until only recently I thought didn't exist."

"That is correct," said Morgaine.

"Madness… that's what it is… madness."

Morgaine took her hand and gazed into her eyes and smiled. "I will enlighten you to your true happiness, if thy assist me in obtaining Excalibur. Should thee not have what thy deserve."

Gwen looked at her nervously and bit her lip gazing over the sunrise. "I don't know…"

"My dear, your heart bleeds for so much more. You deserve more than this world can offer you." She paused and leant close to her, breathing softly in her ear as she spoke. "What can he offer you?" she said teasing.

"Francis," said Gwen frowning.

"Any man. I offer thee the world. If thou will assist me, you can have anything your heart desires. Love, wealth, power! Join me, my dear, and I can offer thee everything. Once I have Excalibur, the world will be mine, and thee can sit by my side as a princess."

46.

Excalibur!

"Save us... what... I mean, how?" stammered Francis.

"It must be you," she said again, "you are the last Pendragon. You answered the calling of Excalibur, you are the one to save us all."

"Yes but who?" Francis could feel himself becoming frustrated at her. "I don't understand who I'm supposed to save. What do you mean save us, the world? What!" he snapped.

"Your impatience will be thy death, if thoust let it."

"Look, I'm sorry, I truly am, but you have to understand this is all a bit much for me."

"You are the last Pendragon," she said again and turned from Francis, walking away through the flowers.

"So, I gathered, but who must I save?" he shouted, then sighed and ran after her.

"You must save us all," she said simply, looking at him frowning. "Surely this is obvious."

"It may be for you, but I'm a bit dim." He smacked his head as he spoke and pulled a face.

"Your mind is addled," she said. "You are the last Pendragon." Her words were slow and methodical as she spoke, "You are the sole heir to King Arthur and by right of bloodline the sword Excalibur shall be yours." She continued her slow walk through the flowers as she spoke, "You bear the responsibilities of your birthright; it must be you that brings the end to us all and it must be you that saves us from our eternal waking."

"How am I to do this?" he asked.

"Once you have Excalibur, the Fisher King will explain."

"Can't you... I mean all this coming and going—"

"No!" she snapped. "It must be the Fisher King. He is the protector; he is the holder of knowledge."

"Can you at least tell me what is going on?"

The Lady sighed and stopped before a small wooden cross. She touched the object and allowed her hands to trail across the bark, and as her hand passed Francis watched a myriad of blooms rise from the wood and gather and stare towards the sunlight. She rested her hand on the top of the cross and smiled at him. "You have his aspect," she said softly.

"Arthur?"

She nodded. "Not his features, but his aura."

"And that's good?"

Again, the Lady nodded as she stroked the cross. "He was a good man, with a kind and gentle heart." The voice was wistful and full of regret as she spoke, "He was destined for greatness before his desire ruled him." Francis knew this was about Guinevere and shuffled uncertain what to do next.

"You were saying... the sword."

"Yes," she stared at him for a moment before speaking. "The battle was bloody," she said, her eyes glazing over as she stared wistfully into the distance, "and final in its resolution. Both sides were devastated. Arthur fought for the country and for valour, Mordred for his own desire and greed. There would be one outcome. In those circumstances there always is..." Her voice trailed off as she looked back at Francis. "We observed – myself, my lover Merlin and Morgaine. We observed the battle from afar, destined not to become embroiled in the conflict. Men fought beasts and comrades and friends fell as the fields of Cornwall became awash of blood." Francis looked around him as the flowers faded and the skies darkened, replaced by a deep brooding sensation. "The armies clashed, and men died for naught, and while the Lords and nobles sat astride their mighty Steeds, the common man fought and fell in the dirt."

"Are you all right?" he asked as she paused in her story.

The Lady nodded and continued, "By the end of the day, all but seven had fallen including the king and Lord Mordred. The king was mortally wounded in battle and taken from the field to rest and heal from his wounds. They never healed and he died, but not before the Lady Morgaine Le Fay cast a curse over the battlefield."

"A curse."

"Yes, all those who survived the battle, are doomed to live an unyielding sleep."

"I don't understand."

"Every one thousand years, the survivors of the battle shall awaken and do battle across the land again until Morgaine can retrieve Excalibur. This would extend to myself and Merlin—"

"But you weren't there," interrupted Francis.

"We were observers," she said simply, "and as much we too are cursed."

"But this doesn't make any sense. If Morgaine wants Excalibur enough to curse everyone who survived, including herself, then why don't we just give it to her?"

"If Morgaine receives Excalibur her power will become absolute. She will be bound by an unholy tie that will extend through a never-ending life and the land will wash in blood."

Francis stared at her for a moment. "Right, let me get this straight, if we give Morgaine the sword, then she will wash the land with blood and if we don't, she will wash the land in blood. So, either way, we're pretty much screwed."

"Thine words have no meaning," the Lady remarked, "but thy meaning is clear." She nodded.

"Then answer me one last thing. If all those who survived the battle are cursed to live an unending sleep of whatever, then why does Mordred live? Ha! Answer that one." He grinned at his own logic and felt immediately foolish at his own outburst.

"Morgaine has unholy powers," the Lady began. "Her gifts are in excess of my own and my Merlin, but only to an extent."

"Like what?"

"She has mastery of dark arts," she explained. "She can create unholy and unearthly creatures and the dead will rise for a while, whilst she lives. But her powers are limited to their time. She can only control what she can see or has a connection with. Her subjects are still of free thought."

"And how do I lift the curse?"

"The Fisher King shall impart that knowledge. I am part of the curse, and I am doomed to obey the calling as is everyone."

"So, I need to return to the cave."

The Lady nodded. "The place of resting," she said softly. Francis watched as she closed her eyes and placed both hands on the wooden cross and raised her head to the sky, closing her eyes. "The time has come!" she called skyward. "The time of restitution. The calling of Excalibur!" Her voice carried as the wind wound its way around her body, whipping up her hair and teasing at the soft fabric which wrapped around her body. "Arthur rises from beyond." Her eyes snapped open, and she stared at Francis as the wind grew stronger, her hands wrapped tighter around the cross as she struggled against the storm brewing around them. "And through thee, the curse shall be lifted!"

The wind screamed around her as her"voic' rose. Francis struggled to keep to his feet, stumbling to the floor as the wind battered his body and as he watched the Lady of the Lake as she continued to scream into the sky, he wished he had something to hold onto.

"All who survive Camlann shall be cursed to live an undying sleep, an eternal life until one comes forth to end thine curse." She stared at Francis… no, through Francis as he fell to the floor and gazed up at her. "Thine youth is that one! Behold! Hidden in plain sight!" She swept forward with one hand towards the cowering youth as she maintained her grip on the cross, the wind growing in strength and her hair billowing in the monsoon. He dug his fingers deep into the dirt beneath his sprawling body and continued to gaze up at the Lady as she shouted in the storm. "Excalibur!" she wailed, her voice raising to a fever pitch, and her hand released the wooden cross.

Francis watched as the bark crumbled from the cross and from beneath the wooden exterior and shining cold hard surface began to shine through the wood like a beacon. The crossed patched bark slowly revealed a smooth silver polished metal which shone in the sunlight and the wind continued to blast its surface, battering away the dullen wood which covered the object. Small jewels protruded through the top of the cross as the hilt of the sword was slowly revealed and a glistening deep gold adorned with a thick leather handle beaconed an impressive sight as more wood fell from the fabled weapon. A deep red encrusted jewel sat in a lone mounting at the head of the handle and glowed, calling towards Francis as the wind continued to grow around them, howling like a wolf at the gates of heaven. The cool metal shone, and the red, green and blue jewels glimmered like beacons as they ran across the handle as the wood fell completely away leaving the sword alone in the clearing; no grass, no flowers could compare to its beauty. It shone, radiant in the broadcast sunlight, dug deep into the soft ground and Francis could hear the voice in his head once again.

"Come to me," it beckoned. Francis looked at the Lady and realised for the first time that the voice was not hers. It was the sword's. Excalibur.

"Come to me," it called again. "Come to me." He looked at the sword and revelled in its beauty… its majesty.

Excalibur.

47.

Words of the Sword

Morgaine strode through the ruins of the castle with her arm draped through Gwen's. The sun had risen over the horizon and bore witness to the couple as they walked slowly back towards the courtyard. Morgaine stopped and glanced up towards the sky, closing her eyes as she smelt the morning air. A smile slowly tracked over her face. "Excalibur," she said softly. "He has it," she breathed in the morning air heavily as she spoke, her breast heaving and exhaling her hot breath.

"How do you know?" asked Gwen quietly.

"I can sense it," Morgaine whispered softly turning to Gwen. "We have much to do."

They strode together in silence through the ruins and Gwen watched her as they moved through the strewn boulders which lay discarded across the courtyard. She looked everything Gwen was not, strong, confident and powerful and Gwen spied her with a slight envious feeling swell in the pit of her stomach.

"Knight Commander!" her voice snapped through the ruins and caused Gwen to start slightly at the sudden harshness of her voice. She watched as a knight ran into the courtyard and came to a stop before her and dropped to one knee, staring respectfully at the ground.

"My Lady."

"It is Excalibur," she said slowly. "I can feel its touch in my mind. After all these years, its call is weak…" She trailed off as her eyes glazed over in a wistful contemplation. "Prepare our forces," she snapped.

"Morgaine." The voice came from behind them, and Gwen recognised it as her persecutor of the last day.

"Mordred," acknowledged Morgaine.

"Is it time?" he asked, eyeing Gwen suspiciously. "What are thoust doing here!" he snapped.

"Hold thy tongue!" snapped Morgaine.

"Forgive me, deathless one. I did not mean…" His fawning betrayed his fear of her and his hatred.

"Yes, Mordred, it is time, and this time we shall have Excalibur." She smiled at Mordred as he strode towards her matching her stare. "We have the means to obtain the sword."

"The girl?" queried Mordred.

"Aye, the girl. She has agreed to aide our cause and with the maiden's assistance the youth will hand us Excalibur without us raising a hand."

"Thoust deny me my vengeance," spat Mordred.

"Perhaps," Morgaine teased, "once we have Excalibur."

"No!" snapped Gwen, finding her voice. "No!" she said again. "If I help you get this sword you must promise you will not harm anyone." Morgaine and Mordred exchanged an amused glance. "Promise or I won't help you."

"I promise," said Morgaine softly.

"Aunt!"

"We promise," Morgaine corrected herself, "and thy shall assist us of thy own free will?" Gwen nodded. "Then no one shall be harmed by our hands."

"And the knights."

"I shall release them."

"Aunt!" protested Mordred again.

"Hold fast, Mordred," warned Morgaine, "it is of my design that they be released. Call it a gesture of good will." She turned to Agravain. "See to it, and bring the knights here to me," she said. Agravain slapped his arm against his chest and turned sharply from the courtyard. "You see, my dear, I gave you my word."

"Thank you," whispered Gwen.

"Now for thy part." She approached Gwen and smiled down at her as she towered over her body. She circled the young woman and stood at her back looking towards Mordred. "We shall allow yon youth to enter the castle. When he finds you, you must delay him until I am ready."

"How do I do that?" asked Gwen biting her lip.

"You will think of something," purred the older woman as she slid her hands around Gwen's young body. She leant her head close to Gwen's ear as she slid her hand down the front of her jodhpurs and into her knickers. She spoke as her fingers toyed and cupped at her groin. "Men are such

256

weak-minded fools," she whispered staring at Mordred as her fingers played beneath the surface of Gwen's clothing. "See how he stares," she teased.

Despite herself, Gwen closed her eyes and bit at her lip as Morgaine's fingers moved slowly within her underwear.

"You shall use your female wiles to entice yon youth." She moved abruptly away from Gwen and stood before a stone plinth which cradled a large crystal ball. "I shall be ready; you be sure you are too," she said, then turned to Mordred. "Take her to the dungeon… and do not harm the girl," she added, shooting him a warning glance. He nodded and moved towards Gwen who flinched under his touch. "Soon," she whispered running her hands over the surface of the sphere.

Gwen flashed a quick glance over her shoulder as she was led gently from courtyard and watched for a moment as Morgaine stood smiling peering into the glass orb, her hands smoothing its surface as she lowered her face close to the sphere and she briefly wondered what she had agreed to.

"'Tis Excalibur," whispered Lord Kay as Francis appeared through the trees of the small clearing, his eyes locked on the object in the youth's hands.

Francis smiled at his two companions and held the sword aloft over his head. "My Lords!" he called grinning wildly.

"'Tis as magnificent as I remember," said Bedivere softly.

"Aye, a noble weapon," agreed Kay as he knelt on one knee before Francis as he approached.

Bedivere moved to copy his actions but was stopped by Francis. "No, no, there's no need for all that," he said.

"But thoust is our king," replied Bedivere as he sunk to one knee and lowered his head.

"I'd like to think that I'm more than your king," said Francis smiling as he extended a hand towards the kneeling knight. "I hope I'm your friend."

"Would be an honour, my Lord," said Bedivere as he accepted his hand.

"Does this mean I'm forgiven?" he asked cautiously.

"We all make mistakes," commented Kay, standing and peering at the boy's hand. "'Tis how we react to atone for thy mistakes that maketh the man."

Francis shuffled uncomfortably for a moment, the sword weighing heavy in his hand and the guilt still weighing heavy in his heart. "I understand," he said eventually.

Kay laughed and slapped Francis on the back. "Don't be so serious," he laughed. "I jest, my Lord." His eyes looked at the sword in his hands and the light glimmered in his eyes. Francis lifted the sword and held the weapon across the palms of his hands. The blade felt cold against his skin and Francis could feel the power within the weapon as it generated an aura. "'Tis a mighty weapon," Kay breathed softly, reaching forward and touching the polish metal of the blade.

"It's beautiful," whispered Francis.

"We must not delay," warned Bedivere, glancing around the glade.

"We have the sword," said Francis casually, "why worry now?"

"If thy hath Excalibur, then Morgaine will know."

"Aye, my Lord Bedivere is correct," agreed Kay, his eyes suddenly darting around the deserted clearing.

"We are safe here," insisted Francis. "The Lady told me."

"But we must yet travel abroad back to yon resting place," snapped Bedivere, his face clouding over with a serious look.

"Let us depart," stated Kay.

Francis nodded. "The scabbard," he said, holding out his hand towards Bedivere. The knight pulled the sheave from his belt and presented it to Francis who weighed it in his hand for a moment before sliding the long blade into the leather shearing. He looked around the island and frowned as the mist seemed to swirl and encase the area, covering the trees and swamping the landscape. "We had better move," he said urgently, "this mist is coming in quick!"

"Does not seem natural," commented Bedivere as he peered into the distance.

"Nay," agreed Kay and pointed through the haze, "methinks the beach is this way."

"Are thee sure?" queried Bedivere.

"It all looks the same," said Francis, peering around as the mist grew thicker.

"My Lord," whispered Bedivere, "which way?"

The two knights looked at Francis expectantly.

Francis closed his eyes and concentrated his thoughts; if the sword had drawn him here then surely it could lead him to the boat. His forehead furrowed into a frown, and he turned slowly in a circle on the spot, the soft dirt digging into his trainers as he moved through the ground. "Merlin," he whispered, "hear me." There was a deafening silence in his head as he continued his slow spin, then drawing the sheaved sword to his chest he whispered again into the leather-bound object. "You're part of me," he urged. "Show me the way." He spoke softly through gritted teeth as he willed an answer. He was aware of the two knights staring at him through the ever-growing fog but continued his silent vigil.

"I hear thee," the voice in his head exploded and Francis could feel himself recoil under the pressure for a moment as the shock of the sudden intrusion invaded his thoughts.

"Merlin?" he questioned the voice, his head moving, his eyes still closed tightly.

"It is I," replied the voice.

"Help me," pleaded Francis.

"You are the last of the Pendragon," the voice replied. "You must do things for yourself; I can only guide you."

"Then guide me now!" snapped Francis, casting curious glances from both Kay and Bedivere. "I... I'm sorry, please, Merlin, help us." He paused as the voice became quiet. "Merlin!" he pleaded as the fog swirled around his ankles.

Gawain stood at Merlin's side and gazed into the depths of the pool, watching as the fog thickened around his comrades and the boy. "Will thoust help?" he asked concerned.

"I can do only so much," said Merlin, his own eyes closed mirroring that of Francis as his hands were spread across the surface of the water.

"Thoust is the boy's consort," stated Gawain. "He needs thy assistance."

"I am aware of his condition," said Merlin testily.

"But your countenance betrays your words."

"My Lord Gawain, I am bound by oath not to interfere—"

"Thoust is a player of words," spat Gawain. "My Lord Galahad was right about that. Your powers can aide the boy, what is thy afraid of?"

"I am Merlin," the old man stated simply. "I do not fear naught." His words betrayed an arrogance to his voice. "I do what I must, and what I please."

"Then if thee does not fear, then help thy Lord Francis. Is that not your position… advisor?"

Merlin's eyes snapped open, and he frowned at Gawain. "Thoust does try my patient, my Lord, but thine words are truth." He closed his eyes and placed his hands over the water again. "I do fear, but not what thee think. I fear the curse."

"We have our own demons to fear," said Gawain softly as he backed away to the back of the cavern and rested against the wall, casting an occasional glance back towards the old sage.

"My Lord Francis," Merlin said softly. "Follow thine heart… it will lead you to safety."

"Follow thine heart," came the voice on his head after what had seemed like an eternity of silence. "It will lead you to safety."

"Merlin, Merlin, Merlin!" called Francis into the air, but no other sound was made through the trees. Francis opened his eyes and gazed at his companions through the mist. The fog had become almost impenetrable under his scrutiny, and he struggled to make out the figures of his companions. He looked about the area and was shocked to see how much visibility had been reduced. What the hell had Merlin meant… follow thine heart? He frowned and looked around. There was no way of knowing which was the way out. His instincts screamed at him, this way and that way, but his mind reasoned against action. The mist grew thicker and swallowed him as he struggled with his conscious mind. "Follow thy heart." The words rang in his ear and played with his senses; what did it mean? All he wanted was to get out… to go home.

Home.

Home.

Home, that was it! Wasn't it?

Home. He frowned and thought of home, his mother sitting watching her soap operas, cradling a cup of colling brown liquid as the television played out its drama.

Nothing.

Home.

He closed his eyes and thought of his room, his bed and the clothes scattered across his floor… nothing…

He tried again and the image of Gwen flashed through his mind, and he immediately chided himself over allowing his mind to wander to a girl that he had only just met, and a girl who probably was out of his league and did not have the same feelings for him. He smiled despite himself; this was a girl who made him feel better just by looking at him. This was a girl who made him smile even when he felt angry at her... in his mind the mist parted and through the clouds a beacon shone through, guiding him home...

His eyes snapped open, and he stared through the mist. "This way," he said pointing into the ether.

"Is thoust sure?" asked Kay staring in the direction indicated.

Francis nodded decisively. "Yes!" His words were firm, and his manner was confident and for the first time in days he felt in control. He strode forward purposely with his two comrades following as the mist rolled in behind them, growing thicker and denser every second.

"What is the meaning of this!" demanded Percival as he was thrust in the centre of the courtyard. He struggled to maintain his balance and composure as he stood before Morgaine. The knight stood defiantly, cuts and bruises marked his skin and the wounds of torture screamed as they condemned his body and the energy fought to flow from his body. His legs could barely support his own weight and his wrists were sore as the shackles had cut deep into his flesh. Tristan fell almost unconscious at his side, his wounds more severe and his treatment worst. He bent to his aide and stared venomously at Morgaine as he placed his hand flat on his friends back as he lay exhausted against the cold harsh ground on his hands and knees. Tristan struggled with his conscious mind and could feel his own energy expel with every breath he took, the broken bones in his chest puncturing as his chest rose and fell in time with the hot sticky breath of the knight. He coughed slightly and droplets of blood stained his mouth as the taste of iron polluted his tongue and he spat a globule of red saliva on the floor by his hand. "He needs rest," begged Percival as he looked on with concern at his friend. "He is dying."

Morgaine swept across the courtyard and knelt beside the knight, her silk cloak trailing across the mud of the floor, and she placed a hand on the back of his head. Tristan struggled to react against her touch and his head sagged beneath her fingers. Morgaine glanced towards Mordred, a flash of anger triggered in her eyes and glared at her nephew.

"He is hurt," she said eventually and looked at Percival with sadness in her eyes, "but he will survive." She shook her head as she spoke the words and moved slightly as the knight coughed again. "Take him," she said softly, "with my apologies." She stood to her full height. "The Lord Merlin may be able to assist his pain and…" Her words trailed away as she was unable to say what was really in her mind.

"Thank you," said Percival slowly and stood, taking Tristan by the arm and pulled his comrade carefully to his feet. Tristan winced with the pain and placed an arm around his ribs, coughing again and looked through swollen eyes at his persecutor.

"Please," said Morgaine softly, "know I do regret this action."

"My Lady," acknowledged Percival and looked at her, tilting his head slightly and frowned. "Indulge my ignorance," he started, "but why does thoust release us? Thy could let us die in thy cells."

"My nephew has acted with dishonour," Morgaine stated. "There is no victory without honour," she said simply. "Thoust should know that." She turned and walked away, pausing by the crystal sphere for a moment and placed a hand on the ball, speaking into the distance. "But mark my words, good Percival, Tristan… next time we meet it shall be thy death. Now if you will excuse me, I must prepare for battle." She smiled and turned her head towards Percival. "Oh, send Merlin my love, and tell the boy, Francis, that I shall have Excalibur and when I do, I will rest his head upon her blade." Morgaine threw her head back and laughed and she pushed her way from the courtyard and into the shadows.

48.

All Roads Lead... Somewhere

The boat seemed tiny as the three men ran down the beach towards the vessel as the waves lapped against the wooden panelling. They ran down the beach, their feet sinking into the soft sand as they moved with a unison across the golden surface. Francis jumped into the vessel, as Kay and Bedivere pushed the boat into the water and slowly the boat moved away from the shoreline and out into open sea. With no oars to assist their passage the two burly knights leant out of the boat; one either side and paddled, forcing their arms through the resistance of the water. Francis held onto the rudder and directed the boat as it drove a path through the sea and cast his eyes back towards the Isle fading in the distance... not just fading in the distance but fading from view completely.

"The Isle," he breathed as he stared under the glare of the sun. Both knights paused in their efforts to follow the gaze of Francis towards the Isle.

"'Tis magic," whispered Kay and turned back from the Isle. "We had best depart post haste."

Francis continued to watch as the mist enveloped the last remaining part of the Isle; its trees and beach completely hidden from view... then slowly as the mist faded the Isle seemed to vanish from the water completely leaving only a still surface. His eyes swept the sea for traces of the Isle but could see nothing behind the boat: no rising hills, no majestic tree line, no rolling beach, no fields of flowers and no Lady... nothing. He rubbed his eyes as the flat water churned and bubbled as the force of the knights brought him back to their present position and he turned to face... land?

The landscape of Cornwall rose out of the water before him and he quickly glanced back, half expecting to have gone in a complete circle, but still there remained nothing of the Isle. He returned his attention to the land in the distance and stared across the horizon at the rising cliffs which stretched beyond his line of vision in both directions. He nodded satisfied that that was truly Cornwall, and soon he thought this would soon be over. He brought the scabbard close to his chest and pulled the blade slightly from the scabbard, allowing his eyes to flirt with the polished metal of the blade. The light of the sun danced off the silver and sparkled in his eyes, reflecting the glare of the sun and mirroring his image in the confines of the metal.

He could see his own image, but that mingled with another, a regal figure, dressed in exquisite robes and finery of which Francis could naught afford… sorry, not afford. He shook his head as he realised, he had corrected his own grammar and stared at the image smiling back at him in his reflection. It could see through the glare of the sun that it was him, but he still frowned at the crown placed upon his head, and the lavish fur around his collar.

"I am you." The whisper almost deafened him, and he glanced at Kay and Bedivere who were still forcing their arms through the water, occasionally glancing up towards the shoreline. "I am your past." Francis looked at the sword and frowned as his image smiled back at him through the metal surface. "I am your future… everything we could be, everything you are… and everything you ever were."

"Excalibur," he said softly, glancing up at the knight with a flushing red tinge growing across his cheeks, then looked back at the sword in his hand.

"I am your destiny," the voice purred again. "The calling." Francis forced the sword back into the scabbard, but the voice continued, "Look at me… look into my soul." Francis slowly drew the sword partially out of the scabbard and stared at his own smiling reflection and frowned as the image clouded. "I am your heritage. You are part of me, and I am part of you," the voice in his head echoed and Francis tried to shake the feeling of madness from his mind.

"When will this end?" he asked out loud.

"My Lord?" asked Bedivere. Francis realised he had closed his eyes and slowly opened his eyes and stared at Bedivere as he stood over Francis. The knight was standing in the centre of the boat and Francis glanced past him towards Kay who was wading through the water towards the shoreline. He had not realised they had reached land let alone had been sitting with his eyes closed.

"Where…"

"We have arrived, my Lord."

"So, I see," murmured Francis, "that seemed quick." He glanced out to sea where the water was still and calm offering no visible sign of the recent events of the Isle itself.

"Aye, my Lord," said Bedivere as he climbed over the side of the boat and placed his hands on the bow alongside those of Lord Kay. "'Tis mystical for sure."

"But how can the Isle disappear like that?" It was more of a comment than a question and he stared at his companions as they pulled the boat up onto the shore. "I mean, the land can't just disappear like that, can it?"

"It is best not to ask questions," stated Kay as his feet sunk in the soft sand. "The Lady has great powers, and it is not wise to provoke them." He glanced up the beach. "The sun is almost overhead; we had best return to the resting place."

"What?" Francis glanced up towards the sky, then his wrist and he examined the small numbers on the watch as the hands marched relentlessly as time continued despite his own actions. It was close to lunch, he realised, and his thoughts drifted once again to Gwen, and he briefly wondered how the other knights had fared in their mission to free her from Morgaine. With one final glance towards the sea, he felt the pang of guilt wash over him as he remembered the sacrifice given by Sir Galahad.

"Your thoughts, my Lord?" asked Bedivere.

"Hmm, oh nothing," lied Francis as he stared across the water.

"It was his choice," said Bedivere softly, "as is all of ours."

"But I never thought he would…"

"We follow you, my Lord, as we followed Arthur." Bedivere smiled and followed Kay up the beach and as he walked Francis watched as his footsteps left a trail along the sand.

For every step they took, the nearer he was to his destiny and with one final glance out to sea he remembered the words of the Lady: "doomed to live an unyielding sleep." Did this mean Galahad was not dead? Only placed once again into a deep sleep until either the curse could be lifted or until the sword called again should he fail? Or did it just mean he was dead? Francis had so many things he wanted to ask, so many things which remained unanswered. He did not know what to do for the best and watched as the waves lapped up against the beach, clawing at the sand. He pulled Excalibur close and turned to face the retreating backs of the two knights and set off after them, his own footsteps matching those of his companions.

"Morgaine," Mordred spoke slowly as he addressed his aunt, his words cast down towards the ground as he kept his head bowed in respectful resolution. "What thine intent?" His hand rested on the hilt of his sword as he spoke, and his fingers twitched over the leather-bound handle of his weapon.

"Nothing," she said simply.

"Explain."

"I need not explain to thee," she spat as she stared into the crystal sphere. "Thy machinations have endangered my plans time and time again. Thee have dishonoured me and shamed me." Her face bore witness to pity, but still she refused to look at her nephew.

"I shall regain my position!" snapped Mordred. "I thirst for power."

"Your ambition is as transparent as your mind," Morgaine responded.

"And your tongue shalt be thy death," he snapped, drawing his sword from its scabbard.

"Thoust dare draw arms against me… your own kin." She said smiling, finally turning to face him.

"Thy coldness hath humiliated me no more, deathless Morgaine."

"Thoust has spirit, Mordred, but no gall." She turned back to the sphere and stared at the mist swirling in the sphere. "But nevertheless, I need thee."

"I shall be king."

"Cease thy endless prattling!" Morgaine snapped. "And place thy weapon away. He will come and we shall have Excalibur… then thee shall receive thy reward."

"The throne."

Morgaine nodded sagely. "I have given my word have I not that thy desire shall be fulfilled and thy shall have what thee deserve."

"What must I do?"

"The Lords Tristan and Percival shall report that we have the girl; this will draw in the boy. Thee shall allow him access to the castle unaided, and once he is within our walls…"

"We kill him and take our reward!" concluded Mordred triumphantly.

"Nay, we offer him the girl."

"I do not understand."

"It is not thy place to understand, Mordred; be sure to keep the men out of sight until my mark." She straightened and walked towards her nephew and placed her arms around his shoulders, drawing him close to her body. "Then, my dear," she said softly stroking his hair, "Excalibur shall be mine."

49.

The Deathly Hallowed

Francis walked through the long tunnel, his feet echoing along the damp condition. Kay and Bedivere walked slowly behind Francis as they stepped into the vast cavern. Francis walked around the stone altar where he was greeted by Merlin and he presented the sword, still encased within the heavily bound leather scabbard. "Merlin," he whispered holding the sword towards the old man.

"My Lord." Merlin bowed his head in respectful discord, before placing his hands on the scabbard. "Excalibur," he breathed closing his eyes. "It has been so long." Despite himself, a smile broke his lined wizened face, breaking through his whiskered features. Francis watched as his two comrades avoided contact with Merlin and instead joined their fellow Knight Gawain at the rear of the cavern.

"What now?" he asked Merlin.

"We await the return of the Fisher King," stated the old man as he handed the sword back to Francis. "He will tell us what you need to do."

Francis nodded. "Do you know anything of the curse?" he asked.

"Nay, only what thy hath been told by my Lady."

"Couldn't you have just told me all of this?"

"My Lord, it had to be the Lady, she held Excalibur and I am bound by my oath to act only as counsel."

A shuffling noise from the mouth of the cavern alerted them to the presence of another body heading down the tunnel. Francis looked through the darkness of the cavern and could see a gorged shape shambling along the long passage. He frowned at the figure; it did not seem as large as it had last time and its body seemed to contort in a variety of ways as the shadow pulled its way along the corridor. The sound of dragging feet was joined by heavy breathing as the figure neared the main body of the cavern.

"Percival," the whisper from the throng of knights behind Francis, broke the silence as the figure… figures broke the dim light and stumbled into the expanse of the central cavern. Gawain broke free of his two comrades and grabbed at the body in Percival's arms.

"He is close to death," whispered Percival, holding his own ribs and struggling against the exertion of the journey.

"Rest," eased Gawain as he took the weight of Tristan beneath his own body, hoisting the figure upon his shoulders and carrying him to the altar. Percival sank to the floor, his back sliding down the wall until his body sat slumped in the patches of water which lay across the uneven floor. "Merlin." He looked at Merlin as he rested the knight upon stone. "Can ye assist?"

Merlin cast his gaze across the crumpled body of Tristan and sighed heavily. "His injuries seem severe," he said at last, before running his hands across the swellings and cuts which protruded through his broken body, "but they would appear only superficial." His words drew blank looks from the knights and Merlin spoke again, "I mean… he should survive. Thoust has lost a lot of blood, but with rest…" His words were disturbed by violent coughing from Tristan. Merlin frowned and pressed his hands against his chest softly, pressing his fingers gently against his body. Tristan coughed again and flinched under the pressure of the old man, dousing his lips with flecks of blood as the air was expelled from his body. "Rest," eased Merlin and he turned from the knight, his head bowed and a resigned look crossing a worried brow.

"What is wrong?" asked Bedivere looking at him from his position across the cavern.

Merlin shook his head. "His wounds are worse than I thought," he admitted. "From the injuries I have felt broken bones within his chest, I cannot do anything for him."

"But you must… you're Merlin!" shouted Francis.

"I cannot defy death," he said sadly.

"But the Lady said—"

"We can still die," stated Merlin. "The curse means we shall be reborn."

Francis looked about the cavern and frowned. "Where's Bors?" he said quietly.

"Bors is dead," whispered Percival from the floor, his head lolled and sagged onto his chest through exhaustion.

"No, he can't be," wailed Francis, "not another." He looked at the question in Percival's eyes and added, "Galahad."

Lord Kay knelt by Percival and placed his head in his hand, gently rising it. "Percival," he whispered putting his head close to his friend's, "how?"

"They were waiting," he coughed as he spoke. "They followed us to the dungeon—"

"Did you find Gwen?" interrupted Francis. Kay shot him a ferocious look and Francis lowered his head ashamed of his outburst.

"Yes, she is safe, but still a prisoner."

"Bors," urged Kay, "what about Bors?"

"They were waiting… they knew we were coming. I was jumped by the mouth of the tunnel; Bors and Tristan made it through into the castle. They found the girl and…" Percival coughed, and his eyes closed slightly. "So tired."

"Percival!" snapped Kay. "What about Bors?"

"Mordred," he whispered, his head sagging forward with exhaustion.

"Sleep, my old friend," said Kay easing his head against the wall and he stood, his eyes remaining on the resting body of Percival against the wall. "Damnation!" snapped Kay.

"It's my fault," whispered Francis staring at his feet. All eyes on the cavern were drawn towards him as he spoke. He looked at each one of the knights in turn before finishing on Merlin. "It's all my fault," he said again. "Galahad, Bors, I sent them both to their death."

"We fight with honour." The voice was crackled and strained. Francis looked towards the injured form of Tristan on the altar. "We fight to die and we die to fight," he said through rasping breaths, coughing between words. Blood dribbled from his mouth and stained his teeth as he smiled through the pain of talking.

Francis leant by the stone altar. "But you shouldn't die for me," he said desperately looking at the knight.

"We… do… not," said Tristan. "We… die… for… glory." He coughed violently again and grasped at Francis' arm, looking deeply into his eyes smiling through reddened teeth. "What… better… way… to… die… than… for… a… maiden." He coughed and fell silent.

"Tristan!" shouted Francis. "Tristan!" His words echoed through the cavern. "Tristan!"

"My Lord," said Merlin softly. "He is gone."

50.

Treachery of the Heart

"That's it," said Francis standing to his feet, "I've had enough."

"What does thoust mean?" asked Merlin.

"I mean I've had enough." Francis could feel his shoulder sag under the weight of expectancy. "The deaths… they are all laid at my door," he said looking around the cavern. "If I am the direct descendant of King Arthur, then I must be held responsible." The cavern was silent as the men inside the cave all watched Francis as he walked around the altar, his eyes never leaving the body of Tristan as he lay unmoving on the slab. "It is about time that I faced my duties," he said, stopping before Merlin and holding out Excalibur in his hands towards the old man. "Therefore, I shall go to the castle and confront Morgaine myself."

"My Lord—"

"Tristan was right," Francis said. "I've been hiding behind all of you every step of the way. I must face my destiny."

"If that is thy desire—"

"It is." He nodded. "And as Tristan said what better way to die than for the maiden you love." He smiled at Merlin. "I've always wanted to be a hero, but never had the guts until now."

"My Lord—"

"No, I'm sorry. But I must do this." He turned to face the knights. "Alone," he added.

"Nay!" snapped Kay. "Thoust cannot."

"I can and I will. I am sorry, Lord Kay, but I will not endanger anyone else. This is something I must do."

"I hope thine maiden is worth it," said Bedivere stepping forward and taking Francis' hands.

"I shall lead thee to the edge of the forest," said Gawain.

"Thank you," said Francis.

"My Lord."

"Yes, Merlin?"

"What of Excalibur?"

"Excalibur shall remain in your care until I return."

"Should thee return," whispered Kay.

"I will return, Lord Kay, and when I do, all this will come to an end, I promise." He passed the sword to Merlin and turned to Gawain and nodded. A deep rumbling from the rear of the cavern interrupted his departure and Francis braced himself another attack by Morgaine. "What is it?" he asked as he peered through the gloom as the noise increased. A pile of rocks moved around on the floor of the cavern, swarming and swelling over the wall and slowly climbed the cavern, embracing the wall forming a large column, stretching up the expanse of the cave wall.

"Our tomb," said Merlin quietly as he watched the rocks forming. Francis watched as they continued to climb up along the wall and for the first time noticed another two similar structures embracing the cavern wall. "These are where we rest until we answer the call of Excalibur." He walked around the altar and placed a hand on the uneven structure as it settled into place. "This is Tristan," he said simply resting his head against the rock.

Francis stared back at the cave in the distance still visibly shaken by the sudden appearance of the stone structure. The body had still lain dormant on the altar, but he knew somewhere in his heart that the words Merlin had uttered had been correct. The curse and the whole "thoust shall live an undying rest" had stricken with him and he knew that the three columns held the sleeping essence of the knights. Somehow, Francis knew they had all died after Camlann; they all had their own personal stories to tell. Galahad with the Grail, Bors and the maiden, so he could conclude that with each death their 'soul' would return to the resting place and await the calling. He looked at Gawain and wondered what his story was. Of all the knights this was the one he knew truly little about, not through the legend of King Arthur, hell if that was the case, he had to admit he knew little about any of them, but he had spent less time with this one than the others; even Bors had stories which he had been told, but nothing about Gawain.

He watched the figure of the knight as he strode through the Cornish countryside confidently pushing through waving grass, as his eyes shone in the sunlight while surveying the surrounding countryside. "We must be wary," he said as he glanced back towards Francis. "There could be Morgaine's troops all around us," he warned.

This had not actually occurred to Francis, but then how else would Morgaine have known where they were on the boat… or at the castle for that matter. He subconsciously looked around him, but only saw trees and grass running through his vision. Gawain moved through the trees and they left the beach area and moved out into the forest. Francis struggled to keep track of the knight as he moved quickly and expertly through the forest, his green armour offering perfect cover against the bushes and the undergrowth and several times he lost track of the knight, only for him to appear by his side time and time again.

"My Lord," Gawain said in hushed tones, his eyes darting around the area. "The castle of Tintagel is beyond that ridge," he said pointing. "It would be my guess that Tristan would have used the secret entrance to the castle on the west wing."

"Not so secret if they were caught," commented Francis wryly but allowed himself to be led away by the knight. "Gawain," said Francis as they moved through the forest.

"My Lord."

"What's your story?"

"I do not understand."

"I mean." He struggled to find the words without sounding harsh. "I know some of the others, but you're a mystery."

"There is not much to tell, my Lord," said Gawain.

"Please."

"Very well, but we must hurry. I wish to make it back from the castle before nightfall." He glanced towards the afternoon sky as he continued to move through the greenery. "I was born to King Lot and Queen Morgause, and I would have been the rightful successor to the throne upon Arthur's death had not it been for my friendship with Lancelot." His eyes flicked over the bushes as they moved while he continued to talk in hushed tones, "I draw my courage and strength from the light of day, and I am by practice a mixer of herbs."

"So, you're a doctor of sorts," said Francis.

"I have studied ailments, I will concede. But I know truly little of medicine… only natural remedies."

"Herbal medicine," murmured Francis, "and you're afraid of the dark." The statement almost slipped out and Francis blushed as Gawain skidded to a halt before him, turning slowly.

"Are not we all," stated the knight, then abruptly turned and ran on. Francis stared after him for a moment, in shock that such a handsome muscular man such as he could be afraid of the dark.

"Explains why he wants to be back before dark," he murmured to himself and forced his way through the undergrowth behind the knight.

He forced himself through the bushes, brambles catching his skin and drawing small traces of blood as the barbs bit at his arm and found himself staring over the castle from above. He stared at the rising turrets, and walls drawing in their magnificence, its stone walls jutting from the rock face of the landscape the monument of ancient Britain stood defiantly looking over the sea. Much of the castle lay in ruins, with most of the structure being lost to time, but elements of the castle remained intact, including several arches and walls. He could see doorways which would have led to exquisite banqueting halls rising from the floor and grass forced its way over the site and invaded the once glorious structure. Through the desolation, a singular structure remained, partially hidden from view by the landscape but unmistakably a hall of sorts. He could see the building rising from the ruins, its four walls almost desolate in construction but unmistakably the remnants of a hall.

"Gawain!" he whispered as he realised, he stood alone before the ruined site. "Gawain."

A hand grasped his arm and pulled him down to the floor and Francis looked around sharply at the knight who was hidden amongst the brambles watching the castle from the safety of the bush. "Be silent!" he hissed through gritted teeth. "We are undetected... let us remain so."

Francis fell to the floor and lay on the grass, his face buried in the soft dirt and his body pressing against the warm ground. He raised his head to follow the glare of Gawain and could see figures in the distance swarming around the outskirts of the ruins. The armour shone in the moonlight and for the first time he realised how much he may have misjudged the whole situation.

"How many are there?" he asked.

Gawain frowned as he peered through the bramble. "Too many to count, my Lord, we are much outnumbered." Francis did not like the sound of that but continued to stare at the scene below. "Is it still thy intent to gain access?" he asked.

Francis nodded. "I have to try," he said, trying to sound braver than he really was.

"Thoust is brave," stated Gawain, "we shall continue beside the mountain path, gaining advantage through the bramble." He indicated to the winding road which ran parallel to the castle. "Then we drop down the cliff to the concealed entrance." Francis nodded and followed the knight making sure the glint in his green armour was always just in sight until they reached the edge of the castle. Gawain pointed through the thorns at a small hole in the wall. "That is yon entrance," he said, "this is where Tristan and Bors would have entered."

Francis placed a hand on Gawain's arm. "Do you think I'm mad?" he asked the knight.

"Nay, my Lord," he said smiling, "thoust is in love." He stifled a laugh and glanced around. "Now go quickly."

Francis nodded and moved quickly across the open ground to the passage and forced his way through the concealed entrance and into the dark confined space of the passage. He had no idea what was waiting for him at the other end, and he could only wish and hope that Morgaine would not expect an attack so soon after the first and in broad daylight at that. He could feel the confines of the passage press down against him as he pushed his way through the roots which gorged their way through the ground and wrapped around the crumbling brickwork and ran his hands over the damp cloisters of the ageing walls wondering how many had walked this way in the past. Judging by the conditions of the ageing passage it had remained hidden from view by the local authorities otherwise it would have been blocked by massive metal poles at either end to stop the unwary tourist. His thoughts wandered to the safety of Gawain who was hidden in the undergrowth behind him before they drifted rather foolishly to himself. He had no idea what was waiting for him at the other end and almost wished he could find Gwen standing their arms spread waiting for him.

He could see a small glimmer of light ahead of him and he felt the final few feet of the tunnel, pausing only to regain his footing as he stepped over the uneven ground. The end of the tunnel, like the rest of it was overgrown with vine, ivy and thorny bramble, but traces of cut creeper alerted him to the fact that Tristan had indeed travelled this way before him. He glanced back through the darkened tunnel and contemplated his retreat before finally pushing his way through the open chasm before him.

He stood in what were the remains of a corridor, and he cast his eyes across the crumbling stonework which laid around the floor around his feet. Vast boulders crushed weeds and flowers as the echelons of time had eroded the building and he ran his fingers along the remnants of the wall, imagining what the castle must have looked like centuries ago. He could imagine scores of men and woman walking up and down this hallway, coming and going from the daily routine much in the way he walked around his own home. He looked up into the sky and could see the sun poking through the remains of the building as though it were watching in progress in silent contemplation. The walls were old and covered in vegetation and travelled in both directions along the ruined site and Francis wondered which way he should travel. He glanced at the floor and could see the heavy indentations made by heavily armoured feet leading off from his position into the bowels of the site. He followed the trail until it led him to a small opening which led downward into darkness, and he glanced around him before plunging headfirst into the thick black confined space.

He moved slowly and carefully down the crumbling stairs, his hands pressing against the rough strewn walls and as his fingers brushed the surface of the brickwork traces of stone fell away from their moorings as it crumbled beneath his touch. He squinted through the darkness as the black swallowed him and placed one foot carefully before the other as each step took him lower beneath the ground and further away from safety. The condition of the passage led Francis to conclude that this was yet another area which had laid hidden from view for centuries and further down he ploughed into the bowels of the site. A light flickered beyond his vision, and he could see shadows dance across the walls, contorting and dancing across the tunnel as the pitch-black condition gave way to a slight glimmer of light. Could this be it? he wondered briefly to himself and continued heading forward towards the radiant light.

Wall mounted torches heralded his arrival and the flame danced and licked at the air as he passed, cautiously peering through the gloom into the small area beyond the passage. It spanned out into the small rooms; two were just an open archway and Francis peered carefully into each, his eyes struggling to adjust to the darkness within each room. He cast his eyes upward as he peered into the rooms and from high above his head, he could make out small vestiges of sunlight cast down from an open ceiling. The third room was covered by a newly fitted door, and Francis ran his hand over the wooden surface, tracing the lines of the grain within the wood and fingering the metal latches before running his hand over the sturdy metal handle. The large black iron ring fell from the latch and Francis took the handle in his handle, weighing the metal in his hand.

He stood on his toes and peered through the small grating mounted high in the actual door and whispered through the grate, glancing back at the tunnel as he did. "Gwen!" he whispered urgently. He hoped his voice had not carried, and he became aware that the passage was his only exit and suddenly wished he had brought Excalibur after all. "Gwen!" he whispered again… nothing. There was no sound from the room, and Francis turned sighing at his failure.

"Francis," the voice was quiet, and he almost missed it. "Francis," again the female voice came through the small grate.

"Gwen!" he whispered again through the grate and into the darkness.

"Francis is that you?" came the voice again.

"Yes," he confirmed and pushed at the heavy door. "Don't worry," he whispered softly as he pressed his body weight against the heavy wooden structure and pushed.

He sighed inwardly as the door shifted under his weight and thanked the lord that it had not been locked. As the door moved under his weight, the thought suddenly struck him, that it was not locked… in a dungeon that would be construed as slightly odd at the very least, but the sound of her sobs pushed the thought from his mind and forced him onward. The door struggled to obstruct its barrier as Francis slowly pushed it open and light spilled into the dark room. As beams of light fell through the small opening, Francis could see why the door had not been barred. Gwen sat on a large bale of hay, her hands tied at her wrist with some form of twine and around her feet, a thick rope secured her to the nearby wall. He forced the door further open, and she smiled as he spilled into the room and stood before her, glancing around the confined area urgently.

"Francis," she said softly, through her clenched mouth. He looked at her face and could see sadness traced across her eyes and the evidence of tears has scarred her pretty features.

"Are you hurt?" he asked as he raced over to her and knelt on one knee, holding her hands in his and gazing into her eyes. She smiled and sniffed back her tears as she shook her head. "You'll be okay now," he said softly as he pulled at the cords around her wrists. "I promise you," he said as the twine fell to the floor, "that nothing will happen to you." He looked at her as she rubbed her wrists and smiled back at him. "I will always be here," he said as his fingers moved over the thick rope and traced one end of the rope to a large metal rind embedded in the wall. His fingers moved over the knot which bound her legs and it fell away easily from her ankle and onto the floor where it rested in the dirty puddles. He looked at her and smiled, brushing a strand of hair from her face. "I promise I will protect you, and I will always try to look after you." He rested his hand against her cheek, and she pressed her face deep into his touch, closing her eyes under his caress.

Gwen looked at him and could feel her eyes swell with emotion, her face breaking into a smile and her hands snaked around his body, drawing him close. She felt safe in his arms, she felt warm... It made what she needed to do so much harder. She smiled at him and looked deep into his eyes, pulling him close to her.

Francis could feel himself swell under her touch and the excitement of his position combined with the warmth of her body. He shook his head as she pulled him close. "We must go," he whispered, but under her touch his body refused to move as he became lost in her eyes.

They shone in the light from the fire outside the cell and he sank in her beauty. Gwen sank deeper in his grip, her arms wrapped around his body and sinking towards his waist. She looked into his face and placed her lips firmly against his, locking their bodies tightly with each other.

Francis reluctantly pulled away and looked into her eyes, a small sliver of saliva falling from their lips as they parted. "We should..." He indicated towards the door.

"We should," she agreed, but her actions pulled him close again, their lips locked in passion and fury as the warmth of their bodies flowed and fought through each other. They pulled apart again and she took a deep heavy breath and rested the top of her head against his chin and looked down the expanse of his body. She returned her gaze to his eyes, and the passion forced their lips together again, excitement rising through the dampness of the dungeon. Her fingers snaked from his waist, and she grasped at the belt around his jeans, her fingers working on the buckle and releasing the leather-bound strap from the small metal clasp.

Francis looked down at her hands and shook his head as it rested against hers as she watched her own movements. "We shouldn't," he whispered. "Not here." His breath was hot against her face as he whispered in her ear.

"Quick," she teased and placed her lips hard against his again, while her hands fumbled across the front of his trousers, forcing the zip down and then moving inside his trousers gripping at his rising body.

"Gwen."

"I'm horny. Fuck me," she whispered, an excited smirk crossing her face as she pulled him from his underwear and out into the open. She gripped at his growing bulge and gently moved her hand along his groin, stroking and teasing him with the softness of her touch. He closed his eyes and the excitement in his growing genitals rose through his body and he found his hand snaking beneath her top, reaching for her soft fleshy breast beneath her bra.

"We don't have time," he insisted as she continued to rub.

"Just make it quick," she whispered as her hand continued to move along his genitals.

He placed his head on her shoulder, closed his eyes and moved his hands down by her side slowly running his hands beneath her jodhpurs and pushing them slightly down her thighs. He looked at her and she forced a smile as she pulled him close to her again, locking in a deep kiss as their bodies embraced in lust and wanting. She closed her eyes and groaned slightly under his touch as she felt him slowly move inside her and his hands moved under her buttocks lifting her slightly onto the bale of hay, their bodies rocking in time with each other. She pushed him away from her mouth as he moved faster between her legs, and she pulled her thighs around his hips and the thrust of his body intensified, moving quicker in time to the rhythm of their passion.

"Ah! the passion of youth!" laughed a female voice from the doorway. "You see, Mordred," chided Morgaine, "'tis how you quench a woman's desire." Morgaine laughed and entered the room moving quickly across to the young couple and placed her hands on his naked buttocks and leant forward whispering in his ear, "So full of energy." She laughed as Francis struggled to pull at his trousers. "Don't stop on my account," laughed Morgaine barely able to contain her joy at the sight of the couple's love. "It has been so long since I tasted the youthful passion. So keen and eager, as I remember, so full of inexperience and so eager to please." She laughed and squeezed his buttocks, smiling at Gwen over his shoulder. She released her grip and allowed Francis to pull his trousers back up over his naked form. "When thy youth is decent, Mordred, see he is brought to me." She turned and laughed as she passed Mordred, standing smirking in the doorway.

Mordred stared at the couple and smirked. "You have done well," he said towards Gwen as he watched her pull her jodhpurs up over her waist.

"Gwen?" said Francis softly, reaching out a hand to her.

"Don't," she warned and covered her eyes with her arm and sped past Mordred into the corridor beyond the door.

"Gwen!"

51.

Ultimation

Francis walked in the courtyard, followed by Mordred and he watched as Morgaine smoothed down the hair on Gwen's head. "My dear, it would appear that your suitor has arrived," she said smiling towards Francis. Gwen shot a glance towards Francis and turned away quickly unable to meet his stare. He felt tortured, his heart died at her betrayal, and he felt heavy in his feelings. He felt his emotion swelling in his gut as a combination of anger and disappointment threatened to overcome him. "Don't blame her, my dear," cooed Morgaine, releasing Gwen's hair from her grasp, "it really wasn't her fault." She glided across the courtyard towards Francis and stood before him regarding the youth carefully. "She didn't have much of a choice." She smiled, then brought the back of her hand sharply across his cheek. The force of the strike thrust him backward and he stumbled to the floor, his hand sneaking to the side of his face. He could taste a slight tinge of iron in his mouth and his hand revealed small traces of blood from his mouth as he pulled his hand away gingerly. "What she did... she did for you," she said softly and turned on her heels and strode across the courtyard back to Gwen.

"Leave her alone," whispered Francis.

Morgaine laughed and grasped Gwen's face pulling her close. "You see, my dear," she cooed in her face squashing Gwen's face between her slim fingers, "he still cares even after you betrayed his trust."

"What do you want?" snapped Francis.

"What makes thee think I want anything from you?"

"Then I'm free to leave," he mocked her and pretended to move away only for Mordred to grab him roughly by the shoulders.

"Let me have this knave and we can dispense of this jest."

"How many times?" snapped Morgaine flashing him a quick warning. "As I was saying," Morgaine spoke directly to Francis, "I wish nothing of thee."

"But—"

"Hah!" she laughed clapping her hands together. "I like thee boy," she said. "Your actions belittle your emotion."

"And your actions betray your words," countered Francis. "I know what you want." He stared at her as he spoke, and the pair stood frozen, locked in a static glare.

"Then let us dispense the niceties and commence to accord." She moved across the courtyard and circled Francis slowly, standing behind him and leaning forward to his ear she whispered, "Excalibur."

"And there we have it!" Francis exclaimed. "Excalibur." He turned his head to look at her. "I don't have it," he said simply.

Morgaine clenched her fists as anger rose through her body and she slammed her hand against his face. He felt his skin bruise as her hand connected with his chin and the pain coursed through his face. "You lie!" she spat. "I know you have the sword!"

"I never said I didn't. I just said I don't have it." He spread his arms offering her a look at his unarmed body.

"So, you do have it," Morgaine purred. "I knew it to be so." Her eyes sparkled with the revelation, and she placed her hands together, closing her eyes. "I shall have it," she whispered.

"No," said Francis determinedly, "I've told Merlin to return the sword if I do not return." The beads of perspiration formed on his forehead as he lied, and Francis hoped Morgaine could not read minds or see through his lie.

"It matters not," dismissed Morgaine, "for we shall take the sword by force if need be." She waved him away.

"Why?" asked Francis. "Why all the killing?"

"It is our way," Mordred snapped. "The throne shall be mine by right of conquest." He strode across the courtyard and joined Morgaine by the crystal sphere. "It is written that once I smite the purge of Arthur, then I, Mordred, shall be king of the Britons." He smiled triumphantly as he slipped his hand into that of Morgaine.

She looked at Francis and smiled. "I offer thee a deal, youth," she said eventually. "Thoust does not wish bloodshed." Her statement brought a resolute shake of the head from Francis. "Then I offer thee this." She released her grip on Mordred's hand and walked towards Gwen who was still standing, silent, watching the exchange between the two parties.

Francis waited, watching Morgaine as she circled Gwen like a vulture slowly stalking its prey. She ran her hand through her hair and leant her head against Gwen's, smiling at Francis as she did so. Her fingers played with the strands of her hair, and they cascaded through her touch. He watched as Morgaine's fingers curled and swiftly, she tightened her grip on Gwen's hair, pulling it down towards her chest. Gwen winced with the pain as her hair was pulled forcibly and a slight scream escaped from her mouth, which caused Francis to step forward slightly from his position only to be barred by the burly arm of Agravain who had moved from the shadows.

"Thoust shall give me Excalibur freely and of thine own will," cooed Morgaine.

"Will I?" commented Francis.

"Thoust will, and moreover thoust shall do it tonight." She smiled and tightened her grip. "For if thy do not, the girl will die." She laughed as Mordred drew his sword and ran it gently across the throat of Gwen, the cold steel pressing against her soft skin.

"Please," Gwen begged, her words unheeded as Morgaine stared defiantly at Francis.

"Your decision."

Francis looked at Gwen and closed his eyes turning his head from her. His mind spun in turmoil; he knew she had betrayed him and led him into a trap but despite it all...

"Francis." Gwen's voice sounded desperate as the blade moved slowly across the skin, producing a small cut below her ear. He opened his eyes and saw Mordred grinning as a small stream of blood flowed down her neck from below her ear.

"All right!" he snapped and stared down at the ground. "Leave her alone," he warned, his voice waivered with emotion. "You shall have Excalibur."

52.

The Heart Desires…

Francis emerged from the tunnel and blinked in the sunlight. He glanced around at the undergrowth and moved into the open away from the tunnel. The cuts on his hands and the bruises meant nothing to him, the pain in his heart grew heavy. "My Lord," whispered the voice from the bushes. Francis looked up from the floor and peered into the bramble where he was greeted by a pair of inquisitive eyes. A figure gently pulled himself free from the thorny bush, his green armour shining in the sunlight. "Where is thy maiden?" he asked as he stared behind Francis.

"I failed Gawain," Francis whispered, tears forming in the corner of his eyes, his hands clenched into tight fists, his fingers curled and his nails digging into the palms of his hands. But still the pain in his heart pounded greater than any physical torment. "She is still in there." He could not bring himself to look at Gawain knowing what he had just agreed to, and he could not bring himself to look back at the castle.

"What do we do now?" Gawain asked.

"We go back to the cave," Francis said simply. "I need… I need… time," he said eventually. Gawain nodded and moved off into the bushes, with Francis following. He stopped and gave the tunnel a quick glance, his heart full of remorse and pain burning through his body.

"Do we trust the boy?" Mordred asked as the image in the crystal ball faded.

"He shall not abandon her," Morgaine said as she moved her hands slowly across the smooth sphere. She looked at Gwen and smiled at her. "I am sorry, my dear, if my nephew hath hurt thee," she apologised and crossed the floor of the courtyard towards her. Gwen flinched as Morgaine raised her hand to her face. "Do not fear me," laughed Morgaine. She pressed her hand against the wound and moved her fingers across the line of blood. "It was a necessity. Nothing more."

"Was that supposed to be an apology?" said Gwen. "'Cause it didn't sound much like one."

"We do what we must to serve our purpose," Morgaine stated simply. "Thy hath assisted me well, my dear, and I have promised you the world once I have Excalibur." She smiled and withdrew her hand from Gwen's neck and examined her blood covered fingers, moving each one in turn, her eyes sparkling and revelling with the flow of crimson down each of her fingers. "I hath given word to protect thine person." She laughed as she licked the blood from her fingers and turned to face Mordred. "Come," she ordered, "we have much to prepare for."

Gwen looked at the crystal ball and could see the image of Francis forcing his way through the bramble and thorns of the bushes and she felt a tear fall from her eye. "So has he," she whispered softly.

The cavern was dark, and the sky overhead was beginning to turn as night was chasing the sun from the sky and day was replaced by the sweet embrace of night. Francis stood on the edge of the tunnel and sighed heavily, his emotion overwhelming his body. He was filled with emotions ranging from love to hate and guilt through to remorse. Each different conflict coursed through his body as he stood on the percipience of decision. Gwen had betrayed his love; could he now betray a group that would follow him blindly to their own death?

"You must do what is right." The voice behind him made him jump and he spun around sharply to come face to face with the huge form of the Fisher King.

"But what if doing the right thing is the wrong thing," Francis commented staring back down the dark tunnel. "For the first time in my life, I've got people looking at me… relying on me to do the right thing and now I don't know what to do for the best."

"What does your heart tell you?"

"Fuck my heart!" snapped Francis. "Look where that's got me." He could feel the tears swell in his eyes again and he wiped away the first drops from his face before they fell.

"Do not be afraid to show thy emotion," stated the Fisher King. "You are the king elect; they will follow."

"But they shouldn't," said Francis. "I mean nothing to them."

"You give them purpose," said the Fisher King placing a decaying hand on his shoulder, "as she gives you purpose."

"What do you know of love?" snapped Francis.

"Do thee think I was always like this?" said the Fisher King. "A helpless cripple? I have known love… I have known heartache. What the heart wants, the heart wants and there is naught we can do about that. It is what you decide to do that will commit the future."

"I don't understand."

"Your decisions here will cause ripples that will spiral across your life. The bigger the decision the greater the ripple, such is the way of the world." He moved his hand and gestured towards the tunnel. "Thoust can hide here… or thy can face thine destiny."

"Maybe hiding is the best thing."

"Sometimes, doing nothing can be worse than doing something." He paused in the entrance of the tunnel and moved his giant frame to stare at Francis. "She will not thank thee, but will she depend on thee. This much I do know. What thoust feel?"

Francis shuffled uncomfortably. He had never really liked to talk about his emotions and always had difficulty opening and now here he was expectant on the very things which scared him. "I love her," he whispered softly.

"As I thought," said the Fisher King nodding.

"Do you think she's too good for me?" Francis spoke directly to the Fisher King.

"That is not for me to decide."

"But she's so out of my league," whined Francis.

"It is your actions and your heart which will win the love of thy maiden… not thine aspect." He pushed Francis down into the tunnel. "Be good," he whispered as they moved slowly through the damp conditions. "Be kind." Francis could see the light cast from the torches ahead. "Be thyself." He could see the shadows move and bounce across the walls of the cavern as they continued their slow trek. "Be true." He could see Merlin talking to Gawain by the altar, their hands a blur of motion as they spoke. "Stay true to thy word."

"I said I would look after her," Francis whispered back through the darkness. "I promised her." His voice was tinged with sadness.

"Thee know what must be done."

Francis paused before the mouth of the cavern and looked at the Fisher King. "They won't be happy."

"They will understand. Do not underestimate their loyalty."

Francis took a deep breath and walked into the cavern and immediately felt a wave of intimidation as five sets of eyes were trained on him. Merlin bowed his head and spoke softly, "Lord Gawain hath told us of thy failure."

Francis nodded and looked about the cavern at the small band of knights. "That is correct," he said, "but it is not over."

"What is thy intent?"

Francis held his hand out towards Merlin. "Excalibur," he whispered.

Merlin stared at the flat palm of Francis's hand and frowned. "My Lord?"

"It is over," Francis said simply. "We have been skulking round in the dark for too long." He grasped at Excalibur and pulled it from the scabbard raising the sword above his head and climbing upon a small boulder addressed the knights around him. "We have hidden in the shadows!" he called staring around the room and the throng of expectant faces. "Now is the time of restitution!" he shouted. "The time of the calling! Now is the time we few stand for justice!"

He could see the level of excitement grow in the cavern as the faces of the knights changed from frowns to grinning champions.

"We march to Tintagel!" shouted Francis over the murmur from the knights. "We take the castle." Lord Kay pulled his sword from his scabbard and raised it in the air, a look of glory crossing his face. "We sweep Morgaine and her forces from the land!" Bedivere pulled his sword from his scabbard and waved it high above his head looking about him in wild delight. "We save the girl!" Gawain helped Percival to his feet and the pair smiled insanely at each other. "And we put Mordred to the sword!" The cavern was rising to a fever pitch as Francis continued. "For Briton!" he called over the chorus of cheering. "For Excalibur!" The sound of cheering was rising to a fever pitch. "For Arthur!" The cheer was deafening as swords were raised in the air above their heads and the joyful expectancy rose in a symphony throughout the darkness.

Only Merlin frowned.

53.

A King's Treachery

The knights spilled from the cavern and into the night air and Francis watched as they flocked out over the beach, their swords reaching high in the air and their voices carrying on the wind. "You don't approve," said Francis standing next to Merlin at the mouth of the cave.

"No," he said simply.

"Why not? Surely you knew it would come to this."

"Mayhap but I still do not approve." Merlin watched the knights wistfully as they ran across the beach to the sandbanks. "I remember Camlann like it 'twas yesterday," he said sadly. "The deaths... the carnage... in the name of what? Mercy? Justice? Revenge?" He shook his head sadly. "Aye, I did know it would come to this, but I had hoped there would be another way," he admitted. "We are all doomed to die one day, let us make sure between birth and death, life is lived to its potential." He smiled at Francis and took his hand in his own. "I do not condemn thy actions, but I implore thee to be safe."

"I had better," Francis said uncomfortably pointing over his shoulder at the disappearing knights.

Merlin watched him run across the sand and felt the presence of the Fisher King by his shoulder. "He is young," he said softly, sadly shaking his head as he watched him run into the distance.

"As was Arthur."

"That may be so, but this is a different age."

"But he faces the same problems."

"Not the same circumstance," countered Merlin.

"They will be back," assured the Fisher King.

"Thoust knows?"

The Fisher King shook his head slowly. "Nay, 'tis but a hope, but I feel they will be back."

"Aye, but how many?"

Francis emerged from the sand grass and stood on the edge of the forest. He scanned the area and cursed his own luck as the knights had all but disappeared, only the markings of their feet marked in the soft ground remained. He knelt and ran his fingers around the deep furrow in the ground, glancing into the dark wood. The branches clawed at the light and around each tree shadows hid, waiting to snatch him. He would have no choice but to enter the forest alone and hope for the best. He was sure he could find the way, but her had no idea if he could catch his comrades as the crashed through the woods. He craned his ear trying to pick up on the noises of the knights, but the air was still only broken by the occasional bird or insect. He stepped through the barrier of the trees and pushed through the branches as they reached for his clothing. He could see a figure laying on the floor, sitting up against an old oak.

"Percival," Francis whispered. The knight opened his eyes and smiled at the youth as he ran over to his prone position. "Are you hurt?" he asked urgently checking his body for signs of wounds.

"Nay, my Lord. I am but still tired from my ordeal in the castle," he admitted.

"Where are the others?" Francis whispered urgently as his eyes flicked across the forest.

"I could not keep their pace," admitted Percival as he struggled to his feet, using his sword as a prop to propel his body from the floor. Percival breathed heavily as he leant on Francis and smiled at the young boy. "So tired," he whispered, placing a finger over his lips.

"You should not have come," said Francis, looking at the bruises beneath his armour.

"And miss this," laughed Percival. "Nay, my Lord." His eyes darted around the forest suddenly alert. "We should be wary," he warned.

"Come." Francis started to move, but a sound from above froze him to the spot. He looked up into the branches of the trees as three large figures dropped from the confines of the tree and stood in a circle around both he and Lord Percival. Francis struggled with Excalibur in the scabbard around his waist and was met by a wall of laughter... laughter?

He glanced around to see the small ring of knights standing around him. "Ha! I told thee; he would not see us!" roared Kay as he slapped Bedivere on the back.

"Have thee, my Lord!" laughed Gawain. "'Tis a fine jest!" He walked towards Francis and placed an arm around his neck and pulled the youth to his chest, placing his head beneath his arm and ruffling his hair.

"Well played, my Lord Percival," commented Bedivere.

"My thanks," said Percival smiling and dispensing his own sword from his hand into its scabbard. Francis frowned for a moment, then despite his best intention, his face broke into a wide grin.

"Idiots," he laughed as he looked around the forest. "How far are we from Tintagel?"

"About an hour's walk, my Lord," commented Gawain. "We could make it before the moon is above our heads."

Francis nodded. "Then I think we had better move."

The knights moved off in single procession through the forest, Gawain at the lead of the group, and Kay bringing up the rear, with Bedivere and Percival each side of Francis as they made their way through the forest. Gawain would stop at every few paces and check the area, before moving off making the progress of the group slow. Francis fingered the hilt of the sword and looked guiltily at the backs of Percival and Gawain. The Fisher King was right he knew what he had to do, and how to do it. He only hoped he was doing the right thing. They pushed their way through the thick bramble and the thorns reached and cut at Francis' skin, but he carried on regardless of the discomfort, his heart still weighing heavy and the guilt gnawing in the pit of his stomach.

"The castle," whispered Gawain from ahead of the party. He glanced back towards Francis. "What shalt we do now, my Lord?" he asked.

"We go the same way as we did before," Francis replied and allowed Gawain to lead the way through the undergrowth and trees to the same patch of land where they had found the tunnel. Percival gazed about uncertainly around him and pulled his sword from his scabbard. "You all right?" asked Francis as he stared at him.

Percival nodded. "Last time I was here, I was attacked and captured." He forced a smile and looked at Francis, pushing his sword back into the scabbard. "I am sorry for the caution."

"That's all right," eased Francis.

"I do not like this," commented Kay at the rear of the group.

"What is it?" asked Francis.

"There are no guards." His sword waved before him like a talisman.

"Morgaine knows we would come."

"She didn't last time," lied Francis.

"Maybe not, but I hasten to add she would know if thoust hath approach with yon sword." He beckoned towards Excalibur as he spoke, his eyes darting around the clearing by the wall. "Let us proceed with caution."

"There is no need to worry," eased Francis. "The last thing Morgaine would expect is an all-out attack on her within her own castle… would she?" He smiled at the knights, hoping they wouldn't notice or understand the significance of his crossed fingers. "She'll never know what hit her." He turned and pushed his way past Gawain into the tunnel. "Now if we could—"

"Wait!" snapped Kay. "What occurred here last time thoust came?" queried Kay, looking at Francis through narrowed eyes. "Thoust hath not explained."

"I went through the tunnel… and I couldn't find her." Francis shrugged and disappeared down the tunnel. The knights paused on the threshold of the passage, watching as Francis was swallowed by the darkness.

"After thee," commented Bedivere towards Gawain.

"Nay, my Lord Bedivere," said Gawain waving the knight before him. "After thee, I insist."

"After me," said the gruff burly voice of Kay as he pushed past the two bickering knights and followed down the tunnel. "I am eager to get thine hands on the knave Mordred." Gawain and Bedivere glanced at each other and drove down the tunnel, with Lord Percival taking up the rear of the party.

They found Francis standing in the ruined corridor, his back against the crumbling foundations of a wall as he glanced up and down the disused castle ruin. He spread his fingers and thrust his hand out beckoning Kay and Bedivere to stop as they emerged from the mouth of the tunnel. The knights paused in the passageway, partially hidden by the hanging ivy falling from the roof of the passage. Their ears could hear the vestiges of conversation drifting down the castle walls from somewhere in the distance. Francis looked at Kay and placed his finger hard against his mouth indicating that they remain quiet as they moved through the castle. Bedivere slipped from the tunnel and joined Francis at the inner wall of castle. He pointed both left and right in mute conversation and Francis paused, remembering the way he had gone earlier that day. He beckoned his hand to there right and glanced towards the mouth of the tunnel, where Gawain and Percival had joined Kay.

Percival was shaking his head furiously and pointing in the opposite direction towards the dungeon area. Francis frowned and shook his head pointing again towards their right. Percival looked both ways along the exposed corridor and ran across the open space and pressed himself hard against the wall. "My Lord," he whispered through gritted teeth. "The dungeon area is this way," he said pointing the opposite way again.

"Gwen is not there," insisted Francis. "I know."

"But my Lord, only the courtyard and great hall lies that way."

"That is where we are going," whispered Francis resolute.

"But I must protest—"

"Excellent!" exclaimed Kay loudly, immediately drawing several eyes at him, all goading him into silence. "Into battle," he continued in a whisper. "I tire of skulking round like a common rat, hiding in the shadows." He leant forward across the open space. "I agree with my Lord, we should attack at the heart of thy enemy."

"No, that isn't it," whispered Francis. "Gwen is that way. I know she is."

"How, my Lord?" questioned Percival as Francis ignored the question and pushed off, pressing his way along the ruins and picking through the debris scattered across the floor. "My Lord," hissed Percival from behind him but he chose to ignore the knight as he moved through the ruins followed by Bedivere and Gawain.

Lord Kay slapped him on the back and leant forward, whispering in his ear, "Make haste."

The knights followed a few feet behind Francis as he slowly picked his way through the ruins. Every few feet, he was sure he caught a glimpse in the shadows of a knight, or the glimmer of armour in the increasing moonlight or even the sound of breathing rasping through the ancient stonework, but most of all he could hear the sound of his own heartbeat drowned out by the sound of his guilt weighing in his stomach. He felt sick the nearer he got to the courtyard and through his own guilt he could see the images of flames cast through the stones and throwing shadows which stretched along the floor.

He held up a hand behind his back indicating for the knights to stop as he moved slowly into the empty courtyard. He strode quietly into the centre of the yard and placed his hand on the crystal sphere cradled in its stone plinth. He spun slowly, taking in his surrounding and searching for signs of Morgaine and her men. His hand fell subconsciously to the sword by his side and small pearls of sweat fell from his brow. He could make out figures, pressed against the walls of the courtyard, pressed in and hidden amongst the shadows and he lowered his head in resolute defeat.

"Come!" he barked the ordered through the night air and slowly the four knights moved as one into the open space.

"Where is she?" commented Bedivere glancing around. "There is naught here."

"I'm sorry," whispered Francis looking at his feet. "They are here!" he called out in the darkness. The knights drew their swords startled by the sudden movement all around them as the shadows detached themselves from the walls of the castle.

"What treachery is this?" hissed Kay as he found himself surrounded by a small group of knights.

"I'm sorry," whispered Francis, his own hand resting on the hilt of Excalibur.

Laughter filled the air and Morgaine swept into the courtyard, her long flowing cloak falling from her shoulders and draped down her back as it floated behind her. "Excalibur is mine!" she declared throwing her hands in the air and laughing as tendrils of blue lightning were emitted from her hands and encompassed her body, swathing her hair and running along her body. Her eyes flashed manically and shone in the electrically charged atmosphere. "Mine!" she screamed as thunder cracked over the castle. "Excalibur is mine!"

54.

Sword in the Heart

"My Liege," said Bedivere imploringly.

Francis struggled to meet his gaze. "I'm sorry," he whispered his apology again and stared at his feet. "I've let you all down," he said sadly.

"Nay," said Bedivere backing closer to his comrades. "Thoust hath only failed thyself," he said. "Was it worth it?"

"No," said Francis softly. "It wasn't."

"Then let us die with honour!" raged Kay, sword in hand and his back pressed firmly against that of his three comrades. He waved his sword at the oncoming attackers and looked around the courtyard. They were hopelessly outnumbered by Morgaine's forces, but if were to die today, best die with honour.

"Hold thy swords!" shouted Morgaine over the heads of the knights. "There shall be no bloodshed!" she called, then looked towards Francis. "Shall there," she purred sweetly and held out her hand, uncurling her fingers in temptation.

Francis shook his head slowly. "You shall have Excalibur," he said quietly, then looked around the courtyard. "Where is Gwen?" he asked, his heart heavy.

"Thy maiden." Morgaine raised her eyebrows as she spoke, "Thoust still hath feelings." She laughed at his discomfort. "How sweet."

"If I am to hand Excalibur over, then I wish to know she is fine." He stood calmly and alone in the centre of the courtyard close to the glass sphere and Morgaine.

"Very well," snapped Morgaine and turned to Agravain. "Bring the girl," she ordered and watched as Agravain sped from the courtyard and into the depths of the castle.

"What will you do once you have the sword?" Francis asked.

"What concern is it of yours?"

"I have people I care about in this world; I wish to know if they'll be safe," Francis said, his grip tightening around the hilt of the sword, his eyes darting around the site.

"They will be spared," said Morgaine. "I give thee my word as a warrior and my promise as a queen." She smiled and held her hand out.

"First the girl."

"Thy doth try my patience!" snapped Morgaine, then her mood softened. "But I shall play thy game for the time being."

The sound of footsteps from beyond the wall alerted Francis to the fact that Agravain was approaching; he listened as metal struck metal as his armour rubbed together in matrimony as he walked into the courtyard. Behind him trailed Gwen and Francis blinked hard as she glided into the moonlight and stood close to Morgaine. Gone were her shirt, jodhpurs and knee length boots and in their place was a long flowing gown, bejewelled in finery of silver and golden embroidered strands running through the gown. The long pale blue gown was offset with lace which ran down her arms and showed her arms through the thin fabric as it fell past her wrists in a large flowing cuff. Her hair fell over her bare shoulders and around her forehead ran a simple plain band with a small blue jewel set at the front of the headpiece. Francis revelled in her beauty as she glided into the courtyard and once again, he felt his heart sink as she looked away as she passed. The sadness in his heart was in evidence and his hand tightened around the hilt of the sword, his anger had subsided and replace with regret and sorrow at her betrayal.

"Morgaine," Gwen said softly and curtsied slightly before her. Morgaine smiled and indicated towards her side for Gwen to join her.

"You see," scoffed Morgaine, "she is safe and well."

"Gwen," said Francis softly. She turned her head away from his voice but remained at Morgaine's side as he spoke. "Gwen, please."

"As you see, she has chosen her side." Morgaine placed an arm around Gwen and smiled, kissing Gwen's head then looking back at Francis. "She is the daughter I never had." She laughed.

"Gwen, at least give me an answer," Francis pleaded.

"I... I'm sorry," she whispered.

"Gwen," he said again, his voice was cracked with emotion and he could hear his own pathetic words spill from his lips.

"She can give me everything I ever wanted," Gwen said looking at Francis, tears welling in her eyes. "What can you offer?" she asked.

"Love," he said softly.

"Is that it?" laughed Morgaine. "I offer her the world, and you offer her love."

"I will protect her," said Francis defiantly. "I will care for her."

"Thoust is a fool," spat Morgaine. "I tire of these games… give me Excalibur!" Her eyes burnt with anger as the fire within her consumed her patience.

Francis pulled the sword from the scabbard and held it aloft in the palm of his hands and stared at the cold metal of the blade. Could he… could he really surrender Excalibur to Morgaine after all he had been through? He looked at Gwen and sighed; even though his heart was breaking he looked into her eyes and remembered. He remembered her smile… how it lit his heart. He remembered her eyes… how they shone and sparkled. He remembered how she made him feel, even after only a couple of meetings, he remembered how he could never be angry with her and he smiled. Yes, he could do it; he could do it for her. "I will give you Excalibur," he said quietly. "Just release her."

"She is free to make her own decisions," mocked Morgaine. "She has chosen to stand with me. Now the sword."

"Gwen," Francis said again. She turned away unable to look into his eyes and he felt his heart swell under the heavy weight of rejection and guilt. He cast a glance towards his companions who stood watching the exchange, swords in hands and ready for a word.

"The sword!" snapped Morgaine.

"I give you Excalibur," said Francis holding out the sword in his hands. Morgaine smiled and stepped forward, her hands reaching for the weapon. "But" started Francis snatching the blade back and pressing its cold steel against his body. "I won't give it to you," he said.

"Explain!" demanded Morgaine.

"I give it to Gwen," he said finally staring at Morgaine. "Let her decide her future."

Morgaine threw her head back and laughed into the air, then looked harshly at Francis. "She will not resist my will," Morgaine warned. "I shall have Excalibur." She placed her hand on Gwen's shoulder and whispered, "I offer thee thine heart's desire… what can he offer you? Love? Love is but a fallacy. Give me Excalibur and I shall grant thee wishes."

Gwen nodded and looked into the face of the older woman and smiled.

Morgaine released her grip on her shoulder and Gwen turned to face Francis, looking at him for the first time since she had entered the courtyard. She glided slowly across the floor and gazed at his face, pity in her eyes. "I'm sorry," she whispered as she stopped before him.

Francis looked down briefly, then looked into her eyes. "Don't," he pleaded as tears welled in his own eyes, "please."

"It's too late," she said softly reaching for the sword. "I've made my choice." She could not look at Francis as she took the sword from his hands. Her hands slid around the blade and hilt of the sword, and she lifted Excalibur slowly and gently from his hands, ignoring the splash of a tear as it struck the metal. She weighed it in her hands for a moment, sizing up the blade and casting her eyes along the steel to the ornate handle.

"Excalibur," breathed the voice of Morgaine from behind her. "At last, after all of these centuries we are reunited." She clenched her fists in victory as the joy overwhelmed her, her face igniting with blind exultation as Gwen turned and smiled at her. "My power shall be absolute," she whispered. Morgaine glanced towards Mordred who stood in the shadows, his face breaking the darkness with the force of his smile. She raised her hand to her shoulder and clicked her fingers, pointing towards Gwen and the sword. Mordred nodded and silently moved into the clearing, peeling himself from the confines of the darkness and strode confidently across the courtyard, his eyes staring mockingly in the direction of the three knights who still stood poised against attack.

His fingers brushed against his own sword as he walked, and he grinned at Gwen through the darkening evening sky. "Brother to Excalibur," he whispered, fingering his own sword, "we shall rule this land." He stopped before the slender form of Gwen and smiled down at her. "The country shall be washed with the blood of the innocent as I seek vengeance," he breathed slowly holding his arms out towards Excalibur, his eyes wavering over Gwen's face before lowering towards the blade in her hands, "and thee shall stand by my side as thy queen."

"I aim to please," Gwen whispered as she took Excalibur in her hands and held it aloft for Mordred. Her hands seemed tiny in comparison the handle in them, and she looked straight at Mordred and smiled. "My Lord, I give you Excalibur," she whispered, her mouth turning from a smile into a determined grimace.

She thrust the sword forward towards his body and shock overcame

Mordred as the metal of the blade forced its way through the chain mail around his stomach as the blade penetrated his body beneath his breast plate and forced its way through the body and severed the metal armour in his back. He looked down at the sword as it skewered his body and his hands grip the blade, cutting into the skin and covering the sword with more blood.

"My Lady," he whispered as his body slowly slid down the blade and his hand floated to her face, where it cupped her cheek.

"Fuck you!" she shouted and spat in his face, watching the saliva as it dribbled across his eyes. Her hands were doused with the warm embrace of his blood as it seeped and flowed from the growing stain spreading across his armour.

Mordred looked at her and smiled through blood-stained teeth and laughed. "You would have made an excellent queen," he whispered, covering her dress with the slight spray of blood as he spoke. His eyes rolled in his head and his arms sagged as blood forced its way through his closed lips and he slid to the ground as Gwen lowered the sword. He lay on the floor unmoving in a pool of his own blood as Gwen stood over his body, covered in the blood of the knight and Excalibur held by her side in the other hand.

55.

Choices

"By all that's holy!" cried Lord Kay as Mordred slid from the end of Excalibur. He turned to his attacker and swung his sword violently against his skull, his sword splintering the metal of his helmet and the blade digging into the bone producing a fountain of crimson to escape and spray over his armour. Bedivere copied his lead and swung his sword at the second knight, his blade connecting with the knight's shoulder and stood with steely satisfaction as the hard metal cut through the soft flesh of the soldier and watched briefly as the man's arm fell to the floor. Percival copied the actions of Gwen and having sunk to one knee he thrust his own blade in an upright arc, stabbing his own guard beneath his breastplate and forced his blade upward. The metal of the sword ran through the inside of his body, severing arteries and puncturing the man's heart before running up his neck as he slid down the blade and protruded from the knight's mouth.

"No!" screamed Morgaine as she watched with horror as the movement around her blurred her vision. Mordred fell… the knights of the round table attacked and the girl… the girl stood there amidst the carnage covered in the blood of her beloved nephew. "Kill them!" she screamed her mind whirling at the scene before her.

"My Lord!" shouted Bedivere as he swung his heavy weapon at another attacker, slicing through the soldier's armour and producing an explosion of crimson across the courtyard floor.

"The land is awash with blood!" yelled Kay as he thrust his sword through another knight. "Only it's thine," he laughed as he watched the knight fall from his blow.

"I think this is yours." Francis turned to the sound of the voice and smiled at Gwen who stood in the midst of the chaos holding Excalibur in her hands.

"We're supposed to be rescuing you." He smiled and took the sword.

"Well don't you think this would be a good time." Gwen ducked as another knight fell close to her from another swing of Lord Kay's sword.

Francis nodded and took a firm grasp of the sword and looked about the courtyard. He could see victims of the knights... his knights fall around them as the battle was quickly becoming a bloodbath. The knights were being slowly forced back towards the edge of the courtyard and close to a wall from the excessive pressure of the relentless forces under Morgaine's disposal. "Bedivere!" he called. The knight waved and smiled as he swung his sword at another attacker, spraying the ground with more blood and littering the area with another corpse. Francis pointed towards the opening close to their position. "We must pull back... there are too many of them." Bedivere nodded and moved across the edge of the wall, followed by Kay and Gawain.

"My beloved," bemoaned Morgaine as she fell to her knees by Mordred's twisted body. She knelt in the dirt and rested his head on her lap, stroking his hair and allowing his blood to stain her elegant clothing. Her hands ran through his hair and her fingers became entangled and matted with blood as her hands ran down his body to his wound. "My dear Mordred," she breathed quietly as the sound of battle overcame her.

Francis stood with his back to the wall, Gwen's hand locked firmly in his and Excalibur in the other. "We need to get out!" he called out to his comrades.

"Thee wish to retreat?" called Kay.

Francis nodded frantically. "Yes."

"Then why does thy not say?" Kay replied as he swung his sword into another attacker.

The limited area that the knights were standing in made it easy to defend their position, but the odds of being overwhelmed were mounting with each attack. Francis could see more of Morgan's soldiers file into the courtyard, and he wondered exactly the size of her army, while here they were four knights, himself and Gwen... and from the look of his comrades they were beginning to tire. Percival was struggling more than most, still ailing from his wounds at the hands of Mordred he leant heavily on the wall as Gawain stood before him fending off an attack. Even Kay and Bedivere were panting hard as the extortion of battle took its toll.

"We must get back to the tunnel," shouted Francis from behind the back of Kay.

"Does thee know the way?" Kay called over his shoulder, keeping his eyes firmly locked on the attacking soldiers.

"Yes, I think so," replied Francis.

"You lead the way, my Lord, we will defend thy rear." Francis nodded and pushed Gwen along the wall towards a low archway and out into the desolate passage. The stones seemed to stare as Francis ran down the grass incline and it struck Francis how calm it felt away from the carnage only a few feet away. He could hear swords clash from the other side of the wall as the fighting continued.

"My Lady," breathed Agravain standing over Morgaine, gazing down at her and the twisted form of Mordred. He could hear her sobs over the noise of battle. "My Lady," he said again and recoiled as she stared at him with venom in her eyes.

"Leave us!" she roared, tears rolling down her cheeks.

"But my Lady… the boy—" Agravain stammered.

"I said leave us!"

Agravain wavered, unsure what his actions should be. He could see the fury and anger of unspent emotion build in her eyes, and he could see the carnage of his men falling around him as they fell in the courtyard… one by one stricken by the experienced knights. He thrust his sword into its scabbard around his waist and glanced across the body laden land and sulked towards the rear of the castle. "By the hand of God," he whispered as he pulled himself into the shadows and fled into the night unnoticed and alone.

Morgaine stared down into the blood smeared face of her nephew. "Dearest Mordred," she whispered, "there shall be a reckoning… of this I swear." She screamed into the air, then silently lowered her head to his and kissed his bloodied lips, smearing her own with his blood.

Francis forced his way through the tunnel, with the sound of footsteps echoing through his head and along the tunnel walls. His hand was gripped firmly around the hilt of Excalibur as he thrust his way through the passage, his mind whirling with new information and new possibilities. His other hand was entwined within Gwen's fingers, interlocked and the thrill of her touch coursed through his body, blocking out the fear which was trying in vain to sweep through his body. He could hear the crash of his comrades behind him as their heavy footsteps stamped over the floor and further behind the first sound of distant pursuers. He could see the end of the tunnel rise into his vision ahead of him as tiny vestiges of moonlight fought its way through the overhanging vines and the outside air caressed the leaves as it drifted aimlessly down the passage. He felt pressure in his arm as Gwen pulled at him, tugging at his arm. He looked at her as he carried on down the tunnel. "What's wrong?" he asked.

"What if they're waiting for us?" she whispered staring past him at the opening of the passage.

Francis shook his head and frowned, hoping she would not see his expression. He had not thought they could be running straight into a trap; he had sort of relied on blind luck that all of Morgaine's force had been gathered in the castle.

"We'll have to risk it," he whispered back, hoping his voice sound confident, while the first thoughts of the potential ambush tripped into his brain.

He held her hand tightly and smiled, feelings flowing through his body that he could do anything. In his mind he pictured himself bursting out of the tunnel and fighting off a hoard of soldiers while holding her hand tightly in his own, he found himself slowly as he approached the mouth of the tunnel and carefully peered through the creepers. He paused as he scanned the area, carefully looking over the vegetation and the moonlight covered the open air. Although the area looked clear, he could not be sure as the darkness crept over the undergrowth and hid the bushes within swathes of shadow. He would have to risk it; he knew in his heart he would have no choice.

With Gwen's hand in his own, and Excalibur stabbing the air before him he moved from the tunnel and stood in the clearing breathing in the air, drinking in the clean air and filling his lungs with the clear atmosphere. They stood alone for a moment and stared at each other. He could feel himself falling in her eyes and as she flashed him a smile which shone like the sun and melted his heart. The crash of Lord Kay and Bedivere emerging noisily from the tunnel brought him sharply back to reality.

"My Lord," said Bedivere, "we should make haste… our enemies are close."

"If we wait here, we can smite our enemies as they emerge!" roared

Kay, revelling in the bloodlust which caught his eye.

"No, I am sorry, Kay," sighed Francis. "We must go. If we're going to end the curse, we have to get back to the cave."

"Aye, perhaps thy is correct," he conceded downhearted and looked back at the tunnel where Gawain was pulling Percival free from the vines.

"The effort is too great," Gawain said softly as he emerged. "His wounds are severe."

"From the attack?" asked Gwen.

Gawain turned his head and sadly shook it as he spoke, "Nay, my Lady… 'tis from earlier."

"Leave me," whispered Percival as he struggled to stand unaided.

"No," said Francis defiantly. "No more deaths."

"My Lord," started Percival, "I am tired, and thy journey will take time with thoust as a hinderance." He indicated across his body as he spoke, smiling at his tortured frame. "Leave me, I will give thee time."

"If you're sure—"

"Francis, you can't," Gwen said imploringly staring into his eyes.

"My Lady do not grieve. This is not my world," said Percival. "It sears my head and rips at my soul," he admitted as the sound of shouting echoed through the tunnel. "I do not fear death… only the unknown."

"I'm sorry," she whispered and leant forward, kissing his cheek smiling through her own tears.

"Do not cry for me," he said softly and held her hands, looking deep into her eyes. "Live thy life." He glanced at Francis and smiled. "My Lord needs a maiden fair of face." He laughed and let go of her hands, turning to face the mouth of the tunnel. "Now go," he said softly.

Francis pulled at Gwen's hand and pulled her through the undergrowth and into the forest. Kay and Bedivere hovered for a moment before nodding in his direction, then followed the couple from sight.

"Thoust are sure?" asked Gawain.

Percival nodded and shook his friend's hand. "Go, my friend," he said and drew his sword facing the tunnel.

"Thoust is a brave man," said Gawain casting one final glance at Percival before the undergrowth swallowed his green armour and he disappeared through the trees.

Percival stared at the tunnel and staggered forward, using his sword as a prop aiding his movement and stood for a moment casting his vision down the passage. He could hear shouting from the confines of the tunnel and sighed, moving inside the passageway and leaning heavily against the soft, muddy wall stared across the ceiling of the tunnel. His eyes followed the arch in the roof, and he stood watching as the tendrils of vegetation thrust its way through the decaying remains of the stonework. With one final effort, Percival forced his sword upward, digging it deep into the earth and moved it around disturbing and breaking the tension cast from the surface. He flinched as tons of mud and soil fell amidst brick as it tumbled from the top of the tunnel casting its baleful glare over the tunnel, the rumble of the subsidence spread through the tunnel, causing a subdued silence as earth shifted and moved in the creation of the underground tomb. Bodies lay twisted and broken beneath the rubble from above and a deathly silence fell over the castle, broken only by a solitary wail of a woman cast from the heart of the castle.

Gwen pulled at Francis' hand as they emerged into a small clearing. He stopped and looked at her, staring into her eyes and smiled, then frowned as she looked towards the floor. He glanced around him for a moment and recognised the patch of land and realised they were close to the beach... and the cave. Kay, Bedivere and Gawain crashed out of the undergrowth and paused at the two figures standing opposite each other.

"Go on," urged Francis.

"Thoust is sure?" queried Bedivere.

Francis nodded. "We will meet you there," he said softly, still looking into her open face.

"Very well." Bedivere cast a quick glance towards Francis as he drove forward towards the beach, followed by the two remaining knights.

"What is it?" asked Francis. "What's wrong?"

Gwen let go of his hand and turned away, tears rolling from her eyes. "Before you came here, I had everything I thought I wanted." She folded her arms as the cold bit into the arms, and the moonlight shone and sparkled off the ribbons cast through her dress. "Then... all the deaths – Dad, Lance, people I don't know." She struggled with her words as her voice trembled. "And then there is you." She turned and looked at him with bloodshot eyes, ringed with a curtain of moisture. "Why?" she asked. "Why risk all of this for me?" her voice quivered, and she looked at him for answers.

"Gwen, don't," he stammered.

"Tell me!" she shouted.

"Gwen, please... I..."

"Please," she begged, "you must tell me!" Her voice rose over the sound of the forest as she shouted, "If you do not, I'll be angry with you!" Her voice softened, "Please, I need you to tell me. You hardly know me."

"I can't describe it," he said softly, taking her hands in his and pulling her close, looking into her eyes as he spoke. "Yes, we have only just met... and yes, I don't really know you. But I want to." He smiled as he spoke, "When I look at you... everything feels right." He struggled with his words as they stood facing each other. "I feel... happy. Is that stupid?" He smiled as she softly shook her head to his words. "I want to be angry; I want to feel scared, but when I see you... it just feels right. It feels good." His arms snaked around her, and he pulled her close to his body, allowing the heat from his body to sink into her. "You make me want to be around you, even if you don't talk to me. Just the odd glance, the look that says... I am here... I care." He pushed her away and held her firmly by the shoulders. "I will be here for you," he promised staring at her. "I will never let you down."

"Thank you," she said softly looking around embarrassed by the sudden burst of words from Francis.

"We should go," he said and placed his lips gently on her cheek and eased himself into the forest with her trailing behind him.

The cave was dark as they walked along the tunnel and entered the cavern. "My Lord... Lady," said Kay smiling at the couple as they moved into the light cast by the flame.

"Kay," said Francis rushing forward and gripping his hand firmly. He looked around the chamber at the occupants and his thought strayed to lost friends; Galahad, Bors, Tristan and Percival and his heart felt heavy for the loss of these men who had sacrificed their own lives for someone they did not really know... only because he was a blood relative of King Arthur.

"My Lord." He turned as the deep voice broke the silence of the cavern.

He felt Gwen flinch under the Fisher King's scrutiny as his figure loomed over them. "It's all right, he's a friend," he reassured her.

"You sure?" she whispered as he stared down on her.

"It is time," the Fisher King said turning his back on her and dragged his body slowly to the centre of the chamber, pausing only briefly to lay his hands against the cold stone altar. Francis released Gwen's hand and moved across the cavern and stood on the opposite side of the altar to the Fisher

King and gazed up the expanse of his body.

"I'm ready," Francis said and removed the scabbard from his waist and draped it over the roughly sewn rock. "What must I do?"

The Fisher King blinked and lowered his head, casting his gaze over the leather-bound casing. "Remove Excalibur," he ordered.

Francis reached for the scabbard and pulled the sword from the sheeve and held it up above his head. The light played around the blade and caught the jewels offset in the handle and threw shadows along the cavern wall. He placed the scabbard back on the rock and lowered the sword placing it gently across the palms of his hands, and he looked up towards the Fisher King and passed the weapon across the stone.

The Fisher King waved the sword away, shaking his head. "'Tis your destiny," he said, turning his back on an uncertain Francis and raised his hands in the air. "We are the few," he spoke, his voice carrying across the cavern and around the waiting throng of people. "The survivors of Camlann. We are the cursed." He lowered his head and closed his eyes as he spoke, "We shall rise through the ages time after time, till the curse is lifted." He looked directly towards Francis. "By a Pendragon." He lowered his hands and turned to face Francis and ran his hands over the top of the blade. "With this blade thee can fulfil your destiny and release our torment."

"What does he mean?" hissed Gwen.

"The sword is cursed," Francis whispered back, "and I am the only one that can end it." He looked at the Fisher King who nodded patiently. "They are locked in an eternal cycle of sleep and battle, never dying." He looked back at Gwen. "I can end this… I can free them."

"You are the one," confirmed the Fisher King. "You are the last Pendragon."

"What must I do?" asked Francis staring at the Fisher King.

"Destroy Excalibur," he stated simply.

"What?"

"Destroy Excalibur… End the curse… Free us all."

Francis stepped back from the altar and looked at the sword in his hands. "I… I… don't know," he stammered.

"Destroy Excalibur," said the Fisher King again.

Francis looked about the chamber at the expectant faces surrounding him. "I don't know if I can," he admitted finally. His eyes looked imploringly at the congregation of knights. "I mean… look at this," he exclaimed weighing the sword in his hands. "It's Excalibur." He searched the faces of those around him and bore witness to silence. "This is history… real history." He struggled with his words. "Excalibur," he whispered looking at the sword. "This is part of our heritage, *my* heritage. This is part of me… this sword. My link to Arthur. You have to understand I don't think I can." He looked at the Fisher King who bowed his head sorrowfully. "Excalibur," he whispered.

"There is but one more way," said the Fisher King simply.

"Without destroying the sword? What is it?"

The Fisher King looked straight at Francis; a heavy sadness tinged in his eyes which caused Francis to gaze down at the sword in his hands one final time. "Thoust must destroy the sword," the Fisher King reaffirmed.

"You don't understand," bemoaned Francis. "This sword is Excalibur." He whispered, "This is my own personal history, my link to the past; it's Excalibur." He looked at the Fisher King. "You said another way?" The Fisher King nodded but remained silent. "Tell me," demanded Francis. "I can't destroy Excalibur… it doesn't seem right."

"There is but one other way to end the curse," said the Fisher King and he looked at Francis directly. "To end the curse, thoust must end the bloodline."